DAVID COPPERFIELD'S
Tales
of the
Impossible

DAVID COPPERFIELD'S

Tales
of the
Impossible

CREATED AND EDITED BY
David Copperfield and Janet Berliner

PREFACE BY
Dean Koontz

HarperPrism

HarperPaperbacks *A Division of* HarperCollins*Publishers*
10 East 53rd Street, New York, N.Y. 10022

Individual story copyrights appear on p. 386

HarperPaperbacks may be purchased for educational, business, or sales promotional use. For information please write: Special Markets Department, HarperCollins*Publishers*, 10 East 53rd Street, New York, N.Y. 10022.

First printing: November 1995

Printed in the United States of America

HarperPrism is an imprint of HarperPaperbacks. HarperPaperbacks, HarperPrism, and colophon are trademarks of HarperCollins*Publishers*.

Library of Congress Cataloging-in-Publication Data

David Copperfield's tales of the impossible/created and edited by
    David Copperfield and Janet Berliner; preface by Dean Koontz.
        p. cm.
    ISBN 0-06-105228-0 (hardcover)
    1. Fantastic fiction, American. I. Copperfield, David, 1956-   . II. Berliner, Janet
PS648.F3D38   1995
813ᴵ.0876608—dc20   95-22709
                                                      CIP

95 96 97 98 99 ❖ 10 9 8 7 6 5 4 3 2 1

Contents

Acknowledgments

THE EDITORS WISH to thank both Harpers—Laurie Harper of Sebastian Agency and HarperPrism—for their support and enthusiasm. And there's the unflappable "Cowboy Bob," Robert L. Fleck, without whose assistance this volume would probably still be in the pipelines. We wish to thank Christy Johnson, Vicki Krone, and Dee Anne Dimmick for so cheerfully and efficiently handling all of the flack. Finally we wish to acknowledge Al Rettig (even if he doesn't know why).

Additionally, David Copperfield wishes to send his special thanks to his parents, Hy and Rebecca, for a lifetime of love and support; to Claudia for being Claudia; and to Janet Berliner for helping to make his vision a reality—now she can get some beddy-bye time.

Janet Berliner extends unending love, affection, and gratitude to Laurie Harper for all of the long hours she put in, the countless conversations, and her invaluable input; to Bob Fleck, her personal assistant, for the coffee and great food when she didn't have time to think about dinner; and to Martin H. Greenberg, arguably the world's most renowned anthologist, for his advice and confidence. Also her mother, Thea Cowan, and her daughter, Stefanie Gluckman. And thank you, David, for making all of this possible. It's been a blast. From one obsessive to another, I hope you miss me, even if it's just a little.

Preface

Illusion, Truth, and the Whole Damn Thing

Magicians and writers of fiction have many things in common. We deal in illusion, we entertain by deception, and we know that art can never be consciously created but arises spontaneously from first-rate craftsmanship and polished technique.

And when we appear onstage, members of the opposite sex throw their hotel-room keys and articles of intimate apparel at us. Panties and boxer shorts, bras and hernia trusses. This can be exciting on some occasions and enormously disgusting on others. But it happens.

Well, okay, that never happens to writers, but only because the short-sighted talent bookers who select the acts for major venues are philistines. They don't realize that a writer sitting at a computer for ninety minutes or penciling changes in a novel manuscript is *riveting* theater.

Illusion. If we magicians and writers have done our jobs well, we leave most members of the audience convinced that what they have seen or read was *real* no matter how impossible it seemed. On one level, they remain sophisticated enough to view the proceedings with detachment, but on deeper levels, they become as gee-whiz credulous as children.

For instance, I myself stopped buying hats years ago because I was afraid that I'd get one of those that produces an inexhaustible supply of rabbits. And since reading Robert Heinlein's *The Puppet Masters*, I slap every new acquaintance on the back several times, as soon as possible after meeting him, to be certain that no alien parasite is attached to his spine. If someone manages to avoid this slapping, I draw my concealed pistol (Heckler & Koch P7, with a thirteen-round magazine) and make him stand with his hands flat against a wall while I frisk him for dangerous extraterrestrial organisms. Fortunately, I have never found any such organisms, no doubt because those vile off-world slugs are aware that I'm onto them and, therefore, wisely steer their controlled human hosts well clear of me.

Deception. Writers reveal secrets about their characters slowly throughout the course of a novel and strive to surprise their readers with story developments; in retrospect, however, the reader must feel that all character revelations and narrative twists were inevitable. Consequently, writers resort to a thousand and one deceptions—just as any magician employs countless techniques to induce the audience to look in precisely the wrong place at the right time.

A few years ago when David Copperfield made the Statue of Liberty disappear in front of a live audience, I was at first distracted by a curious cloud formation and then by a woman in a peculiar hat. By the time I looked at the statue again, he had dismantled the entire thing and hauled it away. (Incidentally, I'm not convinced that the statue he returned is the *real* statue; I think this one was made in Taiwan, not in France.)

Craftsmanship and technique. Practice makes perfect both for a writer and a magician. The more that one writes and the more that one thinks about writing, the better one's writing becomes. To be a great card mechanic, one must spend thousands of hours learning to manipulate cards with faultless finesse. To be an illusionist of the caliber of . . . oh, let me see . . . say . . . David Copperfield requires ceaseless refinement of craftsmanship and polishing of technique.

Mr. Copperfield didn't say to himself, "I'm going to make the Statue of Liberty disappear," and then go out and take a whack at this colossal vanishment the very next day. I'm told by reliable authorities that he first secretly made hundreds of smaller statues disappear from parks across the United States; most were monuments to Revolutionary and Civil War generals, though he was also able to dematerialize three concrete dinosaurs from a roadside tourist trap in the Midwest. (When he caused the brontosaurus, stegosaurus, and T-rex to materialize again, they were turned backward with their butts to the highway, a small error that resulted in the first-ever, Jurassic-statuary mooning.) At Mount Rushmore, something went wrong, and nothing vanished except George Washington's wig and Thomas Jefferson's nose, but by the time Mr. Copperfield got to the Statue of Liberty, he was *smooth*.

The most important thing that writers and illusionists such as David Copperfield have in common is that we seek to impress upon our audiences this truth: that life and the universe are full of mystery and wonder, that all is not what it seems, that there are hidden meanings, that we are capable of transcendence. This is arguably the most important truth with which any art form can deal, because it delights us, exalts us, and gives us hope.

Every time that I watch Mr. Copperfield perform his incredible flying illusion, I am utterly convinced that he can levitate and do elaborate aerial acrobatics. Watching him is hugely entertaining—but more than that, it is also strangely uplifting, perhaps because he convinces me, on some deep level of the heart, that I can fly, too, if not physically then in spirit. His act becomes a metaphor for transcendence. Each time that I read a novel by Anne Tyler or John D. MacDonald, in which characters triumph at least to some degree over their own weakness, over the quiet terrors of daily life (in her books), and over sociopathic thugs (in his books), I am given hope that I, too, can survive the crises of my own life and endure.

It's always possible, I suppose, that David Copperfield *is* able to fly because an alien parasite, attached to his spine, gives him supernormal powers, but I prefer to believe in deeper mysteries than alien parasites—and to cling to the hope of transcendence that is promised in stage illusions and in fiction.

DEAN KOONTZ
Southern California
April 1995

Introduction

THE WAY I SEE IT, there are common threads which bind together all those who aspire to being great artists, be they conjurors whose forum is the theater, or wordsmiths whose illusions are performed in the playhouse of the mind. They are equally obsessed by their craft, equally intent upon capturing the imaginations of their audiences, viewers, readers.

Whether on the stage or on the page, their internal compulsion—their mandate, if you will—is to make the impossible seem possible, to share feelings, to communicate ideas. They are explorers who, childlike in their enthusiasms, are so excited about their journeys that they want to take everyone else along. They want everyone to feel what they feel, to experience their dreams.

This book was conceived because we are grateful to be among the dreamers. To dream is a privilege, to live the dream and to communicate it, the ultimate freedom.

It is my pleasure to invite you to join me and my fellow illusionists as we once again explore the impossible.

—DAVID COPPERFIELD
April 1995

Snow

DAVID COPPERFIELD

We all experience magic in different ways. A hundred years ago, when Louis and Auguste Lumière created the Cinématographe, the first people who saw light and shadow moving on a screen thought it was magic; the first time people heard the voices of their families and friends come from miles away through an instrument they could hold in their hands, or heard music through a box called a radio, they thought that was magic. For me, the first magic was white things coming down from the sky and melting on my hand. . . .

—DC

Snow

ADAM CAREFULLY PILED all of the pillows he could find onto his bed, beneath his window. He wiped circles on the cold glass for his eyes, wedged his chin on the windowsill for balance, and waited.

It seemed like forever before his grandparents came into view. They were both wearing long, black coats, but he knew it was them from far away, because Grandma was wearing her shawl, the mauve-colored one she'd crocheted herself.

They came closer, Grandpa's hand resting in the crook of Grandma's elbow, each supporting the other. Adam jumped off the bed and charged outside in his pajamas to greet them. Grandpa leaned down, picked him up, and gave him a hug.

"He thinks he's still a young man, like you," Grandma said, ruffling Adam's hair and hugging them both.

As Adam turned his head to look at her, a bright, white flash made him shut his eyes tight. When he opened them, Grandma's shawl was dotted with little bits of white stuff that seemed to be floating down from the night sky. Something magical, something he'd never seen before.

"Come in out of the snow," his mom called out.

"Snow." Adam repeated the word. He held out his hands again to catch more of the white flakes.

He watched the white things land on his palm. They were soft and fluffy at first, then wet as they melted into his hand and disappeared. He looked up at the sky, opened his mouth, and put out his tongue, to see if he could catch some.

3

*   *   *

Adam's fourth birthday had come and gone before he saw his grandfather again after that, mostly because Adam had moved to Florida with his parents. Now Grandma had gone away forever, his parents said, and Grandpa was all alone and not feeling too well.

So Grandpa moved from New Jersey—straight into the bed in the guest room—bringing his wheelchair, one suitcase of clothes, the beaten-up rocker, and the mauve shawl.

With the same joyful anticipation he had felt every day since Grandpa had come to live with them, Adam opened the door to his grandfather's room. His grandfather was asleep and snoring gently, so the boy slid quietly onto the old maple rocker next to the bed and settled himself into it.

"Hi, Grandma," he whispered, smiling at the familiar photograph on his grandfather's dresser, the one his mother had taken of him with his grandparents that last afternoon in the house in New Jersey.

On the day of snow.

Adam loved the photograph. It reminded him of Grandma, it reminded him of the three of them, and it reminded him of snow.

He traced the contours of Grandma's face with his fingers, as he had done a thousand times. He knew every hair on her severely coiffed head, every wrinkle on her face. All he could remember about New Jersey was that last afternoon—the white flakes floating down onto Grandmother's shawl, Grandma and Grandpa hugging him, the snow melting on his own palms, and on his tongue.

Adam pulled his grandmother's shawl off the back of the rocker and wrapped himself in it. He snuggled his face into it, loving its softness.

"You got a hug for me, Adam?" his grandfather said, in the hoarse morning voice that the boy loved.

Adam jumped out of the chair and hugged his grandfather, pressing his face against his grandfather's leathery cheek. Without being asked, he put the shawl on his grandfather's bed and poured the old man a glass of water. Then he climbed onto the bed and snuggled happily into the crook of his grandfather's bony arm.

"Wanna play?" he asked, after a few moments.

Grandpa's head had settled back on the pillow. His eyes were half-closed, and he was holding his heart. "Good idea, Adam. Pretty soon I'm gonna get tired, so let's have some fun now."

That was how the boy knew, before he was told, that his grandfather was dying. He wasn't exactly sure what that meant, only that it had to do with not being there any more.

"Think of something special," Grandpa said. "I'll close my eyes and rest a little, and you surprise me."

Adam didn't have to think for long. He knew what would make him happy, and make Grandpa happy, too. He looked around the room for what he wanted. When he saw it, he slid off the bed and, standing on tiptoes, pulled a writing pad off his grandfather's dresser. With intense concentration, he ripped a sheet of paper off the top.

The tearing of paper woke his grandfather. "What you doing, Adam?"

"Making snow," the boy said. More and more quickly, he tore small pieces off the sheet of paper and tossed them up into the air. "Look, Grandpa," he said, palms out, whirling around. "It's snow."

"It's beautiful." His grandfather was wide-awake now, sitting in bed and watching the last bits float to the floor.

Adam continued until every last sheet of paper was shredded and the center of the floor was covered in a layer of white.

When they had admired the snow for a while, Grandpa suggested that Adam clean up before his mother came home. Reluctantly, the boy scooped up the snow and stuffed it in the wastebasket.

For a few days after that, Adam was only allowed to peek into his grandfather's room to say hello. On the third day, Grandpa seemed to be his old self.

"I was so afraid that you were going to leave me, Grandpa," Adam said. He had not planned to say that, but the words came tumbling out.

"Leave?" His grandfather laughed softly and gestured across the bed at his wheelchair, which was folded in the corner of the room. "Where would I go when my heart is here, with you."

He looked at his grandson's face and his voice grew serious. "What is it you're trying to say, Adam?"

The boy was silent. He *wanted* to say, I know that you're going to die soon, and that's not fair, but something stopped him.

"Remember the day you made snow?" Grandpa said, guessing right about Adam's fears. "Remember I told you that one day I would get really tired—"

"Yes, but—"

"Whoa, wait a minute." His grandfather held up his hand, the skin so thin it was almost transparent. "We'll talk later."

He gestured across the room at the fresh, new writing pad that lay on his dresser. Adam started to reach for it, then glanced at Grandpa, who smiled conspiratorially and said, "Make the pieces real tiny."

The window was open, allowing the soft sea breeze to enter the room and keep Adam's snow in the air. He was able to dance around in it for quite a while—so long that neither he nor his grandfather noticed how much time passed. When they did, it was too late. The door opened, and Adam's mother was standing there.

"Oh Lord. Look at this mess."

Adam glanced at Grandpa, who winked at him but said nothing. Without ratting on his grandfather, he said, "I'll clean it up, Mom."

And he did.

The next morning Adam's grandfather was dead. By that evening they had taken him away. Grandpa had been his friend, companion, adviser—his only playmate. Adam felt alone, abandoned, lost.

Going into his grandfather's room was no help, either. His mother had converted it into a sewing room. Except for the photograph and the mauve shawl, it seemed to Adam that his grandparents had never existed. He kept the photograph in his room, the one of the three of them on the day of snow. He slept with it under his pillow, and with Grandma's shawl tucked around him, but it wasn't enough. Grandpa and Grandma were gone, and it wasn't fair.

Every night, he dreamt about Grandpa. His grandfather was always standing in the snow, and his grandmother was always there, too. He'd call out, "Grandpa," and his own voice would wake him, his pillow wet with tears.

One night, after the dream, he wrapped the photograph in his grandmother's mauve shawl and ran onto the beach in the moonlight. He shook out the shawl and placed it on the sand like a beach towel. He was setting up the photograph when a sheet of paper floated toward him in the wind. He grabbed at it and it wedged between his fingers.

Tearing the paper into tiny pieces, he flung them into the air, shut his eyes, and held out his arms, palms facing the sky. He could feel the wind, ruffling his hair.

He opened his eyes. Grandma's shawl was dotted with little bits of white stuff that seemed to be floating down from the sky, and there were flakes on his eyelashes and his nose.

Adam watched the snow land on his palm. The flakes were soft and fluffy at first, then wet as they melted into his hand and disappeared. He looked up at the sky, opened his mouth, and put out his tongue, to see if he could catch some. . . .

Quicker than the Eye

RAY BRADBURY

People always seem to be surprised that while I am serious about my magic, I don't take myself too seriously on-stage. I enjoy what I do, and I want the audience to have as much fun as I am having. I like getting them involved. What I want most is for them to have fun and to lose themselves in the illusions I have created on-stage.

Enter Mr. Ray Bradbury, a long-time master of creating illusions on paper, rather than on-stage. He needs, of course, no introduction, except for me to say how pleased I was when he wrote a story for this volume. He has always loved the magical arts, and has used them more skillfully on paper than I could hope to do in the theater—something he demonstrates here yet one more time in a tale about a middle-aged couple, a magic show, and a pick-pocket who turns members of the audience into rubes.

While the audience laughs, its laughter is tainted by discomfort—for in the actions of the rubes they see reflected their own weaknesses. In his unfaltering way, Bradbury shows us that when we are forced to face our illusions about ourselves and see the reality behind them, we are not always happy with what we find. That it is always easier to laugh at others than at ourselves. And finally that, fortunately for our survival, our minds have the ability to replace the illusions, no matter how shattered.

—DC

Quicker than the Eye

IT WAS AT A MAGIC SHOW I saw the man who looked enough like myself to be my twin.

My wife and I were seated at a Saturday night performance; it was summer and warm, the audience melting in weather and conviviality. All around I saw married and engaged couples delighted and then alarmed by the comic opera of their lives which was being shown in immense symbol on stage.

A woman was sawed in half. How the husbands in the audience *smiled*.

A woman in a cabinet vanished. A bearded magician wept for her in despair. Then, at the tip-top of the balcony, she appeared, waving a white powdered hand, infinitely beautiful, unattainable, far away.

How the wives grinned their cat grins!

"Look at them!" I said to my wife.

A woman floated in mid-air . . . a goddess born in all men's minds by their own true love. Let not her dainty feet touch earth. Keep her on that invisible pedestal. Watch it! God, don't tell me how it's done, *anyone!* Ah, look at her float, and *dream*.

And what was that man who spun plates, globes, stars, torches, Ws elbows twirling hoops, Ms nose balancing a blue feather, sweating everything at once? What, I asked myself, but the commuter husband, lover, worker, the quick luncher, juggling hours, Benzedrine, Nembutal, bank-balances and budgets?

Obviously, none of us had come to escape the world outside, but rather to have it tossed back at us in more easily digested forms, brighter, cleaner, quicker, neater—a spectacle both heartening and melancholy.

11

Who in life has not seen a woman disappear?

There, on the black plush stage, women, mysteries of talc and rose-petal, vanished. Cream alabaster statues, sculptures of summer lily and fresh rain melted to dreams, and the dreams became empty mirrors even as the magician reached hungrily to seize them.

From cabinets and nests of boxes, from flung sea-nets, shattering like porcelain as the conjurer fired his gun, the women vanished.

Symbolic, I thought. Why do magicians point pistols at lovely assistants, unless through some secret pact with the male sub-conscious?

"What?" asked my wife.

"Eh?"

"You were muttering," said my wife.

"Sorry." I searched the program. "Oh! Next comes Miss Quick! The only female pick-pocket in the world!"

"That can't be true," said my wife, quietly.

I looked to see if she was joking. In the dark, her dim mouth seemed to be smiling, but the quality of that smile was lost to me.

The orchestra hummed like a serene flight of bees.

The curtains parted.

There, with no great fanfare, no swirl of cape, no bow, only the most condescending tilt of her head, and the faintest elevation of her left eyebrow, stood Miss Quick.

I thought it was a dog act, when she snapped her fingers.

"Volunteers. All men!"

"Sit down." My wife pulled at me.

I had risen.

There was a stir. Like so many hounds, a silently baying pack rose and walked (or did they run) to the snapping of Miss Quick's colorless fingernails.

It was obvious instantly that Miss Quick was the same woman who had been vanishing all evening.

Budget show, I thought; everyone doubles in brass. I don't like her.

'What?" asked my wife.

"Am I talking out loud again?"

But, really, Miss Quick provoked me. For she looked as if she had gone backstage, shrugged on a rumpled tweed walking suit, one size too large, gravy-spotted and grass-stained, and then purposely rumpled her hair, painted her lipstick askew, and was on the point of exiting the stage door when someone cried, "You're *on!*"

So here she was now, in her practical shoes, her nose shiny, her hands in motion but her face immobile, getting it over with . . .

Feet firmly and resolutely planted, she waited, her hands deep in her lumpy tweed pockets, her mouth cool, as the dumb volunteers dogged it to the stage.

This mixed pack she set right with a few taps, lining them up in a military row.

The audience waited.

"That's all! Act's over! Back to your seats!"

Snap! went her plain fingers.

The men, dismayed, sheepishly peering at each other, ambled off. She let them stumble half down the stairs into darkness, then yawned:

"Haven't you forgotten something?"

Eagerly, they turned.

"Here."

With a smile like the very driest wine, she lazily unwedged a wallet from one of her pockets. She removed another wallet from within her coat. Followed by a third, a fourth, a fifth! Ten wallets in all!

She held them forth, like biscuits to good beasts.

The men blinked. No, those were not their wallets. They had been on-stage only an instant. She had mingled with them only in passing. It was all a joke. Surely, she was offering them brand new wallets, compliments of the show!

But now the men began feeling themselves, like sculptures finding unseen flaws in old, hastily flung-together armatures. Their mouths gaped, their hands grew more frantic, slapping their chest-pockets, digging their pockets.

All the while Miss Quick ignored them to calmly sort their wallets like the morning mail.

It was at this precise moment I noticed the man on the far right end of the line, half on the stage. I lifted my opera glasses. I looked once. I looked twice.

"Well," I said, lightly. "There seems to be a man there who somewhat resembles me."

"Oh?" said my wife.

I handed her the glasses, casually. "Far right."

"It's not like you," said my wife. "It's you!"

"Well, almost," I said modestly.

The fellow was nice-looking. It was hardly cricket to look thus upon yourself and pronounce favorable verdicts.

Simultaneously, I had grown quite cold. I took back the opera glasses and nodded, fascinated. "Crew-cut. Horn-rim glasses. Pink complexion. Blue eyes—"

"Your absolute twin!" cried my wife.

And this was true. And it was strange, sitting there, watching myself on stage.

"No, no, no," I kept whispering.

But yet, what my mind refused, my eye accepted. Aren't there two billion people in this world? Yes! All different snowflakes, no two the same? But now here, delivered into my gaze, endangering my ego, and my complacency, here was a casting from the same absolutes, the identical mold.

Should I believe, disbelieve, feel proud, or run scared? For here I stood witness to the forgetfulness of God.

"I don't think," said God, "I've made one like this before."

But, I thought, entranced, delighted, alarmed: God errs.

Flashes from old psychology books lit my mind.

Heredity. Environment.

"Smith! Jones! Helstrom!"

On-stage, in bland drill-sergeant tones, Miss Quick called roll and handed back the stolen goods.

You borrow your body from all your forebears, I thought. Heredity.

But isn't the body also an environment?

"Winters!"

Environment, they say, surrounds you. Well, doesn't the body surround, with its lakes, its architectures of bone, its overabundances, or wastelands of soul? Does not what is seen in passing window-mirrors, a face either serene snowfalls or a pitted abyss, the hands like swans or sparrows, the feet anvils or hummingbirds, the body a lumpy wheat-sack or a summer fern, do these not, seen, paint the mind, set the image, shape the brain and psyche like clay? They *do!*

"Bidwell! Rogers!"

Well, then, trapped in the same environmental flesh, how fared this stranger on-stage?

In the old fashion, I wanted to leap to my feet and call, "What o'clock is it?"

And he, like the town-crier passing late with my face, might half-mournfully reply, "Nine o'clock, and all's well. . . ."

But was all well with him?

Question: did those horn-rims cover a myopia not only of light but spirit?

Question: was the slight obesity pressed to his skeleton symbolic of a similar gathering of tissue in his head?

In sum, did his soul go north while mine went south, the same flesh cloaking us but our minds reacting, one winter, one summer?

"My God," I said, half-aloud. "Suppose we're absolutely *identical!*"

"Shh!" said a woman behind me.

I swallowed, hard.

Suppose, I thought, he *is* a chain-smoker, light-sleeper, over-eater, manic-depressive, glib-talker, deep/shallow thinker, flesh fancier . . .

No one with that body, that face, could be otherwise. Even our names must be similar.

Our names!

". . . I . . . bl . . . er . . ."

Miss Quick spoke his!

Someone coughed. I missed it.

Perhaps she'd repeat it. But no, he, my twin, moved forward. Damn! He stumbled! The audience laughed.

I focused my binoculars swiftly.

My twin stood quietly, center stage now. His wallet returned to his fumbling hands.

"Stand straight," I whispered. "Don't slouch."

"Shh!" said my wife.

I squared my own shoulders, secretly.

I never knew I looked that fine, I thought, cramming the glasses to my eyes. Surely my nostrils aren't that thinly made, the true aristocrat. Is my skin that fresh and handsome, my chin that firm?

I blushed, in silence.

After all, if my wife said that was me, accept it! The lamplight of pure intelligence shone softly from every pore of his face.

"The glasses." My wife nudged me.

Reluctantly I gave them up.

She trained the glasses rigidly, not on the man, but now on Miss Quick, who was busy cajoling, flirting, and re-picking the pockets of the nearest men. On occasion my wife broke into a series of little satisfied snorts and giggles.

Miss Quick was, indeed, the goddess Shiva.

If I saw two hands, I saw nine. Her hands, an aviary, flew, rustled, tapped, soared, petted, whirled, tickled as Miss Quick, her face blank, swarmed coldly over her victims: touched without touching.

"What's in this pocket? And this? And here?"

She shook their vests, pinched their lapels, jingled their trousers: money rang. She punched them lightly with a vindictive forefinger, ringing totals on cash-registers. She unplucked coat buttons with mannish, yet fragile motions, gave wallets back, sneaked them away. She thrust them, took them, stole them again, while peeling money to count it behind the men's backs, then snatched their watches while holding their hands.

15

She trapped a live doctor now.

"Have you a thermometer?" she asked.

"Yes." He searched. His face panicked. He searched again. The audience cued him with a roar. He glanced over to find:

Miss Quick standing with the thermometer in her mouth, like an unlit smoke. She whipped it out, eyed it.

"Temperature!" she cried. "One hundred-ten!"

She closed her eyes and gave an insincere shake of her hips.

The audience roared. And now she assaulted her victims, bullied them, tugged at their shirts, rumpled their hair, asked: "Where's your tie?"

They clapped their hands to their empty collars.

She plucked their ties from nowhere, tossed them back.

She was a magnet that invisibly drew good luck charms, saint's medals, Roman coins, theater stubs, handkerchiefs, stickpins, while the audience ran riot, convulsed as these rabbit-men stood peeled of all prides and protections.

Hold your hip pocket, she vacuumed your vest. Clutch your vest, she jackpotted your trousers. Blithely bored, firm but evanescent, she convinced you you missed nothing, until she extracted it, with faint loathing, from her own tweeds moments later.

"What's this?" She held up a letter. "Dear Helen: Last night with you—"

A furious blush as the victim tussled with Miss Quick, snatched the letter, stowed it away. But a moment later, the letter was re-stolen and re-read aloud: "Dear Helen: Last night—"

So the battle raged. One woman. Ten men.

She kissed one, stole his belt.

Stole another's suspenders.

The women in the audience—whinnied.

Their men, shocked, joined in.

What a magnificent bully, Miss Quick! How she spanked her dear idiot-grinning, carry-on-somehow men turned boys as she spun them like cigar store Indians, knocked them with her brontosaur hip, leaned on them like barber-poles, calling each one cute or lovely or handsome.

This night, I thought, is lunatic! All about me, wives, hilarious with contempt, hysterical at being so shabbily revealed in their national pastimes, gagged for air. Their husbands sat stunned, as if a war were over that had not been declared, fought and lost before they could move. Each, nearby, had the terrible look of men who fear their throats are cut, and that a sneeze would fill the aisle with heads . . .

Quickly! I thought. *Do* something!

You, you on stage, my twin, dodge! Escape!

And she was coming *at* him!

"Be firm," I told my twin. "Strategy! Duck, weave. Zig-zag. Don't look where she says. Look where she *doesn't* say!"

"Do it! Now!"

If I shouted this, or merely ground it to powder in my teeth, I don't recall, for all the men froze as Miss Quick seized my twin by the hand.

"Careful!" I whispered.

Too late. His watch was gone. He didn't know it. Your watch is gone! I thought. He doesn't know what time it is! I thought.

Miss Quick stroked his lapel. "Back off!" I warned myself.

Too late. His forty dollar pen was gone. He didn't know it. She tweaked his nose. He smiled. Idiot! There went his wallet. Not your nose, fool, your coat!

"Padded?" She pinched his shoulder. He looked at his right arm. "No!" I cried silently, for now she had the letters out of his left coat pocket. She planted a red kiss on his brow and backed off with everything else he had on him, coins, identification, a package of chocolates which she ate, greedily. "Use the sense God gave a cow!" I shouted behind my face. "Blind! See what she's doing!"

She whirled him round, measured him and said, "This yours?" and returned his tie.

My wife was hysterical. She still held the glasses fixed on every nuance and vibration of loss and deprivation on the poor idiot's face. Her mouth was spoilt with triumph.

"My God!" I cried, in the uproar. "Get off the stage!" I yelled, within, wishing I could really yell it. "At least get out while you have *some* pride!"

The laughter had erupted like a volcano in the theater, high and rumbling and dark. The dim grotto seemed lit with unhealthy fever, an incandescence. My twin wanted to break off, like one of Pavlov's dogs, too many bells on too many days: no reward, no food. His eyes were glazed with his insane predicament.

"Fall! Jump in the pit! Crawl away!" I thought.

The orchestra sawed at destiny with violins and Valkyrian trumpets in full flood.

With one last snatch, one last contemptuous wag of her body, Miss Quick grasped my twin's clean white shirt, and yanked it *off.*

She threw the shirt in the air. As it fell, so did his pants. As his pants fell, un-belted, so did the theater. An avalanche of shock soared to bang the rafters and run over us in echoes, a thundering hilarity.

The curtain fell.

We sat, covered with unseen rubble. Drained of blood, buried in one upheaval after another, degraded and autopsied and, minus eulogy, tossed into a mass grave, we men took a minute to stare at that dropped curtain, behind which stood the pickpocket and her victims, behind which a man quickly hoisted his trousers up his spindly legs.

A burst of applause, a prolonged tide on a dark shore. Miss Quick did not appear to bow. She did not need to. She was standing behind the curtain. I could *feel* her there, no smile, no expression. Standing, coldly estimating the caliber of the applause, comparing it to the metered remembrances of other nights.

I jumped up in an absolute rage. I had, after all, failed myself. When I should have ducked, I bobbed, when I should have backed off, I ran in. What an ass!

"What a fine show!" said my wife, as we milled through the departing audience.

"Fine!" I cried.

"Didn't you like it?"

"All except the pickpocket. Obvious act, overdone, no subtlety," I said, lighting a cigarette.

"She was a whiz!"

"This way." I steered my wife toward the stage door.

"Of course," said my wife, blandly, "that man, the one who looks like you, he was a plant. They call them shills, don't they? Paid by the management to pretend to be part of the audience?"

"No man would take money for a spectacle like that," I said. "No, he was just some boob who didn't know how to be careful."

"What are we doing back here?"

Blinking around, we found we were backstage.

Perhaps I wished to stride up to my twin, shouting, "Half-baked ox! Insulter of all men! Play a flute: you dance. Tickle your chin: you jump like a puppet! Jerk!"

The truth was, of course, I must see my twin close up, confront the traitor, and see where his true flesh differed from mine. After all, wouldn't *I* have done better in his place?

The backstage was lit in blooms and isolated flushes, now bright, now dark, where the other magicians stood chatting. And there, there was Miss Quick.

And there, smiling, was my *twin!*

"You did fine, Charlie," said Miss Quick.

My twin's name was Charlie. Stupid name.

Charlie patted Miss Quick's cheek. "*You* did fine, ma'am!"

God, it was *true!* A shill, a confederate. Paid what? Five, ten dollars for letting his shirt be torn off, letting his pants drop with his pride? What a turncoat, traitor!

I stood, glaring.

He glanced up.

Perhaps he saw me.

Perhaps some bit of my rage and impacted sorrow reached him.

He held my gaze only a moment, his mouth wide, as if he had just seen an old school chum. But, not remembering my name, could not call out, so let the moment pass.

He saw my rage. His face paled. His smile died. He glanced quickly away. He did not look up again, but stood pretending to listen to Miss Quick, who was laughing and talking with the other magicians.

I stared at him and stared again. Sweat oiled his face. My hate melted. My temper cooled. I saw his profile clearly, his chin, eyes, nose, hairline: I memorized it all. Then I heard someone say:

"It was a *fine* show!"

My wife, moving forward, shook the hand of the pick-pocketing beast.

On the street, I said, "Well, *I'm* satisfied."

"About what?" asked my wife.

"He doesn't look like me at all. Chin's too sharp. Nose is smaller. Lower lip isn't full enough. Too much eyebrow. On stage, far off, had me going. But, close-up, no, no. It was the crew-cut and horn-rims fooled us. *Anyone* could have horn-rims and a crew-cut."

"Yes," my wife agreed, "anyone."

As she climbed into our car, I could not help but adore her long lovely legs.

Driving off, I thought I glimpsed that familiar face in the passing crowd. The face, however, was watching *me!* I wasn't sure. Resemblances, I now knew, are superficial.

The face vanished in the crowd.

"I'll never forget," said my wife. "When his pants fell!"

I drove very fast, then drove very slow, all the way home.

19

The Conversion of Tegujai Batir

JACK KIRBY

(Extrapolated posthumously from The Horde, *a novel-in-progress by Jack Kirby.)*

Not many people know that the late Jack Kirby, creator, among others, of the Fantastic Four, Silver Surfer, Captain America, The X-Men, had a novel-in-progress that was very close to his heart. With permission from Jack's beloved wife, Roz, and with the writing help of my co-editor, Janet, we have extrapolated from that novel. It is with extreme pleasure that we give you a unique view into the head of the King of the Comics.

—DC

The Conversion of Tegujai Batir

I AM DALIL KHAN. I have been messenger, soldier, and brother-of-the-heart to the Falcon Father, Tegujai Batir. Now I am scribe, and I am glad of it, for what is a man but the product of the written word? The written word that brings him into being. The written word that dictates the pattern of his life, is inscribed at his passing, and continues when he is returned to the dust. It is the essence of all truth, the holy will of Allah, who wrote all that has happened, all that is happening, all that must happen.

I know Tegujai Batir as no one else does. When he looks into my eyes, he sees a mirror of himself, as he once was, and as he is now. He and I are aware that the day must come when he no longer wishes to be reminded of these things. He will kill me then, and someone else will be assigned to finish this writing, which is written from both hearsay and observation, and speaks to the conversion, diversion, and repossession of Tegujai Batir.

Tegujai Batir's father stared into the eyes of his fifteen-year-old son, who sat with young Dalil Khan upon the family's felt mat. "The Reader has come to our home, my son," the father said, speaking of private matters despite Dalil's presence, for the child was both Tegujai's friend and the son of Osman Khan, a revered elder and leader of the tribe.

Tegujai looked annoyed, as if he resented the intrusion upon his evening, which in fact he did.

"This is an honor," his father reminded him.

An honor perhaps, but an intrusion nevertheless, Tegujai thought, as a small man, old by the boy's terms and heavily wrapped in shapeless

23

animal skins, hurtled himself into the room. He appeared to have been propelled forward by physical forces outside of his own body.

"Tegujai Batir. I bid you to grow feet," he shrieked.

The boy jumped to his feet, stood upright, and straightened his shoulders.

"When you have grown a Striking Arm, a Feeding Arm, and Mighty Feet, I shall shout down through the length of your body, and you shall move forward and eat the world," the Reader yelled.

Tegujai balled his hands into fists and held them tightly at his sides, lest they flash to the fur skins at the old man's throat. He imagined himself twisting his fingers tightly to cut off the torrent of words, and could almost feel the throat beat wildly at his fingers, the words fighting to get out.

The old man's eyes rolled about and his lips worked furiously, as if he wished to continue speaking but was unable to do so. Tegujai relaxed his mental pressure on the Reader, a reaction prompted by fear rather than mercy.

At once, whatever possessed the Reader began slowly taking command of things. The sound of it returned in gasps and croaks, and joined with the moving lips to give body to the words. They became fluent, unbroken. A droning litany flowed out to Tegujai who shrank from it, lying down with stomach pains at the feet of his family and their friends.

The outpouring of words continued, directed at the boy who lay stricken on the mat. They were not meant for jinn or man, but for marking Tegujai, damning him, separating him from family, friends, and sun-warmed plain.

"Shacquebai! Shacquebai!"

The Reader screamed these last and most frightening words, knowing the fear the boy felt in hearing them would create a void inside his heart. The jinn, who had led the Reader to the House of Batir, would enter into that void and stake their claim on the soul of Tegujai Batir.

Tegujai had closed his eyes against the onslaught. Upon hearing these words, he opened them and gazed at his young friend Dalil Khan. The younger boy cowered on the corner of the mat, staring as if at a monster.

Thus Tegujai, who had long understood the origins of the jinn, knew for certain that their mark had been put upon him.

I am Dalil Khan. I have been messenger, soldier, and brother-of-the-heart to the Falcon Father, Tegujai Batir. Now, as scribe, it is my duty to record the happenings of that day when the jinn took my friend.

The Conversion of Tegujai Batir

I did not understand it then, but since I was called upon to accept it, it became my duty to learn about them. To say that what I learned terrified me is to say that there is some sand in the desert.

The desert is sand. In the same way, my degree of fear was the definition of terror. Would not any eight-year-old feel that way, in learning that the jinn were brought into being before Adam and were the children of Jann, that the sin of pride drew them from allegiance to the law of the Creator, and that they most often followed Iblix, Ahriman-Sheitan-Satan—who was born among them and was the Grand Master of Immodesty?

These spirits, though lower than the angels, were capable of appearing in human and animal form, and of influencing man for good and evil. In this case, judging by the degenerative behavior of my friend, and the agitation of the Reader, the jinn's intentions were not benign.

Exceedingly perturbed, Tegujai's family searched for a way to exorcise the jinn. After much searching, it was concluded that no Moslem prayer existed that could drive them from their son.

"This can be done only through the force of your own will, your own desire to pursue the goodness of Allah," Tegujai's father told him.

"Where is the goodness of Allah, if He allows such creatures to coexist with him?" Tegujai asked, speaking to his father in a tone of derision such as he would never have dared to use to his elders in the time before the mark was put upon him.

Then, not being of great enough conviction to follow his father's wisdom, he turned to the practices of superstition. He turned from the shamans, who were the spokesmen of Allah, to the Reader.

Having chosen this different method of divination, he at first enlisted Dalil Khan in its study.

Under cover of darkness, they stole from the yurt and went into the hills. When the moon rose, they found the bloodstained tracks of a young wolf, who had apparently strayed from the pack and been injured. Following the tracks, they came upon the beast.

By now, it was bleeding to death, and hardly able to move.

"I wish to return to the yurt," Dalil Khan said, risking the older boy's scorn.

"Well, go then, coward." Tegujai pointed into the darkness. "But you go alone."

Not knowing which was worse, to walk by himself through the black hills or stay with his friend, Dalil Khan watched as Tegujai studied the scarlet tracings flowing from the freshly ripped organ of the beast, studied, absorbed, and was strangely overcome by the symbols of the grisly patterns. The symbols seemed to open a mystic door through which something lunged and possessed him, something which thrashed inside him with unholy life and gave him frightening transports as the jinn clung to him and began the disintegration of all that he was and held dear.

This was a sight from which Dalil Khan shrank in wonder and awe. His decision made, he took off on a solitary journey back to the yurt.

Soon, Tegujai was abandoned in this manner by all who knew him. He was forced away from familiar animal smells and friendly fires, from simple laughter and proud defiance in the face of elemental nature.

This happened slowly, of course, from the day that the Reader left the encampment. Everything Tegujai did or said was interpreted in fearful symbols and colored by his growing anger. Those who loved him and those he loved, those who honored his family, and those whose families he honored, all wore guarded faces and looked fretfully into the gathering clouds of the future.

"I hate all of you," Tegujai shouted, driven by the jinn to lash out at everyone—even Dalil Khan.

Out of this hatred was born the concept of the army that he would form, the one that would become known as the great worm. Its guiding will lived with him and among those who surrounded them.

As word of it spread beyond the tribe, and all men began to live under the shadow of the prophecy, Tegujai's presence could no longer be tolerated.

"You are my oldest friend," Osman Khan told Tegujai's father, in the presence of his son's brother-of-the-heart, Dalil. "It grieves me to ask you to deny your flesh and blood. If you cannot do it, I will do it for you."

"What is it you wish me to do?" Tegujai's father asked, though he knew the answer.

"Your son must be cast from the tribe," Osman Khan said.

Hearing this, I ran to the yurt of my friend to give him warning, for I loved him still and wished to give him the chance to save face. Tegujai took heed at once. After ordering me to leave with him, and after my refusal, he set out without a further word to me on wanderings that would lead him from all that which had once given him joy.

This was the first time I had known life without him. Despite the abruptness of his leave-taking, I listened eagerly for news of him, and committed all that I heard to the deepest recesses of my mind. I am glad of that, for it allows me now to record his journey as if I had indeed traveled at his side.

The Conversion of Tegujai Batir

Tegujai was moving north when the order of things finally crumbled inside him. By then, he had taken up with the few who disdained the tribal life. He rode with them to seek out the cities where, it was told, men mingled in great herds and indulged in unimagined curiosities. Thus he absorbed the poisons of the world from those not of his own kind.

During all of this time, the droning Tegujai had heard in the gloom of the yurt stayed with him. The litany had woven a spell about him, and he seemed unable to escape its gossamer. He found himself enthralled by the new corruptions and delights he was experiencing, and he leaped to the call of war that swept through the Communist lands.

Trekking across the face of the broken earth to Stalingrad, where fighting became an ignoble deed, he learned how man and nature could combine to produce the most horrible agonies. Abominable cruelties enveloped him with a shocking sweetness as he moved onward, through crushed steel and battered, screaming faces, across snows with white hordes shackled to propeller-driven sleds, to the Oder and the Neisse. Farther through East Prussia, sacking, raping, disemboweling, in a devil dance geared to the tempo of the mighty offensive.

There, before him, surged the shaggy masses, and the babble and the clatter of a thousand different strains and dialects.

All of this Tegujai assimilated with a fair amount of ease. Then he reached Siberia. Forming the girding on the Siberian drill fields, he saw something so foreign that he fell to his knees in rank terror—giant machines which rose into the air, and others that crawled and rumbled like jinn monsters.

"What are those things which are metal and yet fly like hawks?" he whispered, voice rasping with fear.

His companion guffawed. "They are called airplanes," he said.

"Airplanes," Tegujai repeated, rising slowly to his feet. "These metal birds, do they carry men in their bellies?"

"They do," his friend said.

"And the ones which crawl like tortoises across the ground?"

"Those are called tanks. They shoot the seeds of hell from their mouths."

As he said this, several of the tanks erupted with noise, and flames issued from them. Again, fear sent Tegujai hurtling onto the earth. Lying there, he determined that his Falcon army would have such metal tortoises and birds.

After that, Tegujai returned happily to the human frenzy of war, which reached its high point with the impaling of the enemy on his own hearth, as men died on the run in the choking dust. The breath came hard from his nostrils. He scrabbled over smoldering rubble, plunged into the darkness of blasted warrens, and heard the screams of straddled women and the rattle of shots tearing into the shadows.

When he emerged, swaying drunkenly from his exertions, he found himself in the world of the white man.

And, for the first time in his life, in the world—and the arms—of a white woman. An Austrian woman.

"*Du bist ein enfaches Kind,*" she said, her great, soft arms drawing him to her unafraid. Her body was large, her face red. "You are a simple child."

In that manner, Anna was able to bridge the barrier of skin and structure and culture. White women could do that, Tegujai decided. They were merely female, dominated by their primary purpose. When they turned to it in bed, they lost fear and found compromise.

Not so, Anna's brother, Fritz, the first white *man* he learned to know.

Fritz fought so subtly in his servility, so openly in arrogance, that there was no basic meeting ground for the two of them. Nor was there any effort Tegujai could make to overcome the instinctive recoil in his make-up.

"*Kaffee?*" Fritz asked, holding the coffee pot poised in his hand. "Cigarette?" Yet in sharing, be it his coffee and his cigarettes, his conversation and hospitality, he sought always to prove his own virtue. The white man was complexity itself, a creature both beautiful and leprous, treacherous and heroic. Beast and angel in one, each devouring the other.

This complexity marked the white man, Tegujai decided. It made him tense and driven, made him strive and hammer and bring into being the big and little wonders of his world, and caused him to foul them and destroy them with equal vigor.

The white man was incredible, but not formidable. Tegujai met him and faced him down with the strength of simplicity, with the serenity and firmness of the rock that lay in his own kind. With the acceptance of things for what they were. Belligerence must be met with belligerence. Love must be returned with equal fairness. There was no compromise in *his* kind. They did what had to be done, did it honestly and unashamedly, with a sincerity the white man lacked.

"Your white man is a sly one, all right," Tegujai announced to Anna on the last night they were together, entering into a diatribe he would repeat years later to Dalil Khan and whoever else was within earshot. "The labels work for him, give him courage when he needs it, wealth when he wants it, and power when he lusts after it. In the manner of all these things, he unleashes his drive and beleaguers the earth and the waters and the sky."

According to Tegujai's perceptions, the white man groveled in excuses. He put labels on his every action. If he did the beast's work, it was done in the name of the angel, who was then run through the gauntlet in order to eradicate the beast.

When an end came to the fighting in Europe, Tegujai could hardly wait for the moment of his return to the tribe. The distance was great, but not for a young mind which placed him already there, in the yurt, at the fire, astride his horse on the open plain. In his youthful imagination he quenched and dispersed the cloud on his name, watched the faces of all light up with pride and happiness as he told the tales of battles and his part in them. He would bring home trophies, and hand them out where all could watch. He would bring home the white man's delicacies, and delight his brothers with the strangeness.

This was Tegujai's dream, but it never bore fruit. Instead, it died in the Russian occupation of Vienna. He was kept by duty among white men, he dallied and waited, he piddled with the intricacies of the army and earned promotion. He marked time in the dimly lit, ghost-ridden streets where cold rain fell from the night and collected in dirty puddles on the cobblestones.

Then, slowly, the return was made. He made it, dragging with him his experiences, the collection of promotions, and the oppressive weight of the white man's leaving which hardened on his back. For His own divine reason, Tegujai decided, Allah had created two kinds of men. The white man, living with his fires; the colored man, with his instincts. If this was so, *he* must live with those facts, at least for the moment. But he determined that the day would come when he would destroy them, all of them—not realizing that it was for this very reason that the jinn had possessed him.

Having made this decision, Tegujai took the route of the military man and served the Communists, for they were everywhere in the Asiatic heartland. He left the Russians as a lieutenant and joined the Chinese as a captain.

Finally, when he had fought in the battles that made the mainland Communist, he poured with them into the Sinkiang, with an added promotion to major and a heart of steel. He was home.

29

He was home, but the sunlit plains were gone. He was home, but his people fled before him, biting his extended hand. They died cursing him, squirming in the snow until they froze in mid-fury. He brought them to his tent, and they died or went mad.

All this passed in the Year of the Tiger. Now it was the Year of the Hare, once-removed. The long flight was over for Tegujai, who had set up his yurt in the lowlands close to the village where he had been raised. The yurt was part of a large encampment; a regiment of seven hundred men sheltered in a wide, semi-circular sweep of yurts, erected and spaced in organized fashion. Within the pincers of the semi-circle were the stockades, log pens built with haste and little enthusiasm by his captives.

Once imprisoned, they were allowed the shelter of cast-off skins and whatever could be spared for rations. When this proved impractical, small hunting parties were organized and the captives provided their own meat under the wary vigilance of mounted tommy gunners. The women and children were kept in separate units, the children receiving the more careful treatment. Tegujai housed them in a large, specially constructed yurt in the charge of details who were under orders to assure the survival of the young. This proved to be a task most harrowing to the guards who, more often than not, would ask for lighter duty among the snapping camels and excitable horses.

The base camp was large, filled with sound and odor and activity, the air in the yurt hot and damp, heavy with odors, and charged with madness. Tegujai himself was plagued by visions, brought to him by the jinn—visions of a future filled with blood and battle. Their voices, squealing inside his head, told him again what he must do. That he must build a maze of tunnels through which a trained army of millions would worm its way to the capitals of the Western world.

Tegujai Batir was never completely alone, for always the orderly sat silently in the corner of his major's yurt. Still, occasionally, he found a moment of peace. During those times, when his tent was silent and the camp sounds had taken over, he convinced himself that his destiny—predicted by shamans and devils alike—was soon to be fulfilled. He sat, relaxed on his mound of skins, and made rapport with the sounds outside, fur-booted feet drawn up to support the overhang of his arms, cigar rolling lazily like cud in the slow rotation of his jaw.

For the most part, however, the visions drove Tegujai to distract himself by filling the tent with an assortment of people.

On one such night, not long after Tegujai's return, the tent held four beside him. One of them was the inert body of Osman Khan who, though the father of his friend and scribe, Dalil, was nonetheless the general who had most recently offended him. The others comprised a sergeant, the orderly, and a slender, young Chinese lieutenant with moody, close-set eyes. Tegujai wore the insignia of a major on the open collar of his uniform. His chunky body, divested of its shapeless quilted field garment, stood well braced and smart in finer garrison cloth. Only his open shirt, which exposed the black hair on his chest, the sags and folds and half-rolled sleeves, only these robbed him of achieving a fully effective military portrait. His affect was that of the type of officer who chose to blend in with his men and render to his superiors what was due them.

And Tegujai Batir delivered. He did so with machine gun, hand grenade, and semi-automatic rifle, rendering up the fleeing thousands who would not live their lives within the new design. He delivered their camels and horses and fat-tailed sheep. He broke the tribe, and when only scattered families remained, he pursued and broke *them*. As for the remnants, half-starved and skeletonized, living on the blood of their exhausted animals, they too would be delivered. They had to be, in order for the tight reins of control to crack over the entire land mass.

Soon it will all be condensed into a crisp, little report, Tegujai thought this night, staring at Osman Khan's body as he absently scraped his fork against the food smears in his mess kit. The long, hard, violent months, the bone-chilling wet, the tortuous dry, the aches and exaltations, a thousand bivouacs, a thousand joltings of the saddle against the body, a thousand rank smells and damnable sights, condensed into nothingness, squeezed into words acceptable to the proper echelons.

The orderly crossed to Tegujai and silently relieved him of the utensils.

"I'll have another cupful of the kumiss." Tegujai's hand glided through the patch of his own fine chest hairs. "Damned if that fermented mare's milk doesn't sit better than whiskey, here in the Takla Makan."

"The wolves can have this desert," the sergeant said. "They can eat the sand in the summer and suck the ice in the winter. I've had my fill of it." The soldier eyed the man lying inert on the floor, a colt's stomach wrapped around his bleeding middle. "That peasant's remedy won't shore up the hole in *him*. Why don't we finish the poor bastard and make him the last of the slaughter. The job's done and—"

"The major will decide when the job is done, Sergeant!" The Chinese lieutenant, sullen and resentful of the latitude allowed these

Mongol troops, spoke like a whiplash, but took no action. "The whores of Urumchi will still be serving the garrison when you return."

"That poultice certainly won't help him, Tegujai." The sergeant spoke through greasy lips, swollen to capacity with meat-gob that shifted in the chewing action to allow for flow of speech. The flesh of the colt was a great delicacy, even to the elevated Mongol of the New China. Considering that the meat had come from the captured herds of Osman Khan, the soldier extended little grace to the man who, by cruel design of misfortune, had supplied the dinner. "Frozen balls of Marx and Lenin, he's just a stinking corpse that needs a bullet to make it official—"

Tegujai was quick to interrupt. He cautioned the sergeant, "Let this go no further, Janim. Make no reply to Lieutenant Chen. He has the right to discipline you and he shall. I have relaxed the rules to make this long pull endurable, but the rules still exist. You must not tread beyond their limits. Let us be comrades—and soldiers."

"I thank you for your support, Major," the Chinese lieutenant put in. "The discipline and dedication of the proletariat spirit has reached a dangerously low level among these men of late. I was beginning to feel like just another man on a hunt, instead of an officer detailed to a military mission."

"Never reject your instincts, Lieutenant." Tegujai took the cup of mare's milk held out by his orderly. "They tell you what the facts are." He sipped slowly. "We've tracked the herd from stamping ground to water hole. What we haven't cut down will be turned over for disposal by the army."

"Then you consider this campaign against rebellious elements such as the tribe of Osman Khan a mere . . . hunt, sir?"

"It's been no more than the flushing of wolves, Lieutenant. Had those been our orders, the tactics would have been no different. Men at the mercy of superior firepower and mobility can inflict only bites, and you must admit that the few bites we've suffered came about through simple lack of caution." Tegujai downed the last of the kumiss and returned the cup to his orderly. With the hairy back of his hand, he erased the creamy outline around his lips. "Glorify this for your military record, Lieutenant. Use it for gain. Just remember it for what it truly was and apply that yardstick to future situations. You will be a soldier with potential, I assure you."

The thin, youthful lieutenant turned to peer thoughtfully into the semi-gloom, hiding the touch of cynicism that manifested itself in a shift of facial expression. Tegujai saw this and was upon him.

"Lieutenant, what would you say was the true value of this . . . mission?"

"For me, Major?"

"Yes, for you, Lieutenant."

"A good working knowledge of the Mongol. . . ."

Tegujai studied his subordinate appraisingly and showed his teeth. "Very good, Lieutenant. Despite the fact that you're the type who would stupidly impale himself on enemy bayonets for the glory of an ideology, you are not lacking in more laudable qualities. What exactly *have* you learned about the Mongol?"

The Chinese lieutenant wheeled and straightened. Facing Tegujai squarely, he spoke with emphatic clarity. "The Mongol, sir, is a brute of the field. As you have said, it's been like flushing out wolves. In and out of uniform I find them unreasonable, ungovernable, and intolerable."

Tegujai chuckled and showed more teeth. He leered into the stony face of the younger man. "Yes, yes, but what are we to do with these beasts who are, after all, my brothers? What are we to do with these wild and superstitious litters of ancient ravagers?"

The lieutenant's eyes narrowed slightly in malice, becoming little black pools of vitriolic liquid in which spots of fire continually sprang into being and flamed out. "The Mongol will conform and contribute, or die. We shall take the animal fat out of his hair, put a muzzle on his mouth, and teach him to do more with his hands than poke about in sheep's dung. That is what must be done with him, though personally I believe the task is futile. The Mongol will resist any effort to make him of value to the state or to himself."

"Really? That's interesting," Tegujai said.

"Yes, and I shall be among the first to volunteer for the extermination squads when General Mao finally throws up his hands and gives the order to rid the New China of this human waste!" The lieutenant had finished and stared rebelliously into space. His anger, released, roamed the confines of the tent and charged it with menace. Tegujai could feel it hang heavily in the fetid silence, see it alive and burning as it touched the men grouped about him. They were Mongols, every one of them, including the major, who could feel the insignia of rank on his collar growing larger until it filled the lieutenant's vision and stabbed home the frailty of his position. There wasn't a man in the tent who couldn't kill him with impunity. It would take little hesitation; another life-spark blown out in the barren vastness of the Takla Makan. Who would know? Who would care? His epitaph would be a closed file. Shot for insubordination, shot for neglect of duty, death caused by wounds suffered in the line of duty, missing in action. A legion of coffin lids had slammed shut on such men whose lives were important only to themselves.

The lieutenant stood in stoic defiance and listened to the cracking of the limb he had sawed through. A liquid streak wormed crookedly down his forehead. The passive eyes of Tegujai followed its downward course; watched it filter through the hair of the eyebrow and form the bright drop that would catch the light as it fell to the floor.

"Go ahead," the lieutenant said and steeled himself for the bullet. "Blow my head off and damn your lice-ridden ancestors."

Tegujai made no move toward his pistol. He allowed his junior officer a moment more in the sweat bath before he spoke. "That's a good show of guts, Lieutenant. For a man like you to sneer at death is commonplace, but this breach of rank is a rarity in your kind. Just isn't done, is it? Like snapping the umbilical cord, I'd say. Well, I'm not going to shoot you for it, although it is my right in such cases. These fourteen months in the field have been harder on you than the rest of us. You've kept to the rules, and this little outburst has been a long time in coming." He scratched at the side of his jaw. "Besides, you couldn't have said what you did if you hadn't turned Mongol. Yes, Lieutenant, you've become a little brother of the Wolf. Watching your behavior when you return among your fellows will be quite amusing."

There was a slight reaction in the lieutenant's otherwise immobile features. Tegujai kept his eyes upon him and poked at the rigid chest with a stubby forefinger. "We've planted a jinn devil inside you, my boy." He grinned. "It will make you cry for blood and send you tearing at your enemies. You'll live twice as hard and die twice as hard . . . and know it hasn't all been for meaningless slogans."

The lieutenant's frame seemed to lose some of its steel. "Will that be all, Major?"

"Yes, I know you want to leave the tent. And you shall in a moment." Tegujai turned to the sergeant. "Hussain!"

There was a movement, the ungainly maneuvering of large bones from a height of seven feet. "Tegujai Batir? Major?"

"Was it you who saw the Reader among the male prisoners?"

"Yes, Sir. I kicked his behind all the way to the stockade. The old fool was working a rifle when we caught up with the last batch at the foot of the mountain. I had a hole in my ear before I yanked the weapon from him and clubbed him with it. Imagine, an old fart of a Reader—"

Tegujai cut him off. "The addition of new captives and livestock will demand a check. The lieutenant will take charge of this. You are to join the detail only to find the Reader and bring him to me."

The tall Mongol shifted restlessly. "As you wish, Major. But hadn't I better stick with the detail throughout the entire check? The lieutenant

may need a hand with the squad when they get in among the women."
Tegujai held him with a baleful stare. "Well you know it's going to
happen. Some hands are going to count crotches instead of heads.
We'll need the regiment to silence the uproar." Still Tegujai said nothing. "That *will* happen unless I'm . . ." Mumbling to a halt, the Mongol
waited.

Tegujai had turned to the lieutenant. "When the check is completed, I shall expect the revised figures."

"Yes, sir." The man was sullen as he pulled into his quilted field
clothes.

"One more thing, Lieutenant . . ."

The Chinese officer's reply was half-formed when the pistol butt
struck him between nose and upper lip. The jolt ran through his entire
body and he lost the support of his knees. He fell upon them, rocking
back and forth. His fingers were pressed to his face as though to keep it
from splitting in two. Then he lurched forward, his shoulder striking
the mat before he rolled over onto his back.

Tegujai coolly returned his pistol to its holster as he surveyed his
handiwork. Between the fingers and the face, the gore came into view.
Tegujai said in a calm and even tone, "An insult to a man's lice-ridden
ancestors demands at least that much, Lieutenant." He motioned to the
others and they understood. The man with his pain and wounds was
removed from the tent. Only the orderly returned to look after
Tegujai's needs.

Now, finally, Tegujai Batir gave his attention to Osman Khan, who
lay as a dead man, stretched full length on the blood-stained mat.
Inside him, memory mingled with pain. The ghosts of the fallen cried
out to him, his wife Milya among them, cut down by gunfire before
she could mount her horse. With what was left of his mind, he thought
of the last pitiful remnants of his tribe, completing the long trek. For
him it was over. He was in hell, bearing his agony in Kazakh silence.

Somber, demon faces hovered and swam across Khan's fevered
vision, and the jinn chose to show them to Tegujai. He at once recognized *his own face,* its boulder-like quality, the skull beneath jutting like
rock through the sallow skin. The soft, almond eyes, the stub of the
nose, the mouth that knew no tender words, these were set in the wide
framework of sturdy bone. There was a slash of black mustache that
hung over each side of his upper lip, and a small chin-beard grown of
fine, soft hairs that lent him the air of a chief. Tegujai Batir, a chief of
demons. Such was his destiny, predicted by shamans and fulfilled by
Tegujai himself.

"Don't stir, Wolf Brother," said the disembodied head of Tegujai, which had separated from Osman Khan and hung like an evil moon over him, emitting high-pitched sounds. "Your wounds are bad, and movement of your body will heighten the pain."

Osman Khan lurched as a great spasm shook him. His eyes closed tightly and his mouth opened and stretched and drew back from his clenched teeth in horrible distortion. The bronze skin glistened beadily on his throat.

Through his agony, the voice of Tegujai penetrated relentlessly. "That is the wrong way to reach for death, Wolf Brother. Even a Kazakh's honor will drain out quickly through shattered bowels. Move again and you'll run to your ancestors screaming like a woman. Lie still. Heed my counsel. Death will come to you soon enough, and I can help you cross into Paradise with dignity."

The man tensed even further. Tegujai's voice seemed to agitate him as would an added refinement on the rack. He could sense the others, too, the jinn, vague beings occupied with unseen tasks. What they were doing was of little consequence, until their sound and movement grew more pronounced, and the smell of raw flesh registered upon him. His eyes remained shut, but it was evident that something was happening, and it involved him.

Tegujai addressed the orderly. "That's it. Careful. He'll go quickly if you're rough with him. Gently—gently there."

The raw flesh odor had strengthened, and Tegujai's voice, clipped and authoritative, shot across the core of what was happening. He seemed to be talking to the jinn. There came a sudden slimy contact with his wounds and Osman Khan recoiled with a hoarse cry. His body lay in that last nebulous state between life and death, then his fingers dug into the felt mat and went limp.

The major rose and crossed to the dying man. He squatted beside him, for the eyes had opened once more. Their fires had dampened. Death was completing the work he had begun. Beneath the sweat, the dirt smears and the raw bruises, the waxen pale had spread.

Tegujai's fingers closed on the cigar and freed it from his teeth. "Soon," he said. "It will be soon, Son of Chiefs. You were not born for these days. You were not of the chaff which rises and flows with the flood. You were of the rock which resists and is torn from the earth to sink in the turbulence." He gazed soberly into eyes that swam in their sockets and could not focus. "How sad it is that you die hating me."

The body trembled and a sound escaped the waxen lips, a ragged sound, thick with the phlegm of body substance, yet Tegujai understood. "World Eater." The sound was just a harsh bubbling in the throat and chest, grating and quickening in the clotting cavern as it

36

moved toward its climax—the ugly noise of departing life. He was slightly startled when it ceased abruptly, for the moment of crossing came with the unexpectedness of birth—an instant in time that was swifter than Man's reflex, the valve of the infinite ejecting and swallowing, operating eternally, independent of mortal design.

"*Shacquebai! Shacquebai!*"

The cries of the Reader broke the death silence and rocked Tegujai from where he squatted. He twisted in fright and fell, tearing at his holster. Shadows leaped in the eerie light, and the sharp crack of blows burst from a flurry of movement.

Tegujai was quickly back on his feet, cold ferocity in tight possession of him, bearing down on the pain in his wrenched back, and forcing the steel of his weapon to the source of the attack.

For all the world, it seemed as though two shaggy beasts, locked in combat, had hurled themselves into the tent. Only a small remaining shred of reason kept him from firing into the rolling bodies. Although shaken, he managed control when the scene arranged itself in proper perspective.

"Forgive me, Tegujai Batir . . . Major . . ." The giant Hussain, his fur askew, disengaged himself from his prey and awkwardly rose to face Tegujai. "The crazy, little dung-eater suddenly got out of hand—" Still angered by his embarrassment, the hulking sergeant leveled a cruel kick at the man on all fours. The impact brought an animal sound, and the man crumpled.

The tableaux was ridiculous. Tegujai, like a man unhorsed, regained his balance and his air of command. He allowed himself the prerogative of outrage, which he hurled in silent bolts at the melancholy face atop its tower of fur.

"What I hear must be true," he said, shaking his head in disgust. "You were formed for birth in a camel's behind."

The tension was draining off. Slowly Tegujai returned his gun, light in his hand, to its holster.

"These Readers see a dying man and immediately go into their routine. They must shout with the departing spirit as he races to his ancestors. They must call them by name at the top of their lungs." Hussain spoke in obvious discomfort. "I beg your forgiveness, Tegujai Batir. Clearly, I entered with the old devil at the wrong moment."

The limbs jutting out of the pile of skins on the floor began to move, and the head of the Reader made jerking efforts to rise, but another kick from Hussain quickly ended the attempt. The sergeant's irritation had not diminished.

Tegujai re-lit his cigar and faced Hussain with narrowed eyes and clenched jaw. When the cottonlike wads of smoke puffed gently into the air, the non-com relaxed. The major, with a good cigar in his mouth, was not a dangerous man. The smoldering belligerence in his expression was merely proper procedure. The incident had reached the level where Hussain could safely breathe. He waited for Tegujai to devise another choice epithet, or hurl an order. What came was an order.

"Forget the Reader, Hussain. Choose a burial detail and dispose of that body. Bury it deep and in a place where it will not be worried by animals."

"We will use rock," replied the sergeant.

Tegujai held him in the grip of his stare as he pulled on the cigar. "It's been a bad day for you, has it not, child of a frozen mammoth?"

The great leather face remained silent in its shroud of melancholia. Army life had taught the brute when not to press his luck. Tegujai drew close to him. He poked stiffened fingers into the giant's middle.

"When the burial has been taken care of, you will attend to one more detail before relieving yourself of further duty for the night."

"Yes, Major. One additional detail?"

Tegujai's rigid fingers struck again. "A woman, you weeping tiger. Find yourself a female among the new arrivals and stay out of sight until morning."

"The tiger grovels before the wisdom and great heart of the Wolf." Hussain's smile was little more than a facial twitch. The huge face seemed unchanged.

"Dismissed," Tegujai said. "Get out of here."

Hussain turned and left, knowing that he hadn't saluted. He also knew that correcting the error would be a greater error still.

The orderly, cleaning his Seminov rifle, glanced irritably in the direction of the Reader, from whom words continued to fall like steady rain. He glanced at Tegujai, standing in indecision above the shattered old man.

The blow will surely come, thought the orderly. If Tegujai does not stop the Reader's babbling, I'll spill the old goat's brains, myself. There was a snap as metal slid where it did not fit. The orderly flung the weapon aside, too angry to finish the job.

"See the worm!" the old man's litany continued. "See his eternal sores! See how his belly knots in hunger! For he lives where the earth is hostile. He thirsts where the water is foul. He prays where there are no prophets. He is not of the blessed. He is not of the sacred. He is not of the chosen. In his blindness, he is but a simple child of Allah."

Something had broken in the old man, something not of the body, for there was already little left of that. The Reader had managed to rise shakily to his bruised knees. His appearance was that of a mangy dog who had suffered horribly from the snapping pack. And so he had. There were few parts of him which had not been wrenched, fractured, or burned. He could no longer control his weeping, his coughing, or the flow of words from his swollen lips. He was climbing to reach his last refuge, and the words were the hand-holds which he grasped. Behind him lay a shattered spirit. To fall back upon it meant enduring the unbearable. So he climbed higher, faster, retreating, retreating, retreating . . .

". . . and it is written that when he with the sword in his mouth has been cast into the fires, when the false prophet, his ally, has been quartered and strung up to the wind, when the dragon has been thrown back into the pit . . ."

Tegujai stood close to the old man and looked down into the wild, staring eyes. "Dung-eater," he rasped. "Dirty old dung-eater! Must that prophecy foul even your final madness?"

"And yet another shall rise, speaking no language, but understanding all. And he shall see the worm, and rouse the worm, and say to it, 'I shall be your will and bid you to grow one Mighty Arm for striking and another with which to feed yourself.' . . ."

A coughing spasm seized the Reader. His body heaved and contracted. The breath whistled in his throat and his lumpy face raised itself heavenward, toward distances beyond Tegujai.

A loud moan escaped Tegujai Batir, and the frightful cry of the damned shook the yurt. Tegujai seized the Reader, who could not feel the contact. He stared into eyes that could not see him. He shouted into ears that heard only the voice of Allah.

"Robber! Fraud!" he shouted at the dead man. "You took it from me! You took it!"

Spittle shot from the redness where the strong teeth were exposed. There was full madness in him. It swept up fiercely and flung him to the Reader, unbridled, inescapable. "I want it back!" Tegujai shouted as blood spread over his hands. "I want the love of my family!"

Tegujai's mouth was drawn back like the Wolf he was.

I am Dalil Khan, messenger, soldier, scribe, and brother-of-the-heart to the Falcon Father, Tegujai Batir. Twenty more years have passed. I still know him as no one else does. The day of our reckoning is upon us, for the Wolf has spawned a Falcon army, selected the site for a tunnel, plucked the Feathers that will make the Falcon fly. He will kill me soon, for even I, who continue to love him like a brother, cannot fill the hole which opened up in him when he cried out and proclaimed his need. I have watched all the love and beauty draining from him, leaving nothing but the hunger. The jinn have seen it, too, and hav-ing the power to do so, they rushed again to fill the void, to reshape the man one more time to their own design.

The brain of the Falcon rests and waits for the signal to be given. The worm that is the army is in readiness—the tunnel at the edge of completion. Soon the worm will curve its way through the tunnel and emerge to devour the white man's world.

Only one thing remains before the jinn's work is done. One more Feather must be sacrificed by the Falcon . . . one more, and the march can begin . . .

Diamonds Aren't Forever

S. P. SOMTOW

Thailand is one of my favorite places in the world. It is also the setting for this story, written especially for this book. S. P. Somtow calls the story a black comedy. Only Somtow, a relative of the Thai Royal House who divides his time between Bangkok and Los Angeles, could so accurately have described Bangkok's strange and fascinating modern-ancient mix.

—DC

Diamonds Aren't Forever

A PRICELESS MING VASE skidded down the marble steps. Fortunately, Rapi, the more swift-footed of the two mezzanine maids, was pushing a mop past the landing at just that moment; she caught it one-handed and, not missing a beat, set it down at the table by the window overlooking the teak pavilion by the canal, where I was just settling down to enjoy a quick breakfast of rice soup, pickled quails' eggs, dried sugar-roasted pork, and ice cappuccino.

"I'm sorry, sir," said the maid.

"What the hell's going on?" I said, turning the vase over and noting that it belonged to the reign of the Emperor Chien Lung. I had only been in Bangkok for a week, and had yet to regain my bearings.

"It's the Khunying," the maid said. "I think she's lost her earrings again. Oh, dear, here comes another." The vase's identical twin came whizzing through the air, narrowly missing a gorgeous, though armless, Khmer statue of an apsara or celestial woman, which stood mounted on a plinth in the center of the landing. The vase shattered against the far wall. "Oh, dear, oh, dear," said the maid, and scurried after the shards.

As she scooped them into a dustpan, she turned to me and went on, "Don't panic, Mr. Shapiro. All these antiques are fakes. The Master has lent all the real ones to the Metropolitan Museum in New York. His nerves, you know."

The Master, Dr. Sukhrip, was my host for this trip. I had met him at a curator's luncheon in New York, where he had given a brief speech on the subject of fourteenth-century Siamese lintels. After welcoming me with a lavish dinner, he had promptly disappeared, leaving me to

45

root about his estate—a palatial complex of Somerset Maugham–like splendor—while he flew off to Singapore to tryst with one of his innumerable wives.

I had been going to the Orient since the 1950s, first as an intrepid young archaeologist's apprentice, then as a buyer for the Metropolitan's Southeast Asian collection, and now as a private dealer in rare art. But I had never been a guest in one of these huge aristocratic family compounds, and I was often at a loss.

I had any number of chauffeurs and servants at my disposal, and I can speak the language tolerably well; but even figuring out which of the seventeen dining rooms, pavilions, pantries, and lunch nooks breakfast was going to be served in each morning was an ordeal. It had never, so far, been served in the same place.

My hostess the Khunying (which is a minor title of Thai nobility) was seldom seen except on her way to some society function.

"Does the Khunying often lose her earrings?" I asked Rapi, who was now kneeling at the low table (I still couldn't quite get used to all this groveling) and refilling my orange juice glass. "What happens next?"

"Oh," she said, "at about ten o'clock she will conclude that one of the servants has stolen them. At eleven, there'll be a police investigation where they'll find us all innocent. At twelve, she'll insist that the investigation hasn't been thorough enough. At one, we'll all take lie detector tests and pass. At two, the tarot card reader will arrive, if she's in town. By five, she'll be calling the shaman."

"Shaman?" I said, my interest piqued.

"Mae Thiap, the shaman," Rapi said. "She's a peasant from the northeast. She's very good at finding things. She usually gets the earrings on the first try; but if she doesn't, the Khunying will have nightmares, forget the lie detector test results, and wake up suspecting one of the servants again, and then the whole chain of events recycles, you see."

At that point, a bloodcurdling scream issued forth from behind us. A door slammed.

"Rapi, you impertinent bitch! How often have I told you *not* to chatter to the honored guests? This isn't the Beaver Bar in Patpong."

Rapi rapidly folded her palms in the universal Thai gesture of respect and said, "Terribly sorry, Khunying."

"My own fault, Midge," I said. "I asked her a few questions."

Midge, as her American friends called her, stood about four-eleven, had the complexion of a fine Sung dynasty porcelain, delicately pouting lips, slender fingers, and enough jewelry to sink the *Titanic*.

"Asking a few questions!" she began in a fury. Then, morphing instantaneously into the perfect hostess, she said, "Is everything all right, Mervin? What time will you need the car? I'm afraid you'll have to take the Benz; I'll need the Rolls to escort the servants to the police station." Then, with renewed rage: "Perfidious lice! Robbing me blind! Fifty American dollars a week I pay these fools, and I can't buy their bloody loyalty!"

"Earrings, was it?" I said.

She turned to me. "And not some silly bauble either; these were three-carat blue-whites, worth around eight hundred thousand baht."

A quick calculation told me that this sum could purchase the services of one of these maids for approximately twelve years and four months. I whistled. "Oh, it's not that they're worth *that* much," she said, "it's just . . . oh! the sense of violation! that one of these creatures actually slunk into my bedroom in the middle of the night . . . it's just too appalling. I'm so sorry about disturbing your breakfast, Moreton—"

"Marvin."

"—perhaps you'd care for some *prosciutto melone?* My cousin just brought back a couple of whole ones from Italy, and I know you can never get decent gourmet food in America—"

"It's all right, thanks. I've got a meeting with a Burmese smuggler at noon, and you know they'll be plying me with—"

"Burmese? Better take some diarrhea pills, just in case. Rapi, go and fetch the big blue bottle from the inner bathroom . . . not the Valium. And the crocodile stilettos for the police station, I think . . . fourteenth ones from the left, third shelf, sixth shoe cabinet."

The maid disappeared silently, and after pursing her lips becomingly for a few minutes, so did the Khunying. It occurred to me that a woman who could pinpoint the exact location of every specimen in her Imeldaesque shoe collection could surely keep track of a pair of earrings.

My rendezvous was a mile away—an hour and a half in Bangkok's stultifying traffic. It was almost evening when I returned, and my chauffeur-driven Mercedes pulled up at the wrought-iron gates at the same time as the shaman came roaring up on the back of a Harley.

The front lawn of the estate was packed. Various staff members were emoting, weeping, gawking, and chattering as police sergeants wandered around interrogating and taking notes.

I left my shoes at the door and was about to go up to my suite when

Midge accosted me. "Oh, good, you're here," she said, while simultaneously speaking in Thai into two cellular phones. "You'll probably enjoy the shaman."

I realized we were right on schedule. "Where?" I said.

"Follow the smell of incense," she said. "I'll join you in a moment. Do you want tea sent up?"

She vanished before I could answer her, trailing a cloud of Samsara.

Incense wafted down from an upper story. As I hesitated, the shaman came trampling past, surrounded by servants bearing silver platters laden with cloths, fruit, flowers, and hard-boiled eggs. Her entourage included a little blind boy wearing a traditional *jongkaben* costume and a white-robed Brahmin priest bearing aloft a silver bowl, as well as a piper, a drummer, and a boy banging on an upturned brass bath bucket. From a lone woman on the back of a motorcycle, she had somehow metastasized into a garish, noisy carnival.

Midge's *faux* Louis Quinze bedroom suite, which she did not share with my host, her husband, took up most of the third floor of the mansion. I sat down at a divan, and a tray of tea and cucumber sandwiches appeared miraculously in front of me. It was served by Rapi, her eyes downcast, on properly bended knee; but when no one was looking, she boldly gazed into my eyes and, with a twinkle, said, "Right on schedule, Mr. Shapiro, you see."

The entourage was setting up shop in an anteroom. Meanwhile, the shaman joined me on the divan. She was a stately woman wrapped in an embroidered *panung,* held in place by a silver belt, and had a no-nonsense look about her, like a yenta on steroids.

"Oh, an American," she muttered to the maid. "I'll have to charge extra."

"I'm afraid I speak Thai," I said.

She giggled at my atrocious accent, then said, "Well in that case, of course, we'll only be charging the down-home rate. Unless you're an anthropologist, of course." She downed an entire cup of tea, and plucked an amulet out of her capacious bosom. "Take this," she said to me, and handed it over. It depicted an intertwined couple—outrageously pornographic, really. "You look as if you might need a little, ah, supernatural assistance in your love life."

"Very kind of you," I said. I peered at it. I couldn't tell if it was old without a magnifying glass. Such fetishes can fetch a fairly decent price in New York, however, so I pocketed it. She waited, presumably for a donation of some kind, but I didn't feel like playing the game.

"You Americans all alike," she cackled in English. "Always show me, show me. All right, tonight you have big, wonderful sex. Then donation. My card." Her business card had a cellular number as well as a fax number, and included the legend "as seen on Letterman."

At that point, the Khunying showed up. She had changed into a casual silk pants suit and slightly less jewelry.

"Oh, Mae Thiap," she said, "I'm so glad you could come!"

"It's nothing, my dear," said the shaman. "And you last saw your earrings where?"

"I don't know, I don't know!" said Midge. "It's those beastly servants, I swear! There's not an honest domestic left in all of Bangkok; the foreigners have hired them all away at grossly inflated wages. I was coming home from the big charity ball, you know, at the Dusit. I'm sure I still had the earrings then. Unless I took them off in the bathroom. But why would I have done that? Or maybe I wasn't even wearing them." Her confusion was genuine, and very discomfiting. "I mean, it's not as if they went *poof!* and just vanished from my ears, is it?"

"Of course not, my dear," she said. "Let's all concentrate our minds." An assistant brought a tray of joss-sticks and garlands. Apparently, I was supposed to join in, so I took seven incense sticks and lit them.

"This part's simply grand," Midge said, clutching my forearm excitedly. "She becomes possessed by the god Phra Isuan—Shiva—who as you know is Lord of the Dance. Then, in the personage of the god, she dances around wildly until she's able to see the true location of every object in the world."

"What if they're not in this room? What if they're stolen?" I said.

"Phra Isuan will rearrange the fabric of reality," said Midge, "and make whatever has happened un-happen. After all, he is the God of Destruction."

"I see," I said dubiously.

The little blind boy came in and presented us with a bowl of sand in which to plant our incense sticks. The room was getting smoky. I tried to look appropriately meditative for a few minutes before carefully placing the sticks in the bowl.

"All right," said Mae Thiap. "Now, children, you must remember that life is a dream; the world is an illusion; that which we call reality is held in place by the chains of karma; but there's a certain elasticity in those chains, and that's what we must rely on. Now, Khunying, if you would kindly concentrate on the earrings . . . try to conjure up a mental picture of them in your mind, a picture so crystal clear that I won't have any trouble plucking it from the maelstrom of your thoughts."

Midge closed her eyes. She folded her palms, blushed a little; her delicate features made me think of celestial women painted on faded

49

murals in the temples of the north of Thailand, one of which I had managed to get smuggled out of the country to a museum in Berlin last year. Not an easy task; to get a mural out, in pieces, you have to dismantle the temple. Crossed a lot of palms with silver that month.

From the antechamber, the pipe, drums, and gong began a bloodcurdling caterwauling. Attendants began a kind of chanting and clapping. The Brahmin priest intoned in singsongy Sanskrit, now and then pausing to asperge us all with lustral water.

As the music crescendoed, Mae Thiap underwent a bizarre transformation. She leaped up. Her arms and legs contorted into strange attitudes and impossible angles. Sideways, she skittered across the carpet. She spun. I could have sworn she had at least four arms. She somersaulted. Her hefty bosom seemed to have a life of its own. She stamped her feet, which jingled with brass anklets. The drums were speeding up now, and at the final crash of the upturned bucket, she was suddenly seated in lotus position on the Sealy Posturepedic under the silken canopy of the four-poster, her arms folded tight across her chest, her neck bobbing up and down like a jack-in-the-box's.

She spoke in a booming voice, the way flying saucer people speak in fifties science fiction movies. "The earrings," she declared majestically, "are right here."

She pointed to one of the pillows.

Abruptly, the music came to a stop. Slowly, Mae Thiap returned to a semblance of human form, then fainted.

There was a moment's silence. The air conditioners hummed. The trails of incense began to settle.

Midge scurried over to the pillow. She lifted it up. Then, with a look of triumph on her face, she held aloft the earrings. "Oh, Mae Thiap, you've done it!" she cried. She knelt beside the prostrate shaman and performed a ritual obeisance and, perhaps because in Thailand one's head may never be higher than the head of a social superior, everyone in the room immediately fell on his knees as well. Except, of course, for me, the token Ugly American. I sat there, staring in bewilderment at the sea of backs that encircled the fat, supine, heaving woman with a fleck of froth on her lips.

That night, I awoke from a fitful sleep to find Rapi inexplicably scrubbing the floor.

"What on earth are you doing?"

Startled, she dropped her mop. "Oh, I'm so terribly sorry . . . I don't know what's come over me. I must have been walking in my sleep again. I'll leave at once."

She did not leave until dawn.

Obviously, there was something to this Mae Thiap's powers. In New York, one wouldn't think of calling in a shaman to find missing objects, but here in Bangkok, you're always right at the borderland of the mundane and the supernatural. I mean, here's a city with fax machines and smog and expressways and buildings shaped like giant robots and the world's highest concentration of shopping malls and all that, but the twentieth century's just skin-deep; scratch it and you're in the primeval past. I love it. Keeps my mind working.

I was musing on all these things as I gazed at the sleek, sleeping young body of the mezzanine maid.

The earrings were an impressive enough feat, but to cause this nubile thing to jump into the bed of a shopworn, sagging, middle-aged Semite was more amazing still. It had to be the amulet.

And if this woman could locate missing earrings, what about something bigger? With the twelve-hour time difference, it was too late to call New York now. I was going to have to wait until after dinner. I had twelve hours or so to cook up a dastardly plan.

I met the Khunying for lunch at the Picasso, a postmodernist café on Sathorn Road whose exterior was a large-scale stucco recreation of one of those brown cubist paintings. Inside, there were pillars that were three-dimensional reconstructions of *Les Demoiselles D'Avignon,* and the walls were a sort of colorized *Guernica*-in-the-round. It was a monument to the cultural hubris of Bangkok in the nineties.

And the Khunying was attired to match: she had the earrings, of course, and a drop-dead Chanel suit set off by a Versace purse of Olympian proportions. It needed to be that big to carry both her cellular phones, which rang continuously during the beluga, and only slowed down when we reached the rack of lamb.

"So how exactly *do* you know my husband, Melvin?" she asked me. I had given up correcting her on my name; I realized now that pretending not to know it was just some roundabout way of insulting her absent husband.

"In New York," I said, "he presented a very fine piece of twelfth-century celadon to the museum's Southeast Asian collection; we've corresponded, on and off, ever since."

"Oh, I see," she said. "You launder his money."

I tried to ignore that, and went on, "And I'm sorry I haven't had a chance to thank him for his hospitality. . . ."

"Oh, I'm sure he's already forgotten," she said. "His whole life seems to consist of trysting with that trollop in Singapore."

We consumed the rack of lamb in silence.

"So you're sort of an Indiana Jones, type, then?" she asked me at last.

"Hardly. But I *have* been known to find . . . objects."

"Lost objects. Like Mae Thiap."

"Ones that have been lost for centuries. But I don't use magic."

"I daresay not; Americans are never any good at magic. No offense, but you're all just too closed-minded."

"I'm not," I said. "Not after what I saw yesterday." And experienced last night, for that matter. But I wasn't sure how Midge would feel about a bed-hopping maid, so I didn't mention it. "That shaman," I went on, "this . . . Mae Thiap. Where did you find her?"

"Oh, she's from up north somewhere . . . all my friends use her. She's not bad, and it's a hell of a spectacle for only five hundred baht. Where in America can you have such a show for twenty bucks? But why do you ask? Have you lost something recently?"

"Found something, more like," I said, remembering the delicious night I had just enjoyed, though the memory was becoming more and more elusive, like a dream that slips through your fingers when you try to grasp it. "She's a fascinating lady."

"Would you like to see her again? We can fax her if you like; I've got my Newton in my bag."

"Has she ever recovered . . . *big* objects?" I fingered the obscene fetish in my coat pocket.

"I don't know . . . well, there was my cousin's Maserati, but there was some doubt as to whether it was actually the right car, you see, and anyway it was stolen again a week later."

Very interesting.

"But what I don't quite understand is . . . didn't you look under that pillow *before* you called her in . . . even before you called the police? I mean, it was a pretty obvious place to have mislaid your earrings. . . ."

"The gods work in mysterious ways, Mordred; such things are beyond me. Yes, I looked there. They must have been there the whole time. Sometimes, if you look at something all the time, you miss the obvious."

That was true enough. But it seemed to me that this was a little more complicated than just locating where an object had been lost. There was something else . . . telekinesis, perhaps. Fixing on the object's true essence, somehow, making it pop through the ether and

52

materialize in its designated place. It was pretty exciting, I thought, as I distractedly munched my crêpes suzette and Midge chatted away on both cellulars.

The journey to Mae Thiap's house was by canal. We were on the Thonburi side of the city, far from the places where tourists congregate; we had to park the Mercedes in the Oriental Hotel and catch a water-taxi. My companions were the Khunying herself, who had managed to get the evening off from her taxing round of charity balls, and Rapi, the maid, who had been brought along to carry the various garlands, incense sticks, fruit and hard-boiled eggs that always seemed to accompany these operations.

I asked Midge about the eggs. "Some of the gods don't like them," she said, "because the higher up they are, the more likely they are to be vegetarians; but with the lesser spirits, they're pretty much de rigeur. The *jao thii,* for example, who inhabits the spirit house at the end of our front lawn."

"But Phra Isuan's pretty big, isn't he? You can't get much higher than Shiva."

"Don't take any of it too seriously, Melrose! We are all Buddhists here in Thailand, which means we don't really believe in gods at all. They're just part of the illusion of reality; they're subject to the laws of karma, too."

"You mean it's all a dream."

"Nothing exists," she agreed, as Rapi poured her a glass of Moët Chandon from the magnum in the ice bucket.

Visitors don't see this side of Bangkok much. The boat eased down the narrow *klongs,* bordered by stilted wooden houses; children leaped naked from overhanging branches, laughing at us; a crone in a passing sampan sold me ice-cold coconut juice.

We docked at one of the wooden houses. The air was heavy with the fragrances of incense, jasmine, and mango. After leaving our shoes on the stoop, we went into a small waiting room that was crammed with suppliants.

"Do we have to wait?" Midge said querulously, but soon the little blind boy emerged from the inner chamber to tell us we could skip to the head of the line. Money talks.

Inside, the walls were lined with statues of Hindu gods, and there were shelves of jars full of strange concoctions: love philtres and the like, no doubt. The shaman was sleeping on a huge heap of pillows, snoring cacophonously, and the blind boy gently prodded her awake.

"Ah," she said, "the Khunying has lost her earrings again?"

"Well, actually, no," said Midge, as we crawled into appropriate positions of respect, "it's my friend Marty from America. He's lost something. Well, *he* hasn't lost it, exactly. It's more that he's never found it, although he knows it has to be around somewhere."

"It's a simple thing, really," I said, pulling out a series of photographs that had just been faxed to me that afternoon. "I have a client in Los Angeles who owns a very interesting set of Buddha images. They date from the late Ayuthaya Period, they're about an inch or so tall, and there are fifty-five in all, each one representing a different *pang* or attitude of the Lord Buddha. It's an absolutely superb collection, possibly the *only* miniature compendium of all the traditional postures of Buddha images done by a single sculptor—"

"But there are fifty-six," said Mae Thiap. "Everyone knows that."

"Yes, indeed," I said. "The one that was never excavated from the site is the *pang peut lok,* the Buddha revealing the three worlds."

"Excavated!" Mae Thiap said. "Stolen, you mean. You're trying to get me to cooperate in the stripping of our national treasures from archaeological sites? You appalling little man."

I gulped. Every now and then one runs across one of those rah-rah do-gooders who wants to repatriate all the antiquities, but to be honest they tend to be starry-eyed Caucasians straight out of Smith College, rather than the more pragmatic natives.

"I'm terribly sorry for offending—" I began, rooting around for some shred of political correctness with which to redeem myself.

"It'll cost a little more," said Mae Thiap. "Let's say, a thousand baht."

"Forty bucks!" I exclaimed in astonishment.

"All right, nine hundred."

"You'd strip a national treasure for nine hundred baht?" I said.

"My child," she said wearily, "life is a dream. Reality is but a figment of the imagination, a baseless fabric, a thing of no substance. And yet, we must keep the wheel of karma turning, must we not? I am merely an instrument of the gods. By the way, I trust that your sex life has improved somewhat?" At which the maid could not help giggling, and the Khunying shot her a look of disapproval.

Then, all at once, the mountain of flesh was dancing up a storm, and the music started banging and tooting from the next room.

She hurled herself across the room with startling agility, working her hands and feet into attitudes more contorted than the fifty-six *pangs* of the Buddha. It was hard to believe that so much poundage could possess so much terpsichorean talent. She somersaulted, cartwheeled, and tied herself into knots. She didn't even appear to sweat, and, sure enough, I was starting to swear she had four arms, though doubtless it was the afterimages of her gestures.

The dance went on a lot longer than before, and I was afraid that the god might give her a coronary before departing her body, but just as I thought she would give out, she shuddered to a stop.

The booming voice of the god spoke to me.

"At the antique shop in the arcade of the Hyatt," said the Lord of the Dance, "on the right-hand side, second shelf down, you will find your missing Buddha image. Go straight there in the morning, though; it has been mislabeled, and is being sold as a modern reproduction, so someone may grab it first."

We all prostrated ourselves, made the appropriate offerings, and took the canal taxi back to civilization.

That night, I woke just before dawn, only to find the lovely Rapi weeping in the moonlight that poured in through the window that overlooked an ancient temple and a large Pizza Hut. She was exquisite in her nakedness; I watched her for a long time before deciding to disturb her melancholy.

"Is everything all right?" I said.

"I suppose so, Master," she said. "I'm just sitting here bewailing my terrible karma, and wondering how many thousands of lives I'm going to have to live through before I can be rich and carefree like the Khunying."

"There's little I can say," I said. "Except to point out that I don't think the Khunying's that happy. Money's not everything. I mean, she's got a husband who's a cad, and . . . a terrible fear of loneliness, too, I suspect."

"Money's not everything! Easy for you to say. You entice me into your bed with a love spell, and next week you'll be getting on that plane and going back to America, and where does that leave me? It's not like you're going to marry me."

"You're right," I said, feeling like a bit of a user myself. "It isn't as if I'm going to marry you."

"Of course you're not, Mr. Shapiro," she said. "Americans always say they come from a classless society, but we all find out pretty soon that that's bullshit."

She was doing a pretty good guilt job on me, almost as good as my mother. This was beginning to sound like the annual Hannukah phone call from Miami. "You're right," I said.

"And anyway, since this entire relationship is just based on a magic spell, you probably don't even like me."

"What are you getting at?"

"You beast! You're gray and withered, and your nose is like a parrot's beak. And to top it all, you're a criminal who gets rich by ransacking other people's cultures."

"That's all very true, but—"

"I hate you!" She flung herself at me, and began pummeling me with her fists. "I hate you, I hate you!" Then she wept passionately, until there was nothing for it but to shake out my weary member one more time and make whoopie till dawn.

To my amazement, the objet d'art in question was exactly where Mae Thiap said it would be, and for a mere hundred dollars, I claimed possession of it. What with bribing a few more officials for the papers necessary for exporting antiquities, and a few other miscellaneous expenses, I was pretty certain I could clear $200,000 for this one.

I was ecstatic. I took Midge out to lunch, dropped a couple hundred bucks on giant crabs flown in from Australia, went down to Fed Ex to ship the relic off to my client, and called the bank to tell them to await an enormous wire transfer within twenty-four hours.

Then I retired to the Khunying's estate to figure out what I should get Mae Thiap to locate next. So many lost masterworks in the world. Imagine if she could dredge up, say, the complete poems of Sappho— even *one* complete poem of Sappho!—or a lost *Pietà* of Michelangelo. And why stop at art? What about the true cross . . . the holy grail . . . the ark of the covenant?

My hands were shaking as I gulped down my chrysanthemum tea and watched a Madonna music video in the Khunying's capacious television room. By now, everyone in the household staff knew that I was having a relationship with Rapi, and schedules had been shuffled so that she could spend more time with me. So she was serving my tea with downcast eyes, every inch the serving wench; after the outburst of the previous night, it was awkward to see her kneeling at my feet, but Thailand is a hierarchical society, and everyone knows his place.

"I wish you wouldn't stare at the floor the whole time," I said.

"I wouldn't presume, Mr. Shapiro," she said.

"What's going on in that complicated brain of yours?"

"Nothing," she said.

I very much doubted that. "Perhaps," I said, "you feel you should give the old classless society a whirl?"

"What do you mean?"

"I'm not saying I'd go so far as to marry you—even at my advanced age, my mother won't let me bring any shiksehs home to meet her—but perhaps a live-in position of some kind. You know, in New York, these kinds of things are done all the time."

"You mean, you're offering me a concubine's position?" she said. "That wouldn't be too bad. I'd have to have my own condo though. It wouldn't do to share the house with your major wife; I'm a respectable woman."

"Your own condo, eh? In New York City?"

"Sir, I've heard that the land in New York is almost as expensive as it is in Bangkok, but surely, with the new antiquities you're planning to 'find', it wouldn't be too hard to—"

True enough, I thought. The girl's mind was devious as hell, and she didn't miss a thing. It wouldn't be bad to have her around the place. She'd look pretty glamorous in one of the Khunying's evening gowns—

"Not to mention the earrings," she said softly.

"You're a mind-reader?"

"Not too hard to read an open book," she said, giggling. "But seriously, it would be wonderful to be your wife, even your minor wife, but there wouldn't be anything I could call my own, would there? The condo, the clothes, the checkbook, it would still be all in your name. I'd only be part of the décor. If only I owned just *one* valuable thing . . . a ring . . . an amulet . . . a pair of three-carat earrings . . . sometimes I dream about stealing them, you know. I mean, I've been interrogated by the police about them often enough, every time the Khunying loses them . . . once, they even beat me."

"Good heavens," I said, empathizing and simultaneously admiring the artful manner in which I was being manipulated. "How awful! Why didn't you quit?"

"But if I had quit, wouldn't they have assumed that I stole them? No, one accepts a bit of police brutality as part of one's karma. I must have stolen someone's earrings in a past life to have been pistol-whipped for stealing earrings in this one. . . ."

The woman was brilliant. If she went on in this vein, I'd have my mother swearing she was Jewish. "You're a remarkable woman," I said, trying to sound noncommittal, telling myself that she was right, that this was a sheerly physical thing, and magically induced anyway, and that there wasn't a shred of *reality* to the passion that even now was welling up once more in my brain, my breast, my loins . . . oh, she was ravishing . . . *and* she had character. She was irresistible. And yet. . . .

I had to think big. The ark of the covenant was all very well, but what about the lost tomb of Alexander the Great? What about the lost treasure of Troy, discovered by Schliemann and spirited behind the Iron Curtain fifty years ago? Could Mae Thiap, perhaps, reassemble lost artifacts as well as find them, so that we could gaze, once more, on the wonders of the ancient world: the Diana of Ephesus, the Hanging Gardens of Babylon? And all for a mere fifty bucks a pop? I imagined she'd need a little more once the scam got going, but who would not mind paying fifty, a hundred, even a thousand dollars for the chance to gaze at, say, the Great Pyramid of Khufu, with all its limestone facing intact and with the pharaoh and his treasure still lying around inside?

"You're daydreaming," Rapi said. "Have some more tea, Master."

"Sure," I said, reaching for my cellular phone. "Sure."

That night, the Khunying's earrings disappeared again.

That night, the maid disappeared.

I was awakened by a scream. The scream came from some distant part of the mansion. I snapped on the light only to discover that Rapi was gone from my side. Was the magic wearing off? Her scent still clung to the bedsheets. I put on a dressing gown and stepped outside.

The lights were on. The house was in an uproar. Valets, maids, and cooks were scurrying about, rubbing their eyes. A Ming vase almost brained me, but I ducked and it flew into an enormous bronze gong that hung between immense ivories. "What's the matter?" I cried.

But I already knew what it must be.

"Those traitrous, disloyal, scheming, greedy, good-for-nothing servants!" The Khunying, robed in one of Victoria's sheerest secrets, was stomping about the landing. "Those earrings were only recovered a few days ago, and now they're gone again! Oh, my terrible karma!"

"Midge!" I exclaimed. Sobbing, she flew into my arms.

"You don't know the half of it," she wept. "It's so difficult . . . the absentee husband . . . trying to manage this beastly estate on a miserable trust fund the size of a rat turd . . . and these damned three-carat earrings . . . I don't know why I ever bought them."

"Calm down," I said. "You know you always recover them."

"Yes," she said. "But the aggravation! The police! Strip-searching the maids! The lie-detector tests! The shamans!"

"Why not cut to the chase and just fax the shaman now?"

"I can't. You have to do everything by the numbers. If it weren't for due process, the whole structure of reality would collapse."

Well, there was little I could say to that.

"Call a roll call," she commanded one of the valets. "I want to make sure no one's made off with the earrings."

Soon, the entire staff was assembling in the front lawn: sentries, scullery maids, dishwashers, laundry women, gardeners, and so on. I knew there were a lot of people working on the estate, but this seemed endless. It was barely light. The faces were ghostly. They muttered and murmured, but the chirping of crickets and frogs and the buzzing of mosquitoes, not to mention the occasional pile-driver doing overtime at the condos going up on the other side of Sukhumvit, overwhelmed their chatter. One by one they were being made to swear, in front of the *saanphraphum* or spirit house which held the displaced guardian spirit of the land, that they had not done the dastardly deed, and calling down all sorts of hideous curses unto the seventh generation if they were perjuring themselves. It was an astonishing spectacle. I looked around for Rapi.

I didn't see her. I went right into the midst of the throng of servants. There were a dozen of her age and build, but none was the woman of my wildest sexual fantasies.

I went to the head security guard, who was doing a roll call and marking the names off on a list. "Have you seen Rapi?" I asked him.

"Not yet," he said.

I was beginning to have a sinking feeling. Hadn't Rapi unburdened herself to me only that afternoon? Hadn't she as much as told me that she lusted after the earrings, yearned to possess them, just so she could know what it was like to own something of value? If she had stolen them, had she fled the house? How long would it be until Midge suspected, and how long could a simple country girl elude a police force so adept at obeying the orders of the rich? Somehow I had to help her get away. Somehow I had to deflect suspicion. I had to get the Khunying to skip the police and go straight to the shaman stage.

At that moment, one of the innumerable Rapi clones—so close, and yet so unlike the real thing—showed up with a cellular phone on a silver platter.

"Hey, Marvin . . ." it squawked. "It's Ross. From Los Angeles."

"Great," I said. "I take it the Buddha image arrived?"

"It came this morning! I installed it in its niche. The whole thing has got to be the most gorgeous assemblage of the fifty-six *pangs* ever collected . . . but . . . but . . . Marvin . . . it's vanished!"

"Vanished?"

"Disappeared out of a locked glass case, in a closed wing of a museum after hours, with seventeen security guards, and . . ."

I began to have a sinking feeling.

How real were the recovered objects? Were they illusions, plucked from the images in our minds? Was it our desperate need to possess

59

these objects that caused Mae Thiap to be able to conjure them out of thin air?

How long did it take for the magic to wear off?

"Midge!" I waved at her as she raged back and forth on the front porch. "Help!" Into the phone I said, "I'll get it back for you. I can't explain *how*, but I'm absolutely sure that it hasn't gotten far. There's more to this than meets the eye."

"Telling me," said Ross, and hung up with a grunt as the Khunying approached me, tearful with fury.

"Look, Midge," I said. "Please. This time you're going to have to skip the police investigation." I wondered if Rapi had managed to make it out of Bangkok yet. "My client in LA just called. His Buddha image is missing, too. Let's just fax the shaman and get her over here pronto."

"It's five in the morning," she said. "I wonder if we can get her a police escort."

Breakfast that morning was grim, though served with an even greater sumptuousness than usual, in a teak pavilion, overhung with orchids, that overlooked a pond. At least, one assumed there was a pond beneath the wall-to-wall lotus pads and blossoms. The Khunying and I were served a rice porridge festooned with giant shrimp and chilies, along with the usual cinnamon-vanilla cappuccino.

We didn't speak. We each awaited the arrival of the shamaness. I felt dread and hope in equal measure. Midge maintained a stolid, aristocratic composure, having far exceeded her quota of *faux* Ming vases. Here, as elsewhere in this household, even a tantrum had to follow set guidelines, or the fabric of the universe would inexorably unravel.

The Khunying had by now learned that my paramour had absconded. Doubtless she was itching to send the police off after Rapi, but now that those stages had been skipped, there was no turning back. Every effort had to be made to restore a semblance of karmic balance.

"Eight hundred thousand baht," the Khunying murmured into her cappuccino.

I was thinking of the two hundred thousand dollars. And the ark of the covenant. And my lost love. Not necessarily in that order.

At last, the steward could be seen walking across the back lawn. He took off his sandals, entered the pavilion, prostrated himself, and informed the Khunying that Mae Thiap had been summoned.

*　　*　　*

In Midge's bedroom suite, I felt a strange sort of desolation. This was the first time I'd ever been in this room when it only contained three people, and its vastness was a little daunting.

Settling into lotus position on the divan, Mae Thiap said, "I'm afraid there's no entourage today, but this is a little sudden . . . not to mention irregular. You didn't call the police inspectors first?"

"Other circumstances . . ." I began.

"I don't know what you're talking about," said the shaman, "but once I am possessed by the god, I'm sure he'll understand everything."

Midge said, "About this unprecedented morning house call . . . there'll be a little extra in the offering, of course."

Mae Thiap waved it all aside. "You're lucky that this is the twenty-fifth century," she said—it took me a second to remember that the Buddhist Era starts five hundred years before our own—"and that I don't actually need a live band." She plucked a CD out of her bosom. "This comes from India," she said, "and there's four tracks: one for summoning Brahma, one for Vishnu, one for Shiva, and one that's sort of a free-for-all. If you wouldn't mind playing track three, there's a dear," she said, handing the CD to Midge, who got up to fiddle with the stereo in the console next to the fifty-five-inch television. Then she put her hand on my sleeve. "My poor *farang* friend," she said. "The lady is missing her earrings, and your friend in Los Angeles is missing his Buddha image; isn't there something you're missing, too? Oh, don't even bother to tell me. The god will see all. What your heart asks, the god will provide. As long as you don't skimp on the offerings." I was about to reply, but she put a finger to her lips. "I almost forgot to tell you. You know, once the god is present, you *may* ask him a question or two. He might answer you, you know. After all, you're a foreigner. How else will you learn anything?"

The dance was even wilder than before. She spun, she stood on her hands, she jiggled her head back and forth, she defied gravity and seemed to hang in the air as she whirled. Arms snaked hither and thither. Now and then, as her robes flapped, her navel glistened like a thousand-faceted jewel. She moved so fast there seemed to be two of her . . . no, more. She boomeranged across the walls. She swung from the drapes of the four-poster bed. There was nothing I could do but stare.

At length, she assumed the lotus position on the bed . . . or was it a couple of inches above the bedspread? . . . I couldn't be quite sure. My vision was blurry. Perhaps it was from all the stress. Or maybe it was because one cannot look directly at the gods.

But this time I wanted answers. True answers. Answers about the very nature of reality. "O Shiva," I said, kneeling with folded palms in front of the possessed woman, "you said I could ask a few questions."

"Yes, my child," she said in the resonant, deep tones of godhood. "I'll answer the questions even before you ask them. The world is an illusion. You want to know whether the earrings I find today are the same earrings that the Khunying lost? The answer to that is simple: if they are perceived to be the same earrings, why would they not be the same earrings? Do you know, my child, what reality is? It is the confluence of all your private illusions. In a world that is already illusion, does the creation of an illusion within that illusion make that illusion less real than the matrix of illusion that surrounds it?"

It sounded a lot like cheating to me. "But—" I began.

"Rest assured," said the god. "The earrings are under the bed."

"Oh, thank you!" said Midge, awed and relieved, and she immediately got down on her hands and knees and started fishing around beneath the Posturepedic.

"Rest assured, also, my pale son," the god continued, "that the missing Buddha image is not far from your friend's hands. He will find it on the next shelf, to the left, above where the cabinet with the rest of his collection is. The mahogany shelf now, not the teak. And this time it will last a while. You see, your friend couldn't quite believe his luck when he opened the package. Illusions, as you know, are fed by the power of our own beliefs. As you Americans say, dreams can come true if you want them badly enough. . . ."

"But this *is* cheating!" I blurted out. "What you're really doing is creating the objects anew, but they're illusions so they're unstable or something and after a while they pop out of existence, and then the owner thinks they've been mislaid and they end up calling you in to create the object all over again, and so Mae Thiap ends up with another forty bucks . . . it's a great big cosmic scam!"

"Oh, you Westerners are *so* Western sometimes. Of course it's a scam. The universe is a scam. You think it's all really there because you think *you're* really there. But you're not, and it's not. A universe lasts a trillion years, and a pair of my earrings lasts a trillion nanoseconds. Both are the stuff of dreams, or dreams within dreams. You should not be too attached to material things, my child. Let them go."

"And—"

"But now I have a question for you, my child. You too are missing something, are you not? Something very important . . . I would go so far as to call it a piece of your heart. Do you want me to conjure it back up for you? Your faith in her is strong. You can probably keep the illusion going for a lot longer than a few days."

I thought about Rapi: her impertinence, her laughing eyes, the delicate odor of the bedsheets. Could I really get her back just by bribing the gods with a few cheap offerings? But if Phra Isuan made her reappear in my arms, exactly the way she was before she left me, would she just be a simulacrum of Rapi, ready to melt into thin air at any moment? Would I be spending the rest of my life paying protection money to a witch doctor in Bangkok in order to keep my woman?

"No," I said. The god was right. If I caused her to reappear, I would only be clinging to the illusion of her that I'd created for myself. "Let her go," I said softly.

"Very karmically correct," the god said. Then, after writhing a little, and foaming at the mouth, Mae Thiap fell into a dead faint, and the audience with Phra Isuan was over.

A week went by. I dreamed about Rapi every night. It wasn't going to be that easy to forget, and the love fetish didn't bring me any more women; it had to be one of those magic spells that only works once.

I never quite had the chutzpah to arrange for the discovery of the ark of the covenant, but I did recover a few major antiquities, thanks to Mae Thiap. I was careful to pick clients who were absolutely fervent in the desire to possess those objets d'art, so there was no recurrence of the vanishing Buddha incident—at least not in the first week. I cleared a cool million, and put a down payment on a penthouse in the upper East Eighties, a building that was being converted to condominiums. So you see, I still hoped.

Midge saw me off at Don Muang Airport. She got one of the VIP rooms opened, so we were able to sit around sipping cappuccino for a while.

"I'm sorry about that maid," she said to me—my first indication that she had any idea I had been hiding the salami in her house. "You know, sometimes a perfectly good maid will up and run like that. I don't understand it. They have much more fulfilling lives with me than back on the farm. Last year it was one of the janitors."

"It's okay," I said, sipping and looking at my watch.

"What can you do?" she said. "After all, slavery's been abolished." She sounded vaguely regretful about that, even though she couldn't possibly have been around back then.

"Here," I said, and I gave her the love fetish I had received from the shaman. "With your husband *still* away, you could probably use this."

"Wow," she said, "thanks." She made sure I still had Mae Thiap's business card and fax number. I made sure that she was still wearing her earrings. Then she gave me a quick peck on the cheek and abandoned me to my karma.

The plane was stalled on the runway for about half an hour. First class was empty, and I downed a double scotch on the rocks, trying to get numb.

Suddenly the curtain was drawn aside and I saw her. I blinked a few times. I wasn't quite sure at first because she was wearing one of those Chanel suits—just like Midge had in her closet—and a two-hundred-dollar hairdo. I'd never seen her with makeup before, either. But that giggle was unforgettable, and the impertinent stare clinched it.

"How—what the—" I said.

"I sold the earrings," she said.

"But—the Khunying—she had them on—Mae Thiap—"

"I stole the earrings at midnight, while the Khunying was taking a soak in the jacuzzi. By the time she missed them, I'd already had the meeting with the jeweler. He ripped me off—I only got five hundred thousand baht for them—but I had to act fast. Once Mae Thiap showed up at the mansion—"

"You sold a jeweler the earrings, knowing that Mae Thiap would cause them to rematerialize in the Khunying's bedroom and the jeweler would get screwed?"

"Dealing hot property is a risky business," she said, and sat down beside me. "You shouldn't drink so much."

"I almost blew it for you," I said. "I got the Khunying to send for Mae Thiap a good eight hours ahead of schedule."

"Thank god I had already disposed of them."

"I'm really going to marry you," I said in wonderment.

"I know, Mr. Shapiro."

"You know!" I wished she would stop calling me Mr. Shapiro.

She smiled. She was beautiful when she smiled. She had the aristocratic bearing of the Khunying down pat—after all, she had spent years observing the members of high society from a kneeling position—but when she smiled, she couldn't quite suppress the farm girl in her. She was full of mischief. She had strength. I really did love her, I thought. I didn't want to say it out loud for fear of looking like an idiot.

The airplane started to move. Goodbye, city of high-rises and stagnant canals, city of shopping malls that look like temples and temples that look like shopping malls, city of beautiful and dangerous women, city of cacophony and tranquillity, city of neon night. I had a piece of that city with me always now. I could hardly grasp it.

"Don't you want to know why I'm here?" she said.

"Because I've put a down payment on the condo in Manhattan?"

She laughed again. "No, silly," she said. "It's because you didn't summon me."

"What do you mean?"

"You had the power. You had Mae Thiap. You lost something, and Mae Thiap can restore *any* missing object. But you didn't ask her to bring me back to you. And you know, she would have, if you had asked. Mae Thiap does not have scruples. She does not have a conscience. At least, not when she is the god. Gods do not have the same morals that mortals do. For the right offering, Shiva would have plucked me from wherever I was, and popped me right back into your arms. You would have had me. Or a reasonable imitation of me. But I would have become a dream within a dream, wouldn't I? I waited for a few days, holed up in a shack in the slums of Klong Toey, with all that cash in a paper bag, thinking, he's going to send for me any minute. But you didn't. And because you didn't, the woman who comes to you now is the same woman you loved before, and the love that I bring to you is not coerced by a magic spell or by your own capacity to weave an illusion of true love. This me is the real me."

Was this Rapi speaking, or was it the voice of the god? I didn't have time to reflect, because she kissed me then, and as I kissed her back we reached cruising altitude, and I started unbuckling her seat belt. . . .

She was real enough for me.

Just Like Normal People

KEVIN J. ANDERSON

When I learned that Kevin Anderson agreed to write a short story for this anthology, I assumed that the story would be hard-edged science fiction, like most of his novels. Instead, Kevin wrote a piece of fiction which can readily be called social commentary. Like Ray Bradbury, his theme deals with what happens when we strip away the disguises people wear, and come face-to-face with the reality beneath the facade; often, says Anderson, what looks pretty on the outside is less-than-pretty on the inside, and that which seems ugly—even deformed—on the outside, is in fact truly beautiful.

—DC

Just Like Normal People

PESTILENCE HAD SPREAD ACROSS the acreage adjacent to the road, through the hilly cornfields half a mile back, and all along the barbed-wire fence lines. It looked as if the Grim Reaper had flown over at midnight and shaken the bad blood off his scythe blade, letting droplets poison the ground.

After years of producing nothing but horrors as crops, the farmer and his family had split up and fled Wisconsin in their separate directions, abandoning the land to seek a normal farm and a normal life.

For a pittance, Collier & Black's Traveling Circus and Sideshows had rented one of the vacant fields.

As the sun thought about setting and the muggy air hoarded its heat, the roustabouts set up tents and rides and midway games and concessions. The sideshow wagons pulled into their slots. The birds and bugs had quieted down for the afternoon; mosquitoes would soon be coming out in full force.

A few people from Tucker's Grove had driven by in old pickups on the county trunk road, slowing down to take a glance, then speeding up as they saw the surly looking strangers pitching the tents and stringing the lights—not the type of people normal folks wanted to be seen with. Some farmhands might finish their chores and creep over to get a preview after dark, but most would wait until crowds and daylight made it safe to look around. . . .

Two of the sideshow freaks hiked away from the main activity with their own peculiar gaits, heading toward the blighted cornfields, as if drawn there. The two had been together a long time, and they knew

69

how to walk side by side, adjusting to each other's pace. Scarecrow remained silent, while his companion jabbered, as always.

"Something ain't right around here," said the Raven, indicating the sick and stunted trees along the fence line with his stubby arm. He scampered ahead with a birdlike gait, jerking his elbows behind him and up in the air. Cocking his head, he added, "Rawwwkk!" for good measure.

The Raven's grotesquely outthrust face made him look like a surly bird. During shows he wore a costume adorned with black feathers, but even without the plumage his dark skin, his mannerisms, and his raucous voice kept him in character. In cut-off trousers for the humid heat, the Raven's short legs looked like drumsticks. His large eyes glinted black as he jerked his attention from one sight to another. "You know where we're going?"

Beside him, Scarecrow sighed. "No. I just want to be away from the sideshow for a while. I'm tired of getting stared at everyplace we go."

He looked into the rows of weirdly rotten corn: freakish corn, as misshapen as he and the Raven. Purple-gray blobs of smut oozed from the cornstalks. One of the ripe ears had split open, showing sharp kernels like the yellowed teeth from an old skull.

Scarecrow shambled along, flopping his many-jointed arms and legs in the choreographed jittery walk he had learned to master. Tall and gangly, he wore patchwork clothes, mussed his blond hair, and see-sawed too much as he moved, like his namesake from *The Wizard of Oz*. But his sunken skull-face and dead-man's skin made no one look at him as a lovable buffoon.

All summer long as the circus worked its way across the Midwest, both he and the Raven would wander around the midway before and after their scheduled appearances in the sideshow tent, handing out leaflets, fascinating the towners, and steering them toward particular shows. The two freaks were comic relief, horrid enough to titillate the customers into wondering what *else* might be lurking inside the sideshow tent.

Today though, with the roustabouts doing all the setup, Scarecrow and the Raven took the opportunity to blow the show for an evening. But Scarecrow wasn't certain if he wanted to come back. What, after all, would they really be leaving behind?

They passed a dead choke-cherry tree so gnarled that it looked as if a huge hand had crumpled it. The bark writhed in the heat, contorting into silent screaming faces. The tall crabgrass hissed like a pit full of snakes. Virginia creepers had twisted into the rusty barbed-wire fence, snapping the posts with slow violence.

Keeping his voice neutral, Scarecrow gestured into the cornfields, toward the low hills. "Let's go straight that way. The farmhouse should be over there."

He plunged into the rows of sharp, drooping cornstalks. When his arm brushed one of the ripe ears, the kernels burst like a line of boils, splattering yellow pus onto his patchwork clothing. A very odd place indeed.

The Raven leaped into the field, knocking down stalks and flapping his stubby arms. "Look! I'm doing your job for you, Scarecrow!"

He startled several crows, which flew toward the sanctuary of trees along the fence line. Through the fluttered blur of black wings, one of the crows appeared to have two heads.

Scarecrow watched, but said nothing.

The dirt lane ended at a cleared yard where the nameless farmer had once lived. An old, dilapidated barn stood near the toppled carcass of a windmill, but only a foundation with burned timbers, broken glass, and scorched ground marked the former location of the farmhouse. The floor had caved in, showing the cellar to be an empty pit.

Scarecrow stared. The air was silent. He heard no birds. The sky bled orange with sunset, and the breeze died down.

"Over here!" the Raven said, hopping up and down beside the hulk of a tractor. One giant wheel had slumped off its axle and fallen to the ground. Black oil oozed from the crankcase into the dust. The rest of the body sagged under its coating of rust.

Flopping his arms and popping his knee joints, Scarecrow ambled over to the tractor. Behind it, a wide rake had been attached, the kind with hundreds of detachable tines used to roll new-mown hay into a long swath that a baler could scoop up. The rake was blood-rust brown, with globs of dust-clotted grease cementing it to the hitch of the tractor.

"Here, here!" The Raven cocked his head and jerked his protruding chin to indicate the rake's claws.

Though dead weeds and clumps of crabgrass covered the farmyard, every scrap of vegetation had been erased in a circular swath extending outward from the rear of the tractor, as if the plants had pulled up their roots and fled.

Scarecrow could not bend down the way other people did. Instead, he marshaled all of his joints and *folded* himself down closer to the ground, wrapping his body into a tighter package so that he could see.

One of the detachable tines was strikingly different, oozing a rainbow-colored light like an oil slick on a dirty parking lot. It was a smooth metal claw, a talon of steel designed to rip into the dirt and tear the soil free for the crops—but this one *felt* different from all the seemingly identical tines on the tractor rake. He touched the cold, weirdly slick metal, the center of the whirlpool of strangeness here. The curved tine seemed to pop off in his hand, jumping into his grasp as if it wanted to be free of its attachment. Scarecrow held it up to the failing light of sunset.

"What is it, Scarecrow? What did we find?"

Scarecrow could feel the fundamental oddness of the piece of metal. Was it a freak of nature? Had it been fashioned from a meteorite fallen from the sky? Or had it been dipped in human blood? Or forged by a blacksmith with murderous thoughts in his heart?

"Something that doesn't belong here," he said, caressing its edge with an extra-long finger. "I wonder if the farmer even knew about it."

Scarecrow held it as he stood up, unfolding and straightening himself, snapping joints into place until he was reasonably sure his body would hold him upright. Scarecrow could not understand it himself, but he felt a kind of affinity for the anomaly, the out-of-place metal. Something that normal people would never understand. "I think I'll take it with us."

The Raven looked toward the darkening sky, at the burned-out ruins of the farmhouse, at the distant field where the traveling circus had set up. "Shouldn't we . . . get back?" he said. He cocked his eye at the dead spot on the ground, performing none of his antics now.

Scarecrow had no interest in returning just yet. "No." He nodded toward the barn. "Let's spend the night here."

Oil-stained rags had been tossed next to rusty coffee cans filled with equally rusty nails. Three empty bottles of Southern Comfort lay label-up in a corner. The upper loft held a dozen old bales of hay, their fresh green-tan turned gray with age.

The Raven scrambled up to the rafters and tucked himself into a V-brace, brushing fat spiders out of the way and wrapping one stubby arm around the beam. He stuck his distended face into his armpit and fell fast asleep.

Scarecrow lay down on the hard-packed dirt floor. He tossed and turned, finding little comfort, but enjoying himself nonetheless just to be spending a night away from the circus tents, the freaks' trailers, and the curious towners.

He clasped the prong-shaped piece of odd metal to his chest, as if it were a treasure, rubbing his many-jointed fingers along the slick surface, like Aladdin rubbing his lamp.

Scarecrow couldn't doze off: his mind crackled with images of the small Midwestern towns the circus had pulled through on its summer circuit, the homey, isolated villages so pleasant and so peaceful, the elm-lined main streets with white Victorian homes, the tire swings in the front yards, the town square with the hardware store and the drugstore and the independent grocer.

Scarecrow remembered in particular the churches, from the high-steepled Presbyterian or Lutheran buildings to the Catholic churches with long purple-prosy names. In Tucker's Grove, as the circus trucks and wagons passed down Main Street, the signboard in front of the Methodist church had caught Scarecrow's eye. "Sunday Service—All welcome." The phrase in quotes denoting that week's sermon read, "We are all God's children!" It struck him with the force of a hammer blow.

All welcome. He wondered if he could believe it. *We are all God's children!*

Scarecrow knew about the towners who came to gawk at the sideshows, laughing and pointing their fingers, saying the same crude comments—he and the Raven had to endure, continue to look freakish because that's what the towners paid to see. But after diverting themselves with the circus, the normal people could go to their normal homes, play their normal card games, listen to their normal radio programs, go to their normal churches.

He drifted on the surface of sleep, with vivid images sprouting in his mind like a bumper crop, and he saw *himself* without his freakish exterior, clothed instead in a normal body. He could have been a steadfast farmer, tall and blond like many of the Nordic settlers of the area, hardworking. He would have suntanned skin, and dirt under his fingernails, and a huge appetite for a home-cooked meal after a day working out in the fields or in the barn. He could have been a pillar of the community, not a leader but just a wholesome, honest worker like these other good folk.

Into his dreams came the Raven, too, but without the defective body-costume his genes had forced him to wear—Raven might have been an eccentric but friendly shopkeeper, maybe running the drugstore or the hardware store, a good-humored stout man who took in strays, fed birds, let kids build a treehouse in the big elm in his front yard. . . .

As dawn brightened the sky, he felt his heart ready to burst with genuine longing and envy. Scarecrow knew he had seen what he and the Raven were really like inside, their true worth—and he was certain the townspeople would see it, too.

Scarecrow picked up a rock and hurled it toward the rafters. It clattered and bounced around the thick beams. The Raven awoke with a squawk and fell to the ground. Some instinct made him flap his stubby arms, as if he had forgotten that he couldn't fly. He landed with a thud and turned a somersault, opening and closing his mouth in silent gapes like a blind chick. "Whaaaaat?!"

Scarecrow tucked the wondrous metal tine into his patched pocket as if it were some sort of treasure; he was sure it had something to do with his vision, a funhouse mirror that brought reality into a clearer focus.

"Come on," he said. "It's Sunday. We're going to church."

They entered Tucker's Grove amid stares of horror, fear, and amazement—but Scarecrow and the Raven were used to stares. They had spent over an hour walking along the country roads, shuffling in the dandelion-choked gravel by the shoulder. A pickup truck roared by, and the driver hurled an empty beer can at them, which banged and clattered on the pavement.

Tucker's Grove Welcomes You! read the sign at the town limits, adorned with emblems of the various civic clubs, the Lions, the Rotarians, the Optimists.

The two companions passed along streets of quiet houses, then up Main Street, where the shops were all closed for Sunday morning. Above their heads, squirrels chattered in the branches of the elm trees. The center of the town drew Scarecrow like a magnet. The curved metal piece in his pocket pulled him along.

Finally, they stood on the well-maintained sidewalk of the whitewashed Methodist church. Scarecrow imagined monthly church gettogethers, families spending a Saturday afternoon weeding, mowing the church lawn, trimming the bushes. A true sense of community and home, the way Scarecrow *should* have felt back at the circus and among the other sideshow people.

He touched the curved tine in his patched pocket. It felt slippery and cold even through the fabric, strange, unusual, wonderful. . . . Maybe he would offer it as an unexpected gift to the kind pastor in charge of this church, set it gleaming in the middle of the offering plate as it was passed from hand to hand. Scarecrow and the Raven could settle down, become part of Tucker's Grove, fit in like real members of the community.

The early church service had already begun. The congregation sang an opening hymn in a group voice that blurred the melody and the words. The organist lifted the singers along with the force of the music.

Scarecrow opened the door just as the congregation fell silent for the opening prayer. Most of the people did not turn around, focused on the service, thinking that perhaps some oversleeping member had arrived a few minutes late.

But children dressed in stiff, uncomfortable clothes squirmed to look at the freaks, eyes widening to the size of plates. The rest of the congregation did not notice until the pastor himself raised his head from the beginnings of a prayer. His jaw dropped and he stopped in the middle of a word.

Scarecrow unfolded his long arm and then unfolded his index finger, indicating the outside. "All welcome," he said. His voice cracked.

This startled the pastor, and his expression changed, as if he found himself trapped by his duty. "Please find a seat," one of the ushers whispered. Scarecrow felt no warmth or welcome from the words.

The pastor raised his hands to the rest of the congregation. "Shall we continue our prayer?"

The people in the pews mumbled along, reading the words of a preprinted prayer in their bulletins. Scarecrow and the Raven went to the empty back pew closest to the door. The ushers stood at attention, perhaps hoping the two would go away. Tentatively, showing some fear, one usher handed Scarecrow a mimeographed bulletin that listed the order of hymns and prayers, a program for the sermon and offertory and benediction.

The pastor was a gray-haired man, clean-shaven, with wire-rimmed glasses that looked sharp on his face. Deep lines around his mouth made him appear to be pursing his lips like a chimpanzee. He finished his prayer and called out the next hymn just after the two newcomers sat down. Scarecrow sighed and went through the process of unfolding himself again to stand up. His many joints ached after having spent the night on the hard dirt floor.

Using his long fingers to shuffle through the pages of the hymnal from the pew pocket in front of him, Scarecrow located the proper hymn before the end of the first verse. Beside him, the Raven jostled and fidgeted, making harsh singing noises without paying much attention to the words.

The congregation members surreptitiously found excuses to turn around and glance at the two. A fat little boy picked his nose and flicked a booger toward the Raven, who lunged forward to catch it in his distended mouth. In the pew in front of them, a prim family shuffled toward the aisle, moving one row up and squeezing in with the already-crowded people there. The pew ahead of Scarecrow and the Raven stood empty, like a barrier between them and the others.

Scarecrow felt a stab of disappointment. They had both joined the circus because the normal world would not accept them, but the small Wisconsin towns had seemed so different, so welcoming, like a place from a fairy tale. An illusion.

The pastor began to read a passage from the Old Testament. It had something to do with demons and the devil walking among men, but Scarecrow found himself staring dreamily at the walls adorned with paper butterflies that had been cut out and finger-painted by Sunday School children. A bright poster said JESUS LOVES ME!

The pastor began his sermon, but his thoughts rambled, and Scarecrow could determine no point to the lecture. The pastor stuttered and lost his place several times, frequently glancing back toward the two newcomers. A sheen of sweat stood out on the man's forehead. Scarecrow felt a heavy ache in the pit of his stomach. Apparently, not everyone was welcome after all.

Raven fidgeted against the hard wooden pew that was not conformed to his lumpy back. As he squirmed, he made cheeping noises that sounded too loud in the sanctuary.

The sermon ended, and the ushers marched up the aisles to take two offering plates from the pastor's extended hands.

Scarecrow fidgeted, realizing that neither of them had any money— but he took out the wondrous, otherworldly tine from his pocket. It would be a strange offering, but it would be magical. Something these people had never seen before. Maybe that would make everything better.

As soon as the Raven realized what the offering plates were for, he hopped to his feet, jerking his elbows up in the air. "Whaaat? They want us to pay?" He looked down at Scarecrow with his black-lacquer eyes. "It ain't even much of a show!" His voice was raucous and loud enough for everyone to hear. "Cheat! Cheat!"

A man stood up three rows in front of them. His face was livid below his greased hair. His suit had gone out of style a decade before. "I've had just about enough of this . . . this sacrilege!" He seemed pleased to have an opportunity to use the portentous word. Several others spoke their agreement.

The ushers stopped their offertory and uncertainly marched toward the back, glancing at each other as if they had never dreamed they might have to act as bouncers. Soon most of the congregation was shouting.

The pastor banged his hands on the lectern for quiet and turned his attention to the freaks. "I think it would be best for you two to leave now," he said. His voice was low and menacing. "You've caused enough trouble in my church."

As he gripped the slick tine with his overlong fingers, Scarecrow heard an echo in his head, shadows of words, as if he could see into what the self-controlled pastor was actually thinking, the phrases the man really wanted to to shout.

We hate you! You're too ugly, too strange! You are not wanted here. Go back where you belong, despicable freaks! You're loathsome. You're not NORMAL like we are.

Scarecrow stood, slowly unfolding himself from the hard pew. His long legs made him appear to be rising, rising, like a cobra from a snake charmer's basket. The Raven hopped onto the pew seat, standing up and glaring at the congregation with his vulture-like face. Saying nothing to the pastor or the people, Scarecrow nodded to his companion, unable to express his disappointment. "Come on," he said, "let's go."

The Raven gave an excited caw and leaped over the back of the pew to the rear aisle. As they walked toward the church door, adjusting to each other's gait again, Scarecrow expected the people in the sanctuary to cheer. The larger usher followed them to the door, but the other merely stared in silence.

All welcome! If any sideshow in Collier & Black's tried such blatant false advertising, Scarecrow thought, the owner would be locked up for fraud.

The morning was fresh and full of sunshine as he and the Raven stepped outside. Behind them, the door closed, and Scarecrow heard the click of the lock. Muffled through the walls, the organist threw herself into playing a hymn so that the whole congregation could heave a joyous sigh of relief.

With the church barred behind them, Scarecrow and the Raven stared out at the masked town of Tucker's Grove. Few other man-made sounds came to them: an occasional car driving by, some people working outside, three children playing. Several blocks away, the Presbyterian and the Lutheran church would be having their services; Catholics would be at Mass. He and the Raven would have received a similar reception no matter where they had gone. *All* normal people *welcome.*

Slowly, feeling it cling to his fingers as if it had been coated with drying slime, Scarecrow pulled the metal tine out of his pocket. The curved shape gleamed like a claw in the humid air. The idea came into his mind, but he couldn't tell if it came from himself or . . . something else.

The Raven hopped a step back. "Whatcha gonna do? Whaaaat?"

"I'm giving them a gift," he said. "A glimpse of something—a show like they've never seen before."

Scarecrow bent at the knees, extended his long body forward, and stretched his arm down to the ground. He thrust the sharp metal end into the manicured lawn with a sound like an ice-pick going into meat.

He hesitated as other, innocent images came to him: church socials with kids and their parents, old people, teenagers laughing and working together, children squealing as they jumped into piles of leaves, bankers and dentists pulling up weeds, housewives serving up orange drink and almond windmill cookies to everyone. He thought of the congregation praying for each other when they grew sick, helping out when times were hard, laughing together at church craft fairs or bake sales or ice-cream socials.

Scarecrow dug the tine into the ground again, as if stabbing a sacrificial knife into the chest of a victim. He pulled the curved piece along as he took a step backward. The lawn and the dirt parted like flesh in a rotten fruit.

With his strangely sharpened vision he saw the tine open a bloody furrow in the earth, splitting the grass and leaving a pulsing red-purple wound that glittered with shadows. Heat and a lava-light rose from the gash with an odor like the breath from a furnace cooking spoiled meat.

"Follow me," he said, listening to his instincts, to what the unearthly artifact *wanted* him to do. He wondered at the destruction at the old farmstead, what sort of poisoned life the farmer had had and how he had been unable to bear seeing the veils slashed away.

With the Raven keeping his distance, Scarecrow worked his way backward across the lawn, ripping the gash open wider. He turned the corner and passed under the stained-glass windows, pulling the furrow along with him. Inside, he heard the pastor reading a passage from the New Testament.

One step at a time, Scarecrow scribed a bloody ring around the church, where all were *not* welcome. When he had dragged the scarlet tip across the clean cement of the sidewalk to meet the beginning of his circle, he thrust the tine into the dirt like a nail holding the ring together. That would be his offering to this congregation.

When he let go of the tine and stood all the way up to survey the raw furrow he had made, he saw nothing other than a scratched line in the dirt.

Inside, the pastor raised his voice in benediction, and the organist played the postlude as the churchgoers buzzed with conversation, no doubt tittering over the excitement they had experienced that morning.

Scarecrow and the Raven stood out near the street under a tall oak tree. "Watch," Scarecrow said.

The doors flew open, and four rowdy—but well-dressed—children burst out, crossing the invisible boundary, and brought themselves to a standstill. Other congregation members strolled out looking smug and self-important as they chatted about their business, the crops, the weather.

A broad-shouldered and jowly man caught sight of the two freaks standing on the sidewalk in front of the church. His face turned florid, and he pointed at them while grumbling to another deacon beside him. Like bouncers in a roughneck bar, they strode forward as the other people emerged from the church.

"Uh, we should go!" the Raven said, flapping his arms in alarm. "Go!"

But Scarecrow remained where he was, rigid and watching. His vision sharpened, darkened—and as the people crossed the line he had drawn in the soil, he watched their masks peel away. He snapped up his awkward head and stared at details he had not seen before.

—The little bald pharmacist, with the twinkle in his eye and sugar-free candy for little kids, who added a little "extra" to some of his prescriptions for people he didn't like, giving them an attack of diarrhea.

—The tallest boy in the choir, desperately clean-cut, out in the darkness of the milking barn with three of his friends, whispering "Hold her steady! Hold her steady!" as he thrust his erection inside the confused cow. The others would each have their turn, after the first had "loosened her up." They had made a pact among themselves never to tell anybody. . . .

The crowd stopped in their tracks, milling about. Some people screamed at what they saw in the faces of those they had known all their lives. Some were appalled by their neighbors, while others were repulsed by *them* in turn. It was a regular freak show.

—The old woman who fed stray dogs hamburger laced with ground glass to "teach them a lesson for pooping on her yard."

—The Sunday School teacher who had been planning how to invite several of the young boys over to his house, where he could have some "fun," the details of which he himself had not yet decided.

—The unmarried bank teller who took a vacation each year to visit mythical relatives in Milwaukee, though her primary objective was to hang out in pool halls and pick up as many city men as possible, preferably two or three a day. Last time she had come back home to Tucker's Grove with syphilis. . . .

As Scarecrow watched, he felt more than vindictiveness or revulsion—he sensed an eerie fascination at these flaws and shames of others. He realized with a start that this must be what the spectators experienced when they came to look and point and titter at the freaks in the circus. He pitied them.

Hearing the babble of frightened commotion, the pastor himself strode out of his church. He looked around, saw the freaks on the outer sidewalk, and then he marched forward, taking charge, intending to throw them off the church property. And then he crossed the line.

—The pastor added false backs to the drawers in his dresser, where he kept bras and panty hose, negligees, and other items of womens' clothing he liked to try on and model for himself in front of a tall bordello-style mirror. Even this morning, as the pastor gripped the lectern, flecks of bright whore-red nail polish clung to his cuticles.

The congregation members turned on him like a wolf pack, shrieking in horror at yet another exposed small-town secret.

As Scarecrow and the Raven turned to leave the screams and commotion behind them, he could still see the shadows of the real people here, the fat women and the ugly men, the pimple-faced teenagers, scarred and retarded people who had no other place in the world. They had turned their scorn upon Scarecrow and the Raven—misfits even worse than they—upon whom they could dump their own shame and revulsion.

"It's only right for them to know just how normal they really are," Scarecrow said.

He also realized that the previous night's rose-tinted dream—him steadfast and hardworking, Raven good-natured though eccentric—was not how things *might* have been without their freakish exteriors . . . but how the two truly appeared in their hearts.

As they walked away, Scarecrow hesitated once, looking back toward the church. He had left the wondrous tine behind, thrust into the dirt. The artifact pierced the masks all people wore, and he could imagine its incredible power.

If he took it with him back to the circus, he would be able to see Collier and Black for who they really were—harried businessmen full of bluster but caring deeply for their show—or the big-hearted fat lady, or the game hucksters who sometimes gave the most wonder-filled kids an extra chance at the games, or the cook who always did his best to help them get by. . . .

No, Scarecrow decided he didn't need the tine after all. He might not be a perfect judge of character, but he knew his friends well enough. He felt the empty pocket of his shirt. The skin on his chest tingled where it had touched the tainted metal.

Scarecrow and the Raven walked without shame down the main street of Tucker's Grove as the day grew brighter and warmer. "If we hurry, maybe we can catch the show before they pack up and leave," Scarecrow said. "I don't think there's any particular need for us to part company with them."

"Nope," said the Raven, who hopped ahead, excited. "Nevermore!"

The Singing Tree

ERIC LUSTBADER

Like all true romantics, I want the magic of a perfect moment to last forever. And I am a romantic, which is why I so often choreograph illusions into vignettes which involve beautiful women, flowing fabrics, dramatic lighting, gestures of love.

Most people don't know that about me. They think of me as an illusionist, a showman. In much the same way, I associated the name Eric Lustbader with best-selling action-adventure like The Ninja *and* Black Blade. *I certainly never dreamed that when asked to write something for this anthology, he would write a bittersweet love story which suggests that a perfect moment cannot be made to last forever; that in fact its magic lies in its very transience.*

—DC

The Singing Tree

FROM A LONG WAY OFF Andy Cooper heard his wife breathing. Closer to hand, across the small, spare hospital cubicle, he could hear the ventilator sighing like an old and rheumy grandparent.

Andy's wife, Melissa, had been hooked up to the ventilator ever since she had gotten out of surgery, chiefly because she could no longer breathe on her own. In fact, the doctors had said they weren't sure Melissa could do much of anything on her own, including think.

Beyond the curtain of the ICU cubicle he could hear the hushed sounds of the central nurses' station. Ranged along the top of a painted metal cabinet Andy had placed all of Melissa's favorite things: a photo of the two of them in Paris where they had first met—a golden-haired, light-eyed couple; the garter she had worn at their wedding; a baby ring that had belonged to her grandmother; a coffee mug from Napa Valley she used every morning she was home; a small beanbag moose he had bought for her on their honeymoon at Niagara Falls. These were artifacts not so much of a life lived but of a loving spirit Andy cherished above all others.

It broke Andy's heart to see these remnants of his wife lined up like so many tin soldiers, abandoned, waiting for their return to life. They looked so mortal. For without Melissa's spirit to infuse them they were only relics of a bygone time.

Andy heard his wife's breathing as from across a great gulf, some metaphysical divide he sensed rather than saw. When the doctors spoke to him of her, they unconsciously slipped into the past tense. By this alone Andy divined that their prognosis for her was grave, for in all other ways they steadfastly refused to give him definitive answers to his

85

many questions. How deeply had she been injured? How serious was her coma? Was her brain impaired in any way, and, if so, how? And perhaps most important of all, would she recover? He desperately needed to know the answers to these questions. Of course, the doctors knew this, but they were in no position to help. But if not them, who?

As far as Andy could determine from speaking to the police, his wife had been shot during an altercation on Broadway and 45th Street. Melissa had had the extraordinary bad luck to be walking past the northwest corner of this intersection eight days, three hours, and eleven minutes ago. A spirited game of Three-card Monte was in progress. The master of this con game, a tall, thin black man with a pencil mustache and a charismatic line of patter, had been successfully hustling tourists for the past six months in this same spot. Nothing untoward had happened. But now, a burly Hispanic, convinced he had been swindled out of his last ten dollars, charged toward the con man, muscling past the shills and spotters. He hauled out a Saturday Night Special and, without aiming, began peppering wild gunfire in the general direction of the con man. Miraculously, the con man escaped all injury. Not so Melissa. Two of the bullets had hit her, one in the throat, the other in her brain.

In truth, it was difficult to recognize the beautiful woman she had been. Her head was swathed in bandages, tubes protruded from her nose and mouth, and what parts of her face were visible beneath the bandages were swollen and black-and-blue. Andy lightly touched the blue veins on the back of her hand as if trying to reassure himself that blood still pulsed through her. He felt her warmth and, therefore, he was closer to her. He closed his eyes against the mechanical pant of the ventilator.

He ran with her in Napa in the cool, clear early morning toward the gaily striped balloon waiting to take them into the sky above precise vineyard rows. He reached out and touched the cable-knit sweater thrown casually across her shoulders. The indigo Irish wool was rough beneath his fingers. It made him think of fields of wind-blown heather. At his touch, she turned back to him and, with the sun on her face, her eyes were the color of honey. She smiled at him, waiting for his kiss, her face turned up like a flower toward the scudding clouds.

He felt a hand on his shoulder and he started.

"Were you napping, dear?"

He looked up into his mother's patrician face. He could detect lines of worry beneath the carefully applied makeup. She was dressed in a black Chanel suit with white piping, making her look even thinner than she was. Around her crepey neck was a black-and-white-striped silk scarf, and she clutched a Judith Lieber crocodile handbag that must have cost an RN's annual salary.

"Just thinking."

"Happier thoughts, I hope." She set down a large wicker basket. "I had Armand at Grace's load me up with goodies for you. All *very* healthy. You have to keep an eagle eye on him otherwise he's liable to slip in a salami or a couple of cannolis." She sniffed. "You might as well just go right ahead and inject the cholesterol directly into your veins."

His mother pursed her lips as she risked a glance at Melissa. But she would not go near the bedside. She had a morbid fear of illness, even the kind that wasn't contagious. She sighed, perched on the edge of a chair facing Andy, her back as straight as a drill sergeant's. "This puts me in mind of your poor father." Andy wasn't surprised. Hospitals always put his mother in mind of her late husband. "It was a tragedy to lose him so young." She sighed again, playing the role for all it was worth. "I never met another man who could hold a candle to him. I made up my mind instantly. He was the only man for me; I'd rather be alone than disturb his perfect memory."

"Mother, Melissa is not dead."

His mother crossed one stick-like leg over the other. "Of course she isn't. I wasn't making an analogy, just talking." That's what she always said. She smiled a shallow smile. "At least I still have my memories, is all I mean. One shouldn't discount the importance of memories." She shook her head. "So many years. In many ways, it seems like yesterday that he was here."

She opened her bag, took out a solid gold compact, began to reapply her makeup. It was an unnecessary ritual that nevertheless comforted her in times of stress. At last, she put away her implements and pursed her lips again. With one last look at herself in the mirror, she snapped her compact closed. "I must fly, darling." She gave him a smile. "Now, we mustn't lose hope." She patted his shoulder. "Be a good boy, as always." That had been her standard reassurance from when he was a child, the implication being if he was a good boy, all good things would accrue to him. A law of nature, just like water running downhill.

When she was gone, he moved the chair closer to the bed and held Melissa's hand. He could feel his lips on Melissa's, could taste the inside of her mouth, heady as wine. But when he broke the kiss they were in the Pool Room of the Four Seasons, alight with those unique bronze chain-curtains. They were sipping champagne; it was the night of their fifth wedding anniversary. They were so completely in love all they saw was themselves.

"I love you," Melissa whispered.

"And I love you," he said. "Nothing will ever change that for us."

And she had replied: "Nothing."

"Andy?"

He opened his eyes.

"Hey."

"Hey," Chris Houghton said from just beyond the curtain. Behind him stood Christian, his three-year-old son.

Andy nodded, beckoned Chris in. Chris took his son's hand and they came in together. Chris, tall and impressive in his three-piece suit, shock of blond hair, and dancing green eyes, took his son up into his arms. "Say hi to Uncle Andy, Christian."

"Hi, Unca Andy," the boy said shyly. He was fair-haired like his father but had the dark, serious eyes of his mother.

"Howdy, pardner." The two of them always played Cowboys and Indians together.

Chris held him out like a bundle and Andy kissed his apple-red cheek. He smelled of baby powder and chocolate.

"Any change?" Chris asked as he drew the curtain shut behind him.

Andy shook his head. Chris set his son down, went over to the bed, bent and kissed Melissa on her cool forehead. "You know what coma is like," Chris said, drawing up a chair and sitting. "One minute they're like this, the next awake and raring to go." He grabbed Christian, who was about to begin exploration of the IV stand, and set him on his knee. "Happens all the time, buddy."

"Sure." Andy found it inside himself to smile. "How're things in the office?"

"We'll have none of that," Chris said with mock sternness. "You promised you'd leave work to me." He grinned while handling a squirming Christian. "What's the matter? Don't you trust me?"

Of course Andy trusted Chris. They had grown up together outside New Haven, had gone to Yale together, had played Saturday softball and touch football together, had even, on occasion, spent the night together with the same girl. Separated, briefly, during law school, they had kept in touch and, when the time was right, when they had paid their dues at prestigious firms, they had formed a partnership. They were young to be out on their own, but a singular talent for mergers and acquisitions had built them peerless reputations in just a decade. That that decade happened to be the eighties was their good luck. Now they had offices on Park Avenue, as well as in San Francisco.

"Hey, guess what?" Chris began.

"Daddy?" Christian interrupted plaintively.

Chris reached into his pocket, took out a candy bar, which he opened for his son and gave to him.

"More sweets," Andy said. "Bonnie will kill you."

Chris kept his grin in place. "She'll never know unless you tell her."

"She'll smell it on his breath," Andy said, hating the fact that he was taking on his mother's role. "She's always suspicious when you bundle Christian off on your own."

"Already taken care of, buddy." Chris held up a box of Tic-Tacs. "Gotta stay one step ahead of the thought police, right?" While Christian was contentedly munching away, Chris produced a pair of tickets, which he waved triumphantly. "Opening night. Rangers versus Oilers. A deuce right behind the home bench. You don't know what I went through to get these, buddy, and they're all ours. What do you say? Tomorrow night. A couple of mouth-watering Porterhouses at Sparks and then the Garden."

Andy felt a million miles away from the kind of excitement that normally would have gripped him. He was a long-time Ranger fan. The firm had a skybox at Madison Square Garden but Andy preferred sitting close to the action. These tickets were the best present Chris could have given him and he couldn't take them.

"I've got to stay here," he said.

"Nothing more you can do for her, buddy," Chris said. "The doctor made that plain."

"The doctor doesn't know squat." Andy tried but failed to keep the bitterness out of his voice. "Melissa knows I'm here, Chris. I'm certain of it."

"Maybe so. But you can't spend the rest of your life locked up in this room." Chris, seeing Andy's angry glare, closed his mouth.

"Tomorrow's *Mefistofele* at the Met," Andy said. Their favorite. The subscription to the opera was one of their most glorious shared moments. No matter how busy the two of them got in business, they always set aside time for the Met subscription. Those evenings of glitter and glorious song had come, somehow, to define them as a couple.

Chris put the Ranger tickets carefully away. "Forget it. Stupid idea, anyway." He put his hand on his son's shoulder. "I'll take Christian and stuff his face with hot dogs until he throws up."

Chris waited patiently for Andy to laugh, but Andy only shook his head. "It's not that I don't appreciate the offer."

"Yeah, well . . ." Chris stood up, putting Christian on his hip. He looked tall and very fit. Father and son seemed of a piece, two chips from the same mold. It occurred to Andy that Chris was holding the future in his arms.

"How about you and me playing a couple of games of handball at the AC?" Chris asked. "Just take an hour, buddy, and you'll see how much better you feel." He was almost pleading. "It'll give you a break and take your mind off this."

"Don't you get it?" Andy said hotly. "I don't want my mind taken off *this.*" He could feel his shoulders hunching with tension and his eyes burned with held-back tears. "You know what's stupid," he said thickly. "I keep remembering this ridiculous argument we had. It was about *Heaven Can Wait,* the Warren Beatty remake of *Here Comes Mr. Jordan.* Anyway, I love that film and Melissa can't stand it. She thinks Beatty screwed up a perfectly fine story." Andy raked his fingers through his hair. "I remember saying to her, 'Honey, you're full of shit.' She got hot, you know, the way she could sometimes. 'Don't tell me I'm full of shit when you don't know the first thing that's going on in my head,' she said. 'Every woman in the world is in love with Warren Beatty,' I told her in my best Bill Buckley voice. 'Not everyone,' she said. 'Someone has to draw the line.'"

Chris shook his head. "The trouble with you is you don't want to feel better." He shifted Christian to his other hip as he leaned over his friend. "Andy, this isn't your fault."

When Andy looked up into Chris's face he found his eyes unaccountably moist. "I know."

"I don't think you do. All you're thinking about is a goddamned fight you had with her—and over what? Warren Beatty, for Christ's sake. Don't you get it?" Chris shook his head. "Don't do this, buddy. Stop beating yourself up." He knelt down beside his friend. "We know each other a long time. We've been through it all together. I know what's eating at you and it isn't a fight you two had over nothing."

"You do?"

"Of course. You think you should've protected her some way. But believe me when I tell you there's no way you could've done that; no one could."

Andy, his head in his hands, was hunched over. "I want it all back the way it was," he whispered.

Chris looked helplessly from his partner to Melissa. Then, impulsively, he grabbed Andy's knee, squeezed hard. "She's going to be all right. I know it."

"Sure she is." Andy nodded, wiping his eyes. He looked at Christian, chocolate and caramel all over his face. He stood up. Suddenly, he wanted only to get away from this conversation. "That's why I have to be here when she wakes up."

"Right." Chris swung his son out so Andy could kiss him goodbye.

"Take care of yourself, buddy." He looked Andy in the eye. "I'll look in on you tomorrow."

Alone again with his thoughts, Andy took Melissa's unresponsive hand. He put aside the image of Christian's face, and in his mind, Melissa returned to life. A year ago their pledge of eternal love almost came undone when the baby was delivered stillborn. There were complications, and the surgeon had had more work than he had bargained for. The result was that Melissa could never again conceive a child. Andy was stunned and frightened by the depth of his despair. He tried to keep it from Melissa, but even sunk within shock and mourning she knew. And like a surgeon wielding a scalpel, she got it out of him. Their marriage had almost spun out of control then.

"You're not yet forty," she'd said, weeping, "and one day you'll wake up and find out you want a child so badly nothing else matters. Even your love for me. Then you'll be gone."

"You're absolutely, one-hundred-percent wrong," he'd told her, wondering in his heart if she was right. What if that time came? he had asked himself. Could he turn his back on her, on their life together and just walk away? He'd seen friends and colleagues do just that. End one life and start another, as if the first one hadn't existed. He couldn't. But what if he felt he must?

And so a gulf began to grow between them, as guilt and uncertainty tainted their once-perfect love. Andy withdrew from Melissa, and she suffered in silence a mounting terror to which she could not put a name.

"Oh, Mr. Cooper. I didn't realize . . ."

Dr. Rothstein's uncertain expression was replaced by the coldly efficient mask the AMA considered professional. She was a small woman in her late thirties with the patented take-charge air of AMA indoctrination. She was quite pretty, in her way, Andy thought absently, with her thick, dark hair and eyes as black as olives. Her complexion had the darkness of the Mediterranean. She had a sharp Roman nose and a wide-lipped mouth. Andy tried to picture her in whites, playing tennis, and couldn't. Melissa, long-limbed and lithe on the clay court at home, could run down balls even at the corners of the baseline. And what a superb horsewoman she was! They had both learned to ride hunter-jumpers in their youth. It was what one did, as a matter of course, in their social circle. The thought of Dr. Rothstein on an English saddle seemed preposterous.

"There's been no change," he said as she checked all the apparatus, IV bags, marking off notations on Melissa's chart. "I've been here the whole time." That chart was a sacred thing, to be seen only by hospital personnel, as if it belonged to God, who would eventually tote up all Melissa's good deeds.

Dr. Rothstein said nothing, busy as she was noting readings that were the same as six hours ago, yesterday, and the day before.

Andy checked his watch. "You're here late." Dr. Rothstein had done the surgery on Melissa.

Dr. Rothstein turned, pressing the chart against her chest. "Mrs. Cooper is my patient," she said softly. "I do not abandon my patients."

Andy knew it would be wiser to let that pass, and in another time, another place perhaps he would have. "I had good reasons for calling in Dr. Matthews to consult," he said.

Dr. Rothstein stood in silence, waiting like a hanging judge.

"Besides being an old friend of the family," Andy pressed on, "he's—"

"A man," Dr. Rothstein offered in her quiet voice.

"He's one of the leading authorities on brain abnormalities," Andy finished.

"So am I. Which is what Bill Matthews told you from the beginning."

"I needed—" Andy paused to correct himself. "I wanted a second opinion. You would have done the same in my position."

Dr. Rothstein cocked her head to one side. "I have no qualms about sharing a patient, Mr. Cooper, especially with someone of Bill's qualifications. I just question the motives."

"Well, don't," Andy said a bit too quickly. "It had nothing to do with you. I just felt more comfortable with a family friend."

Dr. Rothstein eyed him levelly as she passed by him to check Melissa herself. She looked into Melissa's eyes, shone a penlight on the pupils. Andy found himself holding his breath. Dr. Rothstein snapped off the penlight and stood up. She made some more mysterious notations on the chart. "You know, you might as well go home, Mr. Cooper. Nothing will be gained by staying." She looked up. "You can trust the staff to notify you the moment there's a change."

"I can't leave."

"You've got to get on with your life. This could take . . ." She lifted an arm, let it fall. "A long time."

"Why won't you tell me what you find?" He stood squarely between her and the curtain. "You come in, make meaningless small talk while you examine my wife, and then leave without ever telling me what's happening."

Dr. Rothstein stood relaxed and silent, and somehow this posture infuriated Andy. He desperately wanted to get a rise out of her, to break through her glacial reserve and get her to confide something she had no intention of revealing.

"I won't let you go until you tell me."

Dr. Rothstein sighed. "Aren't you being the least bit childish, Mr. Cooper?"

"Don't tell me what's childish!" he shouted. "That's my wife lying there in a coma! What do you know of the pain I'm suffering? Do you have any idea or is this just some medical puzzle to you?"

Dr. Rothstein's gaze dropped for a moment. "To answer your question, I've found nothing, Mr. Cooper. Absolutely nothing."

His heart froze and there was a dimness around the edges of his vision as if the room was closing in on him. "That's bad, isn't it?"

"At this point, I can't say."

"Well, at what point *could* you say?"

"I do not appreciate that sarcastic tone of voice," Dr. Rothstein said. "Perhaps you'd do better in future to communicate with Dr. Matthews."

"Good! Excellent! At least with him I can have a conversation with a human being!" Andy could feel the edge of hysteria in his voice. It was something he had not heard in himself for some time, since his father had died, in fact. He had been thirteen and unprepared for a death so close to home. The thin edge to his voice had an ugly ring in his ears. He wanted to stop, but he couldn't. The floodgates had been opened and nothing was going to shut them now. He'd been sitting here for too long, doing nothing but being terrified that the life he'd known and cherished was over. It seemed to him as if the all-but-perfect life he and Melissa had been leading had been a dream. Had he slept through the past decade? Blind, irrational anger exploded inside him. "In fact," he rushed on heedlessly, "I wish Bill had been on the case from the beginning. Maybe then Melissa would be up and talking now!"

Dr. Rothstein was gripping Melissa's chart with a white-hot fury. "What precisely do you mean by that, Mr. Cooper?"

"Nothing. Forget it."

"I don't think I want to forget it," she said with exquisite pronunciation. "Let me ask you a question, Mr. Cooper. If someone spit in your face, would you be inclined to forget it?"

He said nothing; he felt abruptly exhausted. All the days of tense waiting seemed like stone blocks, an insupportable weight sitting on his shoulders.

"Your highly agitated state excuses many lapses, Mr. Cooper, but insulting me is not one of them." She strode toward him and he backed up, getting out of her way. At the curtain, she turned. "You know, I came to see your wife on my own time. I'm tired. I've done six operations in nineteen hours and I've been at the hospital for just over twenty-six. I should have been home, in bed, long ago. But I'm not. I'm here. Because I have my responsibilities to the people who you seem to think are just medical puzzles to me." She slid back the curtain, then looked back. "Not that you want advice from me, but from where I stand, it seems to me that you're in dire need of a vacation. Try some place far from here, like Montana."

Andy watched as she drew the curtain shut behind her. He smelled some faint trace of her perfume, but he was too paralyzed to think of what it was. He stood without thinking for a long time, but he found he could feel nothing, either. He was in a curious kind of limbo from which there appeared to be no escape. At last, he turned, kissed Melissa on the corner of her cool, dry lips and, taking the wicker basket his mother had left for him, he went home.

That night, he dreamed that Melissa was singing. Perhaps it was an aria from *Mefistofele* or *Carmen,* but he couldn't tell. Instead of words, he heard beautiful sounds—a melody so exquisite that when he awoke his eyes were filled with tears. He was positive that Melissa had been speaking to him, saying, It's not my time yet, hang on.

The phone was ringing.

Still hearing Melissa's strange song, he scrabbled in the dark for the phone and was informed of his wife's death. He was told by the emotionless night nurse the precise time Melissa had expired and was asked if he needed help in making the final arrangements. He put down the receiver without answering.

Chris and Bonnie were of more help at the funeral than was his mother, who, it seemed, was obsessed with getting all the details right: Only white flowers and only roses—carnations and daisies were embarrassingly common; instructing the minister in what to say; rounding up the appropriate people for the requisite number of eulogies. Proper attire was of paramount importance to her; she nearly had to come over and dress Andy herself. Somehow, in her mind, etiquette was synonymous with love and respect.

Andy, numb and unthinking, endured the funeral as if it were an Army training film. He saw people he knew, some well, others not, and dutifully shook all their hands but didn't hear a word they said. He remembered Bill Matthews whispering in his ear, "At least she felt no pain," and Dr. Rothstein in a neat black suit touching his hand, saying something about going far away.

And when, weeks later, he had still not recovered, when he'd been sitting in his office day after day without knowing it, he knew he was in trouble. He felt as numb as if he had been Cryovacced. His windows faced west, and he stared into the setting sun for a very long time, feeling the darkness fall like a mantle on his shoulders.

"Isn't it beautiful, the city at night?"

He recognized Chris's voice without turning around.

"All those lights like a spangle of diamonds."

Andy, who had been contemplating the darkness as if it were an old and unwelcome pal, said, "I've got to get out of here."

"What Bon and I have been telling you, buddy." Chris made himself a small drink of scotch and soda from the wet bar. "Shake those memories out of your head." He came around to where Andy could see him. They existed in companionable silence for some time, Chris slowly sipping his drink, Andy looking out the window into the past.

"I know I'm looking at what you're seeing," Andy said. "I know there's beauty out there, but I can't find it."

Chris shook the ice cubes in his glass. "Tell me something, buddy," he said thoughtfully, "you're not running away, are you?"

"To be honest, I don't know."

"Because that dog won't hunt. You're going to carry your cage around with you wherever you are. Whatever's eating you—"

Andy got up and put on his suit jacket.

Chris put his drink aside. "Where do you think you'll go?" he asked. "Why not take over the San Francisco office? There are a couple of knotty cases that could use your brilliant mind."

"Not Frisco," Andy said without a second thought. "I'm going to Montana."

"Montana?" Chris was clearly stunned. "Buddy, I've got a flash for you, there isn't even a town worth mentioning in Montana. What's a city boy like you going to do there?"

"Lose myself," Andy said, walking out the door.

"That's what I was afraid of." Chris launched himself across the room. "It isn't you you need to lose, buddy." He stood at the door, watching Andy walk away. "You're going the wrong way, you know that, don't you?" He shook his head, muttered, "Shit!" And then in a louder voice, "Hey, am I ever going to see you again?"

✳　✳　✳

The Browning 30.06 was heavy, seven or eight pounds, Andy estimated. But he already had gotten the measure of its balance.

"If you want any chance of stopping an elk, you're going to need a thirty-ought-six, one big rifle," Clay Monitor had said, turning his Chevy Suburban into the Holiday Village Mall on Tenth Avenue, South. Clay's slow Western drawl was as wrinkled and leathery as his wind-burned skin.

That hadn't been the first thing Clay had said to him. At the airport at Great Falls, he'd seen Andy walking toward him with one light bag and no 30.06 of his own, and had slammed his hat against his blue-jeaned thigh. "Shit, your secretary didn't tell me you were a novice."

Clay was tall and reedy, with pale gray eyes that were deceptively soft. He had the kind of face you'd expect on a cowboy: chiseled and wise, except for his nose which was kind of bulbous.

"Sorry," Andy said, handing over his bag. "I didn't think it mattered."

"Well, hell, we get real hunters here, Andy, men who know how to bring down an animal."

Andy had smiled. "Maybe you can turn me into one of them, Clay."

"That'll be the day," Clay had muttered as he'd stowed Andy's bag in the Suburban. On its side was painted: CLAY MONITOR, BACK COUNTRY GUIDE. And then in smaller letters: ELK HUNTS OUR SPECIALTY. The two men had climbed aboard and that's when he'd taken Andy to Sheel's in Holiday Village to get the Browning. Clay recommended the Browning over the Winchester or the Remington, even though it was more expensive, because it was more finely engineered and gave a truer shot. "If I could afford one of these beauties," he said, gripping the Browning Andy had just purchased, "you can be sure this is what I'd use in the back country."

Andy had read about Big Sky Country—he'd even seen a photo or two in travel magazines—but nothing could have prepared him for the sheer wildness of northwestern Montana. For one thing, there were the Rockies: harsh, blue, majestic, snow-spattered. They pierced the clear blue sky like the pillars of heaven. For another, there was the air: cold, clean, bracing. Andy felt as if he'd sloughed off a decade of city toil.

Clay drove out of town, along highways lined with fir trees so dense their green looked black. Occasionally, they'd pass a log roadhouse, featuring $1.99 hunters' breakfasts or charbroiled buffalo burgers. They parked the Suburban at the end of the road inside the Bob Marshall Wilderness, an enormous tract of undeveloped land mandated in the 1940s and protected by the federal government. From there, they rode by horseback thirteen miles to the base camp in the back country eight miles south of Glacier National Park. Clay introduced Andy to the cook and Clay's assistant, who took care of portage and most of the physical work around the camp.

Tents had been set up. A string of pack mules had been used to carry in supplies. A cookfire was blazing and Andy could smell steak grilling. There was still some light, so Clay took him out, loaded up the Browning, and began Andy's initiation into the silent, sacred rituals of big game hunting. Andy, dressed in the thick hunting gear he had bought at Sheel's, learned the rudiments of holding, aiming, and pulling the trigger of a 30.06. The first real shot he fired almost dislocated his shoulder. Clay tried not to laugh at him. In fact, by the time they returned for dinner, Clay said he admired Andy's perseverance. Andy felt good. He'd already seen that Clay was not a man to bandy about the bullshit. A compliment from him meant something.

In his first hours in Montana Andy never felt more distant from his old life. He breathed deeply. He felt his heart beating, the blood rushing through his arteries and veins, the stretch of muscles, the flinch of reflexes. Everything he had taken for granted or had forgotten for so many years now stood out in sharp, almost painful relief.

But at night, after an enormous dinner, his mind drifted from the small talk being bantered around the fire, and he saw Melissa's face floating like a ghostly moon among the bright masses of stars visible through the branches.

He excused himself and turned in. At first, he had a hard time finding a comfortable spot for a body throbbing from his unaccustomed time on horseback. Scents of dinner mingled with the sharp odors of the camp animals, the resiny cinders swirling up from the cookfire to provide a strange but oddly comforting melange. Exhaustion overtook him and he was asleep.

In his dream, he felt Melissa's presence like a whiff of a rushing stream through the pines. He was in Paris, during that long weekend when they'd met. He had been attending a conference on international patent law and he'd run into her in the lobby of the Crillon Hotel. She was finishing up the renovation of an art gallery she'd designed and overseen. They had spotted each other at the same time, and they had smiled, an American recognizing a fellow American in a foreign land. But, obviously, there was more to it than that. They had had drinks, which extended to dinner, then a long moonlit stroll along the Seine, where they'd paused long enough to lose themselves in an ecstatic, languorous kiss beneath the rustling horse-chestnut trees. The moonlight made an ethereal bridge across the river on which they imagined their shadows in embrace. They returned to the Crillon, where they'd made love in his room, then, giggling like kids, had run through the plush, deserted halls to her room, where they made love all over again.

In his dream, Andy could hear her singing softly that strange aria. Now he could make out her words: "Hear my voice, feel my pulse. I am alive."

He awoke with the suddenness of a rope snapping. His heart was racing in the aftermath of her singing. Then, reality hit him all over again: Melissa was dead. And he could not stop the thought that he shouldn't have left her side that night. If he'd stayed, if she'd felt him beside her, maybe she wouldn't have let go.

He was shivering. He sat up, wrapped his arms around his drawn-up legs. He put his chin on his knees, hoping to fall asleep. Instead, he watched the dawning of the world.

Clay took him out just at first light. They'd eaten some steaming hot oatmeal and biscuits with butter and honey, then, taking up their rifles, had headed out into the wilderness. Andy tried to keep in mind what Clay had told him, that for the most part they'd have very little reaction time. You didn't stalk elk, you came upon one and had about a second to swing the rifle up, aim, and fire. "You have to understand what this thing does," Clay had told him, patting the barrel of the Browning. "Once you accept that, you'll be all right. If you can't, you'll never be a hunter."

That day, cool and clear, they came upon two elk and Andy got off three shots. None of them found their mark. His ears hurt from the explosive reports of the 30.06 and his arms ached from holding the rifle. Andy would have liked Clay to tell him how he was doing but since Clay didn't say anything, Andy thought it best not to ask. He was no hunter, he knew, but he wanted to hunt. In fact, he needed it.

That night, after dinner, he tried to ask himself the question: why? He had never killed another creature, discounting that black widow he'd found in a corner of his bunkhouse at camp. Also, that rattlesnake he'd watched his counselor kill a week later as they were hiking in the Adirondacks. He'd held the forked stick down behind the snake's head while the counselor severed it from the writhing body with a Bowie knife. For his bravery, he was allowed to keep the rattle part of the tail after the counselor had carefully dried it. He'd made the mistake of waving it in his mother's face on visiting day. She'd been so appalled she'd gone straight to the camp director and had the counselor fired. His mother could do things like that without any sense of remorse. For his part, Andy arranged for a bucketful of water to drop on the new counselor's head the first time he walked into the bunkhouse.

"How you doin'?" Clay asked, dropping down beside Andy. The cookfire cracked and sparked, sending light and shadow flickering across his lined face.

"Oh, you know," Andy said vaguely.

"I brought you some coffee," Clay said, handing Andy a steaming metal cup. He grinned. "It may not be good but it sure is strong." He took a sip from his own cup, stared off into the night for a moment.

"Feeling a little lost?"

"Yeah." Andy nodded. "Sort of." But not, he thought, for the reason Clay thought.

"Big space out here," Clay said. "Specially for a city man such as yourself. Can be overwhelming, sometimes. Awe-inspiring, I call it."

"That it is," Andy agreed.

Clay took another sip of coffee, glanced over at Andy. "Well, I see you'd rather be alone." He began to get up.

"No, wait," Andy said on impulse. "I'd appreciate someone to talk with." Until that moment he hadn't realized he was lonely.

Clay shrugged, settled himself against the bole of a gigantic spruce. He lit a cigarette, smoked in long, deep drags. "This here is Blackfeet country. Know anything about the Blackfeet, Andy?"

"Not a bit."

"They were the most aggressive of the Plains peoples. The three branches, North Blackfeet, Bloods, and Piegans, roamed all the way from Alberta, Canada, to Mexico. They were horse merchants. The horse is what made them so mobile and so deadly on the plains. Siksikaua is their name: Black Moccasins. Way to the north, where they originally came from, the soil was so moist and black it stained the soles of their moccasins." He smoked thoughtfully, his eyes full of history. "They were decimated by the white man's world, encroaching settlers, liquor, but mainly by diseases previously unknown to them—smallpox, measles, mumps, typhoid, some of them introduced deliberately by the government to 'control' them. The government had a habit of distributing blankets to the People, impregnated with bacteria."

"You sound bitter."

Clay stubbed out his butt, lit another cigarette. "Don't know how it is in the big cities, sonny, but this is Montana. We live free here in the West. I fought for my country readily enough, because I'm a patriot, but I never, ever put my trust in the federal government when it comes to running things." He grunted. "Laws—don't give a rat's ass for 'em. Now, the laws of the West, that's another story entirely. There's a certain code out here you've got to mind."

"I think I understand," Andy said. "The decimation of the Blackfeet is a common story among American Indians, I'm afraid."

Clay nodded as he took a drag of his cigarette. "Law's a funny thing. There's a fine line between justice and inequity. But I expect you know all about that. You're a lawyer, aren't you, Andy?"

"Well, I was." Andy laced his fingers together, flexing them back and forth as he had done when he was a kid. He knew he was trying to figure things out, to disgorge a ball of cold lead that had been forming in his stomach ever since he got the news that Melissa had been shot. "To be honest, I don't know whether I will be again. My wife died, you see, and everything changed for me."

There was a small silence between them. Above, moonlight filtered through the tangle of branches, illuminating the black undergrowth at the edges of the clearing.

"I wonder if you'd tell me something," Andy said. "Did you ever kill anyone, in the war, I mean."

Clay's gray eyes flickered once. "You shouldn't ought to ask a veteran that question, Andy. It's impolite."

"Sorry, I didn't mean—"

"Forget it." Clay finished off his coffee. "I saw my share of action. I came home to Montana to wash my hands, so to speak." He took a deep breath, looked up into the cloudless sky. "This is a place that makes you feel clean. It's a place to find your heart."

Later, in his sleeping bag, just before he drifted off to sleep, it occurred to Andy that Clay had been telling him in his own way that Andy had done the right thing by coming out here. More than anything Andy wanted to find his heart.

The trouble was that Melissa was his heart. He heard her singing again in his dream. She seemed closer this time, her beautiful voice clearer, and he knew that the part of her that could not be quantified or even analyzed by modern science was not dead.

Dawn brought fog and a certain chill that insinuated itself beneath the thick hunting clothes Andy, shivering in semi-darkness, drew on. He ate breakfast in the peculiar charged silence of the pre-hunt. He chewed mechanically and tasted nothing. The second biscuit stuck in his throat.

"Ready?" Clay whispered, taking up his rifle. His breath smelled of coffee and cigarettes. He'd already smoked three cigarettes during breakfast.

Andy nodded, hefting the Browning, and they set out.

The forest seemed eerie, primeval. Color was damped to a minimum, and shapes, half-formed, unrecognizable, kept appearing out of the thick mist. Andy was put in mind of the day he and his family moved into the new house in Connecticut. He was six. His father had just been promoted to chief operating officer of his insurance firm and, to mark the occasion, the ever status-conscious Coopers had moved into a grand house in a prime location. Andy had liked his room well enough; it was larger than his old room, and had more windows. But that night when he'd woken to pee, everything seemed unfamiliar, unrecognizable, and sinister. Shadows took on a presence, and began to move, or so it seemed to Andy. He rushed back from the bathroom and sat in the center of the bed, drawing the blanket around him, safe on his little island amid a dangerous sea of darkness.

Now, he unaccountably had that childish terror again. It was almost as if, keeping a pace behind Clay, he was safe. Clay was his little island of safety amid a sea of shifting fog.

He could hear soft rustlings all around him, but could see nothing. The fog was too dense. It clung to the inside of his nose and mouth; it made his eyes water.

"We could head back to camp, if you like," Clay said from just ahead of him.

"No, it's okay." Andy did not want to be thought more of a city wimp. "Let's keep going." It was curious how he wanted to please Clay, in the same way he'd wanted to please his father. Make him feel proud, like they'd accomplished something together. Andy's father had died before they had been able to do that.

Andy and Clay pushed further into the underbrush. Andy felt drops of moisture dripping onto his bright orange cap, and underfoot the soil was as dark as night. It was a rich mix of leaf mold and shed pine needles, making it springy, ideal for following hoofprints. Clay had shown Andy how to distinguish fresh tracks from old ones that would lead nowhere.

He saw something on the ground and paused, going down on one knee to see it better. He pushed some wild geranium out of the way and recognized a pile of elk scat. It was still steaming. He recognized a fresh hoofprint, saw others that headed off to the right. He stood up to sign to Clay and could not find him. He looked wildly around. He was surrounded by trees and mist. A vireo flew by over his head. Andy called softly once, twice, but heard no reply.

He stood still, in mid-step, as if caught in amber. He felt his heart beating fast, the blood pounding heavily in his temples. There was a roaring inside him. All he could feel was the weight of the Browning. He stared at the elk scat. Then, kicking it over with the toe of his boot, he followed the spoor into the forest.

He tried to remember everything Clay had taught him. He felt the presence of the forest, the breath of it, its heartbeat. He heard the vireo close by, hidden by a welter of branches, and caught a glimpse of a golden-headed bird—a kinglet, according to Clay. He liked knowing the names of things. A real citified dude would have pointed to a bird, not caring whether it was a vireo or a nuthatch; not understanding there was a certain power in being able to identify species.

A real citified dude would have been terrified being alone in a fog-bound forest, out in the middle of the Bob Marshall Wilderness. Andy felt nothing but a strange elation, a growing sense of something coming toward him from out of the darkness. It was something for which he did not yet have a name, something "other," a part of him he had not taken the trouble to recognize. He had been far too busy in Connecticut and New York, fulfilling his parents' dream for his glorious future. The world of LCATs, furious studying, grinding exams, pagers, cellular phones, teleconferencing, legal maneuvering, and getting ahead at all costs did not leave much space for anything else. It was a wonder he'd made time for Melissa.

The elk broke cover almost directly in front of him. He saw it and heard it almost at the same instant and, without thinking, he swung the Browning up. Perhaps he'd been upwind of the beast and it'd scented Andy, or perhaps Andy had made too much noise—that twig he'd stepped on three paces back.

The elk was massive, a bull with arcing horns rippled with great tines like spikes. It was majestic, intimidating. Andy stared into its wild, round eyes for just a split second before he squeezed the trigger. "Try to aim for the lungs," Clay had told him. "The spot just behind the forelegs." The Browning bucked and the roar was deafening. It seemed as if the elk was coming on, undeterred. Had he missed even at this close range? He took a step backward, which was a mistake. His bootheel caught on a gnarled root and he stumbled. Still, the elk came on, and Andy, rising to one knee, got off another shot.

The elk seemed to scream, but in the aftermath of the shot Andy could not tell. The elk, its teeth bared, veered sharply as it went down, first on its knees and then over on its side. Andy, getting to his feet, could see its rib cage rising and falling as it panted and shuddered. Blood pumped out of it, spewing onto its sweat-slick flank. A long drool of mucus snaked out of the snout.

Andy stared, wide-eyed. He was abruptly sickened. He heard the hooves beating a tattoo on the ground, he could see the pain in the elk's eyes as it snorted and heaved. The stench of its dying suffused the forest with a musk that made Andy gag. He knew he should be doing something but he could not recall what.

Some sixth sense made him look up. He saw Clay striding sound-lessly toward him out of the swirling fog. It was such an intrusion in this cathedral-like place that Andy jumped.

"Pull the trigger, son," Clay said evenly.

"What?"

"The animal's suffering." Clay was patient and cool. "Put the Browning up and pull the trigger."

Andy looked down. He had not even been aware he still held the Browning in his hands. He raised the rifle. It seemed to weigh a hundred pounds. He watched the pump of bright blood across the elk's sleek flank. He did not realize until this moment what a beautiful creature it was. He pulled the trigger.

The elk spasmed, then lay still.

"Well done." Clay shouldered past him to peer closely at the beast. "Good shooting."

Andy watched in stunned silence while Clay pulled out his Bowie knife and commenced to field dress the elk. He slit open its belly and removed first the entrails, then the organs. The inside of the carcass steamed into the fog. The stench was overpowering but Andy, gritting his teeth, forced himself to watch. Because the elk was a bull, Clay severed the head, then expertly peeled back the hide so that it could be tanned. Later, at the taxidermist's, it would be sewn back in place around the glass eyes set in the occipital cavities.

But for Andy, the sight of that naked head, ribboned by blood, striped with raw flesh and pale sinew, was like watching his own death. He was never so aware of his own mortality—the vulnerable skin, flesh, and bone of which he was composed. Just like the elk. At that moment, there seemed to be no difference between them.

Clay, crouched and intent as he worked easily over the corpse, quartered the elk. Later, it would be loaded onto the pack mules, taken out of the back country to be processed so that by the time Andy was ready to get on the plane back east, the elk meat would be cut, frozen, and wrapped in convenient sizes.

That night, Andy did not feel like celebrating. He ate dinner in near-silence. Clay seemed to respect the distance Andy had put between himself and the rest of the world. Why not? In a sense, it seemed clear to Andy that Clay, choosing to live out here in the way he did, had done the same thing.

Andy was a long time in falling asleep. He could not get the smell of the carcass out of his nostrils; he worried, irrationally, that he would choke on it in his sleep.

In his dream, Melissa came to him. It was the first time he had felt her, rather than heard her singing. She lay down beside him while he slept, wrapping her arms around him, entangling them both in his sleeping bag. She smelled faintly of sugar and sweet milk. He relaxed into her warmth, immensely comforted that she was so near, that he had come to this part of the world to find his heart and was now so close to finding it.

Then, in his dream, he opened his eyes to find Melissa's body entwined around him. He looked into her eyes and saw, instead, the round animal eyes of the elk, wild with pain. He started, saw to his horror the elk's head and neck emerging from the top of her torso. Its teeth were bared and it looked almost as if it were grinning at him.

He opened his mouth to scream but the only sound that came out was the ear-splitting report of a 30.06 being fired. He reared back, trying to get away, but he was mortally entangled in the bloody sleeping bag and Melissa's limbs. Sweat broke out under his arms, at the back of his neck with the effort of trying to break free. But the more he thrashed, the more entangled he became. He cried out again, another report crashed through his brain. Then, he was alone in darkness. Alone with the singing. It was so close now that it seemed as if Melissa was crooning in his ear. The song was clearer now and it seemed to him more like a chant, the cadences hypnotic, incantatory, holy.

He awoke in a sweat. He could not bear to be alone with the memory of that dream. In the darkness, he made his stumbling way to Clay's tent and, going inside, crouched, shivering, his khaki blanket pulled tightly around him.

"Clay?" he said softly.

"What is it, son?" Clay said without seeming to stir. "Night terrors?"

In the darkness, Andy nodded his damp head.

"It happens, sometimes, after a kill," Clay said, fifteen minutes later, as they sat cross-legged around the cookfire that the guide had coaxed back to blazing life. A pot of coffee was put up, though Andy doubted whether he'd be able to get it down.

"I want you to know something." Clay rubbed his hands in the heat. "You did okay out there yesterday. You stood your ground real well."

"You saw me?"

"Saw it all," Clay said. "What kind of a guide you think I'd be if I let you get in harm's way?" He took the coffee pot off the fire, poured out two cups' worth, handed one to Andy. "Never would have let you go off on your own if I hadn't thought you wanted to." He took a long draught, even though it was scalding. "Needed to, really, is what I figured. There are some things a man's got to wrestle with on his own."

He took out a cigarette and lit it. Then he squinted over the top of the metal cup at Andy. "You find out what it is you're looking for?"

"Maybe." Andy said, appreciating the heat of the coffee, though not its intensely bitter taste. The acid hit his stomach like the punch of a prizefighter. "See, I lost something back in New York. My wife. She was—"

"Pardon me for interrupting, son, but it seems to me you lost something far more important. You lost yourself." When Andy said nothing, Clay continued. "Not to minimize the loss of a wife. I lost mine nine years back and there isn't a day part of me doesn't miss her. But I got on with my life. After I looked death in the face in the war I came home and got on with my life. Only thing a sensible man can do."

Andy looked into Clay's face. "You never . . ." He paused, considering his phrasing. "Didn't you ever want to—I don't know—roll back time to the point before you killed a man, to a time before your wife died?"

"You want to do that now, Andy?" Clay asked. "You had the night terrors. Your sweat was like blood running out of you. I haven't got a doubt in the world that the elk came back to you in some form. Want to go back to the moment before you killed him?"

It was not a question to be taken lightly, and Andy considered his answer carefully. To his complete surprise, he said, "No. I don't."

"Well," Clay said, nodding, "that's progress, ain't it?"

All morning, Clay was busy supervising the collection and packing of the elk meat. The mules, calm as a summer's day, took it all in stride. Andy took the time to sort through his thoughts and emotions. He replayed everything that had happened from the moment he had bulled his way into ICU and had seen Melissa being wheeled in from surgery.

He waited until Clay was finished, then when he was alone, went up to him. "Clay, if you don't mind my asking, why didn't you laugh at me when I mentioned that thing about going back in time? I mean, a man like you—"

"Takes a man like me to understand a question like that." Clay dusted himself off, looked off into the distance. "Anyway, doesn't matter now, does it?"

"But it does to me." Andy was thinking of his dream, of Melissa's closeness. She was by his side now, he knew it. If he could just find a way to reach out, to break the barrier that lay between them. "When you asked me whether I wanted to go back to the moment before I killed the elk . . . I need to know whether it was just an idle question."

"Don't ask idle questions," Clay said. "Got no time for the foolishness of city ways." His gray eyes caught Andy's. "But I expect you already knew that."

"Yes, sir." Andy nodded. "I did." He shuffled his feet. "Then the question . . ." He took a deep breath. Why go on? he asked himself. The idea's nuts. But it was Melissa who drove him on, and this certainty he had that she was so near. "What if I said, yes, I wanted things to reverse themselves."

Clay shook his head. "Thought you were beyond that."

"So did I." Andy held his gaze.

Clay seemed abruptly sad. "It's your wife, isn't it? You can't let her go."

"Or vice versa," Andy said. That was when he told Clay about the singing, how it had started the night Melissa had died, how much closer and clearer it sounded since he'd come to Montana, how it seemed to him like chanting, somehow liturgical, sacred.

For the first time since Andy had met him, Clay seemed startled. "You ever hear about the Singing Tree, son?" he asked after Andy had finished.

"No, I haven't," Andy said.

Clay blew air through his nostrils like a horse. "Well, now you will."

"The Singing Tree exists," Mad Wolf said. "It grows out into the sky from a rocky scree halfway up the path that leads to Grinnell Glacier in Glacier National Park."

"And it sings," Andy said.

"To some, yes," Mad Wolf said. "It sings."

"I heard my wife singing."

Mad Wolf was a Piegan Blackfoot. Clay had taken Andy to see him when they had come out of the Bob Marshall Wilderness. Mad Wolf lived in a small house made of wood and wattle. Out back was a traditional Blackfoot lodge, daubed with symbols such as the broken arrow, the racing bison, the face of the north wind, which was sacred to Mad Wolf. The lodge was conical in shape with an opening at the top, to keep it ventilated and free from smoke. It was made of cowhides, stitched together over spruce poles.

"Your wife, the Tree, it is the same thing." Mad Wolf settled himself against a pile of bearskins. "The Tree grows in space, it reaches toward heaven. White men of science have studied the Tree and still they do not understand how it flourishes, clinging to a bit of rock. Why doesn't a storm blow it down the mountainside? they ask." Mad Wolf cocked his head as if listening to another speak from a great distance. "The Singing Tree is sustained by spirits caught in the land between life and death. It is a kind of lodestone."

Andy's heart skipped a beat. "How do you mean?"

106

Mad Wolf's large, rough-skinned hands opened like flowers to sunlight. "Spirits sustain the Tree; they nurture it through drought and storm. They cry out and it is like the rapture of song. Their bodies have died but their spirits have not yet reached the land of the dead. Who can say why? With each individual it is different."

"So you think this has happened to Melissa."

Mad Wolf said nothing. He was an old man, emaciated and bent-backed, with long hair that gleamed like platinum. He wore a headband of plaited leather from which a single eagle feather rose. He wore beaded armbands and hand-hammered silver cuffs on wrists as slender as a girl's. His face was long and gaunt, pitted and lined by life. His eyes were sunken in his skull and his skin looked like the underbelly of a tortoise. He was so tall he had to stoop to get around his home. It increased the impression that they were in a dollhouse.

Mad Wolf had welcomed them into his home with great ceremony, greeting Clay with a kind of patrician tenderness that gave Andy pause. Andy was unprepared for such gentleness. He had prepared herbal tea for them and had packed a pipe with aromatic tobacco. He had sat smoking, silent and attentive, as Andy described his dreams of Melissa. Clay said nothing, but sat at Andy's side slowly sipping the pungent tea.

"The elk is significant," Mad Wolf said now. "You made a kill and its spirit lay down beside you. Its spirit guided you to the restless spirit of your wife."

"Then she's not dead," Andy said.

Mad Wolf puffed on his pipe. "She is here, certainly."

"Then I want to go to her."

Mad Wolf's eyes flickered once, sliding sideways to glance briefly at Clay. Then they returned to Andy. "I don't think you mean that."

"But I do," Andy cried. "She died a senseless death. Shot down by a stray bullet. It isn't fair. We loved each other so much. Her singing is proof to me that our love transcends circumstance." His heart was so full of anguish no doubt Mad Wolf could see it on his face. "Now I want it all back; I want things to be the way they were before she was shot." Andy leaned forward. "I want you to do this for me."

"The dream of the elk spirit is proof that your words are true. The elk will not attach itself to falsehood or evil. Still, this transformation is not to be entered into lightly."

"I am prepared for anything," Andy said. "I will do anything to get Melissa back."

Mad Wolf's face was utterly without expression. "You must understand the consequences of your request. The Singing Tree is a kind of doorway from our world to . . . another. I can only provide the key to that doorway, you must use it. But when you do, there is no turning back. Events have their own momentum, their own shape and form. I do not predict outcomes; I only provide options." He took a last puff on his pipe. "In the same way you chose to kill the bull elk, you choose this. What will come of it no one can say. But I do offer this guarantee: nothing will ever be the same again." He put aside his pipe. "Take this as a warning or an opportunity, as you will. I have no way of knowing which it is."

His gaze was level as he reached out, touched the tips of Andy's fingers. "Do you wish to proceed?"

"I do." A sudden chill went up Andy's spine.

Mad Wolf turned his pipe over, knocking out the cold dottle onto the packed dirt floor. Rising, he went to a carved chest and extracted a silver box from which he took a packet wrapped in layers of cloth. He returned to sit cross-legged opposite Andy and Clay. He unfolded the cloths with reverence, scooped some of what was inside into the bowl of the pipe. He lit it, handed it to Andy.

Andy pulled the smoke into his lungs without hesitation. Then, at Mad Wolf's signal, he passed the pipe to Clay. When all three men had shared the pipe, Mad Wolf said to Andy: "Do not be frightened but for this journey I must make you ill."

Andy swallowed. "How ill?"

"If you are not gravely ill, you will not be able to pass to the other side, even with the help of the Singing Tree."

Andy looked at Clay.

"You can still bow out, son," Clay said. "No one will think the worse of you."

Andy took a deep breath. He was very frightened now. What had been an obsession ever since Melissa had died was now about to become reality. It had been in his mind for so long—an intimate part of him—the thought of it taking solid form in the real world was terrifying. And yet he heard her singing to him, that same sacred song, and he knew he could not stop now. He did not want to stop. He wanted to be with Melissa no matter what the cost.

Looking deep into Mad Wolf's eyes, Andy said, "What do I have to do?"

He gladly ate the mushrooms Mad Wolf gave him and drank the brackish liquid that tasted like squid ink. The first time Mad Wolf gave him tobacco juice to swallow, he vomited it up for he'd had no food for eighteen hours. Mad Wolf merely produced another bowl and this time Andy was able to keep it down.

Dimly, he was aware that there must be narcotics—peyote or some other natural psychedelic in the brackish liquid he was being fed. He seemed to float on the field of night. Above him, he could see the stars, though surely he must still be inside Mad Wolf's wood and wattle house.

Mad Wolf had daubed his face with a white substance and had garbed himself in the costume of the shaman—fawnskin vest striped by intricate beadwork, deerskin leggings, pricked lengthwise by tiers of colored porcupine quills, a double-strand necklace of yellow bear's teeth. Vertical bars of iron and turquoise hung off him, making him look more like a skeleton than a man.

"Hear my words, A-poi-a-kinni," Mad Wolf intoned. A-poi-a-kinni meant Light Hair. "The first shaman was born from the union of woman and eagle." He now wore a fierce mask made of eagle feathers. He spoke through the open beak. "Shamans are transformed into eagles, attaining entrance into the high realm that arches above all places on the earth." His hands worked the iron and turquoise bars, making them tinkle like raindrops on a glass roof. "These are my bones, the bones of my ancestors. They tell the story of my birth and re-birth, the sacred history of family."

Andy took this all in as if he were nursing at his mother's breast. Indeed, there was a distinctly maternal aspect to Mad Wolf's ministrations that belied his stark and aloof shaman's guise. He was both earth mother and paterfamilias, and Andy felt safe in his presence, lifted up. In this state, he was beyond the pain and suffering of Melissa's death, beyond the guilt that had been eating him alive. He floated in a vast velvet bowl filled with stars and moon, enfolded by a deep blue radiance. As his body became ill, his mind turned pellucid. He began to see for great distances, through the walls of the house. He could see the streams and rivers, the great snowcapped mountains, the rising stands of spruce and fir. Most of all he could see the animals and birds. He listened to their callings with rapt meditation.

All the while, Mad Wolf burned sweet myrtle and sassafras, blowing the smoke across Andy's face while he used rattles made of rawhide stretched over wicker frames. Like the lodge out back, the rattles were daubed with the sign of the north wind. Each time he brought more myrtle and sassafras to be burned, Mad Wolf took up a Prong—a holy forked stick painted red—and used it to draw forth from the fire a glowing coal, which he placed atop the vegetation.

At the end of three days, Andy was so weak he could not stand without support. He could not walk at all. Mad Wolf and Clay carried him out of the wood and wattle house and into the cowhide lodge.

There, they placed him directly beneath the ventilation hole. Mad Wolf built a fire close beside him. At Mad Wolf's signal, Clay left them.

Andy was delirious and lucid at the same time. How this was possible he could not say. He lay as if dead, barely breathing, lost within the incantatory mists, the spiritual condition which was a prerequisite of his journey. It was curious. He had assumed that in this state he would feel even closer to Melissa, but in truth he felt her not at all. What he felt was an almost complete detachment of self. Only faintly was he aware of his heartbeat, the rush of his blood. From a long way off he could hear his own breathing.

Then, he heard Mad Wolf talking to him: "A-poi-a-kinni, you are prepared. It is time for the last stage of your journey to the other side." The rattles commenced their rhythm. "I know you are worthy, for you have been visited by the spirit of the elk. This is rare, A-poi-a-kinni. Exceptionally rare."

The rattles seemed to combine with the sweet smoke to create another world, forming at the ragged edges of Andy's transmogrified vision.

"It is fitting, then, as you embark upon your journey to the Singing Tree that I tell you its origin. In the long time past, before the White man came west, the Piegan were starving. The buffalo were infected with a strange and virulent illness that affected the People when they ate the meat. They were forced to turn to the elk, whom this branch of the People worshipped as sacred. They prayed to Napi, the Sun Power, to forgive them and to make them strong for the elk hunt. The party of warriors went out on horseback, across the prairie to the great glacial forest where the elk dwelt.

"They tried to stalk the elk, but with no luck. For three weeks, they hunted, returning to their lodges without meat to feed their families. The next week, the daughter of Isso-ko-yi-kinni, the head man, was walking down to the buffalo wallow for water, and there she saw the most magnificent bull elk she had ever seen. The elk scented her, but instead of bolting, it turned its head and looked into her eyes.

"'O, great elk,' the head man's daughter said, 'I would take you as my husband if your kind would provide enough meat for my People.'

"She said this out of desperation and as a joke, for she was far too young to take into account the consequences of her words. But to her astonishment, the bull elk lifted its head, its great antlers swinging, and down into the wallow came a host of elk. They were spotted by a pair of warriors who, gathering others to their side, spent the next hour slaughtering the strangely docile beasts.

"Only the great bull was left alive. Somehow the warriors refused to

110

come near it, or perhaps they did not see it at all. When the slaughter was done and the carcasses dragged back to the lodges amid great rejoicing, the head man's daughter and the great bull were left facing one another. It extended its foreleg and said, 'Now you will be my wife.'

"'No! No!' she cried in horror. 'I cannot!'

"'But you swore to me if I sacrificed my herd to your People, you would take me as a husband.'

"Only now did the impact of her imprudent promise sweep over her like a prairie storm. She began to cry as she followed the bull out of the wallow and across the prairie, away from the glowing cookfires of her home.

"During the feasting, the girl's mother noticed she was missing. Her father ordered a search of the village, but of course she was nowhere to be found. Now the village cried for her soul and the wail of the dead resounded.

"'No,' the head man said. 'I feel my child here.' And he pressed a fist against his heart. 'She is not dead.' And, taking up his hunting bow and a handful of arrows, he set out to find her. At the wallow, he discovered a great many elk prints and several prints of a small moccasin he knew belonged to his daughter.

"'She was here,' he said out loud. 'I know it.'

"'Yes,' a voice replied from over his head, 'she was. I saw her.'

He looked up to see a bright-eyed magpie circling. It alighted at the edge of the wallow and cocked its head at him.

"'Have you seen her since?' her father asked anxiously. 'I must find her and bring her back.'

"'In the mountains you will find her,' the magpie said. 'Near the great glacier. I will show you.'

So Isso-ko-yi-kinni marched for three days toward the blue haze of the magnificent glacial mountains, hiking up a mountainside, pausing only briefly to eat wild huckleberries, sharing his meals with the magpie. On the fourth day, they ascended the mountain on which the great glacier had sat for countless years. When they were halfway up to the great glacier, he spotted a herd of grazing elk.

"'There! There!' the magpie cried.

And Isso-ko-yi-kinni bade the black bird fly to his daughter and tell her he was here to take her home. This the magpie did, flying into the center of the herd, hopping along the ground where the girl reclined next to her sleeping husband.

"He hopped and hopped until he got the girl's attention. 'Your father is waiting for you there, along the path. He wishes to take you home. Do you wish to go?'

"'Oh, yes!' the girl replied, but casting a fearful glance at her slumbering husband. 'Tell him I will come as soon as I am able to.'

"The magpie flew off and, some time later, the girl followed. She burst through a stand of spruce into her father's arms, weeping uncontrollably. But when he moved to take her away from the mountain meadow, she resisted. 'No, wait,' she whispered. 'If I leave now I will surely be missed and the elk will come after us and kill you. Better for me to go back and try to sneak out tonight.'

"Reluctantly, her father allowed her to return to her elk husband, but when she returned to his side, he sniffed her and said, 'I smell a person close by. Who have you been seeing?'

"Though the girl used every means at her disposal to reassure the elk she had seen no one, he did not believe her. He gathered all the males and they went down the meadow, through the stand of spruce, where they fell upon Isso-ko-yi-kinni, trampling him so thoroughly that his body was ripped to pieces.

"His daughter, hysterical with grief, fell to her knees, pulling her hair. She tried to find her father's body but could not. She called upon the magpie to find even one shred of him. This the magpie did, pecking through the bloody muck of the trail until he unearthed a piece of Isso-ko-yi-kinni's spine. This he plucked up in his beak and dropped it in the girl's lap.

"She placed it reverently onto the bloody ground and, covering it with a blanket, began to sing. She sang and sang and, after a long time, she removed the blanket. The elk were stunned to discover Isso-ko-yi-kinni's body, inert but intact.

"The girl replaced the blanket and continued her song, which was like a chant, incantatory, holy. And when she removed the blanket a second time, her father stirred and opened his eyes, and was returned to the world of the living.

"In that very spot, where his blood had been spilled, where the magpie had returned the piece of his spine, and where his daughter had sung him back to life there grew in later years a tree, gnarled and ancient-looking, rising each year higher and higher into the sky, defying the white man's notions of law and logic. This the Piegan know as the Singing Tree."

Andy, floating in his blue world, devoured Mad Wolf's words as if they were steak and eggs. He believed the tale Mad Wolf told because he could see for himself the simple truth behind it.

And in that moment, he felt himself rise. Not his corpus, but the essence of himself that was at last free of all physical restraints. He could no longer hear the beating of his heart, the rushing of his blood, and the only sighing he heard was that of the wind rushing through high mountain peaks.

He opened his eyes and saw the hole in the lodge coming closer and closer, opening as if it were some kind of portal. Then he was through it, bursting out into the coal-black sky, lifted on thermal currents like an eagle. And like an eagle he soared far from the lodge, where Mad Wolf still squatted over his prone and inert body. He flew north, toward the brilliant stars and the bright glow of the glacial peaks on the eastern side of Glacier National Park.

He came upon the Continental Divide, saw fulminating clouds rolling down off the sharp serpentine peak like waves breaking against a rocky shore. And then he saw the Singing Tree, gnarled and seeming ancient, as Mad Wolf had said, thrusting impossibly up from rocky scree. Surely there could be no room for roots to form between the shale and limestone. And yet, it reached skyward with its scraggly branches and thick-barked trunk.

Andy knew he was close, now. He could feel a swirl of forces beyond his normal senses, a confluence of unseen currents—electromagnetic, ectoplasmic, psychic. There was an eerie glow, as if from the excitation of molecules. It was as if the very fabric of reality were being warped and bent and—ripped asunder.

Without understanding how, Andy became entangled in the branches of the Singing Tree. He struggled to free himself, but his gyrations only entangled him all the more. He was surrounded by branches. Thicker and thicker they became until they blocked out the moon, the stars, and the sky altogether. There was only an impenetrable blackness.

Andy had been in Mexico City once when an earthquake hit, and this was the somewhat giddy, vertiginous sensation he felt now. The earth, the very air about him felt as if it were splitting apart.

As if they were scenes being presented upon a stage, he saw great fires burning, bloody rivers rising up and overflowing their banks. He heard hideous screams and piteous calls, was witness to mountains shuddering and shifting with a great grinding noise that filled him with a certain dread. Grotesque faces appeared, lit by firelight, forms like shadows gesticulated wildly, menacingly.

Then, as if a curtain had been lowered, darkness returned. He heard the singing. Melissa's voice rose and fell, chanting her sacred song. And he saw her, standing on the spot where the Singing Tree had been. Except, it wasn't exactly as he remembered it. There were subtle but telling differences in the terrain. The colors, for one thing, were all wrong, and the rock was shiny, black as polished obsidian.

"Oh, Andy," Melissa whispered.

"Melissa." He was crying as he took her into his arms. He was overwhelmed with the sensation of holding her again. "I knew you weren't dead. I knew I'd find you." He kissed her hard, and felt her lips open under his. They were as warm and giving as ever. Nothing had changed.

When he opened his eyes, they were in Paris. It was the weekend they had met. He smelled the same flowers in the air, saw the same Bateaux Mouches plying the Seine with their spotlights and amplified commentary. There were the horse-chestnuts rising above their heads as they strolled hand in hand. There was the ethereal bridge of moonlight, stretching across the river to the Left Bank.

They had the conversations he remembered word for word, and he was content to do so. They kissed, long and languorously while the horse-chestnut leaves made a private bower. They went back to the Crillon and he was more than content to begin the physical side of their love affair all over again. He entered her ecstatically. They made love just as he remembered it and, afterward, he felt again the overpoweringly giddy urge to drink champagne. They finished one bottle, took the other down the hall with them, giggling as they stumbled into her room and made love all over again. It was all too wonderful, a dream fulfilled.

But then it began all over again, an identical replay without the slightest deviation. And again. The fourth time they were strolling along the Seine, Andy struggled to break the pattern. He wanted to turn with her at the corner, head toward the Champs Élysées, instead of continuing along the riverbank. He could do nothing but continue on their predestined path.

Beside him, Melissa squeezed his hand, said, "I can feel you struggling. Don't. This is where we are now; there's nothing you can do to change it."

"But where are we?" Andy asked.

"You know where we are," Melissa said. "Paris. We're on our first date."

"But this isn't Paris. It can't be. We're in Glacier Park, Montana."

"Oh, but it is Paris." Melissa smiled. "Look around you. This isn't an illusion. It's real." She hugged him. "We're back in time, back the way we were in the beginning."

"But it's not the same." Andy frowned. "Don't you notice anything odd about this?"

"Odd? Why, no. It's exactly as I remember it." She smiled. "So romantic. So utterly perfect."

Andy wanted to stop in this spot beneath the halo of an iron street-lamp, but he could not make himself do it. The place where they paused to kiss was still several hundred yards away. "But, don't you see, we're not free to come and go as we please."

"But why should we?" Melissa asked. "It was perfect the first time; it's perfect now." She squeezed his hand more tightly. "Don't you think it's heaven, darling?"

"Of course it is." Andy wondered how he could get through to her. "But it seems to be happening over and over again."

"Naturally." Melissa nodded. "This is one point in time and we're reliving it. You can't change the past."

"But I want to." Andy felt an increasing sense of unease.

Melissa seemed genuinely confused. "But why, darling? You're here with me. We're together again. Isn't this what you wanted? To go back to the way it was."

"Yes," he said slowly. "That's just what I wanted."

They paused to kiss, long and languorously, beneath the rustling horse chestnuts. Andy, knowing the small breeze would waft beneath his jacket at this precise instant found himself gritting his teeth. If only it would come a split instant later. But it didn't. If only he could keep himself from continuing to walk back to the Crillon. He couldn't. He began to dread what lay in wait for him. If only he could change one small physical thing. If only he could take a one-block detour—one step in another direction before turning back. But it was impossible. The moment was set in time and they were reliving it.

The fifth time they strolled along the Seine, Melissa said to him, "Darling, you're not happy." She lifted a hand. "No, don't bother to deny it. A woman knows these things."

"It's not that I don't want to be with you," Andy said in misery, "it's that I can't stand the repetition. Don't you have an urge to change just one item in the program—like going to your room first, then mine?"

"I can't think why," Melissa said. "Why tamper with perfection?"

"Because we've already done it again and again," Andy said with some exasperation. "It's driving me nuts and I don't understand why it's not affecting you the same way."

"That's simple, darling. It's because I'm dead. Or, nearly so."

"What?"

"Well, we no longer have the same considerations—like time and *movement*."

"Movement?"

"Yes." She nodded. "That's what life is all about, isn't it? Moving forward. Time flies—or at least it ticks on. Everything changes, the world is in constant flux, a kind of controlled chaos." She lifted a hand to point. "It's different here. Time does not exist. Why should it? It's a human concept, not a cosmic one. And there can be no movement without time. There are no seconds, minutes, hours, days, months, years. Each moment is precisely like the last. Nothing changes."

"Except this discussion," Andy said.

They were coming to the spot where they kissed, but somehow this time Andy had the curious sensation that that moment would be finite. Change would occur there, a path diverging. He recalled Mad Wolf's words: *I do not predict outcomes; I only provide options. What will come of it no one can say. But I do offer this guarantee: nothing will ever be the same again.*

Melissa looked at him gravely. "You have a choice, darling. Now you must make it."

"I don't want to leave you, Melissa."

"Want has nothing to do with it, as you can see," she said. "Having me again means this—all of this, again and again."

He shuddered.

Melissa squeezed his hand again. "Don't you understand, darling? You still have your life to live. You are wedded to movement, not to me. I have passed over."

"But not yet, not yet," he said. "You still live. I can feel your heart beating, feel the heat of the blood in your veins. You're not dead; you exist."

"Yes, I exist," she said. "In this theater." She looked around. "But you can feel how cramped it's getting." She looked at him. "Darling, you've already made your choice."

Andy saw they were fast approaching the spot where they would kiss, where the change would occur. What change? He did not know and that somehow terrified him. It was like the first time you dove into the pool backward. A certain leap of faith was needed; an exemplary courage.

"The truth is we both need to be free," she said in the breathless moment before they paused to kiss. He saw her turn her lips up to him and to the moonlight. He heard the rustling of the horse-chestnut leaves, the faint whooshing sounds of traffic on the Champs Élysées. A spotlight from a Bateau Mouches flashed across their pressed-together bodies and then passed on.

"Goodbye, darling," she whispered.

"Goodbye." Andy almost choked on the single word.

Melissa let go of his hand and, as she did so, she began to rise. Like smoke on a cold winter's morning, she drifted out over the dark ribbon of the Seine. The moonlight danced on the water. She reached that ethereal moonlight bridge. He wondered whether she would look back, and what he would do if she did. He imagined himself running to get her, pull her back. But she did not look back. Strangely, he felt grateful that she did not. His gaze became blurred by tears but he did not lift a hand to wipe his eyes. Tears were necessary now, he understood; they were part of the change.

As he watched, Melissa walked resolutely across the bridge of moonlight, beginning her journey to the other side.

When Andy returned to his Fifth Avenue apartment in New York, it had a strange, musty smell. He spent the next five minutes opening every window, even though the evening was chilly. Then he went into the kitchen, carefully stacked the frozen slabs of elk meat in the back of his freezer. He had given his Browning to Clay, as a parting gift.

Andy stood in the center of his apartment, trying to get a feel for it. The place seemed alien; he was out of sync with everything in it. He looked at the handmade furniture, the fine antique pieces he and Melissa had picked out, the paintings on the walls, the sculpture on marble pedestals. Then he thought of the spruce-filled wilderness out of which he had just come. He thought of the great arch of the sky and the huge sprays of stars beneath which he had pursued his quest for Melissa.

He was inordinately aware of a clock ticking on the mantelpiece. It was as if his strange and eerie passage to the other side had exposed nerves that had long lain dormant. Nerves by which he could discover the passage of unnoticed winds.

He turned in a circle, wondering what he'd do now. Perhaps he'd sell the place and move somewhere. Where? Though the entire world was a possibility, he could not think where he might end up. But that was okay. He knew he was far from where he had been when he'd walked out of here two weeks ago. For the moment, that was enough.

He'd told no one he'd come back and had no desire to do so. He hadn't bothered to pick up his mail. He went to his desk, which was as he'd left it, cleared of all items save for the framed picture of Melissa, laughing in spring sunlight. He stared at her honey-colored eyes, then slowly picked up the tickets for their subscription to the opera, which he'd stuck in a corner of the chased silver frame.

Four messages on his answering machine: Chris wanting him to call when he got back; his mother, her voice all cool concern, wondering when he'd call her; his housekeeper asking if he wanted her to return to work—she'd gotten another offer and wanted to take it. The fourth message was from Dr. Rothstein. Some of Melissa's effects had been left behind and she said he could come by the hospital any evening, since she was there most nights.

While he listened to the playback, he leafed through the opera tickets. The performance of *Mefistofele* was almost two weeks ago, but he saw that *Carmen* was playing tonight. He looked at his watch. It was just past six-thirty. On a sudden impulse, he went into the master bedroom, took out his tux.

An hour and fifteen minutes later, he walked into the grand lobby of the Metropolitan Opera House at Lincoln Center. His beloved Chagall murals welcomed him like old friends. He sat through the performance without hearing much of anything. He was painfully aware of the empty seat beside him. At intermission, he wandered through the beautifully dressed crowd. He drank a glass of champagne and felt a terrible yearning in his chest. He could see again Melissa heading across the moolight bridge that arced across the Seine and, as he stared into the face of every woman he passed, he half expected to hear that strange and haunting melody in his head, the one Melissa had sung to him, drawing him toward the Singing Tree. His heart beat fast to think that he might come across a woman with eyes the color of honey. Woman after woman passed by either ignoring him or giving him a blank New York stare. None had eyes the color of honey; he saw no reflection of Melissa, no hint that she might have come back to him.

He stood in the lobby as the chimes sounded and people began to drift back into the theater. When he was alone with the towering Chagalls, he didn't know whether to laugh or to cry.

The hospital was a dim and quiet labyrinth in the heart of the city. In his tuxedo he was eyed with stoic suspicion by the guard on duty until he asked the woman at the admitting desk where he could find Dr. Rothstein.

"Which Dr. Rothstein? We have two," she said. "Milton or Emma?"

"Emma," Andy said. Funny. She'd never told him her first name and he'd never bothered to find out.

"Try the seventh floor—No, the other way." She pointed. "Take the blue elevators to seven, turn right, go through two sets of doors, across the glass walkway to the Sennheiser Pavilion. Then make a left."

"After that I'm on my own?" Andy said, but she didn't crack a smile. Neither did the guard.

Andy walked the hallways of the Sennheiser Pavilion, which were silent as a library. Occasionally, he passed a night duty nurse or a doctor hurrying by in operating room scrubs. No one gave him a second glance and he was not inclined to ask directions. When he came to a nurses' station he asked for Dr. Emma Rothstein, but no one had seen her. He went on, further into the labyrinth.

He thought about what an idiot he had been to go to the opera expecting to find his dead wife resurrected, like Warren Beatty in *Heaven Can Wait*. He shook his head, recognizing himself for a fool. But a saddened fool for all that. He'd had his time with Melissa and he'd failed to tell her how sorry he was for the way he'd treated her after the baby died. He prayed she knew without his having to tell her.

Andy came upon a man mopping the floor who thought he'd seen Dr. Rothstein heading for surgery but that was, he confessed, some time ago. She could still be there, or she could be in the recovery room. Either way, Andy was headed in the right direction.

"Nice duds," he said to Andy's back. "It ain't New Year's Eve yet, is it?"

Now Andy was in a part of the floor that contained staff quarters, file and supply rooms, conference facilities, and the like. From a long way off he thought he heard singing. He stopped in his tracks, every cell in his body straining as he listened. His blood ran cold. Was that a familiar melody he heard?

He moved forward like a sleepwalker, putting one foot in front of the other. Without conscious volition, he began to walk faster and faster, until he was running full out. And all the while the familiar melody echoed softly down the corridor, filling him with an inexpressible feeling that was equal parts joy and terror.

Outside the door to the surgeon's lounge he stopped. The song was coming from inside. An aria. His and Melissa's favorite from *Mefistofele*. He heard this with more clarity than he had any of tonight's arias at the Met. The voice brought stinging tears to his eyes.

He put his hand on the doorknob, but at the last instant he paused. What would he find inside? Who was playing the opera? He was unaccountably reminded of the moment when he'd kissed Melissa for the last time in Paris. The feeling was curious and unsettling. Could another change be coming?

Then the illusion dissipated and he shook his head. He was kidding himself, just as he had earlier at the Met when he'd been sure he'd run into some reincarnation of Melissa. He'd watched *Heaven Can Wait* one too many times.

He pushed open the door to the surgeon's lounge and went inside. The room was overheated, increasing the reek of burnt coffee and strong disinfectant. Dr. Emma Rothstein looked up. She was reclining on a green leatherette sofa that had looked shabby five years ago and was now way beyond that. She had her legs up, crossed at the ankles. Her shoes were off and her toes were wiggling to the music. She was dressed in a cream-colored sweater and brown tweed skirt. Andy could see she had a lovely body. Her green scrubs lay in a pile in one corner.

She gazed into his eyes and Andy had the distinct impression that she did not recognize him. Then, a subtle shift seemed to occur and something he could not name came into her dark eyes.

She smiled and stood up, framed by the city lights shining through the old-fashioned casement windows behind her. "Mr. Cooper." She extended a hand. "It's good to see you again."

He shook her hand, which was warm and dry. "I got your message. I've been away for a while. I guess I shouldn't have barged in on you unannounced."

"No, no. It's quite all right." She padded barefoot to a metal filing cabinet, which stood next to an old, wheezing refrigerator and a table with a coffee machine and piles of cardboard cups, plastic stirrers, a container of non-dairy creamer and packets of Equal. Dr. Rothstein opened a drawer. "I have your wife's effects. I'm so sorry. I can't imagine how they were forgotten. The hospital personnel are usually scrupulous about such things." She handed him a carefully wrapped package.

"It was good of you to keep them for me," Andy said. He pocketed the package without opening it.

Dr. Rothstein went to turn off the opera, which was playing on a portable CD system, but he stopped her.

"Do you mind? I love *Mefistofele* and I'd very much like to hear the end of it."

They sat together on the green leatherette sofa while the glorious music swirled all around them. Dr. Rothstein assumed her relaxed position, her feet up on a scarred and stained wooden table. Andy noticed what beautiful legs she had. Her eyes were closed to the music, and he studied her face as if seeing it for the first time. She had a kind of cat's face with high cheekbones, a wide mouth, and a narrow chin. It was a strong face but not an aggressive one. He found himself wanting to gaze into her black olive eyes, and he was startled when her eyes opened and he found her looking back at him as serene as if she'd just woken from sleep.

When the opera was over, they sat in silence for some time. At length, Dr. Rothstein cleared her throat. "Would you like some coffee? Or a Diet Coke?"

"No, thanks."

She got up, went to the coffee machine, and poured herself some. "You said you'd been away. Where did you go?"

Andy followed her over and they stood by the casement windows. "Actually, believe it or not, I took your advice. I went to Montana."

The city lights fell upon her face like stardust. "How surprising."

He laughed. "I suppose so. About as surprising as you being an opera buff."

"Why is that surprising?" She sipped her coffee. "Do I look that much of a Philistine?"

"Oh, no. It's just that . . ." He paused, wondering whether to go on. He opened a casement, abruptly overwhelmed by the suffocating heat of the place. "You see, my wife and I . . . We loved opera, but *Mefistofele* and *Carmen* were our favorites."

Dr. Rothstein pushed her hair back off her face. "How odd."

"Yes," Andy said. "That's what I was thinking."

"Well, I'm hardly a buff," she went on. She stared out the windows into the night. A misty rain had begun to fall, pale silver in the streetlights. "I haven't enough time for opera, which is a pity, really, since I live in New York. I've barely been to the Met. But I do love *Mefistofele* and *Carmen*."

"I just came from seeing *Carmen* at the Met," Andy said with a suddenly thumping heart. What was happening here? He had no idea.

"There, you see?" Dr. Rothstein said. "I was deep inside a very swollen brain all evening."

"Bad?"

She looked at him. "Let's just say you enjoyed yourself more than I did."

"I doubt it," Andy said ruefully. "What I learned tonight was that, at least, for me the opera isn't nearly so compelling without someone to share it with."

She drank more coffee. "I'm sorry you didn't enjoy yourself tonight."

"Well . . ." He looked away for a moment trying to marshal thoughts that kept threatening to run off in different directions. "Doctor—"

"Call me Emma. Please."

He looked at her for a moment, then nodded. "I'd like that. But it makes saying this all the more difficult." He took a breath, closed his eyes and thought, here goes nothing. "About our last meeting—"

"At your wife's funeral."

"No, I—" He looked down at his hands. "The truth is I don't remember too much about that day."

"No surprise there."

He settled himself on the metal windowsill. He couldn't seem to wrench his gaze away from his fingers, which were twined about one another like snakes. "The thing is . . . what you said to me about not trusting you—"

"Mr. Cooper, this isn't necessary. You've been through—"

"Andy," he said. "And it *is* necessary, I assure you."

She put aside her coffee cup. To his surprise, she reached out, put her hand over his. "Just say what you have to say, then, Andy. Trust in what's here, now."

That seemed like good advice to him, so he said, "You were right. About everything. I didn't fully trust your expertise, your reputation, your ability because you're a woman. I want to apologize for that."

"Apology accepted."

He looked at her, surprised again. "Just like that?"

"Why not?" She shrugged, then smiled. "It's a lot more than most people are apt to give. It took a leap of faith, an exemplary courage to admit your bias to a stranger." She laughed. "Besides, life's too short to hold grudges." She had a nice laugh, deep and rich. It was the kind of laugh that made you want to join in the fun.

He nodded. "I want you to know that I don't blame you for Melissa's death."

She gave him a wry look. "My insurance company and I bless you for that."

"Don't joke," he said. "I know you did your best with her."

She nodded. "That I did."

Her black olive eyes held his for an uncomfortably long time. What was she trying to tell him? he wondered.

He got up, patted his pockets for nothing in particular, but felt the package of Melissa's effects nonetheless. "Well." He looked around the room. "I guess I should be going."

She perched atop the windowsill. "Why?"

"Pardon?"

Emma smiled at him. "Do you have anywhere else to go?"

"I guess not." Andy sat down beside her.

She crossed her arms over her thighs, sat slightly forward. "Andy, listen to me. I'm not your beloved wife. I never will be. She and I might share a love of operas but that's it. You understand that, don't you?"

Andy tried to swallow. "Sure."

"Do you really mean that, I wonder?" She shook her head. "I can't pretend to know what's going on in your mind, but I don't believe in reincarnation. Neither should you. It doesn't exist."

"The past is over and done with," he told her. "It's a closed book."

She put her head back against the casement. "I'm relieved to hear you say that."

She turned slightly and his heart missed a beat. He could swear something had come in through the open window, a bright mote or a dancing speck of light. But, then, perhaps it was only a reflection of a police car or an ambulance hurtling by far below. The spark or reflection or whatever it was touched her briefly and then was gone.

She turned back to him and he froze. Was it his imagination or were her eyes the color of honey? She moved again and he saw that her eyes were huge and dark and very familiar.

"I'm sorry," he said.

"You already apologized."

Andy shook his head. "I'm so sorry I hurt you. I never meant to but—That last year before you—" He stopped, abruptly embarrassed. Then he put his hand to his forehead. "Aren't you going to ask me what the hell I'm talking about?"

Her eyes were glazed, full of liquid as if she were about to cry. She leaned forward impulsely and kissed him on the cheek. He shivered when he felt her hand at the nape of his neck.

Then they broke apart. Somewhere deep inside him he wanted an explanation of this moment, but if he'd learned anything from his singular journey to Montana it was that some things defied explanation.

Emma regarded him quietly. "I realize I have no business asking this. But, what the hell, it's been a strange encounter so far. So tell me, if you want to, what is it you're looking for?"

Andy considered his answer for a long time. He thought he might as well tell the truth. It didn't require a fanciful imagination to recognize that this woman was somehow different. Like Clay, she wasn't interested in hearing the right answer; she wanted the truth. And at that moment, he realized that this and only this was, after all, what Melissa had wanted from him. "I don't really know."

"Good." She smiled and slipped her hand into his. "Neither do I."

They got up together, and without her needing to ask him, he got her coat. He was content to be with her—with Emma Rothstein, doctor of medicine. It was a good feeling to know he was moving toward the future. He remembered Melissa on the moonlight bridge, disappearing. Where had she gone?

They went out into the dim and silent corridor, heading for the elevators a long way away.

He listened to the echo of their footfalls along the corridor until

Emma said: "How about this? We could grab a bite and then stop at an all-night video rental I know."

"Sounds good." Andy nodded. "Have you ever seen *Heaven Can Wait?*"

She put her handbag under her arm. "Isn't that the remake with Warren Beatty?"

"Right."

"I hate Warren Beatty," she said.

"Impossible," Andy said. He had fallen into a daze, recalling the echo of this conversation as if from a long way off. "Every woman's in love with him."

"Not every one," she said, laughing. Emma's deep laugh and Melissa's musical laugh combined in a delicious swirl. "Someone has to draw the line."

The Hand-Puppet

JOYCE CAROL OATES

When I was a boy, I was a ventriloquist, and used to practice for hours throwing my voice. I created a personality for my wooden partner, so that he could say things that I was unwilling to say for myself. Thus I was able to keep my mask—my protective gear—in place.

I remain grateful for the security lent to me by that other self I created, for I still truly believe that illusion gives us the stuff of survival.

Because of that, I was particularly fascinated that Joyce Carol Oates, Pulitzer Prize–nominee and National Book Award–winner, chose to address that very issue. Her story unmasks a woman who has for so many years been driven by the expectations of others that she has forgotten what lies beneath the mask she presents to the world. In forcing the woman to look at herself, Oates makes us wonder whether dropping our illusions, our masks, would reveal our true selves, or simply a new set of illusions.

—DC

The Hand-Puppet

HOW STRANGENESS ENTERS OUR LIVES. The mother knew that her eleven-year-old daughter Tippi had had an interest in puppets, and in ventriloquism, since fourth grade, but she'd had no idea that Tippi had been working in secret, upstairs in her room, on a hand-puppet of her own invention; nor that the child, by nature a shy, somewhat withdrawn child, planned to surprise her with it in quite so dramatic a way—thrusting the ugly thing into her face when she stepped into the kitchen one Monday morning to prepare breakfast, and wriggling it as frantically as if it were alive.

"H'LO MISSUS! G'MORNIN MISSUS! WHAT'S TO EAT MISSUS!"—the voice was a low guttural mocking drawl, the mother would have sworn a stranger's voice.

The mother was of course taken totally by surprise. She'd had no idea that her daughter had come downstairs before her, and so stealthily! It was all so premeditated, seemingly rehearsed, like theater.

"Oh God!"—the mother responded in the way the daughter must have wished, giving a little shriek and pressing her hand against her heart; staring, for an instant uncomprehending, at the big-headed baby-face puppet cavorting a few inches from her face. Afterward she would recall that, in that first startled instant, the puppet had seemed somehow familiar, the close-set black-button eyes, the leering red-satin mouth, but in fact she'd never seen anything like it before. It had a misshapen body made of stiff felt, a body that was mainly shoulders and arms; the head was bald and domed, like an embryo's; the nose was a snubbed little piece of cotton made prehensile by a strip of wire. How obscene, the mother thought.

"Tippi, how—clever!" the mother said, seeing that the child was hiding clumsily behind a part-opened closet door, her arm, in the flannel sleeve of her pajama top, tremblingly extended. "But you shouldn't scare the life out of your poor mother, that isn't very nice."

"SORRY MISSUS! SORRY MISSUS!" The puppet squirmed in exaggerated delight, stretching its red mouth, making a series of mock bows.

The mother tried to interrupt but the low guttural drawl continued—"MISSUS I BEEN HERE BEFORE YA! AN I GONNA BE HERE WHENYA GONE!" There came then a crackling lunatic laugh the mother would have sworn issued, not from her daughter's mouth, but from the puppet's.

"Tippi, really!"—the mother, now annoyed, but smiling to conceal her annoyance, pushed the closet door open, to reveal the daughter there, mere inches away, breathing quickly, eyes shining, flush-faced with excitement as a small child caught in mischief. "Isn't it a little early in the morning for this sort of thing?"

Boldly, Tippi kept the puppet between her mother and herself, the big domed head and antic face still cavorting—"DID I SCARED YOU MISSUS! SOOO SOORRY MISSUS!"

"Tippi, please. That's enough."

"TIPPI AIN HERE MISSUS TOO BAD! BYEBYE!"

"Tippi, damn—!"

Exasperated, beginning to be a little frightened, the mother took hold of the puppet, grasping her daughter's antic fingers inside the cloth torso. For a moment the fingers resisted—and surprisingly strong they were. Then, abruptly, Tippi gave in, ducking her head. Rarely disobedient or rebellious, even as a toddler, she seemed embarrassed by this display; her sallow skin blotched red and her pale myopic eyes, framed by milky-blue plastic frames, seemed to dim in retreat. She mumbled, "Sorry Mom," adding in an undertone, "It's just some silly thing I made."

"Tippi, it *is* amazing. It's . . . ingenious."

Now she'd regained some measure of control, the mother complimented the daughter on the hand-puppet. What was surprising, unexpected, was that the daughter had been so creative—fashioning a professional-looking puppet out of household odds and ends, pieces of felt, strips of satin, ribbons, buttons, thumbtacks—she who seemed so frequently overwhelmed by school, and whose grades were only average; she whose creative efforts, guided by one or another teacher, and always on assignment, had seemed in the past touchingly derivative and conventional. The mother warmly noted the clever floppy rabbitlike ears, the drollery of five prehensile fingers and a lumpy thumb on each hand. The slightly asymmetrical domed head with a prominent crooked seam like a cracked egg. "When on earth did you make this, Tippi? And your voice—how on earth did you do *that?*"

The daughter shrugged, not meeting the mother's eye. Mumbled again a grave apology, disparaging words about the puppet—"silly, dumb, didn't turn out right"—then she was hurrying out of the kitchen, the puppet carelessly crumpled in her hand. She ran upstairs to get ready for school, a soft-bodied child in flannel pajamas, barefoot, her heels coming down hard on the stairs. The mother, hand still pressed against her heart, stared after her in perplexed silence.

How strangeness enters our lives.

It was in fact, it would remain in memory, an ordinary school day morning. The Monday following the week-long Easter recess in the public schools. Lorraine Lake, Tippi's mother, usually came downstairs at about 7:30 A.M. weekdays to prepare breakfast for her husband and daughter, but on this morning, the morning of the hand-puppet, Mr. Lake, sales manager for a local electronics company, was in Dallas at a convention. So there was just Lorraine and Tippi, whose school bus would arrive at about 8:10 A.M., stopping at a corner up the road. Mr. Lake traveled frequently, so his absence on this morning was not disturbing; in fact, such mornings, mother and daughter exchanging casual remarks as the radio on the window sill played cheery-bright morning music and chickadees fluttered about the bird feeder outside the window, were routinely pleasant, companionable. It might be said that Lorraine Lake looked forward to them. And now, her nerves jangling from the surprise, the oddity, of the hand-puppet, felt subtly betrayed by her daughter.

It was deliberate, she thought, staring out the window above the sink, as into a void. Premeditated. Because I'm alone. She would never have done that to her father.

The Lakes lived in a rural-suburban landscape where, in summer, the foliage of crowded trees created a dark screen, like a perpetual cloud ceiling; in winter and early spring, before the trees budded, the sky was predominant, pressing. Yet it seemed always the same sky—opaque, dully white, layers of stained cumulus clouds like ill-fitting flagstones.

Lorraine Lake stared, and, by degrees, into focus came the needle-thin red column of mercury in the thermometer outside the window—41° F. This too was a familiar fact.

Briskly then Lorraine Lake prepared breakfast. Hot oatmeal with raisins and sliced bananas for Tippi, toast and black coffee for herself. A ritual, and pleasure in it. I am the mother, Lorraine Lake was thinking. I am not '*Missus*'! She was a fully mature woman of forty-two and she was not a woman who believed she might have cultivated another, more worthy, more mysterious and sublime life elsewhere, a life without husband, child; a "true" life without the trappings of the identity that accrued to her in this shining kitchen, this rural-suburban brick-and-stucco colonial house on a curving cul-de-sac lane. If Lorraine Lake had had a life preceding this April morning, this nerve-jangled moment, she did not recall it with any sense of loss, nor any particular resentment.

I do these things because I am the mother.

Because I am the mother, I do these things.

Remembering how, the previous week, Tippi had stayed home, most of the time upstairs in her room. A quiet child. A shy child. A good child who seemed, at a casual glance, younger than eleven—lacking a certain exuberance, a spark, an air of resistance. MISSUS I BEEN HERE BEFORE YA! AN I GONNA BE HERE WHENYA GONE! Tippi seemed to have few friends at school, or, in any case, rarely spoke of them; but there was a girl named Sonia, also a sixth grader, who lived in the neighborhood, who'd sometimes invited Tippi over . . . but had not, recently; nor had Tippi asked if she might invite Sonia over. The realization was alarming. I don't want my daughter to be left behind, Lorraine Lake thought. I don't want my daughter to be unhappy.

Recalling how, as a small child, Tippi had chattered incessantly to herself, sometimes, it had seemed, preferring her own solitary company to that of her loving, doting parents. Thank God she'd grown out of that stage! In later years too the child talked to herself, but usually in private—in her room, or in the bathroom—which isn't uncommon, after all. Now, Lorraine Lake recalled with dismay having heard, just last week, a low guttural voice in the house, a radio or TV voice she'd assumed it must be . . . she'd been on the telephone the other day when she'd heard it, at a distance, and had thought nothing of it. She realized now with a sick sensation that this had been the puppet-voice, the "thrown" voice of Tippi's ventriloquism.

How had the child, practicing in secret, grown so adept? So quickly?

Could one be born with a natural gift for—such a thing?

When Tippi came back downstairs, her face washed, her limp fawn-colored hair combed, she carried herself stiffly, as if she'd been wounded. Her appetite for the oatmeal, and her usual glass of fruit juice, was conspicuously restrained. She wants praise for that ugly thing, Lorraine Lake thought, incensed. Well, she's getting none from me. It was almost 8:00 A.M. Except for the cheery-bright radio music and the excited tittering of chickadees outside the window, there was a strained silence. Finally Lorraine said, with a sudden smile, "Your puppet is very . . . clever, Tippi. And the *voice,* how on earth did you do that?" Tippi seemed scarcely to hear, spooning oatmeal slowly, chewing with apparent distaste. She was a child who loved sweets and often overate, even a breakfast, but this morning her very mouth was sullen. "I had no idea you were making anything like that," Lorraine persisted, enthusiastically. "Was it a secret? A project for school?"

Tippi shrugged her shoulders. Her milky-blue glasses were sliding down her nose and Lorraine had to resist the impulse to push them back up.

Tippi mumbled something not quite audible. The puppet was "silly." Hadn't "turned out right."

Like all the other girls at her school, Tippi wore jeans, sneakers, a cotton-knit sweater over a shirt; Tippi's sweater was so baggy as to resemble a maternity smock. Such clothes should have disguised the child's plumpness, but did not. Tippi's plain prim moon-shaped face seemed to Lorraine to be stiffened in opposition, and in the newly tasted strength of opposition. Lorraine asked, with her bright, eager smile, "But is it a project? Are you taking it to school?"

Tippi sighed, messing with her oatmeal; her pale eyes, lifting reluctantly to Lorraine's, were obdurate, opaque. "No, Mom. It isn't a *project.*" Her lips twisted scornfully. "And don't worry, I'm not taking it to school."

Lorraine protested, "Tippi, I'm not worried. I'm just—" She hesitated over the word "concerned." Saying instead, "—curious."

"No, Mom. I'm not taking it to dumb old school, don't worry."

"I said, Tippi, I *wasn't worried.*"

Which was not the truth, but Tippi could not know. So much of what a mother must say in a household is not true, yet it is always in the interests of other members of the household not to know.

On these mornings, the arrival of the yellow school bus with its invasive sound of brakes was always imminent, awaited. If a child, of the six who boarded the bus at the corner, was late, the driver sounded the horn, once, twice, a third time; waited a beat or two; then drove off, with an invasive shifting of gears. Lorraine Lake had not realized how she'd come to hate the yellow school bus until a dream she'd had one night of its careening off a bridge—sinking into a river—a confused, muddled dream, a nightmare best unexamined. When Tippi had been younger, Lorraine had taken her hand-in-hand out to the corner to catch the bus; Tippi was one of those tearful-sullen children reluctant to go to school, and many mornings a good deal of cajoling, coaxing, kissing, admonishing was required. Now, Tippi was older; Tippi could get to the bus by herself, however reluctantly, and however inclined she was to dawdle. But by custom in the Lake household it fell to Lorraine, the mother, to take note of the time when the time moved dangerously beyond 8:00 A.M.; it fell to Lorraine to urge Tippi to finish her breakfast, brush her teeth, get on her outdoor clothes, and get outside before the bus moved on. Weeks ago, in the dead of February, in an uncharacteristic mood of maternal impatience, Lorraine had purposefully remained silent as if unaware of the time, and of course Mr. Lake, skimming computer print-outs at the breakfast table while Tippi ate her cereal, took not the slightest notice, and Tippi had in fact missed the bus that morning. But the upset to the household, the flurry of accusations and refutations and hurt feelings, the unleashed anger, had hardly been worth it; and the result had been that Lorraine had had to drive Tippi four miles into town, to school—as she might have predicted.

This morning, however, solemn-faced, pouty-mouthed, in her bulky quilted jacket and looking like a mobile fire hydrant, Tippi Lake left the house in time to catch the bus. Lorraine called goodbye after her as always but Tippi scarcely glanced back, and her voice was flat, almost inaudible—"Bye, Mom."

"TIPPI AIN HERE MISSUS TOO BAD! BYEBYE!"

The ugly, jeering words echoed in Lorraine Lake's head.

And what else had the hand-puppet said, his stunted arms flailing and his mouth working lewdly—"MISSUS I BEEN HERE BEFORE YA! AN I GONNA BE HERE WHENYA GONE!"

It was not possible to believe that Tippi had said such things. That she'd been able to disguise her thin, childish voice so effectively, and "throw" it into the puppet. That she'd had the manual skills to create the puppet, let alone the concept. No, it just wasn't possible. Someone else, an older student, perhaps a teacher, had put her up to it.

I know my daughter, Lorraine thought. And that isn't *her.*

After Tippi left on the school bus, the house was unnaturally empty. There was the relief of the sullen child's departure, but there was the strained absence as well. The radio wasn't enough to fill the void, so the mother switched it off. "I know my own daughter," she said aloud, with an angry laugh.

The urge to search Tippi's room was very strong. Yet she resisted. If Tippi said she wasn't taking the hand-puppet to school, then that was so. Lorraine would not violate her daughter's trust by seeming to doubt her, even if she doubted her. And if she found the obscene little puppet in Tippi's room, what then? "DID I SCARED YOU MISSUS! SOOO SOORRY MISSUS!" Lorraine had a vision of tearing it to bits. "BYEBYE!"

Later that morning, Lorraine drove to town. She had an appointment with a gynecologist which she'd several times postponed since an examination of a year ago had gone badly. This morning's appointment was a secret from Mr. Lake and Tippi. (Not that Tippi would have been much concerned: when health or medical matters were mentioned, Tippi seemed simply not to hear. Her eyes glazed, her pert little mouth remained shut. This was a trait fairly common in children of her age and younger, Lorraine had been told. A form of denial.) Lorraine Lake was not a superstitious person but she had a dislike of sharing with others private matters that might turn out happily after all.

As she drove the several miles to town, her eyes moved over the eroding countryside without recognition. More woodland being razed for a new shopping mall, another housing sub-division, Sylvan Acres, rising out of a swamp of frozen mud. Mustard-yellow excavating vehicles were everywhere. Grinding, beeping. Flutter of wind-whipped banners advertising a new condominium complex. When Lorraine and her husband had first moved to their home, ten years before, most of this area had been farmland. Now, even the memory of that farmland was confused, eroded. A trust had been betrayed. This is America, the mother thought. Her mouth twisting. Don't tell me what I already know.

Dr. Fehr's waiting room was companionably crowded as usual. Several of the women were hugely pregnant. Lorraine began to feel stabs of panic like early contractions. But when her name was called— "Lorraine Lake?"—she rose obediently, with a small eager smile.

Undressing as she was bidden in an examination room, clumsy in her nakedness, a woman no longer young, embarrassed by flesh. Rolls of it, raddled and pinched. Drooping breasts oddly yellow-tinged as if with jaundice; the nipples raw-looking, scaly. As if something had been suckling her without her knowledge. How strangeness enters our lives.

A cheerful blond nurse, very young, weighed Lorraine Lake as she stood barefoot, rigid on an old-fashioned scale, weight one hundred twenty-two, then took her blood pressure as she sat, self-conscious in her flimsy paper smock, on the edge of the examining table. Something was wrong with the instrument, or with Lorraine Lake, so the nurse took another reading and entered the data on a sheet of paper attached to a clipboard. Lorraine said with a nervous laugh that she was always a little nervous at such times, so perhaps her blood pressure was a little high, and the nurse said yes, that happens sometimes, we can wait a while and take another reading later. There was a gentle rap of knuckles on the door and Dr. Fehr entered brisk ruddy-faced and smiling as Lorraine recalled him, a man of vigorous youngish middle-age, glittering round glasses and goatish ears in which graying-red hairs sprouted. Asking his frightened patient in the paper smock how she was, nodding and murmuring, "Good, good!" at whatever the answer, looming over her beneficent as a midday sun. Forcing rubber gloves onto his capable hands, he said, just slightly reproachfully, "You've been postponing this a while, Mrs. Lake"—a question posed as a statement.

The examination, familiar as a recurring nightmare, was conducted through a confused roaring in Lorraine Lake's ears. The curious localized pain in the uterus, the physician's invasion to be endured stoically, like a rape by Zeus. The patient was lying rigid on the examining table, head back, jaws clenched, eyes shut; fingers gripping the underside of the table so desperately she would discover afterward that several of her nails had cracked. The Pap smear swab, the chilly speculum, the deep probing of Dr. Fehr's strong fingers . . . seeking the spongy tumor, grown to the size of, what?—a nectarine, perhaps. After all these months.

Whatever words Dr. Fehr was saying, kindly or chiding or merely factual, Lorraine Lake did not hear. Blood roared in her ears like a crashing surf. She was blinking enormous hot tears from her eyes, tears that rolled down her cheeks onto the tissue paper that covered the examining table. She was thinking of the pregnancy that had inhabited her body nearly twelve years ago. The enormous swelling weight of the baby. The pressure, the billowing radiant pain. They praised her, who had not after all been a young mother, not *young* as such things are measured. They insisted she'd been brave, tireless, pushing! pushing! pushing! for more than eighteen hours. Giving birth. As if birth were something given, and given freely. In truth, Lorraine Lake had wanted to say that the birth had been taken from her. The baby forced itself from her. A vessel of violence, of hot unspeakable rage. And the terror of such knowledge, which she could share with no other person, certainly not the man who was her husband, the baby's "father." And the forgetfulness afterward, black wash of oblivion. *God never sends us more than He knows we can bear* one of Lorraine's older female relatives assured her. Lorraine laughed now, remembering.

Dr. Fehr, vigorously palpitating uterine tissue, seeking the perimeters of the spongy tumor, must have been surprised. The laugh became a cough, the cough a fit of sobbing, unless it was laughing, a gut-wrenching laughter, for in addition to experiencing pain the patient was being roughly tickled, too.

Through a teary haze the alarmed faces of doctor and nurse stared. Then, urged to lie flat, the weeping patient was quieted; no longer hyperventilating; the mad pulse in her left wrist deftly taken by a man's forceful thumb. "It's just that my body isn't my own," Lorraine Lake was explaining, now calmly. "I'm in it, I'm trapped in it, but it isn't my own. Someone makes me speak, too—not these words, but the others. But I'm terrified to leave my body, because where would I go?" This question so earnest, Lorraine began to laugh again, and the laughter became helpless hiccuping that lasted for several minutes.

It was decided, then, when Lorraine Lake was herself again, and upright, able to look Dr. Fehr unflinchingly in the eye, that, yes, of course, she would have the operation she'd been postponing—a hysterectomy. The fibroid tumor was non-malignant, but steadily growing; it was in fact the size of a nectarine, soon to be a grapefruit; not dangerous at the present time, but of course it must come out. Lorraine Lake was a reasonable woman, wasn't she. She had no phobias about hospitals, surgery, did she? "A hysterectomy is a common medical procedure," Dr. Fehr said gently.

"Common as death?" his patient inquired.

Frowning as he scribbled something onto the sheet attached to the clipboard, Dr. Fehr seemed not to have heard.

"No. I guess nothing is as common as death," his patient said, with an awkward laugh. She may have believed herself a person with a reputation for drollery and wit, in some other lifetime.

In any case, the examination was over. Dr. Fehr, in his white physician's costume, his round eyeglasses glittering, got to his feet. The patient would call his office, make arrangements with his nurse, for the next step preparatory to surgery. "Thank you, Doctor," Lorraine said, stammering, "—I-I'm just so sorry that I broke down—" Dr. Fehr waved away her apology as if it were of no more significance than the female hysteria that had preceded it, and was gone. Left by herself, Lorraine wiped her eyes on a tissue, wiped her entire face which stung as if sunburnt. She whispered, "I *am* sorry, and it won't happen again." She crumpled the tissue, along with the ridiculous baby-doll paper smock, and dropped both into a gleaming metallic wastebasket.

*   *   *

"A common medical procedure."

Driving then, not home, for she could not bear the prospect of *home,* but in the direction of Tippi's school. The midday sky had lightened somewhat but was still stippled with clouds, a pale luminous sun like a worn-out penny.

It was noon recess. Boys and girls everywhere in the vicinity of John F. Kennedy Elementary School—in the playground, on the school's steps, milling about on the sidewalks. Traffic moved slowly here, monitored by crossing guards. Lorraine looked quickly for Tippi, but did not see her; no doubt, Tippi was inside the school building, in the cafeteria or in her homeroom. How gregarious these children were! Lorraine braked her car, moving slowly along the curb, avidly watching the children, strangers to her, who were her daughter's classmates. Were any of those girls Tippi's friends?—did any of them even know Tippi Lake?—or care about her? Lorraine felt a mother's dismay, seeing how pretty, how assured, how like young teenagers many of the girls seemed, hardly Tippi's age at all. Some of the girls appeared to be wearing make-up—was that possible? At the age of eleven? Poor Tippi! No wonder she disliked school, and was reluctant to discuss it, if these girls were her sixth-grade classmates.

It was as she passed the playground that she saw Tippi.

There was the quilted jacket, there the familiar fawn-colored hair and short plump shape, at the edge of the playground not more than ten yards away. At first, it looked as if Tippi was in a group of children, then it became clear that Tippi was by herself, though advancing aggressively toward the children, who were younger than she; she was unaware of her mother, of course, or of anyone watching. The several children, all girls, shrank from Tippi as she thrust something toward them—*was it the hand-puppet?* Lorraine stared in disbelief. Tippi's face was fierce and contorted as Lorraine had never seen it, and her body was oddly hunched, tremulous with concentration, appalling to witness. The younger children moved away from Tippi, not amused by the puppet, but staring at it, the object animated on Tippi's right hand, with looks of alarm and confusion. *What was the puppet saying? What foul threatening words issued from its lewd red-satin mouth?* Two older girls, witnessing Tippi's behavior, approached her and seemed to be challenging her, and Tippi whirled upon them savagely, wielding the puppet like a weapon. Lorraine could see the very cords in her daughter's throat work convulsively as Tippi "threw" her voice into the big-headed baby-faced bald creature on her hand.

"Tippi!—my God."

Lorraine would have shouted out the window of her car, but by this time she'd driven by; traffic bore her along the narrow street, and there was nowhere to park. Her heart was beating so rapidly she was terrified she might faint. The panic of the physical examination washed back over her. *That child is mad. That is the face of madness.*

No, it's harmless, just a game. Tippi gets carried away by games.

Lorraine drove through an intersection—blindly through a red light—a car horn sounded in annoyance—she was trying to think what she should do. Drive around the block, approach Tippi a second time, call out her name and break up the incident—my God, it was unthinkable, her own shy, sensitive daughter bullying and frightening smaller children! But at once Lorraine changed her mind, no of course not, no she could not, dared not confront Tippi in the playground of her school, in such a way, so public—Tippi would be humiliated, and Tippi might be furious. Tippi would think Lorraine was spying on her—she would never trust Lorraine again.

The profound shock was: Tippi had taken the hand-puppet with her to school, after all.

Tippi had lied to her. Deliberately, shamelessly, looking her mother in the eye.

Still, Lorraine could not confront her daughter, not now. Better to think of it later. Another, calmer time. She decided to continue with her errands in town, as if nothing out of the ordinary had occurred, for perhaps nothing had. In any case she was damned if she was going to cry again, become hysterical a second time within an hour—no thank you, not Lorraine Lake.

That afternoon, waiting for Tippi to return home, she prowled the house, restless, agitated. A cigarette burned in her fingers. Several times she believed she heard, in the distance, the sound of the school bus grinding its ugly brakes—then nothing. Her aloneness would soon be violated by the child's noisy entry.

How happy, alone. Smoking a cigarette—as she hadn't done in twelve years. Her husband and her daughter would be shocked, disapproving, and she herself would have been so, in other circumstances. The sharp nicotine charge in her lungs was like a thrust of love, imperfectly but passionately recalled. *Why not?—we don't live forever,* the mother thought. Except, mouthing the words to herself, what she actually said was, "We don't love forever." She heard this, and laughed.

She was passing by Tippi's closed door. She had not entered before, and she would not, now.

Instead, she climbed to the third floor, to the attic. Where rarely she went and then only on an errand of strict necessity; never for such a purpose—simply to stand, heart beating quickly, before a grimy window. Not knowing where she was exactly except it was a place of sanctuary, solitude. The sky was closer here, drawing the eye upward. She smoked her cigarette with a lover's abandon, coughing a little, wiping at her eyes. She was free here, she was safe here, wasn't she!—when Tippi came home, Tippi would not know where she was. Tippi would want to hurry to her room to hide the hand-puppet and she, the mother, would not be a witness to the child's stealth; each would be spared. But really she did not care. She was not thinking of Tippi, or of the loathsome hand-puppet, at all.

How beautiful! The gray impacted clouds had begun to separate, like gigantic boulders, shot fiercely with flame. There was to have been an afternoon thunderstorm, but the northeast wind out of Canada had blown it past. The mother stared, in a trance. She knew there was something behind her, below her; something imminent, threatening; a grinding of brakes, a jeering nasal child-voice . . . But, no; she was alone here, and she was safe. She leaned forward breathlessly; she saw herself climbing into the sky of boulders. As a girl, so long ago, she'd been wonderfully physical—athletic, self-assured. What buoyancy to her step, what jubilation, like that of a soul coming home! Her tall figure receded into the radiant distance, and never a backward glance.

Then she heard it: "MISSUS WHEREYA HIDIN? DID I SCARED YA MISSUS! SOOO SORRY MISSUS!"

It was in the attic with her, its voice coming from all sides. Or was it in the very sky, the jeering words quivering with flame?

140

ROPED

F. PAUL WILSON

Physician-novelist F. Paul Wilson's eerie novel, The Keep, *was made into a movie in the early eighties, shortly after I began my career in magic. His most recent best-seller,* SIBS, *is no less fascinating. That he agreed to write a story for this anthology pleases me enormously, even if the question he poses is not an easy one to answer. How much, his story asks, might a man be willing to risk for the ultimate piece of magic, one that will effortlessly make him rich and powerful beyond his wildest dreams?*

—DC

DAYFD

TRUE TO HIS WORD, the first installment of Dennis Nickleby's *Three Months to Financial Independence* arrives exactly two weeks after I called the toll-free number provided by his infomercial. I toss out the accompanying catalogs and "Occupant" bulk mail, then tear at the edges of the cardboard mailer.

This is it. My new start. Today is the first day of the rest of my life, and starting today my life will be very different. I'll be organized, I'll have specific goals and a plan to achieve them—I'll have an *agenda*.

Never had an agenda before. And as long as this agenda doesn't involve a job, that's cool. Never been a nine-to-fiver. Tend to ad lib as I go along. Prefer to think of myself as an *investor*. Now I'll be an investor with an agenda. And Dennis Nickleby's tapes are going to guide me.

Maybe they can help me with my personal life too. I'm sort of between girlfriends now. Seem to have trouble keeping them. Denice was the last. She walked out two weeks ago. Called me a couch potato—said I was a fat slob who doesn't do anything but read and watch TV.

Not fair. And not true. All right, so I am a little overweight, but not as overweight as I look. Lots of guys in their mid-thirties weigh more than I do. It's just that at five-eight it shows more. At least I still have all my hair. And I'm not ugly or anything.

As for spending a lot of time on the couch—guilty. But I'm doing research. My folks left me some money and I'm always looking for a better place to put it to work. I've got a decent net worth, live in a nice high-rise in North Jersey where I can see the Manhattan skyline at night. I make a good income from my investments without ever leaving the house. But that doesn't mean I'm not working at it.

145

Good as things are, I know I can do better. And the Nickleby course is going to take me to that next level. I can feel it. And I'm more than ready.

My hands shake as I pull the glossy vinyl video box from the wrapper. Grinning back at me is a young, darkly handsome man with piercing blue eyes and dazzling teeth. Dennis Nickleby. Thirty years old and already a multimillionaire. Everything this guy touches turns to gold. But does he want to hoard his investing secrets? No way. He's willing to share them with the little guy—guys like me with limited capital and unlimited dreams. What a *mensch*.

Hey, I'm no sucker. I've seen Tony Robbins and those become-a-real-estate-millionaire-with-no-money-down infomercials. I'm home a lot so I see *lots* of infomercials. Trust me, they roll off me like water off a duck. But Dennis Nickleby . . . he's different. He looked out from that TV screen and I knew he was talking to me. To *me*. I knew what he was offering would change my life. The price was stiff—five hundred bucks—but well worth it if he delivered a mere tenth of what he was offering. Certainly a better investment than some of those do-nothing stocks in my account.

I whipped out my credit card, grabbed the phone, punched in his 800 number, and placed my order.

And now it's here. I lift the lid of the box and—

"Shit!"

There's supposed to be a videotape inside—lesson one. What do I find? An audio cassette. And it's not even a new one. It's some beat-up piece of junk.

I'm fuming. I'm so pissed I'm ready to dump this piece of garbage on the floor and grind it into the carpet. But I do not do this. I take three deep breaths, calm myself, then I march to the phone. Very gently I punch in Mr. Nickleby's 800 number—it's on the back of the tape box—and get some perky little babe on the phone. I start yelling about consumer fraud, about calling the attorney general, about speaking to Dennis Nickleby himself. She asks why I'm so upset and I'm hardly into my explanation when she lets loose this high-pitched squeal.

"*You're* the one! Ooh, goody! We've been hoping you'd call!"

"Hoping?"

"*Yes!* Mr. Nickleby was here *himself.* He was *so* upset. He learned that *somehow* the *wrong* kind of tape got into one of his *Three Months to Financial Independence* boxes. He instructed us that should we hear from *anyone* who got an *audio* cassette instead of a *video* cassette, we should tell them not to worry. A brand new *video* cassette of *Three Months to*

Financial Independence would be *hand* delivered to them *immediately!* Now, what do you think of *that?*"

"I . . . I . . ." I'm flabbergasted. This man is on top of everything. Truly he knows how to run a business. "I think that's incredible."

"Just give us your name and address and we'll get that replacement to you *immediately!*"

"It's Michael Moulton." I give her the address.

"Ooh! Hackensack. That's not far from here!"

"Just over the G.W. Bridge."

"*Well,* then! You should have your replacement *very* soon!"

"Good," I say.

Her terminal perkiness is beginning to get to me. I'm hurrying to hang up when she says, "Oh, and one more thing. Mr. Nickleby said to tell you *not* to do *anything* with the audio cassette. Just *close* it up in the box it came in and *wait* for the replacement tape. The messenger will take it in *exchange* for the videotape."

"Fine. Good—"

"Remember that now—close the audiotape in the holder and wait. Okay?"

"Right. Cool. Good-*bye.*"

I hang up thinking, Whatever she's taking, I want some.

Being a good boy, I snap the video box cover closed and am about to place it on the end table by the door when curiosity tickles me and I start to wonder what's on this tape. Is it maybe from Dennis Nickleby's private collection? A bootleg jazz or rock tape? Or better yet, some dictation that might give away one or two investment secrets not on the videotape?

I know right then there's no way I'm not going to listen to this tape, so why delay? I pop it into my cassette deck and hit PLAY.

Nothing. I crank up the volume—some static, some hiss, and nothing else. I fast-forward and still nothing. I'm about to hit STOP when I hear some high-pitched gibberish. I rewind a little and replay at regular speed.

Finally this voice comes on. Even with the volume way up I can barely hear it. I press my ear to the speaker. Whoever it is is whispering.

"*The only word you need to know:* ROGUE."

And that's it. I fast-forward all the way to the end and nothing. I go back and listen to that one sentence again. "*The only word you need to know:* ROGUE."

Got to be a garble. Somebody erased the tape and the heads missed a spot.

Oh, well.

Disappointed, I rewind it, pop it out, and close it up in the video box.

So here I am, not an hour later, fixing a sandwich and watching the stock quotes on FNN when there's a knock on my apartment door. I check through the peephole and almost choke.

Dennis Nickleby himself!

I fumble the door open and he steps inside.

"Mr. Nickleby!"

"Do you have it?" he says. He's sweating and puffing like he sprinted the ten flights to my floor instead of taking the elevator. His eyes are darting everywhere so fast they seem to be moving in opposite directions—like a chameleon's. Finally they come to rest on the end table. "There! That's it!"

He lunges for the video box, pops it open, snatches the cassette from inside.

"You didn't listen to it, did you?"

Something in his eyes and voice tell me to play this one close to the vest. But I don't want to lie to Dennis Nickleby.

"Should I have? I will if you want me to."

"No-no," he says quickly. "That won't be necessary." He hands me an identical videobox. "Here's the replacement. Terribly sorry for the mix-up."

I laugh. "Yeah. Some mix-up. How'd that ever happen?"

"Someone playing games," he says, his eyes growing cold for an instant. "But no harm done."

"You want to sit down? I was just making lunch—"

"Thank you, no. I'd love to but my schedule won't permit it. Maybe some other time." He extends his hand. "Once again, sorry for the inconvenience. Enjoy the tape."

And then he's out the door and gone. I stand there staring at the spot where he stood. Dennis Nickleby himself came by to replace the tape. Personally. Wow. And then it occurs to me: check the new box.

I pop it open. Yes sir. There's the *Three Months to Financial Independence* videotape. At last.

But what's the story with that audio cassette? He seemed awful anxious to get it back. And what for? It was totally blank except for that one sentence—*The only word you need to know:* ꞥꞸꞮꞤꞤ. What's that all about?

I'd like to look it up in the dictionary, but who knows how to spell something so weird sounding. And besides, I don't have a dictionary.

Maybe I'll try later at the local library—once I find out where the local library is. Right now I've got to transfer some money to my checking account so I can pay my Visa bill when the five-hundred-buck charge to Nickleby, Inc. shows up on this month's statement.

I call Gary, my discount broker, to sell some stock. I've been in Castle Petrol for a while and it's doing squat. Now's as good a time as any to get out. I tell Gary to dump all 200 shares. Then it occurs to me that Gary's a pretty smart guy. Even finished college.

"Hey, Gary. You ever hear of QAYPB?"

"Can't say as I have. But if it exists, I can find it for you. You interested?"

"Yeah," I say. "I'm very interested."

"You got it."

Yeah, well, I *don't* get it. All right, maybe I do get it, but it's not what I'm expecting, and not till two days later.

Meantime I stay busy with Dennis Nickleby's videotape. Got to say, it's kind of disappointing. Nothing I haven't heard elsewhere. Strange . . . after seeing his infomercial, I was sure this was going to be just the thing for me.

Then I open an envelope from the brokerage. Inside I find the expected sell confirm for the two hundred shares of Castle Petrol at 10.25, but with it is a buy confirm for *two thousand* shares of something called Thai Cord, Inc.

What the hell is Thai Cord? Gary took the money from Castle Petrol and put it in a stock I've never heard of! I'm baffled. He's never done anything like that. Must be a mistake. I call him.

"Hey, dude," he says as soon as he comes on the line. "Who's your source?"

"What are you talking about?"

"Thai Cord. It's up to five this morning. Boy, you timed that one perfectly."

"Five?" I swallow. I was ready to take his head off, now I learn I've made nine thousand big ones in two days. "Gary . . . why did you put me into Thai Cord?"

"Why? Because you asked me to. You said you were very interested in it. I'd never heard of it, but I looked it up and bought it for you." He sounds genuinely puzzled. "Wasn't that why you called the other day? To sell Castle and buy Thai? Hey, whatever, man—you made a killing."

"I know I made a killing, Gary, and no one's gladder than me, but—"

"You want to stay with it?"

"I just want to get something straight: Yesterday I asked you if you'd ever heard of **ᖴᗩᐯᗴᗴ**."

"No way, pal. I know ParkerGen. NASDAQ—good high-tech, speculative stock. You said Thai Cord."

I'm getting annoyed now. "**ᖴᗩᐯᗴᗴ**, Gary. **ᖴᗩᐯᗴᗴ**!"

"I can hear you, Mike. ParkerGen, ParkerGen. Are you all right?"

At this moment I'm not so sure. Suddenly I'm chilled, and there's this crawly feeling on the nape of my neck. I say one thing—*The only word you need to know*—and Gary hears another.

"Mike? You still there?"

"Yeah. Still here."

My mind's racing. What the hell's going on?

"What do you want me to do? Sell the Thai and buy ParkerGen? Is that it?"

I make a snap decision. There's something weird going down and I want to check it out. And what the hell, it's all found money.

"Yeah. Put it all into ParkerGen."

"Okay. It's running three-and-an-eighth today. I'll grab you three thousand."

"Great."

I get off the phone and start to pace my apartment. I've got this crazy idea cooking in my brain . . .

. . . *the only word you need to know:* **ᖴᗩᐯᗴᗴ**

What if . . . ?

Nah. It's too crazy. But if it's true, there's got to be a way to check it out.

And then I have it. The ponies. They're running at the Meadowlands today. I'll invest a few hours and check this out. If I hurry I can make the first race.

I know it's completely nuts, but I've *got* to know . . .

I just make it. I rush to the ten-dollar window and say, "**ᖴᗩᐯᗴᗴ** in the first."

The teller doesn't even glance up; he takes my ten, punches a few buttons, and out pops my ticket. I grab it and look at it: I've bet on some nag named Yesterday's Gone.

I don't bother going to the grandstand. I stand under one of the monitors. I see the odds on Yesterday's Gone are three to one. The trotters are lined up, ready to go.

"And they're off!"

I watch with a couple of other guys in polo shirts and polyester pants who're standing around. I'm not too terribly surprised when Yesterday's Gone crosses the finish line first. I've now got thirty bucks where I had ten a few minutes ago, but I've also got that crawly feeling at the back of my neck again.

This has gone from crazy to creepy.

With the help of the Daily Double and the Trifecta, by the time I leave the track I've parlayed my original ten bucks into sixty-two hundred. I could have made more but I'm getting nervous. I don't want to attract too much attention.

As I'm driving away I can barely keep from flooring the gas pedal. I'm wired—positively giddy. It's like some sort of drug. I feel like king of the world. I've got to keep going. But how? Where?

I pass a billboard telling me about "5 TIMES MORE DICE ACTION!" at Caesar's in Atlantic City.

My question has been answered.

I pick Caesar's because of the billboard. I've never been much for omens but I'm into them now. Big time.

I'm also trying to figure out what else I'm into with this weird word. *The only word you need to know . . .*

All you need to know to *win*. That has to be it: the word makes you a winner. If I say it whenever I'm about to take a chance—on a horse or a stock, at least—I'm a guaranteed winner.

This has got to be why Dennis Nickleby's such a success. He knows the word. That's why he was so anxious to get it back—he doesn't want anybody else to know it. Wants to keep it all to himself.

Bastard.

And then I think, no, not a bastard. I've got to ask myself if I'm about to share the word with anybody else. The answer is a very definite en-oh. I get the feeling I've just joined a very exclusive club. Only thing is, the other members don't know I've joined.

I also get the feeling there's no such thing as a game of chance for me any more.

Cool.

The escalator deposits me on the casino floor at Caesar's. All the way down the Parkway I've been trying to decide what to try first—blackjack, poker, roulette, craps—what? But soon as I come within sight of the casino, I know. Flashing lights dead ahead:

PROGRESSIVE SLOTS! $802,672!!!

The prize total keeps rising as players keep plunking their coins into the gangs of one-armed bandits.

I wind through the crowds and the smoke and the noise toward the progressive slots section. Along the way I stop at a change cart and hand the mini-togaed blonde a five.

"Dollars," I say, "even though I'm going to need just one to win."

"Right on," she says, but I can tell she doesn't believe me.

She will. I take my dollar tokens and say, "You'll see."

I reach the progressive section and hunt up a machine. It isn't easy. Everybody here is at least a hundred years old and they'd probably give up one of their grandkids before they let somebody use their damn machine. Finally I see a hunched old blue-hair run out of money and leave her machine. I dart in, drop a coin in the slot, then I notice the machine takes up to three. I gather if I'm going to win the full amount I'd better drop two more. I do. I grab the handle . . . and hesitate. This is going to get me a *lot* of attention. Do I want that? I mean, I'm a private kind of guy. Then I look up at the $800,000-and-growing jackpot and know I want *that*.

Screw the publicity.

I whisper, "ዪ◍ም**Ⴒ**ᴮ," and yank the handle.

I close my eyes as the wheels spin; I hear them begin to stop: First window—*choonk!* Second window—*choonk!* Third window—*choonk!* A bell starts ringing! Coins start dropping into the tray! I did it!

Abruptly the bell and the coins stop. I open my eyes. There's no envious crowd around me, no flashing cameras. Nobody's even looking my way. I glance down at the tray. Six dollars. I check out the windows. Two cherries and an orange. The red LED reads, "Pays 6."

I'm baffled. Where's my $800,000 jackpot? The crawling feeling that used to be on my neck is now in the pit of my stomach. What happened? Did I blow it? Is the word wearing out?

I grab three coins from the tray and shove them in. I say, "ዪ◍ም**Ⴒ**ᴮ," again, louder this time, and pull that handle.

Choonk! Choonk! Choonk!

Nothing this time. Nothing!

I'm getting scared now. The power is fading fast. Three more coins, I damn near shout, "ዪ◍ም**Ⴒ**ᴮ" as I pull the goddamn handle. *Choonk! Choonk! Choonk!*

Nothing! Zip! Bupkis!

I slam my hand against the machine. "Damn, you! What's wrong?"

"Easy, fella," says the old dude next to me. "That won't help. Maybe you should take a break."

I walk away without looking at him. I'm devastated. What if I only had a few days with this word and now my time is up? I wasted it at the track when I could have been buying and shorting stocks on margin. The smoke, the crowds, the incessant chatter and mechanical noise of the casino is driving me to panic. I have to get out of here. I'm just about to break into a run when it hits me.

The word . . . what if it only works on people? Slot machines can't hear . . .

I calm myself. Okay. Let's be logical here. What's the best way to test the word in a casino?

Cards? Nah. Too many possible outcomes, too many other players to muddy the waters.

Craps? Again, too many ways to win or lose.

What's a game with high odds and a very definite winner?

I scan the floor, searching . . . and then I see it.

Roulette.

But how can I use the word at a roulette table?

I hunt around for a table with an empty seat. I spot one between this middle-aged nerd who's got to be an optometrist, and a mousy, thirty-ish redhead who looks like one of his patients. Suddenly I know what I'm going to do.

I pull a hundred-dollar bill from my Meadowlands roll and grip it between my thumb and index finger. Then I twist up both my hands into deformed knots.

As I sit down I say to the redhead, "Could I trouble you to place my bets for me?"

She glances at my face through her Coke-bottle lenses, then at my twisted hands. Her eyes dart back to my face. She gives me a half-hearted smile. "Sure. No problem."

"I'll split my winnings with you." *If I win.*

"That's okay. Really."

I make a show of difficulty dropping the hundred-dollar bill from my fingers, then I push it across the table.

"Tens, please."

A stack of ten chips is shoved in front of me.

"All bets down," the croupier says.

"Put one on **RAPED**, please," I tell the redhead, and hold my breath.

I glance around but no one seems to hear anything strange. Red takes a chip off the top of my pile and drops it on 33.

I'm sweating bullets now. My bladder wants to find a men's room. This has got to work. I've got to know if the word still has power. I want to close my eyes but I don't dare. I've got to see this.

The ball circles counter to the wheel, loses speed, slips toward the middle, hits rough terrain, bounces chaotically about, then clatters into a numbered slot.

"Thirty-three," drones the croupier.

The redhead squeals and claps her hands. "You won! Your first bet and you won!"

I'm drenched. I'm weak. My voice is hoarse when I say, "You must be my good luck charm. Don't go anywhere."

Truth is, it *could* be luck. A cruel twist of fate. I tell Red to move it all over to "ᛯᛟᛁᛈᛔ."

She looks shocked. "All of it? You sure?"

"Absolutely."

She pushes the stack over to the 17 box.

Another spin. "Seventeen," the croupier says.

Now I close my eyes. I've got it. The word's got the power and I've got the word. *The only word you need to know.* I want to pump a fist into the air and scream "YES!" but I restrain myself. I am disabled, after all.

"Ohmigod!" Red is whispering. "That's . . . that's . . . !"

"A lot of money," I say. "And half of it's yours."

Her blue eyes fairly bulge against the near sides of her lenses. "What? Oh, no! I couldn't!"

"And I couldn't play without your help. I said I'd split with you and I meant it."

She has her hand over her mouth. Her words are muffled through her fingers. "Oh, thank you. You don't know—"

"All bets down," says the croupier.

No more letting it ride. My winnings far exceed the table limit. I notice that the pit boss has materialized and is standing next to the croupier. He's watching me and eyeing the megalopolis skyline of chips stacked in front of me. Hitting the winning number two times in a row—it happens in roulette, but not too damn often.

"Put five hundred on sixteen," I tell Red.

She does, and 22 comes up. Next I tell her five hundred on nine. Twelve comes up.

The pit boss drifts away.

"Don't worry," Red says with a reassuring pat on my arm. "You're still way ahead."

"Do I look worried?" I say.

I tell her to put another five hundred on "ᛯᛟᛁᛈᛔ." She puts the chips on 19.

A minute later the croupier calls, "Nineteen." Red squeals again. I lean back as the croupier starts stacking my winnings.

No need to go any further. I know how this works. I realize I am now the Ultimate Winner. If I want to I can break the bank at Caesar's. I can play the table limit on one number after another, and collect a thirty-five-to-one payout every couple of minutes. A crowd will gather. The house will have to keep playing—corporate pride will force them to keep paying. I can *own* the place, damn it!

But the Ultimate Winner chooses not to.

Noblesse oblige.

What does the Ultimate Winner want with a casino? Bigger winnings await.

Winning . . . there's nothing like it. It's ecstasy, racing through my veins, tingling like bolts of electricity along my nerve endings. Sex is nothing next to this. I feel buoyant, like I could float off this chair and buzz around the room.

I stand up.

"Where are you going?" Red says, looking up at me with those magnified blue eyes.

"Home. Thanks for your help."

I turn and start looking for an exit sign.

"But your chips . . ."

I figure there's close to thirty G's on the table, but there's lots more where that came from. I tell her, "Keep them."

What does the Ultimate Winner want with casino chips?

Next day, I'm home in my apartment, reading the morning paper. I see that ParkerGen has jumped two-and-one-eighth points to five and a half. Sixty-one percent profit overnight.

After a sleepless night, I've decided the stock market is the best way to use the word. I can make millions upon millions there and no one will so much as raise an eyebrow. No one will care except the IRS, and I will pay my taxes, every penny of them, and gladly.

Who cares about taxes when you're looking at more money than you'll ever spend in ten lifetimes? They're going to take half, leaving me to eke by with a mere five lifetimes' worth of cash. I can hack that.

A hard knock on the door. Who the hell—? I look through the peephole.

Dennis Nickleby! I'm so surprised, I pull open the door without thinking.

"Mr. Nickle—!"

He sucker punches me in the gut. As I double over, groaning, he shoves me to the floor and slams the door shut behind him.

"What the *fuck* do you think you're doing?" he shouts. "You lied to me! You told me you didn't listen to that tape! You bastard! If you'd been straight with me, I could have warned you. Now the shit's about to hit the fan and we're both standing downwind!"

I'm still on the floor, gasping. He really caught me. I manage a weak, "What are you talking about?"

His face reddens and he pulls back his foot. "Play dumb with me and I'll kick your teeth down your throat!"

I hold up a hand. "Okay. Okay." I swallow back some bile. "I heard the word. I used it a few times. How'd you find out?"

"I've got friends inside the Order."

"Order?"

"Never mind. The point is, you're not authorized to use it. And you're going to get us both killed if you don't stop."

He already grabbed my attention with the punch. Now he's got it big time.

"Killed?"

"Yeah. Killed. And I wouldn't give a rat's ass if it was just you. But they'll come after me for letting you have it."

I struggle to a crouch and slide into a chair.

"This is all bullshit, right?"

"Don't I wish. Look, let me give you a quick history lesson so you'll appreciate what you've gotten yourself into. The Order goes way back—*way* back. They've got powers, and they've got an agenda. Throughout history they've loaned certain powers to certain carefully chosen individuals."

"Like who?"

"Like I don't know who. I'm not a member so they don't let me in on their secrets. Just think of the most powerful people in history, the movers and shakers—Alexander the Great, Constantine, some of the Popes, the Renaissance guys—they all probably had some help from the Order. I've got a feeling Hitler was another. It would explain how he could sway a whole nation the way he did."

"Oh," I said. I knew I had to be feeling a little better because I was also feeling sarcastic. "An order of evil monks, ruling the world. I'm shaking."

He stared at me a long moment, then gave his head a slow shake. "You really are an ass, Moulton. First off, I never said they were monks. Just because they're an order doesn't mean they skulk around in hooded robes. And they don't rule the world; they merely support forces or movements or people they feel will further their agenda. And as for evil . . . I don't know if good or evil applies to these folks because I don't know their goals. Look at it this way: I'll bet the Order helped out the robber barons. Not to make a bunch of greedy bastards rich, but because it was on the Order's agenda to speed up the industrialization of America. Are you catching the drift?"

"And so they came to you and gave *you* this magic word. What's that make you? The next Rockefeller?"

He seems to withdraw into himself. His eyes become troubled. "I don't know. I don't have the foggiest idea why I was chosen or what they think I'll accomplish with the Answer. They gave me the tape, told me to memorize the Answer, and then destroy the tape. They told me to use the Answer however I saw fit, and that was it. No strings. No goals. No instructions whatsoever other than destroying the tape."

"Which you didn't do."

He sighs. "Which I didn't do."

"And you call *me* an ass?" I say.

His eyes harden. "Everything would have been fine if my soon-to-be-ex-wife hadn't raided my safe deposit box and decided to play some games with its contents."

"You think she's listened to the tape?"

He shrugs. "Maybe. The tape is ashes now, so she won't get a second chance. And if she did hear the Answer, she hasn't used it, or figured out its power. You have to be pretty smart or pretty lucky to catch on."

Preferring to place myself in the former category, I say, "It wasn't all that hard. But why do you call it the Answer?"

"What do you call it?"

"I've been calling it 'the word.' I guess I could be more specific and call it 'the Win Word.'"

He sneers. "You think this is just about winning? You idiot. That word is the *Answer*—the *best* answer to any question asked. The listener hears the most appropriate, most profitable, all-around *best* response. And that's power, Michael Moulton. Power that's too big for the likes of you."

"Just a minute now. I can see how that worked with my broker, but I wasn't answering questions when I was betting the ponies or playing roulette. I was telling people."

The sneer deepens. "Horses . . . roulette . . ." He shakes his head in disgust. "Like driving a Maserati to the local 7-Eleven for a quart of milk. All right, I'll say this slowly so you'll get it: The Answer works with all sorts of questions, including *implied* questions. And what is the implied question when you walk up to a betting window or sit down at a gaming table? It's 'How much do you want to bet on what?' When you say ten bucks on Phony Baloney, you're answering that question."

"Oh, right," I say.

He steps closer and stands over me. "I hope you enjoyed your little fling with the Answer. You can keep whatever money you made, but that's it for you."

"Hey," I tell him. "If you think I'm giving up a gold mine like that, you're nuts."

"I had a feeling you'd say something like that."

He reaches into his suit coat pocket and pulls out a pistol. I don't know what kind it is and don't care. All I know is that its silenced muzzle is pointing in my face.

"Hey! Wait!"

"Good-bye, Michael Moulton. I was hoping to be able to reason with you, but you're too big an asshole for that. You don't leave me any choice."

I see the way the gun wavers in his hand, I hear the quaver in his voice as he keeps talking without shooting, and I flash that this sort of thing is all new to him and he's almost as scared as I am right now.

So I move. I leap up, grab the gun barrel, and push it upward, twisting it with everything I've got. Nickleby yelps as the gun goes off with a *phut!* The backs of his legs catch the edge of the coffee table and we go down. I land on him hard, knocking the wind out of him, and suddenly I've got the gun all to myself.

I get to my feet and now I'm pointing it at him. And then he makes a noise that sounds like a sob.

"Damn it!" he wails. "Damn it to hell! Go ahead and shoot. I'm a dead man anyway if you go on using the Answer. And you will be too."

I consider this. He doesn't seem to be lying. But he doesn't seem to be thinking either.

"Look," I tell him. "Why should we be afraid of this Order? We have the word—the Answer. All we have to do is threaten to tell the world about it. Tell them we'll record it on a million tapes—we'll put it on every one of those videotapes you're peddling. Hell, we'll buy airtime and broadcast it by satellite. They make one wrong move and the whole damn world will have the Answer. What'll *that* do to their agenda?"

He looks up at me bleakly. "You can't record it. You can't tell anybody. You can't even write it down."

"Bullshit," I say.

This may be a trick so I keep the pistol trained on him while I grab the pen and pad from the phone. I write out the word. I can't believe my eyes. Instead of the Answer I've written gibberish: ℞⊕⅂ℇⅅ.

"What the hell?"

I try again, this time block printing. No difference—℞⊕⅂ℇⅅ again.

Nickleby's on his feet now, but he doesn't try to get any closer.

"Believe me," he says, more composed now, "I've tried everything. You can speak the Answer into the finest recording equipment in the world till you're blue in the face and you'll hear gibberish."

"Then I'll simply tell it to everybody I know!"

"And what do you think they'll hear? If they've got a question on their mind, they'll hear the best possible answer. If not, they'll hear gibberish. What they *won't* hear is the Answer itself."

"Then how'd these Order guys get it on your tape?"

He shrugs. "I don't know. They have ways of doing all sorts of things—like finding out when somebody unauthorized uses the Answer. Maybe they know every time *anybody* uses the Answer. That's why you've got to stop."

I don't reply. I glance down at the meaningless jumble I've written without intending to. Something big at work here. Very Big.

He goes on. "I don't think it's too late. My source in the Order told me that if I can silence you—and that doesn't mean kill you, just stop you from using the Answer—then the Order will let it go. But if you go on using it . . . well, then, it's curtains for both of us."

I'm beginning to believe him.

A note of pleading creeps into his voice. "I'll set you up. You want money, I'll give you money. As much as you want. You want to play the market? Call me up and ask me the best stock to buy—I'll tell you. You want to play the ponies? I'll go to the track with you. You want to be rich? I'll give you a million—two, three, four million a year. Whatever you want. *Just don't use the Answer yourself!*"

I think about that. All the money I can spend . . .

What I don't like about it is I'll feel like a leech, like I'm being kept.

Then again: All the money I can spend . . .

"All right," I tell him. "I won't use the word and we'll work something out."

Nickleby stumbles over to the sofa like his knees are weak and slumps onto it. He sounds like he's gonna sob again.

"Thank you! Oh, thank you! You've just saved both our lives!"

"Yeah," I say.

Right. I'm going to live, I'm going to be rich. So how come I ain't exactly overcome with joy?

Things go pretty well for the next few weeks. I don't drag him to the track or to Atlantic City or anything like that. And when I phone him and ask for a stock tip, he gives me a winner every time. My net worth is skyrocketing. Gary the broker thinks I'm a genius. I'm on my way to financial independence, untold wealth . . . everything I've ever wanted.

But you know what? It's not the same. Doesn't come close to what it was like when I was using the Answer myself.

Truth is, I feel like Dennis Nickleby's goddamn mistress.

But I give myself a daily pep talk, telling myself I can hang in there. And I do hang in there. I'm doing pretty well at playing the melancholy millionaire . . .

Until I hear on the radio that the next Pick 6 Lotto jackpot is thirty million dollars.

Thirty million dollars—with a payout of a million and a half a year for the next twenty years. That'll do it. If I win that, I won't need Nickleby any more. I'll be my own man again.

Only problem is, I'll need to use the Answer.

I know I can ask Nickleby for the winning numbers, but that won't cut it. I need to do this myself. I need to feel that surge of power when I speak the Answer. And then the jackpot will be *my* prize, not Nickleby's.

Just once . . . I'll use the Answer just this once, and then I'll erase it from my mind and never use it again.

I go driving into the sticks and find this hole-in-the-wall candy store on a secondary road in the woods. There's a pimply faced kid running the counter. How the hell is this Order going to know I've used the Answer one lousy time out here in Nowheresville?

I hand the kid a buck. "Pick 6 please."

"You wanna Quick Pick?"

No way I want random numbers. I want the *winning* numbers.

"No. I'll give them to you: ꝗ⧄ᴪꝑꞜ."

I can't tell you how good it feels to be able to say that word again . . . like snapping the reins on my own destiny.

The kid hits a button, then looks up at me. "And?"

"And what?"

"You got to choose six numbers. That's only one."

My stomach lurches. Damn. I thought one Answer would provide all six. Something tells me to cut and run, but I press on. I've already used the Answer once—might as well go all the way.

I say ꝗ⧄ᴪꝑꞜ five more times. He hands me the pink-and-white ticket. The winning numbers are 3, 4, 7, 17, 28, 30. When the little numbered Ping-Pong balls pop out of the hopper Monday night, I'll be free of Dennis Nickleby

So how come I'm not tap-dancing back to my car? Why do I feel like I've just screwed up . . . big time?

* * *

I stop for dinner along the way. When I get home I check my answering machine and there's Nickleby's voice. He sounds hysterical.

"You stupid bastard! You idiot! You couldn't be happy with more money than you could ever spend! You had to go and use the Answer again! Damn you to hell, Moulton! They're coming for me! And then they'll be coming for you! Kiss your ass good-bye, jerk!"

I don't hesitate. I don't even grab any clothes. I run out the door, take the elevator to the garage, and get the hell out of there. I start driving in circles, unsure where to go, just sure that I've got to keep moving.

Truthfully, I feel like a fool for being so scared. This whole wild story about the Order and impending death is so ridiculous . . . yet so is that word, the word that gives the right answer to every question. And a genuinely terrified Dennis Nickleby *knew* I'd used the Answer.

I make a decision and head for the city. I want to be where there's lots of people. As I crawl through the Saturday night crush in the Lincoln Tunnel I get on my car phone. I need a place to stay. Don't want some fleabag hotel. Want something with brightly lit halls and good security. The Plaza's got a room. A suite. Great. I'll take it.

I leave my car with the doorman, register like a whirlwind, and a few minutes later I'm in a two-room suite with the drapes pulled and the door locked and chained.

And now I can breathe again. But that's about it. I order room service but I can't eat. I go to bed but I can't sleep. So I watch the tube. My eyes are finally glazing over as I listen to the same report from Bosnia-Herzewhatever for the umpteenth time when the reporter breaks in with a new story: Millionaire financial boy-wonder Dennis Nickleby is dead. An apparent suicide, he jumped from the ledge of his Fifth Avenue penthouse apartment earlier this evening. A full investigation has been launched. Details as soon as they are available.

I run to the bathroom and start to retch, but nothing comes up.

They got him! Just like he said they would! He's dead and oh God I'm next! What am I going to *do?*

First thing I've got to do is calm down. I've got to think. I do that. I make myself sit down. I control my breathing. I analyze my situation. What are my assets? I've got lots of money, a wallet full of credit cards, and I'm mobile. I can go on the run.

And I've got one more thing: the Answer.

Suddenly I'm up and pacing. The Answer! I can use the Answer itself as a defense. Yes! If I have to go to ground, it will guide me to the best place to hide.

Suddenly I'm excited. It's so obvious.

I throw on my clothes and hurry down to the street. They probably know my car, so I jump into one of the waiting cabs.

"Where to?" says the cabbie in a thickly accented voice. The back seat smells like someone blew lunch here not too long ago. I look at the driver ID card and he's got some unpronounceable Middle East name.

I say, "**ⓡⓞⓥⓟⓑ**."

He nods, puts the car in gear, and we're off.

But where to? I feel like an idiot but I've got to ask. I wait till he's made a few turns, obviously heading for the East Side.

"Where are you taking me?"

"La Guardia." He glances over his shoulder through the plastic partition, his expression fierce. "That is what you said, is it not?"

"Yes, yes. Just want to make sure you understood."

"I understand," he says. "I understand very good."

La Guardia . . . I'm flying out of here tonight. A new feeling begins to seep though me: hope. But despite the hope, let me tell you, it's tres weird to be traveling at top speed with no idea where you're going.

As we take the La Guardia exit off Grand Central Parkway, the driver says, "Which airline?"

I say, "**ⓡⓞⓥⓟⓑ**."

He nods and we pull in opposite the Continental door. I pay him and hurry to the ticket counter. I tell the pretty black girl there I want first class on the next flight out.

"Out to where, sir?"

Good question. I say, "**ⓡⓞⓥⓟⓑ**."

She punches a lot of keys and finally her computer spits out a ticket. She tells me the price. I'm dying to know where I'm going but how can I ask her? I hand over my American Express. She runs it through, I sign, and then she hands me the ticket.

Cheyenne, Wyoming. Not my first choice. Not even on my top twenty list. But if the Answer tells me that's the best place to be, that's where I'm going. Trouble is, the flight doesn't leave for another three hours.

It's a comfortable trip, but the drinks I had at La Guardia and the extra glasses of Merlot on the flight have left me a little groggy. I wander about the nearly deserted terminal wondering what I do now. I'm in the middle of nowhere—Wyoming, for Christ sake. Where do I go from here?

Easy: Trust the Answer.

I go outside to the taxi area. The fresh air feels good. A cab pulls into the curb. I grab it.

"Where to, sir?"

This guy's American. Great. I tell him, "RAPED."

He says, "You got it."

I try to concentrate on our route as we leave the airport, but I'm not feeling so hot. That's okay. The Answer's taking me in the right direction. I trust it. I close my eyes and rest them until I feel the cab come to a halt.

I straighten up and look around. It's a warehouse district.

"Is this it?" I say.

"You told me 2316 Barrow Street," the cabbie says. He points to a gray door on the other side of the sidewalk. "Here we are."

I pay him and get out. 2316 Barrow Street. Never heard of it. The area's deserted, but what else would you expect in a warehouse district on a Sunday morning?

Still, I'm a little uneasy now. Hell, I'm shaking in my boxer shorts. But I can't stand out here all day. The Answer hasn't let me down yet. Got to trust it.

I take a deep breath, step up to the door, and knock. And wait. No response. I knock again, louder this time. Finally the door opens a few inches. An eye peers through the crack.

A deep male voice says, "Yes?"

I don't know how to respond. Figuring there's an implied question here, I say, "RAPED."

The door opens a little wider. "What's your name?"

"Michael Moulton."

The door swings open and the guy who's been peeking through straightens up. He's wearing a gray, pin-striped suit, white shirt, and striped tie. And he's big—damn big.

"Mr. Moulton!" he booms. "We've been expecting you!"

A hand the size of a crown roast darts out, grabs me by the front of my jacket, and yanks me inside. Before I can shout or say a word, the door slams behind me and I'm being dragged down a dark hallway. I try to struggle but someone else comes up behind me and grabs one of my arms. I'm lifted off my feet like a Styrofoam mannequin. I start to scream.

"Don't bother, Mr. Moulton," says the first guy. "There's no one around to hear you."

They drag me onto a warehouse floor where my scuffling feet and their footsteps echo back from the far walls and vaulted ceiling. The other guy holding me is also in a gray suit. And he's just as big as the first.

"Hey, look," I say. "What's this all about?"

They don't say anything. The warehouse floor is empty except for a single chair and a rickety table supporting a hard-sided Samsonite suitcase. They dump me into the chair. The second guy holds me there while the first opens the suitcase. He pulls out a roll of silver duct tape and proceeds to tape me into the chair.

My teeth are chattering now. I try to speak but the words won't come. I want to cry but I'm too scared.

Finally, when my body's taped up like a mummy, they walk off and leave me alone. But I'm alone only for a minute. This other guy walks in. He's in a suit, too, but he's smaller and older; gray at the temples, tanned, with bright blue eyes. He stops a couple of feet in front of the chair and stares down at me. He looks like a cabinet member, or maybe a TV preacher.

"Mr. Moulton," he says softly with a slow, sad shake of his head. "Foolish, greedy, Mr. Moulton."

I find my voice. It sounds hoarse, like I've been shouting all night. "This is about the Answer, isn't it?"

"Of course it is."

"Look, I can explain—"

"No explanation is necessary."

"I forgot, that's all. I forgot and used it. It won't happen again."

He nods. "Yes, I know."

The note of finality in that statement makes my bladder want to let go. "Please . . ."

"We gave you a chance, Mr. Moulton. We don't usually do that. But because you came into possession of the Answer through no fault of your own, we thought it only fair to let you off the hook. A shame too." He almost smiles. "You showed some flair at the end . . . led us on a merry chase."

"You mean, using the Answer to get away? What did you do—make it work against me?"

"Oh, no. The Answer always works. You simply didn't use it enough."

"I don't get it." I don't care, either, but I want to keep him talking.

"The Answer brought you to an area of the country where we have no cells. But the Answer can't keep you from being followed. We followed you to La Guardia, noted the plane you boarded, and had one of our members rush up from Denver and wait in a cab."

"But when he asked me where to, I gave him the Answer."

"Yes, you did. But no matter what you told him, he was going to bring you to 2316 Barrow Street. You should have used the Answer before you got in the cab. If you'd asked someone which cab to take, you surely would have been directed to another, and you'd still be free. But that merely would have delayed the inevitable. Eventually you'd have wound up right where you are now."

"What are you going to do to me?"

He gazes down at me and his voice has all the emotion of a man ordering breakfast.

"I'm going to kill you."

That does it. My bladder lets go and I start to blubber.

"Mr. Moulton!" I hear him say. "A little dignity!"

"Oh, please! Please! I promise—"

"We already know what your promise is worth."

"But look—I'm not a bad guy . . . I've never hurt anybody!"

"Mr. Nickleby might differ with you about that. But don't be afraid, Mr. Moulton. We are not cruel. We have no wish to cause you pain. That is not our purpose here. We simply have to remove you."

"People will know! People will miss me!"

Another sad shake of his head. "No one will know. And only your broker will miss you. We have eliminated financiers, kings, even presidents who've had the Answer and stepped out of line."

"Presidents? You mean—?"

"Never mind, Mr. Moulton. How do you wish to die? The choice is yours."

How do you wish to die? How the hell do you answer a question like that? And then I know—with the best Answer.

I say, "RAYED."

He nods. "An excellent choice."

For the first time since I started using the Answer, I don't want to know what the other guy heard. I bite back a sob. I close my eyes . . .

. . . and wait.

Switch

LUCY TAYLOR

Lucy Taylor's story is a bizarre, contemporary take on one of my favorite movies, The Wizard of Oz—*with more than a hint of Plath's* The Bell Jar *thrown in for good measure. Once you've read this, the next time you awaken from a deep sleep feeling disoriented, you will experience a moment of terror.*

—DC

Switch

IN HER SLEEP, twelve-year-old Erika heard the wind scream like a woman being slashed. She wanted to wake up, but she couldn't. She was trapped in the dream.

"Pick a card, any card," cooed the magician. His voice was oily and wheedling. He wore a crimson beret and white gloves that were frayed at the fingertips. His face looked as yellow as old mayonnaise. His breath smelled fruity and bitter at the same time, like marmalade. He leaned down toward Erika, offering the cards spread out in a fan shape in his gloved hand.

"Which one?" she said nervously, fearing a trick.

"Any one!" he grinned back fiercely, showing so many teeth, that she thought he was going to bite out a chunk of her flesh.

She reached out toward the cards. Which one to pick?

"Gotcha!" cried the magician before she could choose. He flung the cards high into the air. All the colors of the rainbow, all the designs her imagination could conceive, tumbling helterskelter, hither and yon, all swirling around like gaudy leaves cast to the wind. She saw places and names hurtle past and faces—some that she didn't recognize and some that were schoolmates and neighbors and family.

Like seeing the world through a kaleidoscope designed by a lunatic.

All out of sequence, in wild disarray.

With a cry of dismay, Erika fell to her knees, tried to gather the cards and put them back in their proper order. They were slippery and fell through her fingers.

169

She started to pray.

The magician laughed till he screamed.

She awoke from the nightmare to the shriek of a furious chinook, the fierce dry wind that blew down onto the plains of Colorado from the eastern slope of the Rockies in the winter and spring. Like a hundred freight trains thundering past, it rocked and pummeled the house.

Living out on the plains of eastern Colorado, Erika had heard the chinooks before, the wild winds that blew off loose shingles and rattled the windowpanes in their frames. They terrified her, the way they rushed past the house like something savage and out of control, diabolical in their frenzy.

Tonight, though, the wind was worse than she'd ever heard it, brutal and angry and purposeful, like a madman pounding the roof with a ball-peen hammer while he tittered and hissed. Like a giant pugilist throwing combination punches at the walls.

Erika clutched the covers over her head and chewed on the tip of one braid, a habit she'd picked up when she was small and her brother Brock teased her for sucking her thumb. She hated herself for acting like a little kid—*I'm almost grown-up,* she reminded herself—but the chinook was shaking and battering the house now, violently seeking entry. The bed, the floor, began vibrating, creaking. Erika stopped trying not to be scared and screamed for her parents.

No one came.

She yelled for her brother Brock, whose room was right next to hers. He didn't answer.

Maybe they can't hear me for the wind.

She got up and ran first to Brock's room and then to her parents'. Their beds looked slept-in, but they were empty.

Fear felt like a hand wriggling down Erika's throat all the way to her belly. The wind was tearing things loose from the house, shaking the house like a salt shaker and, if it didn't stop, Erika was afraid she and her family would fall out the broken windows and doors like so many grains of white salt.

Her vision blurred. Smeary colors dripped from the ceiling and streamed down the walls. Her flesh seemed to be liquefying into long, goopy strands. Her bones felt as flimsy as Styrofoam, as though she was about to be tossed away like one of the cards she'd seen in her dream, pitched high in the air to land where the winds of chance blew it.

She knew only one way to protect herself. She shut her eyes and tried to duplicate the trick she'd used years ago, when Uncle Dub came visiting from Garden City and put his hand down her panties when he took her out to the Dairy Queen: she pretended her head was a TV set and she clicked it off and unplugged it.

Then she was safe. Or had seemed to be.

She'd watched what Uncle Dub was doing to her and tried to convince herself it wasn't real, it was only an illusion. *Real* was up here in her head, not down there, where Uncle Dub's hand groped in her panties.

She escaped that way now, her consciousness sliding out of the spot between her eyebrows and drifting up through the shifting colors and shimmery walls into the overpowering screech of the chinook.

Out the window she could see shingles and trash can tops, children's toys sailing high in the air, spinning in the moonlight. They looked like light bright shiny cards.

Her sleep was like a gauzy twilight, where dreams flickered instead of stars. She was in the school gym doing push-ups. A squinty-eyed woman with sparse lips and no chin was yelling at her to do the exercise faster. "I can't, dammit, leave me alone!" Erika yelled. The woman with no chin grabbed Erika by her braids and yanked her head back. She had a witch's sharp nose and nailfile-on-glass voice. "Go to the principal's office!" she shouted. "Now!"

Then Erika was as wide-awake as if someone had snapped their fingers inside her head. She sat up. The wind had died down. She was afraid the clock might have stopped during the eyeblink-brief night, but it said a little after seven o'clock and the digital display changed as she watched it.

But the house itself—the *aliveness* of the house seemed to have come to a halt in some mysterious way. There was no sound, no clatter of breakfast dishes, no doors being slammed, newspapers folded. The silence expanded and deepened, like the vibrations of a great bell tolling in a deaf ear.

She remembered the night before—the empty beds in her parents' and brother's rooms. Wherever they'd gone last night, surely they were back now.

She lay there listening intently, listening for all the things she should have heard but didn't. The house, the street outside, were draped in silence thick as a fog, a solid, pregnant quiet dense with its own profundity.

When she was very young, Erika's older cousin Penny had teased her with a terrifying threat: if she were bad, one day when she was asleep or in the bathtub or watching TV, Ma and Pa and Brock would slip quietly out of the house, get into the car and drive away, leaving her behind. She knew now that Penny was just being mean, but now the awful words came back to her. What if Penny had known something she didn't? What if her parents and brother had really left her?

"Ma?" Erika whispered.

No one answered.

"Ma! Pa! Where is everybody!"

The silence rang in her head like a taunt.

Trembling, Erika got out of bed. She found her parents' and Brock's bedrooms were still empty. So was the kitchen, where this time of day Ma would be cleaning up the breakfast dishes, maybe nibbling a waffle or piece of toast that somebody'd left on their plate.

Today there was only that unbearably rich, fertile silence, silence like turned earth roiling with creepy-crawlers and worms. Silence like the inside of a coffin.

Erika put on her jacket and buckled her fanny pack around her waist. In it were her allowance money and hairbrush, a tube of Tooty-Fruity Lipgloss, half a dozen POGs, and some photos she'd taken of her family's recent trip to Yellowstone, which she was planning to show Denny Capshaw, a seventh grade boy she was starting to like.

She walked next door to the neighbors' and banged on the door, shouting hello. No one came. Not even a dog yapped. So it was with all the houses on the block, no amount of tearful screaming and pleading and shouting brought the slightest response from any of the locked, mausoleum-like houses.

Erika started to run. She ran through the deserted streets to Buford Junior High School, but she already knew . . . she *knew* . . . the school was still locked from the day before. The playground was barren, the classrooms, when Erika peered in the windows, were empty as well.

For an instant, standing on the glass shards of a broken bottle as she looked through a window into the empty gymnasium, Erika remembered the dream in which she was lying on her belly, sweaty and exhausted, struggling to do push-ups while a witch in blue shorts and white tennis shoes yelled at her. Now she remembered more: scribbling a nasty poem about the witch on the wall of the girl's restroom and then trudging to the principal's office, where a frowning secretary with bubblegum pink lips phoned her parents to come get her.

Had she dreamed that part, too?

Erika gazed at the deserted school, the empty streets, and neighborhood. She picked up a sharp-edged piece of glass off the ground, closed her eyes, and thrust the jagged fragment into the heel of her hand. Pain jolted her. Blood bloomed in her palm like a rose plucked from the air by a magician.

She didn't wake up.

They've really all gone. The whole world's disappeared. I'm all alone.

She could not imagine enduring such awesome aloneness for long. Never to see her parents again, her brother, her friends. Never to hear a human voice except her own. She looked at the piece of glass she was holding and thought about what she must eventually do—it was a sin, but God would have to understand.

She sat down on the bench by the bus stop and sobbed until her throat felt like she'd swallowed a mouthful of kitty litter.

The cold wrapped itself around her like a shawl. The wind, that strange yowling chinook from the night before, was beginning to clamor again. It swirled trash through the air and blew grit off the playground into Erika's face. Her eyes stung with tears and the school and the houses around it grew blurry and bendable, the way they had on the previous night, like soft toys made of rubber. Everything seemed to be losing its substance, turning to shadow and smoke.

The chinook kicked gravel at Erika as she fled to the nearest house and huddled under the porch, shielding her face with her jacket. She considered running right out into the wind, letting it sweep her away, but she couldn't make herself do such a foolhardy thing. She was afraid to find out where the wind might take her.

The wind shrieked like a witch with a toothache. It filled every cranny and space of the vast, thrumming silence. It poured into her ears, into her head like shards of blood red, glassy sand.

Please don't take me away, too, she thought, and that was the last thing she knew.

Pick a card, any card, said the magician in his sly, singsongy voice. His grin was like Uncle Dub's. Erika wasn't so sure she was dreaming this time. The magician offered her the same wide fan of cards. The cards gleamed like polished tiles, like bright, miniature stained glass windows. Each one gem-perfect and brilliant.

Pick a card.

Erika reached out her hand.

That's it now, pick a card. It won't bite you.

The magician's leering face, his phony-sweet whisper were just the way Uncle Dub's had been. Suddenly Erika knew—it was another trick. She would pick the wrong card. She knew it! The trick was set up so she had to pick the wrong card, because the Erika card wasn't there in the deck at all. She'd somehow held onto her card during the terrible wind when all the other cards had blown away and everyone disappeared. And now . . .

The magician hopped up and down like a maddened toad.

He hurled the cards down and they fell end to end in a line, like a road paved with jewels snaking off into the distance.

Pick a card! Pick a card! Pick a card!

Erika woke up beneath the porch of the strange house, hugging her knees to her chest. Her hand throbbed where she had deliberately cut herself. The wound was covered with a crust of dried blood.

She listened. And her heart leaped with hope because she could tell that the world had returned. Cars were rolling by in the street. Children played ball. Somewhere a radio was playing and a couple of women were chatting about whether or not to henna their hair.

Everything sounded like it was supposed to, the way it had sounded *before.*

Why, then, was she still so afraid?

Erika stretched her stiff, tired muscles and started for home.

Or to where home used to be.

She turned east on Demeres Road and walked north for four blocks on Prestwick Drive till she got to her house. There was a strange Buick in the drive, but she figured her parents had guests, maybe someone left homeless when their roof had blown off. Marching up the steps, she rang the bell, which responded, not with its usual raspy buzz, but an unfamiliar, bell-like trill.

A woman Erika had never seen before opened the door. She was big-boned and blonde with deep smile lines etching her eyes and a missing side tooth. Her nails were long and fake and polished the color of cinnamon buns. She stared at Erika.

"Lizbeth," she said. "What are you doing home from school this time of day?" Her bluesy voice had a soft, West Texas drawl. "You sick or somethin'?"

Erika blinked hard, said nothing.

"Well, come on in the kitchen. I just took a tray of brownies out of the oven. You can tell me what's going on while we eat."

Erika bit her lip to keep from crying. She followed the strange woman into the kitchen.

Did she have the wrong house? Could the woman possibly be so nearsighted that she mistook Erika for her daughter Lizbeth?

But it wasn't the wrong house, it was *her* house, Erika realized, right down to the hat tree in the hall and the dark, star-shaped stain on the rug in the dining room where Brock had once spilled a mug of hot cocoa. Except the furniture . . . the furniture was all wrong. It was flowery stuff with bright patterns and ruffled lamps, whereas theirs had been pale blue and white French Provincial. And in the kitchen was a big butcher block table and a cage with two parakeets in it instead of the TV that Ma liked to watch while she cooked.

"I . . . I think I must have the wrong house," Erika said in a small, skittish voice.

The blonde woman looked up from slicing the brownies. "Oh, come on, it hasn't been *that* long since I baked brownies."

"No, I mean really . . . who lives here?"

"Lizbeth, that's not funny no more. I don't care for sarcasm, okay?"

"Hey, Lizzie, what are you doin' home?"

A man opened the back door and strode in. He was tall and broad as a Kodiak bear and almost as hairy, with a full reddish beard sprouting out of his fleshy jowls and chin. "You been sent home for sassin' your phys. ed. teacher again?"

"She's in a mood," said the woman. "Bein' smart-assed."

The big man, who reminded Erika of a picture she'd seen in a story-book of Paul Bunyan, scowled. "Now you know what I told you would happen if you got sent home from school again. I don't care if you do hate phys. ed., you gotta take it to graduate. Did you get punished with push-ups again?"

Erika felt the fear inching up her spine like a cockroach parade. Her tongue felt blistered and dry. She drew herself up and tried to speak in the clear, strong voice of the trial attorney she hoped to be when she grew up. "I don't know who you are or what you're talking about. My name's Erika Spence, and this is my home, and I want to know what have you done with my parents, Sarah and Jim Spence and my older brother, Brock Spence? Where are they? Who are you? What have you done with them?"

The man and the woman stared at her. The woman spoke first, timidly, "Lizbeth, honey, what—" but the man cut her off. "What are you talkin' about? What the hell is this, some kinda game? Who the hell are these Spence people?"

Erika reached in her fanny pack and pulled out a photo of Ma and Pa and Brock at Yellowstone the month before. She'd taken it with her favorite Christmas present, an instant Polaroid camera.

"These are my parents and my brother," she said. "They're supposed to be living here. What have you done with them?"

The blonde woman had set down the knife and come around the

table. She looked at the photo for a long time and frowned, showed it to the man. They exchanged puzzled looks.

Then the man shrugged and started unbuckling his belt with hairy, thick-knuckled hands.

"You got one more chance to explain yerself, Lizzie, to cut out this foolishness or I swear, you ain't too old to take upstairs, you ain't too old to . . ."

"Hank, please," said the woman.

"Now, Prudy, just stop, let me handle this, okay? I don't know what damn-fool game she's playin' or where she got that picture, but—"

"Hank, I don't think it's a game. I think . . . Lizzie, just talk to me. Tell me what's going on."

She reached out to Erika.

"Don't touch me!" Erika smacked the strange woman in the mouth. The woman yelped as blood streamed from her lip. The man bellowed. Erika dashed for the door.

She plunged into the street, dodging a furniture van that swerved and squealed its tires to avoid her, then darted between two houses and hid under some box-bushes in the backyard while the man named Hank and the woman named Prudy searched for her. Her heart was double its size, slamdancing her throat. She bit her tongue to keep from crying.

Afternoon shadows crawled over Erika's hiding place. It had been over an hour since she heard the man and the woman calling for her. She crawled out from under the bushes.

A white Scottish terrier wearing a green collar and tags approached Erika. She recognized the dog at once: the Barrys' Scotty, Felix the Lion-Hearted, who could catch a mean Frisbee despite his short legs and stout body. Erika fed him and walked him whenever the Barrys went out of town.

She dropped to her knees.

"Felix, come here. Are you lost, too?"

Felix flattened his ears. His snarl looked like a smaller version of a pit bull ready for battle. Erika stood up and jumped backward as Felix sprang. His pint-sized killer dog teeth pierced her socks and punched through the skin of her ankle.

Erika screamed and kicked Felix away. He came at her again. She ran to a parked car and climbed onto the trunk. She waited there until Felix lost interest and wandered away, then her tears flowed. Felix the Lion-Hearted had been like her own dog.

She climbed down from the car hood. Her shoe felt squishy and weird. She looked down and saw it was filling with blood.

Up ahead, she saw a mailman turn the corner and start up the block. It was a skinny, olive-skinned man, not the regular mailman, Mr. Simms, but she ran up to him anyway.

"Do you know where . . . ?"

The olive-skinned man stuffed a handful of letters into a mailbox and tugged on the fat lobe of an ear that stuck out from the side of his head like a miniature satellite dish. "Lizbeth Buchanon, I just passed your folks a few blocks from here and they're lookin' for you. Your dad, he looked madder'n a wet hen. I'd head on home if—Lizbeth, Lizbeth wait, where you goin'? Didn't you hear what I said? Your parents are lookin' for you! Hey, what happened to your foot?"

Erika darted across the street and ran through several backyards until she could no longer hear him yelling. Her heart was pounding the way it did the summer before when she had to go off the high diving board at the public pool and then just stood there, toes wrapped over the edge, looking down into the terrible bottomless blue.

She was hungry and thirsty. There were four dollars and change in her jeans pocket, but she didn't dare walk to the convenience store up the street for fear the strange people who thought they were her parents would be there.

Assuming, of course, the convenience store was still where she remembered it to be. Maybe that had changed, too. And maybe her mind was altered, too, making her have memories about being punished in gym class that really belonged to some girl named Lizbeth Buchanon.

That was the scariest notion of all.

She was entering an unfamiliar neighborhood, one of tall close-spaced apartment buildings with tiny, sparse yards. A group of girls shot basketball on a litter-strewn court. They had sleek, coltish muscles and scolded each other in some language that Erika did not understand. The street signs now were written in a language other than English.

Erika paused at the corner to look in the window of a small grocery store. The bins on display were full of items she didn't recognize: fat, bulbous yellow fruit and long tuberous things that might have been gigantic string beans or maybe monstrous, deformed melons. The signs identifying these objects were written in fanciful red letters that looked like small houses pierced with a variety of slashes and strokes. They ran up and down, not left and right.

Erika peered in and squinted.

Erika's Grandma Bertie hobbled to the door of the shop and stared out. Part of her face hung lopsided, like she was made of Play-Doh that somebody'd stretched out to make a funny-ugly face. That was the result of Grandma Bertie's stroke the year before. Erika flung her arms about the old woman.

"Grandma Bertie? Grandma Bertie, it's me! It's Erika."

The old lady acted like Erika'd puked on her. She jabbed the knob of her cane into Erika's chest, hissing spittle and strange words at Erika. The words made no sense and seemed to be grouped into one long period-less paragraph. The syllables sounded stretched out and melted together like Grandma Bertie's face.

"Grandma, why are you talkin' like that. Speak so's I can understand you, Grandma, please!"

The old woman chattered and glowered and banged Erika on the shin with her cane. Erika squealed.

A man with round owlish eyes and a mouth like a slit in a piggy bank ran up and dragged the Grandma Bertie person away from the door.

"Did you hit that girl? Did you? Good Christ, May, you senile old bag, do you want to get us sued again?"

The old woman began to gibber her birdcall-like words.

"Are you all right, miss?" the slit-mouthed man asked. "She didn't hurt you, did she? No problem here, right? Okay?"

Erika shook her head, backing away.

"Come here and let me take a look at your leg."

He wiggled slim, spidery fingers. *Come here.*

Erika ran.

The strange part of town with the people who spoke funny words began to peter out, but the roads here were no less unfamiliar, narrow and two-laned. Some were dirt roads leading out toward a horizon as flat and dark as the edge of a ruler. Erika tried not to wonder what had become of Denver, whose downtown buildings could normally be seen silhouetted against the sky like some far-off magical kingdom.

A familiar-looking, brown convertible bore down on Erika. She recognized it at once—she could never forget it. It belonged to Uncle Dub. Last time she'd sat in it had been when his thick, cold fingers—chilled from holding the cup of vanilla/chocolate swirl—had wiggled and waggled in the niche between her legs.

But to Erika's relief and amazement Uncle Dub wasn't driving the car—which he had proclaimed loudly and often could not be driven by anyone but himself. Behind the wheel sat red-haired Darlene Markson, Erika's math teacher. Darlene was a plump, pan-faced lady whose hobby was jigsaw puzzles. Her husband Bruce, who coached Little League, collected Civil War relics. Erika liked the Marksons and their sons, Wayne and Jeff. She'd spent two weeks with them once when Ma and Pa had some difficulties and split up temporarily and Ma said she needed time to herself "to think." During that time, Darlene Markson had taught Erika how to make pies from scratch and how to play chess. The Marksons all liked to quote Scripture; they prayed before every meal and read the Bible together at night. So when Darlene Markson pulled the car to a stop alongside her, Erika was so happy to see her that she got in without saying a word.

"Is it . . . is it really Erika Spence . . . or are you some other girl now?" said Mrs. Markson hesitantly.

Erika jumped at the sound of her own name as though it were something foreign to her.

"Yes, yes! It's Erika! I can't find my parents or my brother. I don't even know where I am any more, and I'm hungry, and my foot's hurt and everything's changed. Can you help me?"

Mrs. Markson stared at Erika so hard it was like she was trying to see through her skin.

"Yes, of course, Erika. I'll help you. Come home with me first, I'll get you something to eat." She added in a small, strained voice, "Bruce and the boys, I haven't seen them since last night."

It was a different house from the one that Erika had visited before, a big gawky frame house with a huge oak tree in the front yard, but Erika didn't remark on this. Inside, she noted that Mrs. Markson had several jigsaw puzzles going at once, just like she always did whenever Erika had visited her at the old house, wherever that was now. Darlene Markson washed Erika's foot and gave her a pair of her own satin bedroom slippers to wear. Then she put out a big plate of cold fried chicken and coleslaw and potato chips and they sat at the dining room table. Erika ate ravenously.

"Do your parents know where you are?" asked Mrs. Markson.

Her real parents, Erika wondered, or those strangers Prudy and Hank? In either case, the answer was no. She shook her head.

"So you just took off on your own?" said Mrs. Markson, forking pink, stringy coleslaw into her mouth.

"There was a wind," Erika said softly. "It blew real hard and either it blew me to a new place or it blew everybody else far away. Things got all confused and mixed up. Nobody has the right name now. Nobody lives where they're s'posed to. The magician did it, I think. He sent the wind. Did you hear it?"

Darlene Markson sank small white teeth into a lip that look swollen and bitten. "You know, then."

Know what, Erika wanted to ask. She chewed her food and stayed silent.

179

"Yes, I heard the wind," Mrs. Markson continued. She gave a choked laugh. "Matter of fact, it blew so hard, I think it blew Jeff and Wayne and Bruce clear away. Some other man tried to get in here, said he was my husband, but I wouldn't let him in . . ."

"The people, they all got switched around," said Erika quietly. "What happened? Where did they go?"

"I don't know," murmured Mrs. Markson. "I don't understand this. Bruce and me, we were expectin' the Rapture, when God takes His own up to Heaven, but not this. Not everyone all stirred up and put back wrong." She got up and walked over to a completed jigsaw puzzle on the card table next to the TV. "Like God got bored and He went and did—*this.*" She gave the card table a terrible smack with both fists. The puzzle bounced and broke apart. Pieces fell to the floor, rolled this way and that. "And the worst part is, we don't know if this is the first time or if . . . if it's been happening all along . . . things getting switched around . . . and nobody ever remembered it had been any different."

Erika cringed from the ferocity behind Darlene Markson's blow. "So why didn't it happen to you, too?" she asked finally. "How come you're still you?"

Darlene Markson put her bleeding fist to her mouth. "I'm not sure. I was real tired and blue the night the wind started up and I took a whole handful of my pills . . . Bruce doesn't know I take pills, he'd say it was unChristian, but I need them, I need my pills to relax and . . . I dreamed God came down all painted up and evil and he mixed everyone up. But he couldn't touch me, 'cause the pills had washed over my mind like an ocean and he . . . couldn't get to it." She stared at Erika as if suddenly realizing something. "What about you? Did you hide your mind, too?"

"Kind of," said Erika, wishing for the first time that maybe she hadn't used the power she'd learned from her experience with Uncle Dub, wishing she'd just let the wind take her, blow her someplace new, into some other girl, maybe that girl named Lizbeth who hated phys. ed. and had a mama named Prudy and a daddy who looked like Paul Bunyan.

"What should we do?" asked Erika.

"I don't know," said Mrs. Markson. "I've got enough sleeping pills left . . . if things get real bad . . . if I never find Bruce and the boys again . . . maybe I could . . ." she trailed off.

"I've thought of that, too," Erika said, "but I don't want to die. I want my family back. I want *everything* back the way it was before."

"I don't think it can go back," said Mrs. Markson. She put a hand under Erika's chin, lifted it up. "And we can't tell people everything's different now, because they won't believe us. They'll think we're crazy. But we can stick together—we've got to. There may be other people like us—people who didn't get switched around for some reason, who remember the way it was. Right now I think we should pray. We'll pray for courage to get us through—"

The doorbell rang.

Mrs. Markson jumped up. "Maybe it's Bruce and the boys."

Erika stayed at the table nibbling chips, but she could hear Mrs. Markson opening the front door and saying hello. By the tone of her voice, Erika knew it wasn't her husband or sons at the door.

She heard a man talking, then a woman. She heard her own name! She jumped up, recognizing the voices. It was Ma and Pa, asking to see her.

Erika burst into the hallway, ignoring the two police officers who stood straight as tin soldiers on either side of the door. She threw her arms about her mother, sobbing. Her mother bent down, comforting. "There, there, hon, there, there."

Erika suddenly stopped crying and whirled around. One of the policemen was clicking handcuffs onto Mrs. Markson, the other reading her something like the cops on TV—"My Randy" rights, Brock called them sarcastically.

"What are you *doing?*"

"They're just going to question her, honey," said Erika's mother. "About the kidnapping and all . . . a bulletin was put out that you'd run away and then the policeman saw you go by in Mrs. Gordon's car . . ."

"Mrs. *Markson,*" screamed Erika, "her name's Mrs. Markson!"

". . . like I was saying, in Mrs. Gordon's convertible, so then Hank and Prudy called us and . . ."

"She didn't kidnap me. She was taking care of me. Don't hurt her, please."

They took Mrs. Markson away, still calling her by the wrong name. She was begging and babbling about needing to go back for her pills.

"I'm glad we found you," said Erika's mother. "So glad . . ."

Ma took Erika's hand on one side, Pa took the other. They walked out the front door—

—into the arms of Paul Bunyan and Prudy, who looked sour and scared, but broke out in nervous, relieved laughter when they saw Erika emerge from the Markson house.

"It *was* her! You found her!" boomed Paul Bunyon.

"Thank God," said Prudy. "And thank you so much, both of you, for helping us out. I don't know what's happened, if she's on drugs or what, but she stood right in our kitchen and swore up and down that Sarah and Jim Spence were her parents and then she showed us your picture. Don't know where she got it from, but we recognized you, of course, the Hollys from the PTA and the bridge club. But she'd got your names wrong, said your name was Spence. Then when the police called to say they'd seen her go into the house with Mrs. Gordon . . . I thought maybe it would calm her down if you should be the ones to approach her and pretend to be these people she thinks are her folks."

Erika's father looked at the photo Prudy showed him. "That's one of the pictures got lost after our trip to Yellowstone last year. Our boy Peter took it."

Erika's mother shook her head. "At least now you can get help for the poor confused child. God bless you."

"I know the name of a top-notch psychiatrist," said Erika's dad. "He specializes in delusional psychosis. I could give you his number."

"We'd appreciate that," said Prudy, squeezing Erika's hand. "I can't imagine what's happened to her—maybe Mrs. Gordon's been giving her pills—it sounds to me like the woman has a drug problem."

"Lizbeth's gonna need plenty of treatment to straighten her out," growled Paul Bunyan.

"Let me pick a card! Let me pick a card!" pleaded Erika.

The magician held the deck up high out of her reach. "It isn't time yet," he singsonged. "It isn't time yet to reshuffle the deck."

Still, Erika leaped for the cards in his hand. Leaped like her life depended on it.

The magician made a tsk-tsk sound with his pursed, purple lips. He closed the cards up into a neat deck and turned away.

Erika awoke in her bed in the place that smelled like cough drops and pee, the place where everything was bolted down—the chairs, the bed, the TV set. They were so afraid you were going to hurt yourself with something, pick something up and hit somebody with it that they had everything fastened down.

And the people, they were fastened down, too. With straps across their wrists and locks on their doors, with pills the doctors said would keep their minds from bolting away like so many spooked horses, but really just made them sit there like scared-looking dolls.

Please make it all go away, Erika thought.

Put everything back like it was.

Put it back.

Erika turned her face to the strange wall in the strange room in the strange world.

She prayed for the wind to come back.

The Eighth of December

DAVE SMEDS

Dave Smeds' alternate history story opens in Berlin, in December, 1995. In this Berlin, the Cold War has not ended; the Wall is still a fact of life. Using Rock & Roll as a backdrop, Smeds forces us to reexamine the sentiments of the sixties. Was the hope of love and peace that was set into motion simply an illusion?

—DC

The Eighth of December

WEST BERLIN WAS DRAPED in gray as the band's limousines rolled through the streets. An unbroken mantle of clouds threatened a downpour, but held on to its bounty like an avaricious politician, turning the last hour of daylight into outright gloom. Faded buildings paraded by. People huddled at bus stops, toying with umbrellas as if certain they would need them at any moment. No smiles.

Vic Standish consulted his watch. In less than twenty hours he would be boarding his Lear jet and be done with this city. Most of that time would be filled playing the gig or holed up in his hotel room, with only one necessary detour in between. He was ready to be gone. In the past two days the Bürgermeister's liaison had shown him and his mates the best the city had to offer, but its façade held too many cracks: The barbed wire and guard turrets were still there at Checkpoint Charlie. A policeman stood at nearly every major intersection. The smear of paint on a brick wall didn't quite conceal the swastika graffiti underneath. Seated next to Vic, his drummer Lenny was reading a paper containing a bold headline about the deepening crisis in Yugoslavia. The Soviets had just delivered more armaments to the Serbs. The U.S. was contemplating increased air strikes to aid the besieged Islamic enclaves. The United Nations had given up its attempts to mediate.

Saturday, December 2, 1995. The Cold War was casting a frigid shadow. The citizens of West Germany wore haunted, worried faces of stone. Vic had no doubt it was the same a few miles away on the communist side. Their mental photo albums were open—if they were old enough—to pages showing tanks rumbling into Hungary in 1956, into

187

Czechoslovakia in 1968. Closer to home, they were remembering the Wall going up, splitting the city, never to come down.

Vic knew something of what they must be feeling, though as an American, his corresponding memories were of the Cuban Missile Crisis, of umpteen civil defense drills during his teenage years, and of his father building a bomb shelter beneath their house. How had the world become so hostile again? There had been a time, after Nixon went to China, after the Vietnam War ended, after détente, after Jimmy Carter brought Israel and Egypt to the table at Camp David, when people and nations had steered toward a gentler course. That was in another lifetime, Vic reflected. Back when he owned a different name. Back when he used to tour Europe with his old band. Back when people listened to a different kind of rock 'n' roll.

Everything had changed, and trying to recapture the past was futile. In the here and now, he had to concentrate on what was possible. Maybe the music wasn't the same, but at the very least, he could help take the crowd's mind away from the concerns of the moment. Wasn't that his job?

As the quartet of limousines approached the stage entrance of the coliseum, a cluster of several hundred fans cheered and waved banners. VICTORY! GREATEST BAND EVER! said one sign, which brought a wry shake of the head from Vic. Faithfulness was one thing, but exaggeration was another. He remembered a concert in '69 when he and his sidemen had had to sneak in through a maintenance tunnel to get backstage, and even that didn't compare to what he'd witnessed at Beatles and Stones gigs.

Lenny was grinning, though. For him, the adulation was a brand-new experience. The band's fourth album was emptying off the shelves as fast as it could be restocked. The tour was cresting a wave of momentum that would put them in the public consciousness for good. No more one-hit wonders, no more promising journeymen, destined to vanish as soon as someone new came along. Even if the band never cut another track, Victory would not be forgotten.

Vic let a smile nudge the corners of his lips. Yes, it *did* feel good, didn't it? Even to an old fart who had seen it all before. It set his blood to flowing, made him think of tight young groupie bodies—even though he didn't indulge in the latter's charms any more—and made his hand itch for the hard, phallic shape of a microphone in his grip.

"We're gonna blow 'em away," Lenny boasted.

"Yeah." Vic accepted it as an obligation. "Let's do it."

*   *   *

The Eighth of December

The audience reaffirmed that English-language rock 'n' roll acts could make it no matter where in the world they played. The crowd rose to their feet as Victory lit into its self-referential piece—a minor hit on the radio, not even released as a single—but one that always made a connection during the live show with its long, repeated chant: "Victory! Victory! Victory is here!" It was two-thirds of the way through the show. Vic was stomping back and forth across the stage, sweat streaming down his bared chest, shouting the lyrics, egging the Berlin residents to a higher and higher pinnacle of frenzy.

The pounding in his heart came from three separate stimuli. First was the euphoria of being center stage, holding the attention of so many at once. Second was the nostalgic high of being successful at a craft at age fifty that he had been master of since age twenty-one. Third, he was terrified.

He was afraid because he wasn't in command of the mood. It had gone beyond him, driven by the screaming guitars, the heavy metal arrangements, the visceral beat of the drums. The Germans were releasing their pent-up tension, letting it flow out in waves. Glorious and necessary as the catharsis was, Vic knew it had the potential to spark a riot. He fought back visions of trampled twelve-year-old kids, of eyes being jabbed out. His bouncers at the edge of the stage, huge men who had once played football or hockey at semi-pro levels, were earning every bit of their salaries now—throwing overexuberant fans bodily back into the upraised arms of the hundreds who had abandoned their seats and mobbed the front of the stage. Those arms waved back and forth, their owners' eyes gleaming with worship as Vic stalked back and forth. That awe would turn to rage if Vic did what he wanted to—which was to run for the nearest exit. God help him if his voice were to falter or if a fuse blew and killed the speakers. The people had come to purge their demons. The process was in full swing, as unstoppable as an orgasm in mid-ejaculation. If he denied them their release, they would rip him to pieces.

He had no choice but to keep going, keep pretending that he was the one orchestrating the moment. If the horde lost the focus he was providing, the best description of the result would be chaos.

The song reached its final, crashing note. Vic sobbed. He wanted desperately to switch to a ballad, quiet the savage exultation, put some moderation into the waving fists, the screaming women, the feedback loops from the amps. But he couldn't.

Victory didn't do ballads.

*   *   *

189

The band had blown them away, all right. Vic sat in numb awe in his dressing room, dismissing the invitations of the other members of the band. They were heading off to celebrate with one final night of alcohol and Berlin women, and if they had any brains left, condoms as well. He was in no mood to extend the altered state of consciousness. He would let it dissipate while he had the strength to survive it. Vic's body ached. He took a final swallow from a bottle of Evian. Two liters down his throat since the end of the encore and he was still dehydrated. A fifteen-minute shower in the ludicrously tiny stall in the back of the room had merely diluted the layer of brine that hugged him like a second skin. Fresh perspiration was still oozing from his pores, though where he was finding the fluid to produce it, he didn't know.

A knock sounded on the door. Hurriedly he picked up the wig he'd removed prior to the shower and refitted it with an expertise born of countless repetition. He'd need to adhere it better before he went out, but it would hold for the length of time needed to deal with a visitor.

He rose and unlocked the door. Fred Brownell, his manager, slipped inside. Vic restored the deadbolts.

Fred was beaming, his bowling-ball torso resplendent with a silk cravat and a suit that must have set him back a few thousand deutsche marks. He set his valise down on the makeup counter and opened it, showing a sheaf of box office receipts next to his laptop computer.

"You're back at the top again, kid. I knew you could do it. You just topped this place's Guns N' Roses attendance record."

Kid was a relative term. Fred was sixty-one years old, his skin as tough as old leather from too many years of lying on beaches and from too many drugs—though he had forsworn both when he turned forty-five.

"I'm back?" Vic asked, groaning from fatigue as he eased into a folding chair. "What are you comparing it to? We don't talk about those days, Fred."

"Oh, fuck the rules," Fred replied mildly. "One time won't hurt. There were a lot of good times back then. I would think you'd be glad to get back to home base."

"Home base? I never hung around any scene like *this.*"

"Don't be such a glum asshole." Fred raised his arms, spun in a circle, as if to point out that neither of them was in his grave. "All I meant was, it's good to see you out of retirement."

"We've been recording and touring more than five years now, Fred. It's not a recent development."

"Victory never did anything like this before," the fat man insisted.

"This tour is hitting that old level. You moved those people out there, kid. Even with fake hair and a fake voice, you worked magic. They were there for you."

Fred obviously hadn't seen what Vic had. From backstage, the manager had watched the energy rise, gotten a boner at the thought of all the profits, and pictured reality the way he wished to.

"Bullshit. They were there for themselves," Vic said. "Don't make it into something it's not. I'm just a guy with some songs. The rest of it is just an illusion. It is now and it was back then."

"People don't buy tickets just to hear songs," Fred said. "They could play their copies of your CDs if all they wanted was the tunes. They came for Vic Standish the man. Maybe it *isn't* the way they used to come for Brad Taylor. But it's close enough in my book."

"Whatever you say." It wasn't worth arguing the point. Fred was Vic's closest associate and he loved him like a brother, but the man couldn't be talked out of anything. That's what made him such a good negotiator of contracts. Let him believe what he wanted to.

After Fred left, Vic pulled off his wig, reverting once again from a long-haired dark brunet to a short-haired blond with a deeply receding hairline. He popped out his contact lenses, which altered his brown eyes to blue. His eyebrows were that shade of variegated brown that worked with either type of coloring, especially after he donned his thick-framed glasses.

"The old days," he muttered, checking himself out in the mirror. In the old days, his body had been lean and taut. Ribs would show when he removed his shirt. His cheekbones had stood out and his arms had been ropy with veins. He hadn't totally gone to pot since then, but the thyroid problem had taken its toll. He looked nothing like he had in his youth, and now with the wig and contacts gone and his body stuffed into an overcoat that exaggerated his bulk, he barely resembled the man who had been on the stage ninety minutes earlier.

He slid out the door unobserved. The security men were concentrating on the entrances, per orders, Vic having learned that the best way to give fans the slip was to be where the guards weren't. He avoided the limousine waiting out back. Instead he filtered through the fringes of the group by the exit, parting them like the stern German corporate executive he appeared to be, and grabbed a regular taxi. No one gave him a second glance.

Cautious habits died hard. Rather than stay with the same vehicle that had taken him aboard at the ICC, he got out at a major hotel and furtively slipped into a second taxi. This car delivered him to an older, two-story home depressingly close to the Wall. The building was well-maintained, but across the street was more agonistic graffiti overlaid upon vestiges of World War II bomb damage.

Despite the late hour, the lights were on. A stout housekeeper bedecked in apparel just as no-nonsense as her expression led Vic to a bedroom that looked and smelled like a patient's room at a hospital, complete with an adjustable bed on rollers and an oxygen tent covering the upper body of the man on the mattress.

"Hi, Andrew," Vic said. The invalid opened his eyes, smiled, and waved the housekeeper away. She left with a Teutonic glare at Vic that implied in no uncertain terms that he should not exhaust her charge. Both men waited until the sound of her footsteps confirmed that she had descended the stairs, out of conversational hearing range.

"How's it goin', Brad?" Andy asked, rubbing at his eyes. He didn't seem to have been sleeping, though the dark purple semi-circles under his lower lashes hinted that he should have been. "Or should I say Vic?"

"It's Brad to you," Vic said, unfamiliar as it was to hear the name roll off his tongue.

"Hated to miss the concert," Andy said. "Kept trying to talk the doc into letting me go with my portable oxygen. I hope you brought down the house."

Vic shrugged. "You could say that. Those young bozos I perform with know how to rock. Sometimes I still wish I had you and the other guys behind me, though."

"Well, we all make our choices, don't we?" Andy gestured at his wasted body. "Guess I took some detours I would have avoided if I'd known what I was in for."

"I wouldn't say we had any options about what either of us did. Things happened. Things bigger than any of us. We couldn't have known what would come down."

"Oh, the world is a motherfucker, that's true. But that don't mean there's no component of responsibility." For the first time, the sick man seemed to locate a reservoir of strength. His tone carried weight as he asked, "Have you thought about my idea? You'll be in London on the eighth. It's the perfect place."

"I'll think about it. I've got . . . a bit more to lose than you."

"True," Andy replied. "But also more to gain." He coughed, and with it came a gurgle from deep in the lungs.

"Shit," Vic said. He handed his friend the glass of water from the bedside. "That sounded bad."

"Oh, I'm not dying yet," the other man joked. "They say I'll probably make it through the winter. I've got a New Year's party planned. Can't let people down."

The Eighth of December

* * *

Back in his hotel room, Vic brooded. He had managed to be chipper and good-humored through the last of his short visit with Andy, but now the unfiltered pain of seeing his friend in a terminal condition was keeping him awake. That, or he was still juiced with adrenaline from the show, even though by rights he should be deep into the rebound by now, catatonic until the alarm clock forced him to get up and head for the airport.

He turned on the television. An actress who looked like she'd never had a period disrupt her adult life cooed over the latest development in tampons. He reached for the remote, annoyed—didn't northern Europe have any commercial-free stations? Perhaps, like everywhere else, the local government simply wouldn't fund that sort of thing any more. A change of channels brought him an old American movie, with John Wayne speaking German in a high nasal voice that tended to go on long after his lips had stopped moving. He killed the volume and let the picture flicker at the corner of his visual field. Hell. It wasn't as if he didn't know why he was restless. Andy had resurrected a ghost.

The clock on the nightstand had long since rotated its digit counters into the A.M. half of the night. December 3rd. Five days short of fifteen years since the turning point.

Vic unfolded the clipping that Andy had given him just before they had said good-night. It was a rock critic's essay from *Rolling Stone,* written in 1975, analyzing who had been the greatest movers and shakers of the past decade.

Vic Standish was unknown, of course. Brad Taylor headed the list, up above Lennon and Dylan, Jagger and Hendrix. On the first page of the article, there was a picture of a lean, fair-haired, thirty-year-old man with a speck of hazel in the iris of his left eye, right where Vic Standish had an identical mark.

A spokesman, the critic called Taylor. The voice of a generation.

The essay's tone was so reverent it sounded like a eulogy. In some ways, it might as well have been one. Vic recalled the writer's name from a later issue of the same magazine, the special edition that appeared a few weeks after the murder of John Lennon—the one with his naked body wrapped around Yoko Ono. When Vic had first seen the cover on a newsstand, Lennon's closed eyes and damp washcloth posture, along with Ono's somber gaze-into-space, had led him to conclude that it was a photograph of the corpse. He had nearly set fire to the whole stack before he learned that it had been taken by Annie Leibovitz hours before the murder, and that Lennon himself had suggested the pose.

That issue had also contained a mention that in East Berlin, the state radio station had broken its usual ban on Western rock music and aired ninety minutes of Beatles songs as a memorial. That little snippet of trivia had bubbled to Vic's mind when his plane had touched down for the current gig. More than one aspect of his life seemed to be closing full circle this weekend.

May, 1981: Fred was sitting with him in a Los Angeles patio café, doing his best not to be stunned by what Brad had just announced. To his credit, Fred did not try to protest. He nodded mournfully and leafed through the pieces of paper Brad had just given him.

"This is how I see it," Brad said. "John Lennon and I shared way too many similarities. We're both rock 'n' roll legends. Both us had fans literally tear clothing off our bodies to have a piece of us. He took a hiatus. So did I. We both lived in New York most of the last five years. Now there are these."

Fred's frown evolved into a scowl. The papers he'd been handed were death threats, written by at least three separate lunatics, only one of which the police had been able to track down.

"These are as bad as you said," Fred muttered. "It's really got you spooked, eh, kid?"

"Damn right it's got me spooked." Brad's hand shook as he reached for his coffee, just thinking about it. "I'm not going to become a target for another Mark David Chapman."

"So you're going to fake your own death." Fred didn't phrase it as a question; he spoke as if anchoring the concept firmly in his brain. He was a perceptive man. He had caught on that his client had made up his mind and nothing he could say was going to change it. The one thing he might fuss about was the financial loss, but the plan, as Brad had delineated it, would give Fred quite an income flow over the long haul.

"Yes."

Fred sighed and reached out to shake Brad's hand. "It's been a fun ride, kid. I think you're crazy, but you have my support. Where are you going to do it?"

"Grand Cayman."

Grand Cayman is an island where all sorts of things can be bought. In June, 1981, Brad Taylor's body was found, throat slit, in the kitchen of a bungalow on the beach several miles from George Town, a vacation residence he had owned and visited frequently for several years. At least, the public was led to believe the body was that of Taylor. It actually belonged to a derelict purchased from a morgue, but to pin it with a different identity required active lying by only two individuals outside Vic's tight-knit circle—a police detective and a coroner, both well paid for their falsehoods.

Reported missing were several important pieces of Brad Taylor memorabilia, including his favorite guitar. Naturally Vic—as he would henceforth be known—had taken these articles with him, but their absence was attributed to robbery by the same man who had done the killing.

The search began for the thief/murderer. Several of the island's usual suspects were rounded up and questioned in the "guilty until you pay us off" style of the local authorities. A description of a man who had supposedly been seen near the bungalow on the day in question was distilled out of that activity, but the artist's composite showed a lanky, dark man with dreadlocks, a description that applied to so many transients in the region that it was useless as a means of narrowing the list of suspects. Then a radio station in New York received what purported to be an anonymous letter from the guilty party. It rambled on in a fashion reminiscent of the Zodiac killer, saying that Brad Taylor had been murdered for his immorality and decadence. In the envelope was a lock of hair that matched that of Taylor, and an exact list of the missing items from the bungalow.

The media had a field day, but when the excitement ended, the authorities had no leads. The case went as cold as the ashes, supposedly those of Brad Taylor, that were scattered over New York Harbor in early July.

December, 1981: Vic, still lying low in the Caribbean, rendezvoused with Andy on Tobago.

"I wanted to tell all my old bandmates," Vic said as they shared dinner at The Beachcomber. Parrots sat on perches just outside the open windows of the restaurant. Palm trees waved in the slight breeze. The last of the sunset was vanishing, and a soca beat could be heard from the disco next door. "Maybe I will later. But the more people who know, the more likely it is that the whole scheme will fall apart. I'm sure I can count on your discretion."

"Of course," Andy said. "Always." Setting down the crab leg on which he'd been nibbling, he shook his head at the bizarre circumstances. "So . . . how many people *do* know?"

"Just the folks whose cooperation I can't do without if I'm going to keep pulling it off," Vic explained. "My ex-wife. My executor. They get cash to me bit by bit, siphoning it to me from my estate. And Fred, of course. I have to have somebody like him to look after the tape archive and make sure the music gets licensed in a way I can live with. I might not be Brad Taylor any more, but I'll be damned if I'll let my work be turned into Pepsi jingles and background noise for used-car dealers' ads."

"Amen to that." Though Brad had essentially been a solo artist, writing all his own songs, Andy's bass guitar work was on the definitive recordings of seventy percent of those tunes, and he obviously didn't care to have his legacy diluted.

A bat sailed through the restaurant, over their table, scooped up a pair of fruit flies, and vanished in the direction of the beach. None of the staff or old-time island residents gave the flying mammal a second glance. After all, these were the tropics.

Vic turned back to the table to find Andy frowning.

"Aren't you lonely?" the bassist asked.

Vic coughed. "Yeah. That's why I had Fred arrange this meeting."

"In that case, how long you gonna keep this up?"

The "dead" man took a long, slow swallow of rum. "Don't know. Couple of years? Maybe by then, Lennon being gone won't sting like it does now. Doesn't it leave you feeling stung, Andy?"

"Stung by fire ants, my man. And it was even worse when I heard that *you* had died." He stared pointedly at his old boss.

Vic blinked, then cleared his throat. "Sorry," he muttered into his empty glass. "I just felt . . . mortal. I needed a break. Some time away, unhounded by fans, able to walk around without feeling like someone is looking at me every second. You know what I mean?"

Andy smiled wryly. "I quit being your back-up man seven years ago next Tuesday, you know that? Even after all that time, even being off to the side like I was, it still takes hanging out in corners of the world like this to have any privacy at all."

"Well, there you go," Vic said. "Being dead is the most out-of-the-way corner I could find. I want to rest awhile before I go back to the rat race. Ask me again in a year. Maybe I'll feel differently then."

A year might have been enough. Vic grew tired of never being able to call up old acquaintances. But 1982 contained the April from hell: Bob Dylan was machine-gunned to death outside his front door in the presence of two of his children. Donovan Leitch was next, shot by a mental-hospital escapee who accused him of stealing the lyrics of "Sunshine Superman" and threatening to execute a host of other rock icons for similar "crimes."

McCartney was the last, but also the worst for Vic. It wasn't just that the bullet left him in a vegetative state, unable to die and unable to live. It was that Vic hadn't realized how much the other leader of the Beatles had meant to him until he was taken out. Vic had always been a Lennon fan, except to compare Yoko Ono's voice unfavorably with that of a macaw. Yet when he overheard a man joking that McCartney had always been a vegetable, he'd loosened the bastard's teeth for him and spent the next few hours at home playing "Yesterday" and "Got to Get You into My Life" and "The Long and Winding Road," forcing his bloodied, swollen knuckles to coax the tunes from his guitar or his piano.

Every megastar in the industry ducked into seclusion or hired the entire army of France to guard them. Caution reigned for a long time. Elton John gave up touring, releasing sporadic albums recorded at home behind barred gates. George Harrison vanished into his mansion for the next seven years.

Any thought Vic had of revealing himself disappeared. Brad Taylor remained victim number two on a list that had grown far too long. Vic Standish walked the planet in his place. He was rich. He lived a comfortable life. He wasn't going to fuck with that. His collaborators, who might have become careless and let something slip under other circumstances, understood the stakes, and kept their lips sealed.

In 1986 the detective on Grand Cayman confessed to his part. Annual, untraceable deliveries of cash, part of the original bribe, had not been enough; he thought he could get more money by selling his tale. The tactic did not harm Vic. For one thing, the detective did not know what name Brad Taylor had adopted, and second, the man was widely known as an unreliable witness. His testimony had been bought in more than one court case, which was a reason Vic had selected him. Fortunately, the coroner could offer no corroboration. He had already died, and better still, had passed away quietly of natural causes in a hospital, providing little fuel for conspiracy theorists. Only the *National Enquirer* and other tabloids paid any attention to the detective, and they only milked the story for two weeks. The reputable media shoved it in the same basket as Elvis sightings.

The likelihood of being exposed grew increasingly remote. With that sense of security, Vic ultimately could not resist the narcotic of having an audience. With a body gone overweight, minus the pretty-boy face of his younger days and with various cosmetic adjustments, he slid back into the music scene in 1989, given entrée by a few careful behind-the-scenes maneuvers by Fred.

Using Fred was a risk, because it linked him to his former identity. But Fred managed dozens of acts at any one time, and had hundreds in his résumé. Taking on another client set off no alarms. Without Fred, the goal would not have been approachable. Otherwise Vic used none of his old colleagues, and only two of the new crew—his sound man and his chief roadie—were added to the list of those who knew the real history behind Vic Standish, again because the scheme would fail without their assistance.

And here he was. Victory's first album had gone nowhere, but the band had gained a touring reputation. The second album contained a hit single. Then the third went platinum, and now the fourth was into the stratosphere.

The success was the biggest surprise. All Vic had cared about was having the chance to get out there in front of a few thousand fans. If he had dreamed it would get this big—still not as big as his heyday as Brad Taylor, but huge by objective standards—he might have reconsidered the whole project, because it exposed him to the risk of discovery.

But the fact was, no crazed fan had gunned down a rock 'n' roll star in over a decade. The fad, Lord be praised, seemed to have gone the way of all fads. Or maybe, thought Vic, shutting off the hotel-room TV and tucking the folded clipping into his valise, it was just his own paranoia that had gone away. Not that he didn't have his roadies observe heavy security precautions, but in hindsight his reaction to the events of December 8, 1980, seemed . . . excessive. Perhaps he'd been snorting too much coke.

He was clean now. He was clear-eyed. And he might not have enough excuses for denying the wish of a dying friend.

"God damn you, Andy," Vic muttered.

Finally his eyelids were getting heavy. He undressed, shut out the lights, and listened to the rain batter at the window. Tuesday was the gig in Amsterdam. Best not to think beyond that. One hurdle at a time.

Empty seats dotted the rear of the upper level. Judging by album sales, the Dutch fans were as loyal as those elsewhere, but it was a Tuesday night and sleet was falling. Vic breathed a small sigh of relief. As proven so recently, a capacity crowd generated a peculiar energy that was difficult to control. Here, the vacancies left echoes and reduced the hubbub from the drone of a hornet's nest to that of a few honey bees dancing between peach blossoms.

The concert hall was also smaller than the stadiums Victory played on its weekend stops. The venue reeked of hashish; the haze was so thick it dimmed the glow of the exit signs. The members of the band stepped gingerly across the darkened stage to claim their instruments. Dim blue, violet, and green spotlights roamed across the crowd, gradually shifting toward warmer colors of greater intensity as they prepared to converge where Vic waited on a dais in front of the huge array of drums.

Already the Amsterdam denizens were proving how little like the Berlin horde they were. Women stood and flashed their tits, knowing this was the one time when Vic could see clearly out into the galleries. Nearly half the attendees had long hair. Some wore tie-dye shirts. He was sure he even saw one or two middle-aged types raising their fingers in the rabbit-ear symbol for peace: God, how long had it been since he'd seen *that?*

The beams struck him. The lead guitarist launched into the screaming opening chord of the title song from the group's third CD, and Vic raised the microphone to his lips.

His deep, potent voice matched the pulse-pounding music. Victory was a kick-ass band. For the ten-thousandth time, Vic made the mental adjustment needed to recognize that the lyrics bellowing from the speakers came from his mouth. It was *not* his true voice. He was a tenor, and there was no way he would have sounded like anyone other than Brad Taylor if his head tech hadn't modified the signal coming from the microphone. Though he was singing normally, what the audience heard was an entire register lower.

The crowd clapped and stomped their feet. First song down, the band lit into its second and third. By then, Vic was puzzled, though he tried not to let it show. These people were enjoying the performance, but they were doing it in a way no Victory fans had ever done. In simplest terms, they were *non-violent*.

The distinction was subtle. It was more a feeling than an observation, because the lights in his face kept him from picking up some of the visual details. But he'd been up there in front of so many people in so many cities that he could read an audience the way another man could read the emotions of a dear lifelong friend. When they screamed, they did not have their teeth bared and the neck muscles tensed; they were smiling. When they flailed their bodies to the drumbeat, they were not shoving the people beside them; they were swaying in unison. Far fewer asses than usual were encased in black leather; instead they were tucked into faded blue denim. And some of the women were *still* topless, without converting nearby males to testosterone hyperactivity.

It doesn't fit, Vic thought. The lyrics pouring out of his mouth weren't the paeans to love, the sly political commentaries, the personal transformation odes of Brad Taylor. They were supposed to be as far removed from Brad Taylor as possible. Nowadays he sang about fast chicks, hot motorcycles, or bitchin' scenery. When composing, he couldn't avoid inserting occasional clever turns of phrase, but such flourishes were buried within a cascade of primal drums and frenetic guitars, and no one had yet made the comparison between Vic Standish and any of the peace/love/dope generation of rock lyricists. Most of his fans didn't even know what the words to the songs were. They listened for more visceral reasons.

For the sixth number, Vic pulled out a harmonica, a rare departure, like his occasional use of a tambourine, from his role as vocalist. For five years he had avoided playing guitar or keyboards in public, because those were Brad Taylor's habits, but he was thankful for the feel of an instrument in his hands now. The concert was stirring old memories at a time when he was unusually vulnerable to their effect.

In a way, it all made sense. It jibed with what he had seen on the streets of the city the previous day and a half. Amsterdam was the last bastion of the Dream—the one that went "All You Need Is Love." Here the courts did not send recreational drug users to prison for decades. Prostitution remained legalized. The society tolerated alternate lifestyles, promoted the arts, provided sex education to minors. Yet Vic caught an undertone of desperation out in the seats. The Dutch were running scared, behaving with an exaggerated sense of abandon that recalled the stories he'd heard of the decadent moments in pre-Nazi Germany right before the iron fist squeezed shut. Individuals from many nations had thronged to the city of the famous painters, coming to the one place that was withstanding the tide of repression. In this milieu the free spirits of Europe could congregate in the open.

As Vic lowered the harmonica and bellowed out the first stanza, he faltered, almost forgetting the lines. He was only half in the moment. The rest of him was free-floating, touching upon events and conclusions of the past fifteen years.

America had once given him scenes like this. Then something had happened. The pendulum swung. Reagan came into office. The Republicans won a majority in Congress and never lost it. Now Bush was wrapping up a second term and the momentum was *still* gaining toward the right. The Pentagon's budget had increased every year. Social Security was being phased out. Carriers of HIV were required to wear ID bracelets to alert the general public to their malady—a public health issue, not a personal liberty concern, according to the new surgeon general. Abortion was illegal again in eighteen states.

Vic's stomach lurched. His knees went watery. What was it Andy had said about responsibility? Surely the period of hope between '65 and '80 was nothing over which he had control. People talked about the Beatles fueling societal change. They quoted lines from Brad Taylor and Bob Dylan. Sometimes they even threw into the mix the Doors and the Eagles, Jackson Browne and Crosby, Stills, & Nash. But that was all horseshit. No one had that kind of power.

Or did they? Vic Standish was worried. He looked back and saw a cusp point. The spirit of the sixties had faltered most visibly after its leading balladeers were cut down. Not until Lennon was taken out did the metamorphosis settle in, and then . . .

The heavy metal noise surrounding him turned sour to his ears. Not because it was bad music, or badly played—quite the contrary—but because it wasn't *him*. And because it symbolized a personal cowardice. He was envisioning a world in which he hadn't run for cover. What if he had contributed to the tide of events? What if his faked murder had set up the streak? With Lennon gone, then him, was that enough to establish the fad of offing rock stars? Was that what had given that series of deranged lunatics the confidence to go after Dylan, Donovan, and McCartney?

Absently he waved to the crowd. They cheered in spite of his wobbly performance of the last song. Did they see something in him that he didn't? Vic Standish was a fantasy, not a true identity at all. If they could cling to their faith in him in the face of a lie, who knew how much more could be birthed by the truth?

He fell back into his music, astir with a thousand thoughts. The songs were the same that Victory always played. He couldn't change that yet. But December the 8th was only three days away.

London. Wembley was nearly sold out. Half an hour before the show, Vic peeked out as ticket-holders gravitated toward their assigned seats, many of them finding their places with a restrained, funeral pace. This wasn't Berlin, and it wasn't Amsterdam. These were the citizens of the country which had given life to John Lennon, and this was the anniversary of his death. Any rock event—heavy metal or not—

that took place on December 8th carried a unique sort of emotional baggage.

Through binoculars, Vic saw fans running their fingers along their souvenir programs, noting the black trim. Only the very youngest attendees needed an explanation. All knew whose life and passing was being commemorated, though there was no indication that the accent had been added at Vic's instructions.

Vic was thankful only one death need be mourned. He was still worrying about Andy, no matter that the latter had assured him in a phone call that afternoon that he was doing well and yes, the odds of being able to host his New Year's party were still in his favor.

It was bad to be losing a friend, but it would be far worse if Vic lost this one before the month was out. The concert tonight was being recorded for a Christmas pay-for-view broadcast. This would be the one show of the tour that Vic's old bandmate might have a chance to attend, if only in the remote sense.

He counted down the minutes, conscious of each breath. Finally the moment came to step on stage.

The video cameras served as a wake-up call for musicians already riding a high. Victory pushed the envelope of its talent. Vic paced himself, maintaining the structure he wanted of the evening, openly asking the listeners to clap or sing along at precisely the places he wished them to. The crowd, dutiful as the English could be, let themselves be wooed, all without losing their boisterousness. Vic was in sync with his listeners in a way he hadn't been since the last full-scale tour Brad Taylor had mounted in 1974, before Andy and a couple of his other long-term sidemen had gone their own way. Or maybe it was earlier still—perhaps since that fund-raiser for peace in '72, the last time he had tried to make a concert more than just a musical event.

After nearly two hours, the lights went down. The roar from the seats was deafening even to ears shielded to protect them from the Pete Townshend syndrome. Vic and his mates walked off. Everyone knew they'd be back—Victory always did an encore of three songs.

"Still planning a surprise?" Lenny asked Vic in the tunnel backstage. In the stadium the cheers were turning into a chant: *Victory! Victory!*

"Yes," Vic said. "I'll give you the signal."

Even his colleagues didn't know what was coming down. Vic wasn't sure anything was. He was proceeding step-by-step. When the moment arrived, he might let it pass. Fighting the inertia of years was not a simple thing.

After the appropriate pause, before the fans became impatient, the band marched back onstage. The lights rose and Victory sailed into a high-energy rendition of their first hit, the song that had led the encore at every stop of the tour.

Anticipation rose. Sweat trickled down Vic's back. Hands reached for him, held back by the height of the stage and by the bouncers. Faces glowed. The third song, they all knew, was supposed to be Victory's new single. It had just gone to number one and was the most popular piece the band could offer at that particular time and place. They had not played it so far that night.

The second song ended. The sweat on Vic's body turned arctic. The plan now was *not* to follow with the expected song, but he saw that to deviate from expectations would be a mistake. Were he to defy the crowd that way, they would turn on him. He had to give them what they wanted, earn their gratitude.

He nodded to his bassist, and led off with the wild-man scream of the number one song. The crowd raved, able at last to reach the climax of their adoration. Vic shuddered, realizing how close he had come to fucking up. Now, more than ever, the Wembley faithful were with him.

The band stretched out the four-minute piece to six, repeating the chorus until the steel beams of the structure groaned from the decibel level.

The lights went down. The crowd cheered and held up cigarette lighters and burning matches, calling for another encore for the sake of form, even though they knew Victory didn't do second encores. A few practical souls made an early break for the exits.

A single, wide spotlight came back up. There was Vic, all alone on the stage. He held a guitar.

"Wait," he said softly, the amplified voice barely audible over the buzz.

The tumult gradually tapered off, if only because no one knew what to expect. Vic Standish didn't do solos. He didn't play guitar. And if he did, it wouldn't be an acoustic instrument with those strangely familiar gold frets and pearl white face, monogramed with an elegant "B.T." One by one the people sat and waited, murmuring among themselves.

"I would like to share something with you," Vic said. Methodically, he lifted his wig from his head, put his contact lenses in their case, and placed a pair of granny glasses on his nose.

A handful of people among the crowd gasped as the gigantic viewscreen behind the stage lit up with a close-up of Vic's face, showing a heavyset, worn, balding version of a legend thought deceased. They paused, stunned, as Vic arranged microphones near his mouth and near his guitar strings—a different mike arrangement than he used as the front man of Victory.

The first soft notes flowed from his guitar. Utter silence fell over the crowd. They waited for the fourth measure when, if this were the song it sounded like, the vocal would begin. Exactly on cue, Vic opened his mouth.

He sang clearly, on-key, using the arrangement made famous in the original 1969 recording. His timbre had changed a little in twenty-six years, but there was no question whose voice it was.

The crowd began to stir as more and more people figured it out. The rumble was low and pregnant with meaning, as if everyone wanted to speak at once, but no one dared shout for fear of drowning out the anthem coming from the stage.

Vic reached the second chorus. A drum joined in, along with base and rhythm guitars—gently, as befitted the tune. Startled, Vic glanced behind him and found his bandmates in their places. They had never rehearsed the song with him, and had no warning he would bring it out tonight, but no player of rock 'n' roll, from the most acidic punkrocker to the schmaltziest Barry Manilow clone, hadn't learned the piece at one time or another in their garage band days. Vic grinned, and fell back into the song with renewed inspiration.

By the third and final chorus, the audience joined in. The voices, in a harmony rare for such a huge group of singers, mounted to a choir-like holiness, speaking of love and imagination and hope for the future. Vic—Brad—was thrust back to the era when he had composed the lyrics, back to a moment when he bled a drop of himself into every syllable.

The words were a kind of worship, but not the mundane syco-phancy of fans toward a celebrity. Brad had never written them to make the world love him, but to show the world the beauty of itself. It was *his* worship of All That Out There.

The occupants of Wembley understood. They were on their feet, some hugging each other, some calling, "Brad! Brad!" Some praying, some shaking their heads—not in disbelief at what they were seeing down there on the stage now, or at what they were feeling in their hearts, but in wry self-reflection on what they had believed up to this point.

The euphoria spread. Brad could sense it washing out into London, over the island, skimming the English Channel and, in the other direc-tion, gathering into a wave that would crash across the entire width of the Atlantic Ocean. It was not an illusion. It was a living force.

Out there, somewhere, a pendulum began to lag, no longer swing-ing unchecked. A tide was turning.

Brad caressed his guitar, letting the music flow from it, from him. He was no longer confused about his role or his identity. The choice was simple. The world needed a dreamer with a voice. He would serve as best he could.

Expert Advice

LARRY BOND

Larry Bond's first novel was a coauthorship with Tom Clancy,
Red Storm Rising. *Since then his name has hardly ever been
absent from bestseller lists around the country and, indeed, the
world.*

*When Larry was asked to be in this collection, he modestly
countered that he had only once before published a short story,
but that he'd give it his best shot.*

*He has fired right on target with this piece of military sleight-
of-hand which uses the fact that, in warfare as in magic, one of
the best weapons is the element of surprise. While the US cre-
ates the illusion that they are operating by the book, the plan
they actually put into effect is uncharacteristic—and deadly.*

—DC

Expert Advice

THE BLACK-AND-WHITE PHOTO was fuzzy, grainy, and poorly composed. Its appearance wasn't helped by being projected on a six-foot-wide screen at the end of the theater. It showed a group of men in baggy, drab uniforms on a bare, rocky hillside.

The man in the center of the photo was instantly recognizable. Round-faced, with a thick dark mustache, his face almost a caricature of itself, Saddam Hussein was surrounded by a cluster of uniformed men. It was obvious, even in this poor-quality picture, that one of the men was not Arabic.

The briefer, Colonel Frank Dolan, referred often to an analysis of the photo. Almost ten pages long, it verified the authenticity of the image without compromising its source, parameterized the date, speculated on the reason for the gathering (watching armored exercises outside Baghdad), and most importantly, identified the individuals in the photo.

Dolan was "Deputy J-2 for the Joint Chiefs of Staff," a complex title that meant he was the number-two man to the Intelligence chief for the Joint Chiefs, a body made up of the highest-ranking member of each of the armed services. Tall for a fighter pilot, Dolan brought the same energy to his job that he did to flying.

Dolan was finishing a very early morning brief to his boss, who would shortly have to go in and brief the Joint Chiefs themselves. The briefing theater, deep inside the Pentagon, was a well-appointed room, long with rows of leather seats facing one narrow end, where the screen was mounted. Dark wood paneling was softened by a dark blue rug and matching drapes that absorbed sound. Color was provided by dozens of unit plaques that covered one long wall. An aisle down the middle led to the podium where Dolan now stood. Other members of the staff occupied some of the back chairs, but the object of the brief sat in the front row.

General Mike O'Neill, the J-2 himself, listened to Dolan with a sour expression. He wasn't happy.

"Is there any doubt in your mind that it's Connor?" demanded O'Neill.

"I've redone most of CIA's analysis myself, sir. Everything checks. The liaison to CIA said they'd even shown the photo to Connor's ex-wife, and she'd confirmed it."

O'Neill nodded reluctantly. "I was hoping you'd found a flaw somewhere, but hell, I recognize him. I knew him over in Saudi during Desert Storm."

The general was an army officer, a tanker, short and compact, with black hair cut short in defiance of a receding hairline. He'd commanded an armored division in the Persian Gulf, where Connor had been one of his company commanders.

Captain Harry Connor was a strapping ex–football player, an intelligent and competent officer. The problem was, Connor thought he was brilliant, George Patton and Stonewall Jackson reborn in a single body.

He'd actually received a medal in the Gulf, the Army Commendation Medal for a short, vicious action with a Republican Guard unit. Hundreds of others had also received the same decoration, and there were many higher awards.

That didn't matter to Connor. He'd played it up to the hilt, claiming that his decoration entitled him to special promotions, the pick of assignments, and general adulation from anyone in earshot. It hadn't, of course, and his attitude had reflected that.

The downsizing that swept through the armed forces had no sympathy for Harry Connor's injured feelings and he'd found himself out on the street. "The army got a little better that day," mused O'Neill.

There was no official record of his movements after that. Investigators, picking over a cold trail a year later, talked to old friends (few) and family members. They all described the same man—angry with a service and a country that he felt had betrayed him. Connor had described himself as "a war hero destined for a general's stars," according to his older brother.

Six months after his discharge he'd drawn his few savings from the bank, sold his car, pawned a few belongings, and borrowed some cash from his family. He'd bought a plane ticket to Rome. The first sign of his intentions might have been a clumsy attempt to falsify his identity.

Although his passport read "Harry G. Connor," the ticket was made out to "Andy F. Connor."

The CIA in Rome was still trying to trace Connor's movements there, but the next time there'd been any word of him was a rumor of an American near the Turkish border. Repeated and retold until it was picked up by a US agent in Ankara, it simply told of an American accompanying an Iraqi unit in the northern part of the country. It hadn't been linked to Connor until much later, and even then it was just supposition, but subsequent events seemed to confirm it.

This embittered army officer had apparently sold his services to his former enemy, and was advising and training Iraqi troops. There were only a handful of sightings, but each placed him higher and higher in the military and political hierarchy. The latest sighting, the photo they were all staring at, seemed to show Connor at the side of Saddam Hussein himself.

The American wore an Iraqi-style uniform, even a beret like his new master's. He held a pair of binoculars in one hand and pointed ahead of the party, presumably toward the exercising troops.

The most chilling thing to Dolan, O'Neill, and to everyone who had seen it was that Connor was talking, possibly explaining or commenting, and Saddam Hussein was giving Connor his complete attention. His hands were clasped behind his back, his body half-turned to the American, and his attention fixed on Connor's words.

How long had Connor had his ear? What was Connor telling him? Almost certainly the "American" way of war. How to train his soldiers, how to build a competent staff. How to organize logistical support. Was Saddam listening?

Harry Connor thought so. He hadn't known his picture was being taken that day outside Baghdad, but if he had, he'd have asked for an eight-by-ten glossy to put on the wall.

Connor often remembered that day, almost six months ago, the first exercise of a brigade trained according to his recommendations, and Saddam watching its every move. The brigade, a first-line armored unit, had started out for one objective, but at the first phase line had received a surprise change in orders. With no confusion, the brigade had steamrollered over the Republican Guard unit acting as the "enemy."

After that, Connor had been on the gravy train. He'd moved into a big office in the presidential palace, he had weekly, sometimes daily meetings with the Man himself, and Iraqi generals took their marching orders from him, ex-Captain Harry G. Connor, ex–US Army. Saddam was still being a little vague about the rank, but had promised him at least a colonelcy, and swift promotion after that.

Connor smiled at the thought of his elevated position, his rapid advancement. How long would those know-nothings in the army have sat on him, holding him back because he hadn't spent enough time polishing the CO's brass? It had taken two, almost three years of hard work to get to this office, but back in the States he'd be a major at most.

He'd never liked the army, he decided. He liked the work, and he loved combat. It was his chance to shine. He was good at his job, but too good for the system. In a way, it had been the best move he could make to leave the army. It had freed him up for this job, with the money and rank he'd always deserved.

Connor had seen the opportunity, and taken it. He knew Saddam Hussein. The Iraqi president was an impatient, violent man. He believed in the simplest solution to a problem. During the war with Iran he'd tried to buy sophisticated weapons, spending money like water to upgrade his armed forces' capabilities and ensure a quick victory over Iran.

It hadn't worked, of course, because Hussein neglected other details, like training and planning. A ruinous decade-long war had left him with nothing more than a ruined generation and a mountain of debts.

He'd tried to solve the debt problem like the war. Rather than pay back the banker, Kuwait, he'd just invaded the country. That hadn't worked either, the only results being more deaths and more debts.

Connor understood impatience. He also understood Saddam's need for revenge against the United States. He'd shown up a little over three years ago, offering his services to the Iraqi government as an independent advisor. Although he'd posed as an English mercenary, the Iraqis had quickly penetrated his legend, and seemed happier in the knowledge they were being advised by an old enemy.

Connor was the perfect solution to Saddam's problems. He was apolitical, interested only in coin, hated the United States, and seemed to have the answers Saddam's army needed. Mixing ex-Soviet doctrine with Western tactics, he'd shown a keen sensitivity to Hussein's need for political control.

Now he sat in a fancy office behind a desk that cost more than he'd made as a lieutenant. Photos of himself with Saddam and other Iraqi generals covered one wall, and a two-foot model of a T-72 sat on a side table, guarding a pile of operations orders he was reviewing.

Those op orders brought another smile to his face. They were the fruit of seeds he'd planted months ago, the result of Saddam's growing confidence in him and the Iraqi armed forces. Connor had always hated paperwork, but this batch of paper was the answer to his prayers. He'd show the US Army what he was capable of. He'd show them what they'd lost. Very soon.

General O'Neill faced the Joint Chiefs of Staff and wrestled with the age-old dilemma of the intelligence officer. Like a seer, these men expected him to tell them what was in the enemy's heart and predict the enemy's next move. Well, he'd left his Ouija board in his other suit.

The Iraqi Army was on the move. Several armored units had left their garrisons and were moving south. The Iraqi Air Force, still not recovered from their pasting in Desert Storm, was also moving south, consolidating at airfields in the southern half of the country. He'd laid out a lot of information. Some of it raw, some heavily processed and analyzed. It was a good brief, with as much meat as he could arrange. It just wasn't enough.

What was Saddam up to? From an analyst's point of view, it was a straight indications and warning problem. If the enemy does this and this, then he's probably getting ready to do that. For instance, if an army unit leaves garrison, but without a lot of repair or logistic support, then it's probably just a short exercise. If the enemy starts constructing trenches and bunkers, they're going on the defensive. If they start stockpiling ammunition and fuel, they're planning to attack.

This movement was still in the early stages. It could go several different ways, including the one everyone worried about: Desert Storm Round Two. These five men, though, didn't want to hear that.

They desperately needed to know if a state hostile to the United States was about to take actions harmful to their nation's interests. Time was at stake. Time was money, time was lives. Let the enemy get too far along in his plans and it would be too late to stop him. Time was also distance. Iraq was almost on the other side of the world.

The Joint Chiefs, who advised the President on matters of military policy, would shortly have to go into the Oval Office and tell the President what the Iraqis were doing, and suggest what the United States should do about it. He thought about Connor, and the photo. Connor's existence and nature were well established, and like Hussein, he was no friend of the US.

O'Neill finally summarized, "Whatever Iraq is doing, it will not be helpful to the USA, and might be very harmful. While it may be just a large exercise, it may also be the beginnings of an offensive buildup. We will not be able to tell with certainty for some time, and I would recommend that in the meantime we proceed assuming a worst case."

The CNN piece was sandwiched in after the news of a tornado in the Midwest and an investigation in Washington. The announcer read it with the mix of interest and concern that marked it as news, but not big news.

"Sources near Fort Bragg have reported that the 82nd Airborne Division has been put on low-level alert. Part of America's rapid-reaction intervention force, it would be among the first units deployed to an international trouble spot."

The announcer's face was replaced with a map of the Persian Gulf region. "This may be related to rumors of new activity inside Iraq. Department of Defense sources have hinted that the Iraqi army is showing unusual activity, but are vague as to its purpose.

"When questioned about the alert, DOD officials refused to comment, and would not say if there have been any alerts among air force or navy units. We take you now to Loren Carey, in Mountain Home, Idaho."

A line of F-15s parked on a concrete apron replaced the map. Loren Carey was a tall, dark-haired woman in her thirties, who managed to look good in an air force camouflage jacket over an expensive suit.

"Mountain Home Air Force Base is the home of the 366th Composite Wing. Made up of fighters, bombers, and special purpose aircraft, it is specially trained and equipped to be the first into any trouble spot, flying and fighting within hours of arrival."

As she described the 366th and its mission, the camera slowly panned over the ranked aircraft, the hangars, and the runways, where a scream of jet engines marked each landing or takeoff. The images conveyed an impression of great strength, but not great activity.

"Colonel Tom Arndern, operations officer of the 366th, has assured us that although they are ready to move, no special orders have been received from the Pentagon."

The camera shifted to show a square-faced, ruggedly good-looking officer, a bit shorter than Carey. He wore a camouflage jacket like Carey's over an olive-drab flight suit.

"We are always working at maintaining or improving our readiness. You can't just get ready and then be ready. It's a twenty-four-hour-a-day job."

"How quickly can you deploy, if you have to?" asked Carey.

"We can send an 'A' package, about a quarter of our strength, within six hours. We can send the whole wing, all the maintenance personnel, spare parts, communications gear, even a field hospital, within forty-eight hours. With other wings, it can take a lot longer. We are specially trained and equipped for a rapid-deployment mission."

"I know you've said you have no special orders for deployments, Colonel, but given the volatile situation in Iraq, do you expect to get word to move?"

Arndern smiled, and with just a tinge of fighter pilot drawl, replied "Ma'am, nobody knows what the future holds, and I don't try to guess."

"Thank you, Colonel."

The image shifted back to the announcer at CNN headquarters in Atlanta, and, smiling, Connor zapped the TV with his remote control.

It couldn't be better. The US was reacting exactly as one would expect. In response to unspecified actions on the part of Iraq, the JCS was increasing the readiness of its rapid-reaction units. Action and reaction. In military terms, it was called "the initiative," and right now, before the first shot was even fired, he and the Iraqis had it.

Harry Connor was well-versed in US Army, in fact, in all US armed forces doctrine and practices. He was a fast study, and the information he needed wasn't even classified.

For instance, the alert system of the 82nd Airborne was common knowledge inside the army, and was available to anyone else for the price of a phone call to the division's public affairs officer. Its exact status was supposed to be classified, but anyone who understood the army and watched CNN could make some shrewd guesses.

Connor could hardly hide his glee. The United States of America was reacting to his actions, dancing to his tune. If they loved that, they'd love his next move.

Intelligence analysts pored over satellite photos. Each one showed a bridge or road junction, natural choke points that would slow traffic and give them the best chance of catching any Iraqi military movement.

Ninety percent of the photos showed nothing but empty road or civilian traffic. The times and places of these photos were logged for later analysis, but it was the other ten percent that were the payoff.

"Look at this one," one analyst remarked. Displayed on a large-screen color monitor was a line of rectangular blobs, each with a small round blob on top. Other shapes were less regular, but each held meaning. He pointed to the head of the column, then counted back along its length. "I see forty-seven tanks, with trucks and support vehicles. Discounting a few that probably broke down, this is the book strength of an Iraqi armored battalion."

Other photos showed the tail ends of columns or the heads, but they could still give valuable information in patterns and directions of movement, traffic flow, and other military information. Of the dozens of photos that showed equipment, there were three clear shots that showed an entire convoy. The evidence was there. The Iraqis were moving south in real strength. It was no longer a rumor.

Scooping up prints of the three best images, the editor headed for the door. Behind him, the team turned back to their work. There'd be another batch of photos coming from SPOT in an hour.

The *Times* ran it as a front-page story. "Iraq Masses for Second Invasion." There was nothing tentative or qualified in the article's analysis of the situation. Backed up by the commercial satellite shots, it described an army on the move. It did not speculate on other possible reasons for the movement, or whether the troops' movements were supported by logistics and other preparations, but it made its point.

Colonel Frank Dolan thought the article was clean, concise, and far beyond the expertise of most newspaper reporters. It wasn't up to J-2 standards, of course, but he had an edge in experienced staff and better raw material.

Dolan held up the paper, folded so that the front page showed one of the three photos. He held a glossy printout next to it, which coincidentally showed the same bridge, although about an hour later. About half the convoy was across in his, which was much sharper. Among other things, the two photos together helped him measure the efficiency of Iraqi traffic control, but that was minor.

Dolan was going to go into the briefing theater in a few minutes and agree with the *Times* article, much as it galled him to be scooped by a newspaper. He and his staff had identified elements of ten divisions now beginning to move south.

A buildup by a hostile state was worrisome, of course, but what concerned Dolan more than that was the pattern of the buildup. Construction equipment had been busy at several southern logistics dumps, and maintenance crews were repairing roads near the border as well. There were things any Western planner would do as a matter of course. In fact, they were things the Coalition forces had done in Desert Storm. Now they were being practiced by an enemy.

Dolan scratched his chin thoughtfully. Had Saddam learned a lesson from his enemy? Possible, but not likely. Was Connor helping him with his planning? Also possible, and scary. *That bastard was going to cost us some lives.*

General Andrews's brief was succinct and to the point. "We have classic indications of an Iraqi buildup near the Kuwaiti border. Along with satellite photos, there is increased radio traffic, increased aerial activity, and," nodding toward a CIA liaison in the corner of the room, "reservists are being recalled to active duty.

"Based on their present rate of buildup, which is well planned and deliberate, they will be able to launch an offensive with one division in a week." Nobody in the JCS thought that was a real possibility, but as a threat, it could not be ignored. The real problem came later. Dolan continued, "In two weeks, they'll have three divisions, in four weeks, they'll have ten, all first-line.

"It is also my opinion that Harry Connor has taken an active role in planning this operation. There is no reason to assume that he has not assisted in the offensive planning as well."

Jason Thomas, a four-star general and chairman of the Joint Chiefs, had listened to Andrews's brief impatiently, fidgeting with the newspaper in front of him. He'd received nothing but bad news, and now political pressure was forcing them to act openly.

In other situations, a buildup on one side had been matched by a quiet buildup by the United States. If a dictator realized that he was going to be opposed, or could not get the overwhelming edge most bully states needed to win, he often slunk away, his forces going back to garrison. Many US exercises were designed to show hostile governments that we could get to a distant trouble spot quickly when we needed to.

Now the quiet buildup would become a public confrontation. Congressmen, invoking the "will of the voters," wanted to know why the Pentagon hadn't acted.

Well, now they had to act. Thomas sighed tiredly. "All right. I'll recommend to the president that we send the ready brigade of the 82nd and the 366th immediately, and that we prepare for a general deployment to Kuwait."

He looked around the room. "Gentlemen. It looks like we might have to do it again."

As the meeting broke up, Thomas pulled his Intelligence chief aside. "Mike, I want to see everything you've got on Harry Connor. See if we can get the FBI or someone to do some more digging as well. We've got to know what he knows, and we've got to shut him down."

Connor and his Iraqi aide toured the logistics base. One of many dotting the southern part of Iraq, it was organized using a blend of Iraqi, Soviet, and Western techniques. Most importantly, it was built to resemble a complex of commercial-style warehouses near a new factory. Stocked slowly over many months, it contained enough ammunition, fuel, and spare parts to supply a brigade for a week in the field. A new rail terminal, which would be finished in a few days, supposedly served the factory, but would also allow rapid resupply of the depot.

Activity had just started at the other, established supply dumps. The feverish buildup there would be photographed and documented by American satellites, but Connor himself had chosen these sites. While not an intelligence analyst, he knew that if the site didn't look like a supply dump, and if shipments to it were made when satellites weren't overhead, the chances of it being spotted were very small. Iraq is a big country. Instead, watching the known dumps, the Pentagon would get one of the many "signatures" of a future offensive.

Much of the Pentagon's assessment of the Iraqi Army's readiness for an offensive would be based on the level of its supply dumps. A general may be a great tactician, but logistics makes it possible for him to be on the battlefield and lets him stay there. A tank can only go a few hundred miles before it needs more fuel, and it can burn through its ammunition in one battle. Getting that tank resupplied keeps a successful battle from turning into a failed offensive.

Although the old, well-known dumps were half-empty, these hidden dumps were all fully stocked. To the Americans, the units heading south were hobbled until their logistical support built up. Instead, each Iraqi formation was ready to go the moment it reached the border, a cocked pistol pointed at Kuwait, Saudi Arabia, and at America.

Bravo Three Nine loafed along at an easy four hundred knots at twenty-five thousand feet. Randy McCall, the command pilot, grumbled to himself that an RC-135 certainly didn't tax his flying skills. Of course, the RC-135 had actually started out life an Air Force C-135 cargo plane, and the C-135 was nothing more than a militarized Boeing 707 airliner.

A few changes had been made, though. The airline passenger seats had been replaced by tons of electronic equipment, computers, generators to power it, and air conditioners to keep it all cool. The fuselage's clean lines were marred by a forest of antennas, each designed to pick up a particular brand of electromagnetic energy . . . energy like radar beams, and radio and microwave communications signals.

It also carried very precise navigation equipment. The GPS receiver was one of the plane's most heavily used instruments. Especially near the Iraqi border, it paid to know *exactly* where you were. Right now they were skirting the Iraqi border.

Bravo Three Nine was a spy plane, pure and simple. Like an eavesdropper listening at the enemy general's tent, it recorded countless hours of radio transmissions. It plotted the location and type of any radars it detected.

The radar data was more immediately useful, since it simply had to be plotted on a map as part of the Iraqi defense net. The communications tapes had to be translated, sifted, and analyzed. A lot of the good stuff was in code, McCall knew. Maybe we could read their mail, maybe not, he thought, but even the pattern of communications was useful. "Traffic Analysis" had been a useful tool back as far as WW II. With computers, McCall was sure the analysts drained those tapes dry.

The nav system alerted him to an upcoming waypoint. He'd make a one-eighty turn in sixty seconds. Slow and smooth, so as not to ruffle the techs in the back, it would set them up on another leg.

McCall knew it was important, maybe even vital work. It was still boring.

Dolan's brief to O'Neill and Thomas was concise and convincing. "Connor has had an effect, and a rather thorough one, throughout the Iraqi armed forces. You can't really see it in the line units, but the organization of several Republican Guard divisions has been standardized and altered. Command and control relationships have been improved as well. We are seeing more sophisticated radio networks, more flexible than the Russian pattern. I really don't think Saddam could have come up with this stuff on his own."

Dolan leaned forward to emphasize his point. "All the changes have been to more Western, and in some cases, clearly American lines. The high command's comm system is almost a duplicate of the one used by Schwarzkopf in Desert Storm."

He passed a satellite photo to the two men. "This shows a reorganized Republican Guard division in garrison two weeks ago. It's one of the ones that's now moved near the border with Kuwait. The maintenance units use exactly the same number of trucks, workshop vehicles, and so on as a US armored division. This is completely new and very atypical for an Iraqi unit. One of the reasons why only a few units have been changed to this organization is that they had to strip the rest of the Iraqi Army to get the gear they needed."

Dolan passed a packet of material covered with classification stickers and intelligence warnings to Thomas. "This is everything we've been able to collect on Connor and his influence on the Iraqis. There are definite patterns here. He's the wild card—or better yet, a trump card, and the Iraqis are playing it. We've gotta stop him."

The president's face looked grave. Unhappy and doing his best to look even unhappier, he stood in the East Wing, along with the secretary of defense and the chairman of the Joint Chief of Staff. The secretary of state was in Kuwait.

"My fellow Americans, the price of freedom is eternal vigilance. In spite of our best efforts at deterring a tyrant, it appears that he is planning another attempt to violate the sovereign territory of a neighboring country.

"Strong Iraqi forces have moved south in the past few weeks, and there is evidence," he asserted, nodding toward the secretary and the chairman, "that this is much more than an exercise.

"At the request of the Kuwaiti government, I have today ordered the Pentagon to deploy whatever forces they think are necessary to protect the sovereignty of that country and vital US interests in the region. Under the name DESERT RAMPART, American and other allied troops will deploy to Kuwait and assist in its defense. General Thomas will now provide you with a general overview of the operation."

The television in Hussein's office carried the press conference live, subtitled in Arabic. As Thomas pointed to the map and listed units, Connor tried to pay attention, and at the same time answer Saddam Hussein's questions. There was an urgent, impatient streak to the general that would not go away.

They sat in the President's opulent office, surrounded by "battle trophies" and symbols of his office, along with the Iraqi general staff, all political toadies without a shred of initiative. Now, at the moment when the operation seemed ready to succeed, Hussein wanted to throw it away and move on impulse.

Hussein stood in front of a map of the area, affecting a strategic air as he studied the border. "They are weak and we are ready to strike now! You said so yourself, Connor. We will attack now!"

"With only one corps, Mr. President?" Connor tried to control the emotion in his voice. Everything he dreamed of would be ruined.

"We can't hold Kuwait with a force of that size. All we'll do is repeat past events." He carefully skirted any direct mention of the previous invasion of Kuwait, or Desert Storm. Such references would have to bring up the failure of an operation planned by Hussein himself.

"That corps was trained by you, Connor, and you have said it is a match for anything the Americans have."

"Not if the Americans are allowed to build up in Saudi Arabia as they did last time, and then launch a set-piece attack. The crux of this plan is that they are allowed to deploy forward. Political and tactical considerations will converge and they will deploy into Kuwait, the ostensible target of our forces."

He paused, then looked around the room. They were quiet, and watching him. He had them.

"The Americans will deploy into Kuwait, in close proximity to the border and our forces. They are in a hurry, and will rush light, mobile forces like the 82nd and the 101st into the region. The heavy units, with tanks and APCs, will take longer. In fact, we know exactly how long it took last time." He looked around trying to take them all in. A few were nodding.

"They will be vulnerable, but will accept that chance, because their intelligence tells them we are not yet finished with our preparations." He smiled.

"According to our intelligence, the alert brigades of the 82nd and the 101st Airborne are loading now, and should be arriving in Saudi Arabia and Kuwait sometime tomorrow. The lead elements will be at the border forty-eight hours after that, and the two brigades should be finished deploying two days after that.

"That's when we have them!" Connor's grin was predatory, and infectious. He stood before Hussein, like a lawyer arguing his case.

"Think about it. Two lightly defended brigades, frantically digging in, setting up communications, trying to establish themselves in a strange place. I know how and when the brigades will deploy, how long it will take to perform each task. Spies at the airfields, the docks, and among the population can also track their progress."

His voice became even more intense, more enthusiastic. "Three days from now, before either brigade is completely deployed, there will still be about two-thirds of each one up, but not fully dug in.

After midnight, when the men who can are asleep and the rest of them are tired from days without sleep, we will hit them with a reinforced corps . . . four armored divisions, in a set-piece attack, supported by aircraft and artillery.

"It'll be a bloodbath! There will be hundreds killed, three times that in wounded, and many, many prisoners. Our corps then withdraws back across the border and digs in. After a defeat like that, the US may abandon Kuwait. We will claim it was a preemptive strike, forestalling another American invasion of Iraq.

"At a minimum, it will take a lot of time for the US to reorganize and then carefully build up. By that time, we will have finished massing the forces we need not only to take Kuwait, but Saudi Arabia as well."

He paused. "If they are willing to fight us at all." His voice addressed them all, but his eyes were aimed at Hussein. "None of you have an appreciation for the power of public opinion in the United States. A disaster like this will paralyze the US government and give you a free hand. Iraq will have punished the United States for its aggressions, and you will have shown yourself to be the kind of leader the entire Arab world needs."

Connor looked at Hussein. The president was nodding, slowly, thoughtfully rubbing his chin, but smiling. The American relaxed a little, inside. Saddam just needed to be reminded of the plan, he thought.

"All right, we will wait." Hussein's decision let a wave of relief flow through the American. He should have more confidence in his skills, he chided himself. He had had to run through the plan with Hussein every few days, keeping him focused. Well, he wouldn't have to do that much more. Events were in motion.

The CNN anchor looked different in a khaki jacket, outside in the desert air instead of in his high-tech Atlanta studio. His backdrop was the massive gray side of a transport plane, so big that the camera could only capture the front third of the fuselage and a bit of wing.

The scream of jet engines was a possible interference, but it was also "color" and gave an air of urgency to his report.

"I'm Jan Moore, and I'm at an undisclosed airport somewhere in Kuwait. Jet transports like the one you see behind me have been landing every few minutes since last night, although we have only been here since dawn. The area is crammed with troops, all collecting equipment and moving out in small convoys.

"I'm not allowed to identify the units here or their destination, except that these are part of the American reaction force operating as part of DESERT RAMPART. The men we approached were all in a terrible hurry, but seemed motivated and ready for battle. They were not pleased about being here, but seemed to accept the need. To a man, they all expressed a desire to 'do the job right this time.'

"This is Jan Moore, for CNN."

Frank Dolan took a gulp of lukewarm coffee, more out of habit than any hope it would actually keep him awake. His only comfort, and in fact a great comfort, was Mike Andrews's face across the table, eyes as red as his.

They were both in one of the most secure spaces in the Pentagon. The steel-walled room, an intelligence center in the basement of the Pentagon, held more secrets than Dolan cared to think about. The center's staff had been working for hours with the two men, running down leads, making up statistical summaries.

The results of their efforts lay half-formed between the two officers, a pile of photos and computer printouts competing with an empty pizza box.

The air-conditioned, fluorescent-lit room was literally lined with steel to prevent electronic eavesdropping. It was not a comfortable place to think, but Dolan knew that if he went anyplace comfortable, he'd probably go to sleep.

Their first hint had been, as Dolan suspected, logistics. Since the supplies were an important means of measuring the readiness of Iraqi units, the two had decided to look at the production and import of military stores. There wasn't that much in the supply dumps, so if they knew the production capacity of the munitions factories and such, they'd be able to figure how long it would take to produce what Hussein needed to launch an attack.

Those figures were available, but didn't jibe. The factories were going full blast, but there weren't enough of them to fill the dumps in less than a few months. Why move units up now if they wouldn't be ready to attack? Cheaper and safer to keep them in garrison.

Maybe there's a lot in transit, they thought, so the two had spent hours studying the rail net. Photos and computer analysis had been backed up by a late-night call to a government transportation expert.

There'd been a lot of construction. That was only to be expected; they were still repairing damage from Desert Storm. In addition, though, a lot of new tracks were being constructed, much heavier than would be expected. Small factories, ones whose output would not normally need a dedicated railhead.

Neither man noticed it until the third one cropped up—all in the south. Way south. "See how many there are," said O'Neill.

According to the printout, about seventy percent of the Iraqi rail system was covered by photos less than a month old. The US spent a lot of time and effort watching its old enemy. In all, they found seven new railheads, all near factories, all in the south. The photos, when compared with older images, usually showed other construction, usually warehouses.

It was five in the morning when they'd run it down as far as they could. "Let's go up to my office and get cleaned up," O'Neill suggested. "We'll brief Thomas in half an hour."

Randy McCall rubbed the sleep from his eyes. Theoretically, they were supposed to get eight hours of crew rest between missions, but with the Iraqis kicking up so much dust, the brass were all screaming for information. He couldn't blame them.

The Incilirk, Turkey, airbase was bustling. Dozens of combat aircraft, Falcons and Eagles, had landed, and indeed were still arriving as he entered the operations building. He hadn't heard anything about it, but he was almost glad that some of the US moves weren't making it onto the evening news.

He stopped in the squadron offices long enough to grab coffee and a roll, trying to maximize the six hours of sleep he'd managed to grab since the debrief of his last mission. Dressed in a flight suit, he stepped into the briefing theater, filing past a group of Falcon drivers on their way out.

The briefing theater was a rough-finished room covered with squadron insignia and detailed maps of Turkey and the surrounding region. The rangy, sandy-haired pilot sat down in the front row, along with his co-pilot and navigator. The rest of the crew had already started their pre-flight inspection, which would last several hours. In the meantime, the plane's command crew would go over every inch of their flight plan.

"This is a special mission, even for you folks," the colonel announced. "It will be a deep penetration flight, and will concentrate on communications, although you'll be recording radar data as a matter of course. We're putting a few extra comm techs on your bird, and an Iraqi linguist. Also, one of the techs is a full colonel and will be mission commander, Randy."

McCall nodded. Having a bird colonel as a back-seat driver didn't bother him. He was nothing more than a driver anyway. A highly skilled and talented one, he mused, but he really just flew where they told him to. Many of the missions carried a ranking officer, usually an intelligence specialist, who called the shots.

The operations officer started going over the route, which penetrated several hundred kilometers into Iraqi territory. That was unusual enough to make McCall pay close attention.

It took another forty-five minutes to go over the route, radio frequencies, weather, escape and evasion procedures, and dozens of other details. One indication to McCall of the importance of the flight was the addition of two F-15s as close escort. Other combat aircraft would be sitting on the pad here at Incilirk if needed. Also, a Pave Low rescue chopper would be standing by at an advanced base near the border, if they went down.

Harry Connor trailed along a discreet distance behind Saddam Hussein. The Iraqi leader was touring an armored battalion only a few dozen kilometers from the border, and was surrounded by a cluster of officers and photographers.

It had been Connor's idea to make these inspections, but he was happy to be pushed out of the limelight. While seeing Saddam Hussein at "the front" hopefully motivated his men, Connor climbed over armored vehicles, and through his aide questioned officers on their preparations. Connor had noticed that the farther away Saddam was, the more honest and accurate their answers were. Still, it helped to have the dictator nearby, as a reminder of Connor's authority.

There was much to be done, even at this late hour. Still, these troops were light-years ahead of where they'd been a year ago, and Connor was sure that under his leadership he'd teach the Americans a lesson they'd never forget.

Hussein's chief of staff rushed over. The man was always breathless, Connor observed, as if speed were evidence of his loyalty. "He is ready to go back to Baghdad."

"All right," Connor replied, and quickly finished his discussion with an armor officer. It was not a good idea to keep Saddam Hussein waiting. By the time he trotted over to the helicopters, the two escorting gunships were already airborne, and the first machine, with Saddam in it, was just lifting off.

The Russian-built Mi-17 was uncomfortable. The helicopter carrying Hussein had been upgraded, of course, almost to the point of opulence, but this machine had little more than canvas seats and a metal map table. They were command variants rather than troop carriers, though, and carried extensive radio gear.

Connor used that table now to organize his notes and prepare for the evening briefing. He personally briefed Hussein on the status of preparations twice a day, before he retired and again in the morning. There were always problems to solve, priorities to juggle, even in a well-run army. The Iraqis presented much more of a challenge.

He was up to it. The American ordered his aide, "Get on the radio and contact the 32nd Division's chief of staff. Find out how many vehicles are down right now, and how many they'll have fixed by dawn tomorrow." The aide, an English-speaking captain, nodded and left. They'd inspected the 32nd Armored Division yesterday, and in spite of all his efforts, poor maintenance was keeping almost a quarter of the unit's tanks from being fully combat-ready. He expected the number to be much higher today.

Connor glanced at his watch. It would be sunset in an hour. They'd be back in time for prayers, then a light meal and the brief. After that, Hussein disappeared. Nobody would ever say where he was, although he could of course be reached in an emergency. Rumors abounded of families turned out of their homes in the middle of the night, or hotels finding the dictator under a false name in one of their luxury suites. It was a given that he never slept in the same place twice.

Randy McCall nervously glanced at his GPS receiver. So far its information had been perfect, but his neck was riding on it.

No airline flying this time. Bravo Three Nine was over a hundred miles inside Iraqi territory. They'd tanked just before crossing the border near Tall 'Afar. The northeast border of Iraq was mountainous, and Bravo Three Nine's route traced the valleys and passes, once in a while popping up to an altitude where their antennas could "see" the radar and radio signals. As soon as the mission commander, whose name McCall had not been told, said they had enough, McCall headed down again, fast.

"All right, Major McCall." Randy heard the colonel's voice in the headset. He didn't know much about the officer, but he'd bet money he'd been born west of Amarillo. "This time we're staying high. Climb to two five thousand and head for waypoint one eight alpha."

"Roger," was the only answer McCall could give, but a chill on the back of his neck threatened to move down and take over his spine and the rest of his body. Iraq's air defense system would have no trouble picking up the large, slow, intensely vulnerable reconnaissance plane.

As he climbed and turned to the new course, he saw that it was to the northwest, away from Baghdad, but nowhere fast enough to suit him.

In the back of the plane, the colonel and mission commander turned to his communications officer. "Call Hightower. Tell them we have a positive detection on the target. Confirmed at site Alpha." The lieutenant nodded and picked up the scramble headset. "Hightower" was the call sign to the Joint Chiefs' comm center at the Pentagon.

In Hussein's Baghdad command bunker, Harry Connor was just about to begin his brief. His aide came running up with the figures for the 32nd Division. "Just in time," muttered the American. Scribbling, he handed the officer a new list. "Here, we need counts on these items from all the logistics bases. Try and have some of them by the end of the brief," he demanded.

Obviously dismayed but nodding silently, the Iraqi captain sped off.

Connor hurriedly finished his preparations as the last of the Iraqi generals filed into the room. As Connor had been doing for the past two weeks, he was about to brief Saddam Hussein and the Iraqi general staff on the status of the plan. Normally this would be handled by Saddam's own chief of staff, but that general, nothing more than a political appointee, was more than willing to let Connor get all the attention. They were all convinced Connor's plan would fail, and wanted no part of the blame when it did.

The American opened his mouth to begin when Saddam Hussein motioned for him to wait. He called over an officer, who handed him a small box. The dictator stood.

"Harry Connor, you have lived and worked among us for a long time now. You have shared your skills with us, and you have shown in many ways your loyalty and devotion to our cause. As we prepare to strike at our enemy again, it is only right that we show our appreciation and trust in you."

Connor didn't quite believe what was happening, but as Hussein approached, he snapped to attention.

The Iraqi president stopped in front of Connor and opened a small box. Inside were the insignia of an Iraqi general. Connor stood speechless as Hussein pinned the small stars on his shoulder tabs, and everyone applauded.

The warm glow of congratulation was suddenly interrupted by a buzzing alarm. An aide picked up a phone, listened for a moment, then relayed, "An aircraft has been detected a hundred and fifty miles north of the city. It is at high altitude."

Memories of the Coalition's air attacks were still very fresh in everyone's mind, and for a moment Connor thought they were all going to bolt from the room. Where, Connor wasn't sure. The bunker, rebuilt after Desert Storm, was four stories down, and protected by almost as much steel and concrete as Cheyenne Mountain.

All eyes were on Hussein, and for a moment he paused, considering. Was this the first phase of some new American air campaign?

"What is the aircraft's destination?" demanded Hussein.

"North and west, Mr. President, headed for Turkey. Its speed is over eight hundred kilometers an hour. Air defense needs your permission to intercept, sir."

"Probably a reconnaissance aircraft," suggested Connor. They were used to US and other spy planes lurking near the border. A penetration this deep, if that's what it was, would be very unusual. Could it have dropped Special Forces by parachute? If so, why be so obvious about leaving?

Still, Connor was convinced he was right. "It can't be an attack. The US doesn't have enough planes here yet to even begin an air offensive. Besides, they wouldn't want to create an incident we could use to our advantage."

"All right, 'General.'" Hussein smiled. "I agree. I also do not wish to provoke an incident . . . at this time." He ordered the aide, "Track its movements but do not attack it. Let me know if it changes course."

He turned to the group. "Let us begin the meeting."

Two hundred feet over the Iraqi desert, Ted Sandstrom did his best to hug the rolling, barren landscape below him. All the electronics in the world could not, and should not, replace his eyes and mind as they guided his jet and, by default, the rest of the package across a hostile landscape.

They cruised at just over four hundred knots, nowhere near their top speed, but the optimum speed for the altitude, air temperature, and distance they had to fly. It looked fast enough to him with the desert flashing by only a heartbeat below him.

Skimming the landscape, even at this relatively low speed, felt like a roller coaster. Every rise made him pull up, and with even the slightest climb the g-forces pushed him down. A dip in the terrain lowered the nose, and "negative g" lifted him up out of the ejection seat.

In addition to the uneven terrain, the sun-baked landscape created columns of heated air that bounced the plane like a bumpy road. It was tiring, and sweat was pouring off of him in spite of the air-conditioning. He told himself it was just fatigue, and not tension.

Colonel Ted Sandstrom, call sign "Python," didn't dare look behind him. His backseater, Captain "Wreck" Rayford, could, but didn't bother. In theory, there were fifteen other F-15Es back there, but they'd only be able to see two or three. The rest would be hidden by the terrain. Spread out in trail formation, the sixteen fighters were spaced out in a column exactly nine-and-a-half miles long.

The whole point behind flying so low was to hide their planes not only from each other, but hopefully from the Iraqis as well. Their route snaked south over the Iraqi landscape, dodging radar stations and any other location that might possibly raise an alarm. Sensors on his aircraft would tell him if they were detected by radar, but electronic spy planes overhead would know almost as fast if he'd been spotted. They could also see much farther, and provide him with the "big picture" he lacked.

"Comanche Lead, this is Hightower." Although his flight would not reveal itself by transmitting on radio, the Pentagon had gone to a great deal of trouble to make sure they could talk to him. "Confirm site Alpha. You are still clean. You are go to target. Do not acknowledge this transmission. Good luck."

Rayford spoke over the intercom. "I copy. Just over two hundred klicks to target, fourteen minutes out."

Sandstrom acknowledged the information, which confirmed his own navigation display. He didn't mind hearing it twice. There was no room for error.

A small cluster of buildings flashed by under his wing. Their inhabitants were in for a sixty-second airshow and some broken windows, thought Sandstrom, and imagined their confusion as the stream of fighters roared overhead. He regretted having to overfly the town, but as they closed on the target, the landscape was becoming more settled. Besides, they were too close for it to matter now.

In the JCS briefing theater, Colonel Dolan waited nervously near a telephone. A computer display had been projected on the screen, showing a map of Iraq, overlaid with symbols. It showed known Iraqi aircraft, Bravo Three Nine, and the Comanche group. E-3 radar planes patrolling near the border gave them a God's-eye view of the area, but all the electronics in the world couldn't take away the risks of war.

Out of the corner of his eye, Dolan studied General O'Neill. The tanker sat calmly, chatting with the service chiefs, who had assembled to watch the Comanche flight. This had been his idea, and many lives, as well as his own career, were riding on the next few minutes. Dolan admired his patience.

General Thomas, the Chairman, also sat near a phone. The President, when he gave permission for the raid, had not wanted to give any sign by changing his schedule, so he was in Detroit, addressing a police group. Thomas would contact him with the results seconds after they were known.

They would tell him whether or not a war had started.

Harry Connor had just finished listing the units deployed along the border when Wreck Rayford reported, "Initial Point, seven minutes." Colonel Sandstrom, expecting the mark, advanced the throttles and pulled back gently on the stick. Behind him, seemingly erupting from the desert, the rest of the strike package climbed as well. Leveling out at medium altitude, the sixteen strikers, all F-15Es, assumed a more conventional formation. The four F-15C escort fighters split into two pairs and angled off to the sides. At those altitudes the raid would normally be picked up by radar within moments.

Fifty miles behind them, a hundred miles apart, two EF-111 Raven aircraft also popped up within seconds of each other, and of the Comanche package. They climbed higher, and as they climbed the right-seater, an electronic warfare officer, turned on the Raven's jamming equipment.

"Turn on" was too weak a term to describe the result, Colonel Sandstrom thought. Antennas built into the airframe poured out electromagnetic energy powerful enough to kill an unprotected person within a hundred feet. Hundreds of miles away, radar antennas built to receive microwatts of energy were overloaded by a thousand times that much and were blinded.

Because of past reconnaissance by planes like Bravo Three Nine, the jamming planes knew where the radars were and what frequencies they used. They were the radars that could have detected the Comanche package, but all the radar operators would see now was a pie-shaped wedge of white static.

Connor was listing the American units now known to be in Kuwait when the alert phone buzzed again. An aide picked it up and listened for a moment, then paled. "The air defense radars near Baghdad are being jammed!"

"Why? By whom?" demanded Hussein. As he spoke, an air force general ran over and grabbed the phone from the aide.

"Tell me what you know," the general demanded. He listened for a minute, then reported, "Jammer aircraft to the north are attacking our air defense radars. We don't know their exact location, or if there are any other aircraft with them."

Hussein snapped, "I don't care what they know. Put the air defense forces on full alert, and warn all the armed forces to watch for signs of a sneak attack."

The general nodded and spoke hurriedly into the phone. He listened again, then hung up.

"All air defense units will be at battle stations in five minutes. We do not have too many fighters on alert, but they will also be up in five minutes. The rest will take longer."

Hussein nodded even as he turned his head to stare at Connor, who had watched the proceedings along with the rest of the staff. "What is happening?" Hussein demanded.

Connor was puzzled. He'd made a point of studying the air campaign of Desert Storm, and air force tactics in general before coming to Iraq. Something was going down, but what?

Better to err on the safe side, he thought to himself. "It's probably an air raid, Mr. President. There could be stealth fighters or Tomahawk missiles coming in right now. They could hit air defense sites or communications facilities. Depending on the target, they could be followed by other strike aircraft."

"Could it be a nuclear attack?" asked Hussein.

"Not a chance, sir. The political costs of a nuclear attack are more than the US government would be willing to bear."

Hussein seemed less than convinced. He wasn't used to thinking about the people's opinion in making a decision.

"Besides, sir, the first time we would know of a nuclear attack would be the detonation. You don't need jamming for an ICBM."

That convinced the dictator, but he immediately demanded, "Where, then?"

"I don't know, sir. I upgraded the command radio net. If you'd let me improve the air defense communications . . ."

"That's not the issue right now," Hussein snapped. "Are we the target?" A few generals cast nervous glances around the space.

Connor shook his head. "Doubtful, sir. American doctrine doesn't include attacking a head of state, and US forces have never targeted one."

* * *

231

"Three minutes from target," Rayford reported. Sandstrom didn't bother speaking. He was far too busy trying to follow the dancing symbols on the heads-up-display. Half told him vital information about his plane's condition, the other half told him how to steer to a precise point in the sky. He also had to watch the few tracers coming up from the cityscape below. None was close, but that could change quickly.

"Laser targeting is up and programmed. The weapon is selected." Collins's steady tone showed no trace of excitement.

Sandstrom checked the heads-up-display. The lower left corner contained the letters "GBU" and a line on his heads-up display traced a path through the sky.

"Target is locked," Rayford reported.

Sandstrom risked a glance at the radar display. In ground-mapping mode, it showed a cluster of buildings, almost as clear as a television image. Rayford had zoomed in the image and centered it on the Iraqi high command's headquarters.

"Drop in thirty," coached the backseater, and Sandstrom leveled the Eagle's wings. He made a minute correction in heading and watched the display. The lines, squares, and circles all merged in the center directly over the headquarters building and he thumbed the release. The Eagle shuddered and leapt upward, freed of its two-and-a-half-ton load.

A sensor on the weapon's nose immediately detected laser light reflecting from the side of the headquarters building. Steering vanes on the bomb compensated and steered it straight in. Above, Comanche Lead turned away, the laser illuminator slewing to hold the beam on target. The second aircraft, half a mile behind, approached the release point.

In the bunker, they could hear the air-raid sirens. An aide was on the phone with air defense headquarters, relaying news about the attack overhead. The reports were fragmentary, based only on poor radar and visual sightings. Aircraft had been seen headed for city center. Hussein looked worried, and Connor was about to reassure him again when a rumbling crash shivered the walls. The lights dimmed for a moment, then came back up.

"They *are* trying to hit us," he marveled. He was concerned, even interested. He'd never been under attack from the air before. He was not afraid. Not four stories down.

The GBU-28 laser-guided bomb had hit within a foot of the laser spot on the headquarters building. The two-and-a-half ton weapon, specially designed to penetrate fortifications, had only been used twice, in the last days of Desert Storm. It could penetrate one hundred feet of earth or twenty feet of reinforced concrete, which was enough to take it down two stories into Saddam Hussein's bunker. A massive explosion sent shock waves throughout the structure, but it held.

Then the second weapon hit. Striking within a few feet of the first one, it took advantage of the path made by its predecessor and went even deeper.

In the lowest level of the command bunker, Connor and the others felt the second shock three seconds after the first, the time it takes a jet at six hundred knots to fly half a mile. The third came another three seconds later.

Like a giant's sledgehammer, each blow seemed stronger and closer. Connor began to worry when the lights went out for good on the third impact. Dimly lit by emergency lanterns, he saw the ceiling crack with the fifth, and felt fear. The last thing he saw was the overhead dissolving into yard-wide chunks raining down on him, Saddam Hussein, and the rest of the Iraqi general staff.

In total, ten of the twelve weapons worked as advertised. The sixth weapon penetrated but did not explode, and the ninth failed to guide, hitting a nearby building. The others were more than enough.

In the JCS theater, the secure channel came alive, and Dolan heard a voice, which he recognized as Ted Sandstrom's. "This is Comanche Lead. Shingle. I repeat Shingle. Out."

The pilot's voice was accompanied by digital images transmitted from one of the strike aircraft and relayed via satellite. The six-foot-square picture showed the now-familiar headquarters complex with the central building completely gone. The three above-ground stories had collapsed into a massive crater over a hundred meters across. The bombs' successive hammer blows had done their job.

There were a few cheers among the usually dignified four-star generals, and a lot of handshaking and smiles. The colonel looked at Thomas, who had the secure phone in one hand and used the other to urge his colleagues to be quiet.

All the tension flowed out of Dolan, and he suddenly wanted to sleep. One of a string of nonsense words, "Shingle" meant no casualties to the attackers and many bombs on the target, a completely successful operation.

He pulled himself together. It didn't mean he could stop work. They had to prepare a brief for the President, and monitor the Iraqi armed forces. And someone was going to have a field day trying to track political developments in Iraq.

Dolan felt no sorrow for Connor and Hussein. Their plans for the US were buried with them. They'd tried to catch America by surprise, but sometimes the best surprise is just not following your own rules.

Geroldo's Incredible Trick

RAYMOND E. FEIST

Ray Feist is the author—among many other books—of the runaway bestseller The Magician. *His childhood was imbued with magic, and his love of it is a lasting part of his life. He is dedicated to what Samuel Taylor Coleridge calls ". . . the willing suspension of disbelief," and told me, ". . . it's delicious to believe in magic."*

As for his story, anything explicit I might say would only spoil it for you. For that reason, I will simply say that it is incurably—enjoyably—Ray Feist.

—DC

Geroldo's Incredible Trick

THE COMIC WAS BOMBING. Nagafia had been a British colony at one time, so language wasn't his problem. Some of the jokes were too "American," but more than cultural differences were working against him. Simply put, he was awful.

"They sound like they're going to riot," Jillian said as she leaned forward to inspect her stage makeup.

"It's a raucous house," said the Great Geroldo.

"Only Quincy Monrow would book us into a civil war," said Jillian, waving her hand before her face, as if to clear away the almost-permanent haze of smoke which filled the tiny closet that passed for a dressing room of the Victoria Theatre in the city of Dafa-el-bara.

Geroldo moved past the young woman to stand before the mirror and check his own appearance. He spoke to her reflection over his shoulder in the mirror. "It's not a civil war." He pulled down one lower eyelid, as if doing so allowed him to see himself better in the dim light the single overhead bulb afforded. "It's simply their politics tend to . . . the rough side. Quincy swore this would be our last . . . difficult booking, if we did well. He said there were summer fairs in Europe that would prove profitable."

"I swore I heard gunfire," said Jillian as she inspected her costume prior to leaving the dressing room.

"Fireworks," answered the magician. "Besides, the notice from the State Department only urged caution . . ."

"Notice?" said Jillian, her features darkening in anger. "You mean there's a State Department Advisory on Nagafia and you didn't tell me?"

239

Geroldo turned and smiled, his make-up and badly capped teeth making him look like nothing so much as a badly made-up clown rather than a master magician. "I didn't wish to alarm you, dear."

"You didn't wish to alarm me?" she shouted as she crossed to stand before him, leaning forward so as to be nearly nose-to-nose with him. "You mean you knew I wouldn't come, you drunken idiot!"

"I will not be spoken to in that manner, young lady! I am your father!"

"You are not my father. You're the man Mom was married to when she died. Not the same thing."

"I'm your step-father," he said unblinkingly, holding her gaze.

Jillian sighed and closed her eyes. After a silent moment she opened her eyes and said, "Yes, you are, and you've been a good one in the ways that count." She let her anger flow away as she always did with Jerry and kissed him on the nose. "But try to behave. This is a Muslim country and they don't like drinking."

"I haven't had a drop—"

"Since breakfast," she finished.

"Just a drop, then, to soothe my jet-jangled nerves," he said, returning to inspecting his face in the mirror.

"After we get home, I think you'd better start looking for another girl," Jillian said.

Geroldo turned. "Why?"

"I'm thinking of quitting," Jillian said. "What did you think: we'd need two idiot girls in this act?"

"Why are you thinking of quitting?" he asked.

"Because I'm thirty-two years old and look forty-two!" said Jillian, studying her reflection. Her face was thin, and she kept herself fit, because the stage work for her was strenuous. Still, she knew she wasn't what any man would call pretty. Interesting, attractive, even "handsome," but never pretty. "The only men I meet are comics, saxophone players, and agents. They're all married, gay, drug addicts, or dumber than dirt." Her voice turned softer, despite the crowd's shouts of anger coming through the door. "I'd like to find a man, get married, and have kids, Jerry. I don't have that many years left."

Geroldo was about to say something when the door opened. "Don't you knock?" shouted Jillian to the theater's stage manager as he shoved open the door.

"You're next," he said, ignoring her question, though he seemed to be taking inventory of every spangle on her costume. Wearing nude tights under the brief outfit gave Jillian the appearance of being scantily clad, despite the fact that she was covered from neck to toe. "I urge you to be good," he continued in his oddly Etonian accent, made all the more incongruous by his almost cliché Arabic appearance. "The audience didn't care for the comic, I'm sorry to say."

Suddenly loud shots rang out from behind the theater. Jillian jumped, putting her hand to her mouth. "What was that?"

"That was the comic, I'm *very* sorry to say," said the manager, looking nervous. "Colonel Zosma is in the audience tonight. *He* thought the comic was very bad." He shook his head. "Bad performance. Very bad. You should strive to be very good for the colonel. Our leader can be . . . unpredictable," he finished as he moved through the door.

The door closed and Jillian said, "Zosma! He's that murderer . . ."

"Now, Jillian," said Geroldo, as he stood. He patted her hand in a reassuring fashion. "We'll dazzle them. I'm sure these rustics haven't seen any of our wonders."

"These rustics have automatic weapons," said Jillian, anger mixed with terror on her face. "And they're obviously inclined to use them. You've never had theater critics like these, Jerry."

"Well, we shall simply do our very best, shan't we?"

As he turned to leave the room, Jillian pulled on his hand. Softly, but urgently, she said "Since I was a child, Jerry, you've been telling me about what you called your 'incredible trick.' Now might be a good time to use it."

Geroldo stopped. "It's a difficult thing to do, Jillian, and far too subtle for a room of this size. And, above all, the timing must be absolutely perfect." He was silent a moment, then said, "Besides, I haven't practiced it in years. Though I don't know if practice is required." Shaking his head, he added almost absently, "I'm sorry, but I can't imagine how that particular trick could help us."

He moved down the narrow, dark hall to the side of the stage, as the theater crew finished moving his props to the locations he had marked out that morning. Jillian overtook him and said, "Before I die, I'd like to know what it is."

Patting her hand again, he said, "Someday I'll tell you."

He peeked through the side of the curtain and Jillian leaned down to see from below his chin. The theater had been built during the English colonial period; the stalls were filled with common folks, most wearing white shirts and black pants, though a few suits could be seen, as well as traditional robes. The dress circle was packed with men in military garb, all carrying side arms. Each aisle was guarded by soldiers carrying automatic weapons. In the box overhanging the far side of the stage a large man with a ridiculous number of medals on his chest sat grinning.

That grin caused Jillian to shiver.

Then the sound man started their pre-recorded music and Geroldo said, "We're on."

As the curtains parted, Jillian said, "Jerry, I'm frightened."

Geroldo smiled his broadest smile and said, "Courage, daughter. We shall endure."

He strode out to the center of the stage, greeted by a murmur of voices. When Jillian followed, several men laughed, while others hooted and cheered what appeared to be an ample display of Western female flesh. Jillian wished she had worn black tights instead of the nude ones.

The audience stared with expectation, their features made all the more alien by the reflected stage lights. Half-darkened, half-revealed, they resembled a jury of demons far more than an audience desiring entertainment. Jillian put aside her fears and let years of stage rehearsals take over; focusing on the act took her mind away from fear.

The act started as it always did, with some rings, silk scarves, and cylinders, moving quickly to more elaborate illusions. The equipment was old, but well cared for, and while the choice of illusions would have seemed old-fashioned, even quaint, and commonplace in the United States, the Great Geroldo and his step-daughter had been playing rural theaters in small countries for years, to a steady if not significant financial reward.

But there was something different about this night. Colonel Izar Zosma, recently "elected" by a narrow margin in a one-man race, with his armed men counting the ballots, sat grinning at the performance. There was, however, nothing mirthful in the man's expression. His dark features were made even more sinister by a week's growth of unshaved beard. He sat motionless, his smile never fading, and as each moment passed without reaction from the crowd, Jillian knew their lives were in jeopardy.

Then things started going wrong. Stage magic is always a matter of rhythm, timing, and even a half-second delay can ruin the effect of an illusion. A prop not handled deftly, a fumble on an exchange, and Geroldo and Jillian were playing catch-up. The tape recorder was unrelenting. Where a canny live conductor might have covered a mistake, as each new gaffe was made the recording made the compounded errors all the more obvious to the audience.

By the time they reached the climax of the act, the entire theater was silent. Only the music from the tape recorder reverberated in the hall. The sound of equipment scraping across the badly finished stage sounded unnervingly loud to Jillian as she readied the last illusion. Geroldo's constant narration echoed through the theater as if they were in an empty hall. Jillian tried not to shiver.

Geroldo began the final stage in preparing for his Trunk-of-Death illusion. He was showing the razor sharp blades he used, the ones Jillian would be shoving through the trunk as he expertly bent his body around them, when Colonel Zosma stood.

Every eye in the house turned toward the dictator, who stepped over the edge of the balcony and dropped easily to the stage. A hefty man, he walked lightly on the balls of his feet, as one would expect a powerful athlete to move, to where Geroldo waited. The soundman turned off the music.

The colonel held out his hand and Geroldo put one of the blades in it. He gripped the hilt of the stage sword, then slashed through the air suddenly, causing Jillian to step back. He cut through the air an inch from Geroldo's nose, but the old magician didn't flinch.

With a surprisingly cultured accent, Zosma said, "I've always loved this trick." He slapped the flat of the blade against his hand. "Always wondered how you magicians did it."

Geroldo smiled and said, "A magician never—"

"Reveals his tricks!" shouted Zosma and the entire audience drew in a breath. "I could have you shot if you don't tell me."

Geroldo said, "But, Your Excellency—"

"Colonel!" The man almost hissed his title. "You," he said to Jillian. "Open that box!"

Jillian hesitated only an instant, then opened the trunk. The colonel glanced inside, ran his hand around the inner surface, then stood upright. "Get in," he said to Geroldo.

Jerry looked at Jillian, who was now ashen, and said, "Courage, daughter."

He stepped inside and, if anything, looked more dignified than Jillian had ever seen him look in her life. A drunk, a depressive, and by any measure only a mediocre sleight-of-hand merchant, he was still the only family she had, and she loved him. Now some madman was on the verge of killing him before her eyes.

"*I* shall insert the swords!" shouted Zosma as Jillian closed the trunk on her step-father.

To Jillian, Zosma said, "You Westerners think us fools! I know that this trick works because he knows where you will place the swords, first one there, then another, then a third, and he artfully drapes his body around them. Let's see how he likes surprises!"

243

Turning, Zosma circled the trunk, selected one slot at random, and drove the sword into it. Jillian gasped, but the audience remained silent. Jillian could barely stay on her feet as her knees trembled. The slot was one that was used for the fifth sword, and if Jerry had been in the wrong position, it would have skewered him like a turkey on a spit.

But the sword slid through and no sound issued from the trunk.

Jillian hoped Jerry was listening to where the madman was walking, trying to anticipate where the sword would next appear. As if reading her thoughts, Zosma grabbed up another sword off the table and almost tiptoed around the trunk, then inserted the blade in another slot, pushing it through quickly. There was a slight hesitation, as if he were meeting resistance, then the blade slid home. No sound came from the man inside, and Jillian forced herself to breathe.

Nine swords would enter that trunk and as each was added, Geroldo was required to assume a more difficult position. Part of what made it possible for him to survive the illusion was pressing his body hard against the already-inserted blades, against the flat or back of the blade. The order of insertion was critical.

Zosma quickly inserted the third, fourth, and fifth blades, but still no noise came from inside. Jillian worried that Jerry might have been killed by the first blade, and that was the reason for his silence.

Zosma slowed, as if each added blade would be the killing one. The sixth slid home, the seventh, the eighth.

Then the last blade. Zosma lingered over the top slot, the one which would have been the final blade in the normal course of events. But if Jerry had to be out of position to avoid the first eight, he would be in line for a killing blow.

Colonel Zosma inserted the blade, paused, then slammed down hard. It met with resistance, and Jillian felt her knees threatening to buckle. That was part of the act, an effect that got a reaction from even the most blasé of crowds. And it worked again, as a gasp escaped from the heretofore silent audience.

Zosma drove the sword to the hilt, then waited.

He walked around the trunk, saying at last, "Remove them."

Jillian prayed silently, removing the blades in the correct order, so that if Jerry was still alive he would have a chance of escaping injury. When the last blade was removed, Zosma said, "Open the trunk."

She reached toward the latch, her hand trembling visibly. She released the catch, flipped it, and pushed open the trunk. Like a giant upright clamshell, it swung wide to reveal its contents.

The Great Geroldo, master illusionist, the toast of five continents, self-appointed member of the Magician's Hall of Fame, sat crouched inside. "Give us a hand, will you, Jilly dear," he said. "I'm a bit cramped in here."

Jillian reached in and put her hand under Jerry's arm, giving him some support as he climbed out of the trunk. Whispering, he said, "The good colonel was so slow I got a bit stiff waiting for the finale."

The audience went wild.

Zosma stood there a moment like a man defeated in a contest, then suddenly his mad grin was back. "Wonderful!" he said.

He slapped Geroldo on the back and said, "You are very good, my friend. Very, very good. I am very pleasantly surprised!" He turned back to the box where his entourage waited for him. To one of the officers in the box he shouted, "Give this man some money. See he and his assistant get safely back to the airport tomorrow!"

He signaled that he was departing, and the soldiers in the audience moved quickly to provide coverage for him, as the curtain closed on the magician and his step-daughter.

Geroldo adjusted his clothing, and turned slowly toward the dressing room. His knees appeared to be weak and Jillian hurried to help him. "You look terrible," she whispered.

"Not here," he answered, and they were silent as he slowly let her half-carry him to the dressing room.

As Jillian helped Jerry sit, a knock came at the door. She opened it and found a soldier outside; he handed her an envelope. She closed the door and opened the envelope. "Jerry, there's over ten thousand pounds here!"

"Good," said Geroldo. "We're going to need it. Now, be a dear and send for the house manager. Have him quietly fetch a discreet doctor and bring him post-haste."

"Doctor?" said Jillian. "What's wrong?"

Geroldo, never one to let a theatrical moment pass untouched, slowly stood, then held opened his swallow-tailed coat, revealing his pristine white shirt. After a moment, Jillian saw a red stain appear, then another, then suddenly blood flowed and Geroldo went pale.

"The best trick I know, daughter, the one I've never wished to show, is one that really has had, until now, little theatrical relevance." He slowly lowered himself back into his chair. "I learned it one summer from a Hindu fakir, actually." He was on the verge of fainting when he said, "It's really quite a strange little thing, but under the right circumstances I can keep from bleeding for periods of time."

Jillian was moving to the door to call the house manager as the Great Geroldo slid from his chair. His last thought before unconsciousness swept over him was that this had been a very unlikely venue, and a less than ideal audience, before which to finally, after years of secrecy, reveal his incredible trick. After the doctor patched him up, he'd have to think of a way to incorporate it into his act. Still, he thought as darkness closed in around him, the timing *was* perfect.

Dealing with the Devil

ROBERT WEINBERG

I can't think of anyone who does not have some fondness for stories about making a deal with the devil; who among us has not thought of that possibility, or at the very least been fascinated by Faust and Dorian Gray, to name but two who did what most of us are far too sane—or afraid—to do.

In his story, Robert Weinberg pits a priest with a Carny background against a dead card shark who exists in the real world courtesy of his deal with the devil. His mandate is to deliver ten souls each year into the hands of his Master. The way he figures it, he'll get extra points, perhaps even extra time on earth, if he can deliver up the soul of a priest. . . .

—DC

Dealing with the Devil

"WHAT DO YOU THINK you are doing, my son?" asked Father Stevens, focusing his flashlight directly on the man crouching in front of the open safe.

Startled, the burglar, a big, burly man in his mid-forties, turned and stared at the priest. Shakily, he rose to his feet. His hands, clutching a wad of greenbacks, trembled. "Forgive me, Father," he said, his voice quivering with emotion. "I-I had to do it."

"Nonsense," said Father Stevens, stepping closer. One hand holding the flashlight, he reached out with the other and tugged the bills out of the thief's fingers. The robber offered no resistance. "No one is forced to disobey God's commandments. You know that, Ernest Jones. I've said it many times in my Sunday sermons."

The priest's voice grew stern. "Sermons delivered at services that you attended ever since you were a child." Ignoring any possible danger from the thief, the diminutive priest bent down and replaced the money in the open safe. Shoving the door closed, he spun the combination lock. Only then did he look again at the would-be robber. "I want a full explanation of your actions, my son. *Immediately.*"

A wizened little black man with skin the color of dark chocolate and hair the color of freshly fallen snow, Father Stevens was dwarfed by the burglar. However, the force of the priest's personality was such to cower giants. His high cheekbones, sharp nose, and thin lips gave his face a quiet dignity, accented by his advanced age. Dark brown eyes contained wisdom and compassion gained from more than five decades spent serving the poor and downtrodden of Chicago's far south suburbs. Father Stevens was nearly eighty years old. He was a Windy City

251

institution, as famous in his own way as Al Capone and the original Richard Daley.

"I wasn't stealin' the money," said Ernest, his voice dull and filled with despair. "I was just hopin' to borrow it for a few weeks. Planned to pay it back, Father. Swear to God, I did. I swear."

"Do not use the Lord's name in vain," snapped Father Stevens. He gestured with the flashlight at a nearby chair. "Sit."

It was 2:00 A.M. and the two men were alone in the priest's study. Troubled by the aches and pains of old age, Father Stevens was a light sleeper. The noise made by Jones fumbling with the safe's lock had been enough to wake him in his bedroom across the hall. A man without fear, he had come investigating armed only with his ever-abiding faith. Catching the thief had been easy. Now, the priest wanted to know the motive behind the attempted crime.

"Speak," he commanded in a tone sharp enough to break bones. A gifted orator, Father Stevens spoke with a righteous passion. He used words like weapons. "Tell me what pressing need *forced* you to commit this crime? You know that money is to help the needy, those unfortunates in our community without food and shelter. You were not stealing from the church, but from the poor."

"I had to do it," said the big man, breathing heavily. His gaze was firmly aimed at the floor. He could not stare Father Stevens in the eye.

The priest's voice dripped with sarcasm. "What necessity moved you to rob from your brothers and sisters, my son? Drugs? Women? Liquor?"

Jones shuddered, his whole body shaking. "Please, Father, I didn' mean no harm. I was gonna pay it back. I was, I was. Just couldn't face the thought of burnin' to hell. I was scared, real scared. That's why I done it. Really."

"Hell?" repeated Father Stevens, frowning. "Explain yourself."

"I be a gamblin' man, Father," said Ernest Jones intently. "You know that. It's my one sin. Can't help myself. I love them cards. Play poker whenever I can. Usually two, three times a week, after I leave work. There's always a game goin' on in the back room of Little Joe's Tavern. I lose some, win some. Depends on the way my luck is flowing."

Jones paused, sucking in a deep breath. "Lately, my luck's been bad. Real bad."

Father Stevens said nothing. But his eyes narrowed with concentration as he listened to Jones's story. The big man had been a member of Father Stevens's congregation all of his life. He was a solid citizen, levelheaded, and extremely honest. Jones was not the type to steal church funds. Which was what had the priest so concerned. What evil lurked behind this attempted robbery?

252

"There's a new player in town," said Jones. "He's been sittin' in the game the past few weeks. Tall, thin dude, talks real fancy. Sounds like you, Father. Man is murder with them cards. Fast hands, fastest hands I ever did see. He's been winnin' night after night. Took me for all I'm worth. The other regulars too."

"You came here to steal church funds to continue this gambling," said Father Stevens, shaking his head unhappily. "I thought better of you, my son."

"No, Father," said Jones, unable to hide the anguish in his voice. "I done learnt my lesson. I don't want no money to keep on playin'. It's the note I already signed that has me shakin'."

"Note?" said the priest. "What note?"

"I lost, Father," said Jones. "Like I said, I lost real bad. Got caught up in the game an' bet more than I should—more than I had. End of the evenin' found me a thousand dollars short. So I signed a note promisin' to pay this gamblin' man the money I owed him in a month. Or forfeit my collateral."

Father Stevens felt the coldness in his heart expand, fill his body with a nameless fear. "What did you pledge, my son?"

Wordlessly, Jones dug into his pants' pocket and pulled out a crumpled piece of paper. Smoothing it out, he handed the sheet to Father Stevens. "Gamblin' man, he gave me a copy. Just to keep it legal, he said."

Carefully, the priest scanned the document. His bright eyes widened in astonishment.

"Your *soul?*" he whispered. "You promised your immortal soul for a gambling debt."

Jones nodded. "Me and Hightower, Carver and Stokes, we all done it these past ten days. Card shark gave us to the end of the month to raise the money. *Or we forfeits our souls to the gamblin' man.*"

The next evening, just before midnight, Father Stevens stepped up to the long bar that extended front to back of Little Joe's Tavern. Wearing a long dark coat and wide-brimmed black hat, he attracted little attention from the few regulars bent over their drinks in the far end of the room.

"Good evening, my son," he said softly to the huge man perched on a high wood chair behind the counter. "We've missed you at services lately."

"Father Stevens?" said Little Joe Winter, the establishment's proprietor and sometime barman. Tonight, a young man with a shaven head, wearing a white apron, served the drinks, while Little Joe sat in his chair and surveyed his kingdom. "Why am I not surprised."

Some men had nicknames that fit them like a glove. Others went in the opposite direction. Little Joe belonged to the latter group. A huge man with barrel chest, bullet-shaped head and no apparent neck, he weighed close to four hundred pounds. Though slow speaking, with a moon face and simple expression, Little Joe was nobody's fool.

Always calm, with a ready smile and a hearty laugh, Little Joe maintained an iron grip on his tavern. Underage drinkers were politely but firmly shown to the door. Hookers acted like ladies on the premises or were refused admittance. Drugs, and those who sold them, were strictly forbidden.

Gambling took place in the back room. Little Joe provided the cards and protection from the police for a small cut each night from the pot. Too many complaints about a particular player's honesty, and the individual was politely asked to leave. On his feet or off them, depending on the circumstances. Little Joe employed no bouncer. He was big enough and mean enough when necessary.

Father Stevens liked Little Joe. The big man was reasonably honest and obsessive about his bar's reputation. The barkeep would never allow a dishonest game in the back room. Which signalled to the priest that something much more sinister was taking place at the tavern.

Father Ben Stevens took his title seriously. He considered his parishioners his children, in spirit if not in flesh. The priest felt personally responsible for their well-being. When outside forces threatened his flock, he responded. Which was why he had come to the tavern tonight.

"What do you mean, my son?" he asked Little Joe. "Are you implying you expected my visit?"

"Surely was," said Little Joe, with a knowing nod. The giant waved a ham-sized hand to the young barman, summoning him over. "I knew you would be in sooner or later. What with the trouble brewing for Carver, Jones, and the rest of them fools. Can't say I like it myself."

"Get you a . . ." began the bartender, cheerfully as he approached the two men. The sentence died on his lips. "Uh . . . Father Stevens?"

The priest nodded, a faint smile crossing his lips. "Leroy. It is nice to see you are working.

The young man's jaw hung open in astonishment. A member of the church choir, he appeared shocked to see Father Stevens in the bar.

"Wherever the need, I come," said the priest, as if answering the bartender's unasked question.

"Yeah, that's the way of it," drawled Little Joe. "Now fetch me a Bud Light and Father Stevens a glass of our best red wine."

The giant snorted in disgust. "*Light* beer. Light on taste as well as calories." The huge man patted his immense stomach. "I'm on a diet. Doc says I need to lose some weight or my heart ain't gonna last much longer."

"You got a big job ahead of you," said Father Stevens.

"Tell me about it," said Little Joe, chuckling. "I'm glad to see you, Father. This trouble in the back room has been causing me problems. It's hurting my business and my good reputation. Willie Carver was arrested two days ago, trying to rob a 7-Eleven. Damn fool was lucky he wasn't shot. Moe Hightower's been talking to the loan sharks, trying to get a loan. Jim Stokes doesn't say a word, but there's a funny look in his eyes. And Ernie Jones been outta sight for days. People are starting to talk. And talk ain't good for a place like mine."

Father Stevens took a sip of wine. "They are all middle-aged men, not young fools. None of them are involved in drugs. All work hard, have good jobs. Pious souls, they attend services regularly. I find it difficult to believe they are willing to sacrifice everything for money."

Little Joe looked around, as if making sure no one was close enough to hear their conversation. "Well, Father," he drawled, softly, "problem with all those fellows is that they share a common passion. They love poker. These brothers take it damned serious. From what I hear, they dug themselves into a hole so deep that climbing out is impossible."

"I know these men," said Father Stevens, with a shake of his head. "I've known them all their lives. They have been playing draw poker for twenty years or more. They're not professionals, but they're not amateurs either. How could they have lost so much money in so short a time?"

Grunting, Little Joe leaned closer to Father Stevens. The wood chair groaned in protest as the huge man shifted his weight. An odd, apprehensive look crossed the giant's features. "I hear what you're saying, Father. That's the problem. They're just outclassed. A stranger arrives in town ten days or so ago. He comes in each night, plays cards with the regulars. Never hear a complaint about him from anyone. He plays an honest game, best I can tell. But, he keeps on winning. Night after night, he keeps on winning."

The big barkeep wiped one huge arm across his forehead, drying off invisible beads of sweat. "I can't kick him out. Doing so would make it look like the game was rigged, and that would destroy my business. Still, you know the trouble he's brought. I wish he'd pack up and leave. He's been cleaning out my long-time customers, then taking their notes when they run out of cash. The situation puts me in a real quandary. I'm damned if I do, damned if I don't. If you can do something about it, I'd consider it a real favor."

"Does this stranger have a name?" asked Father Stevens.

"He calls himself Mississippi Slim," said Little Joe. "Tall, slender dude, with pencil moustache and thin, thin eyebrows. Coldest eyes I've ever seen."

Father Stevens felt a sharp knife slide into his ribs. He drew in his breath, suddenly feeling the weight of his years. "This man dresses very neat? He always wears a long black waistcoat with a big red handkerchief tucked into his top pocket?"

"Yeah, that's him," said Little Joe. "You recognize this hustler, Father?"

"I was born and raised in a carnival," said Father Stevens, his voice soft and introspective. "In my youth, I knew a man by that name, who dressed in such a fashion. However, it cannot be the same man. He's definitely not the original Mississippi Slim. It must be someone imitating his famous style."

"One sure method to find out," said Little Joe. Ponderously, he pushed himself off of his wood chair. He waddled around the bar. "Follow me."

The huge man led the priest to a door in the rear of the tavern marked "Employees Only." The portal opened into a small kitchen used primarily to prepare the few hot snacks the tavern offered.

"Take a look through there," said Little Joe, pointing to a glass panel. "I installed a one-way mirror years back just to keep an eye on things. Didn't want customers getting out of hand. You should be able to spot this Mississippi Slim character with no problem."

Father Stevens stared through the glass into the other room. There were several tables visible, but only at one was there a game in progress. Four middle-aged men sat hunched protectively over their cards. Occasionally, they glanced up at the dealer, waiting patiently, cards face down on the table, arms folded across his chest.

The blood drained from the elderly priest's face. It couldn't be and yet it was. There was no mistaking the gambler's features. Carefully, Father Stevens watched the game progress. The dealer won the hand with three jacks. The pot was a small one, but most of the chips visible on the table were already stacked up in front of him. Casually, the man called Mississippi Slim picked up the deck, expertly shuffled the cards for a few seconds, and dealt out five of them to each player.

Silently, Father Stevens turned away from the peephole. He had seen enough. An impostor might alter his appearance to look like Slim. But no one could duplicate the easy manner with which the notorious card shark handled a poker deck. The cards jumped from his fingers. He had a style uniquely his own.

"Well?" asked Little Joe. The big man hesitated for an instant. "You recognize him, Father?"

"That's Mississippi Slim," said the priest, shuddering. "In my misbegotten youth, I served as a shill for gamblers working the carny. Mr. Slim was with us for several years. He taught me a great deal about poker. Without question, he was the most talented player I had ever seen."

"I thought you stated it couldn't be the same man," said Little Joe. "Why not?"

"Mississippi Slim died of cancer sixty years ago," said Father Stevens, slowly. "I know that for a fact. I saw him buried."

After completing several errands the next morning, Father Stevens spent the rest of the day in prayer. He knew without a doubt that Mississippi Slim's appearance at the tavern was no coincidence. The souls of Ernie Jones and his friends merely served as bait to catch a bigger prize. The priest suffered from no false modesty. He had served the Lord for more than half a century. It was *his* spirit that the Father of Lies wanted. And Father Stevens knew, that despite his misgivings, he had no choice but to risk it to save his flock.

As he walked to Little Joe's Tavern, the little priest let his mind drift back to his days working the carnival circuit. His father, an acrobat on the midway, had never approved of his shilling for the cardsharps who traveled with the show. Though not a religious man, Jacob Stevens had more than once warned his son about the perils of his youthful folly. One particular maxim had been repeated time and again by the elder Stevens in describing the risks involved in dealing with the devil. Father Stevens smiled. Tonight, he hoped to put the advice given to him by his parent sixty years ago to good use.

The poker game at Little Joe's started promptly at eight o'clock every evening. Father Stevens stepped into the bar at a quarter to the hour. He nodded to the bartender and the owner, then proceeded to the back room.

Three men sat around one of the card tables. Glancing up at the new arrivals, they blanched when they spotted Father Stevens. All three were members of his congregation.

The stately priest said not a word. He merely glared at the trio and gestured with his head toward the door. The resulting scramble resembled a scene from a Three Stooges film.

Father Stevens dropped into a chair and tried to relax. Despite the chill of the evening, he was dripping with sweat. He felt incredibly tense. It was one thing to lecture his congregation about the evils of consorting with the Father of Lies. It was quite another to sit down at a card table and play poker with him.

The priest knew he had no choice. Demanding Mississippi Slim leave town was no solution. He had to get back those promissory notes from the gambler. And, even if he did, chasing the dead man away would only allow him to set up shop in another town, snaring other innocents in his nets.

The only way to banish sin was to face it squarely. Father Stevens had preached that credo all his life. Now, the time had arrived for him to prove its truth.

A few minutes before the hour, Little Joe Winter ambled into the room and settled down on an overstuffed lounger in the rear of the chamber. "Good luck," he said to Father Stevens.

"Thank you, my son," replied the priest. "Your good wishes are appreciated."

Mississippi Slim entered the room exactly at eight o'clock. A light-skinned black man, with pencil-thin moustache and eyebrows, his eyes were black stones of ice. He paused for an instant, then took the chair across from his sole opponent. Removing the bright red handkerchief from his coat pocket, Slim meticulously wiped any stray dust and sweat from his fingers. Only then did he look at Father Stevens.

"Jacob Steven's son, Ben," he said after a moment. His voice was rich and smooth, like butter melting on hot bread. He had a Southern accent, slurring his words together in a manner unchanged in sixty years. "What a pleasant suh-prise. It's been a long, long time, sir, since last we met. You've grown a good deal older since then."

"You have not," said Father Stevens, his tone flat and unfriendly. Confronting Slim, he felt his doubts slip away. "You look the same as the day you were buried."

The gambler chuckled. "I see you took to religion. That's a shock. I never figured a carny shill would become a man of the cloth."

"The world is full of surprises, my son," said Father Stevens. He picked his words carefully. "Your return to the land of the living, for example."

Slim smiled, a slow, knowing smile. "Sometimes even death is a gamble," he replied. "If you make the right connections afterwards, the grave isn't permanent."

"You serve the Prince of Darkness," said Father Stevens softly. "There is no honor in assisting such foulness."

"That, sir-rah, depends entirely on your point of view," said Slim, undisturbed. "To you, it's a terrible sin. I, on the other hand, consider it a damned fine bargain. Each summer I deliver ten new souls to my boss. In return, he grants me another year here on Earth. I'm a free agent, acting entirely on my own, relying on my particular skills to remain active."

The gambler chuckled. "It may not be the best existence possible, but it sure the hell beats the alternative."

Carefully, Slim stuffed his handkerchief back into his pocket. Though the room was well lit, a patch of darkness seemed to hover over the gambler's right shoulder. "Enough chatter. I'm abiding by the rules, as dictated in the holy books. Nobody's forced to play with me. Nor do I use any magic in my game. It's all perfectly straight. There's nothing you can do to stop me."

"I'm not here to stop you, Slim," said Father Stevens, reaching into his pants pocket and pulling out a wad of hundred-dollar bills. "I've come here tonight to clean you out."

Mississippi Slim's eyes narrowed. He glanced down at the money and then back up at the aged priest's face. "I do believe you're serious," he said, sounding astonished. "Serious but crazy. No man living, or dead for that matter, can beat Mississippi Slim at draw poker."

"I am willing to bet everything I have to prove you wrong," said Father Stevens.

"Including your immortal soul?" asked Slim, with a smirk of satisfaction. The words echoed through the small room. Hearing them, Father Stevens knew he had not guessed wrong. This entire scam had been aimed at him, not his parishioners. The devil worked in cunning ways. The patch of darkness behind the gambler was bigger now, more menacing. The lights grew dim.

"If necessary," said Father Stevens. He knew it was the only possibility of forcing Slim to play.

"I never backed down from a bet," said Slim. "No matter the costs. But I never lost a game that mattered."

"I'll take that risk," said Father Stevens. "Get the cards and deal."

Slim signalled Little Joe. The big man knocked once on the wall of the room. In seconds, the young bartender appeared, carrying a sealed deck of playing cards. Taking it, Slim tapped the package on the table.

"For luck," he said. "Good or bad."

Opening the deck, he shuffled the cards. His long thin fingers moved with lightning speed. Satisfied with the mix, he offered the deck to Father Stevens. Nodding politely, the priest cut the deck.

"Straight draw poker," declared Slim. "Nothing wild, no limit to the bets."

He pulled a thick stack of crumpled greenbacks from his coat pocket. "No reason for chips in a two-man game. We'll use straight cash."

"And we'll pass the deal with each hand," said Father Stevens. "Just to keep things fair and square."

Slim paused. "You accusing me of cheating, preacher-man?"

Father Stevens smiled. "I said no such thing. But, I know too well the deeds of your unholy master. All my life I have studied his works. We pass the deal or we do not play."

The gambler grimaced, his features twisting in annoyance. Then, greed won out over caution. He shrugged. "I'll abide by your rules, sir-ruh. Let's play cards."

In the soft white light of the back room, they played draw poker. At first, only Little Joe Winter watched. Then, as word spread that a big game was taking place involving Father Stevens and the gamblin' man, other men drifted into the chamber to watch silently. After an hour, nearly a dozen spectators followed the flow of the cards.

The game ebbed and flowed. Father Stevens played cautiously, carefully pondering each bet, weighing each decision as if it were his last. Slim, in contrast, wagered without hesitation, tossing his money into the pot with the casual air of a man convinced he couldn't lose.

There was magic in Mississippi Slim's fingers. Long and delicate, his digits seemed to have a life of their own. The cards flowed from them smoothly, gliding across the table as if propelled by a gun. He shuffled effortlessly, working the deck faster than the eye could follow. Watching the gambler was seeing a master craftsman at his best.

Father Stevens possessed no such skills. The elderly priest shuffled slowly, methodically. There was little magic in his precise, careful dealing. He was not a showman like Mississippi Slim. But Father Stevens knew how to play poker. That was what mattered.

Gradually, a pattern emerged. Father Stevens won steadily, but usually small hands where little money changed hands. Slim took in a few large pots, mostly when he dealt. After an hour, Father Stevens was richer by a few hundred dollars, but neither man held much of an advantage over the other.

"Time for another deck," declared Slim, leaning back in his chair. "And a snort of your best whiskey."

With a nod, Little Joe tapped his knuckles on the wall twice. A few seconds later, the bartender appeared, with a new package of cards and a filled shot glass. Slim's requests had obviously become routine at the bar over the past few days.

Stretching, Father Stevens rose from his chair. Wordlessly, he mouthed a silent prayer.

"Hoping to change your luck, sir?" asked Slim, grinning. "Your Lord can't help you now. Cards are the devil's tools."

"You talk much too much for a man facing the fiery pit," said Father Stevens sharply. He resumed his seat, his expression grim. "Shuffle the cards and deal."

The second hour of playing progressed at a much faster pace. The priest appeared to play more aggressively, as if stung by Slim's comments. He bet more often, taking greater risks on often questionable hands. However, the brief break seemed to pay off. He won steadily on his deals, while losing slight amounts on those of Mississippi Slim.

The gambler continued to wager with abandon. He couldn't entirely disguise the look of satisfaction from Father Stevens's eyes. The priest, trained by a lifetime of dealing with liars, sinners, and cheats, recognized that Slim was letting him win, setting up the big scam. It was part of the show. The gamblin' man was an expert at his craft—not playing poker but enticing fools. However, Father Stevens had prepared a few tricks of his own.

When Slim paused after two hours, his stack of bills was noticeably lower. Except for the twinkle in his dark eyes, he appeared angry and annoyed. The black cloud that hovered behind his shoulders had faded to a wisp of shadow, hardly visible in the crowded room.

"Another deck and another whiskey," he demanded, sounding properly distressed.

"I will have a glass of wine," added Father Stevens, his gaze meeting that of Little Joe's for a moment. The big barkeep nodded and rapped the wall four times. Drinks were served along with a fresh deck of cards. Barely glancing at the deck, Slim rapped it hard on the table twice.

"Time for my luck to change," he declared.

But the cards proved otherwise. Father Stevens continued to win. The priest seemed to know when to bet and when to fold. He bet on hands that seemed sure of losing, and threw in others that looked to be sure winners. In nearly every case, his decision proved to be correct. Abandoning the last semblance of caution, he risked more and more on each deal. The stack of money in front of him grew steadily, until it dwarfed Mississippi Slim's bank.

Nearly three hours after the start of the game, Slim took the deck and shuffled it thoroughly. Carefully, he dealt out the cards. Father Stevens glanced down at his hand and nodded. He had been dealt three queens and a pair of fives. A full house, drawn on the deal. It was the best hand of the evening.

Looking up, he stared intently at Mississippi Slim. Finally, he glanced over at the deck of cards resting on the table. The priest muffled a shiver of apprehension. The moment of reckoning had arrived.

"A thousand dollars to stay," said the elderly priest, his voice trembling slightly with emotion. Despite all of his plans, he was scared. The Master of Lies was no fool. Anxiously, he pushed a stack of bills to the center of the table.

"A decent wager, sir-ruh," said Slim, no longer sounding distraught. "I'll see your thousand and raise it two."

Behind the gambler, the patch of darkness had returned. It had grown in size and shape. Cloudy, mist-like, it resembled a man but was definitely not human. Slim's boss had come to watch the play.

Staring intently at the darkness, Father Stevens murmured a few words and made the sign of the cross. The shadow shivered but remained hunched behind Slim. "None of your mumbo-jumbo, preacher-man," growled the gambler. "My boss is merely observing. He enjoys a good game as much as the next. More so, perhaps. He's always been known as a gambler."

Slim counted out the money. The bet left him with less than a hundred dollars in his bank.

Father Stevens gathered his courage. The fiery pit was very near. The room was filled with the sickly smell of brimstone. But, he had absolute faith in his God.

The priest counted out his entire stack of money. "I will see your two thousand and raise you three more."

Mississippi Slim grinned, suddenly looking very satisfied. Behind him, the shadow grew darker, more substantial. Reaching into his inner coat pocket, the gambler pulled out four folded pieces of paper.

"These are notes due for one thousand doh-llars each," he said, dropping the slips to the table. "I believe they are the items you came seeking tonight, preacher-man. I'll see your bet and raise you one thousand."

Father Stevens drew in a deep breath. He knew that Slim had been working carefully all night to bring about this final confrontation. He had to match the bet or forfeit the hand. There was only one way to do that. The unholy lust on Mississippi Slim's face was frightening to behold as the elderly priest uttered the fateful words.

"I'll call your bet with my own note," said Father Stevens. He scribbled a few words on a piece of paper and tossed it in the center of the table. "Same amount. Same terms."

"Agreed," said Slim immediately. His grin stretched from ear to ear. "The soul of an innocent man is always a fine catch. However, the spirit of a preacher-man who's spent his life in the service of the meek, now that's a prize worth a whole lot more. My master will reward me nice and proper for my doings here tonight. Show your cards, preacher-man."

"You forgot to ask how many cards I require," declared the priest, calmly.

"What?" said Mississippi Slim, the first trace of doubt creeping into his voice. "Cards?"

"I'll take one card," said Father Stevens. Reaching into his hand, he discarded one of the pair of fives, breaking up his full house.

Licking his lips, the gamblin' man dealt the priest one card. Eyes narrowed, Mississippi Slim shook his head in bewilderment.

"I'll stand pat," he said, spreading his hand on the table. "Full house. King's over."

With a smile, Mississippi Slim reached for the pot.

"Four queens," said Father Stevens, revealing his cards.

"It-it can't be," said Mississippi Slim, his dark eyes bulging in astonishment. "I dealt you a . . ."

"You dealt me a full house, queens over," said Father Stevens. "A sucker hand, for sure. Placing my faith in the Lord, I discarded a card and picked up the fourth queen. All of your cheating was for naught, my son."

Slim sighed, a heavy sigh, the sound of a man knowing he was doomed to hell and that there was not a thing he could do to prevent it. He glanced over his shoulder. The black shadow was gone. It had vanished when Father Stevens' cards touched the tabletop. "My boss won't like this, won't like it one bit." He shrugged. "He's not the forgiving type."

"You made your bargain," said the priest. He signalled to Little Joe. "Another drink for Mr. Slim. Where he's going, they don't serve whiskey."

Three knocks brought the bartender. This time, he carried only the shot glass, no cards. Raising the tumbler to his lips, Slim shook his head in annoyance.

"I don't understand it, sir-ruh," he said, more than a trace of curiosity in his voice. "I bottom dealt, false cut, double discarded, palmed out cards, and rang them in, but you still beat me. Time and again, I played you for the sucker and each instance you escaped my trap. And then, in the end, you beat me at my own game."

Slim never heard Father Stevens's reply. With a flick of the wrist, he swallowed his drink. Instantly, beads of sweat exploded across his forehead. Eyes tearing, he gasped for breath.

"What was in that glass?" he choked out, as flames engulfed him. White lightning flashed and Mississippi Slim disappeared in a puff of red smoke. Only his red handkerchief remained.

"Holy water," said Little Joe Winter, answering the question, his voice sounding very satisfied. "I don't take kindly to man or devil cheating in my tavern."

Deliberately, Father ripped the five notes into shreds. "That cancels those debts," he declared. He scooped up the cash. "The money will go to those foolish enough to have lost it."

The crowd of onlookers, their expressions baffled and astonished, dissipated quickly. Father Stevens's unyielding stare sent them scurrying for safety. Soon, only the priest and Little Joe remained in the room.

"He never guessed," said the big barkeep. "I thought for sure Slim would catch on."

"Mississippi Slim saw me as a priest," said Father Stevens. "Nothing more. That was his mistake. He dismissed the fact that I was raised in a carnival. I knew all along that he would cheat. I expected that. But, with your cooperation, it didn't matter."

"I thought he'd explode when he saw those four queens," said Little Joe, chuckling.

"He tried several times to set me up with similar hands," said Father Stevens. "Each instance I refused to rise to the bait. It wasn't until I spotted the fourth queen resting on the top of the deck that I knew my salvation was at hand."

"Damn fool never realized that when he called for cards, we slipped in the deck you marked earlier today," said Little Joe. "From then on, you were able to read every card dealt. Plus the top card on the playing stack."

"In his arrogance, he ignored the basic rule of cardsharps everywhere," said Father Stevens. He took a sip of wine, remembering the wise words spoken decades ago to him by his father. "*If you're dealing with the devil, make sure you bring the cards.*"

Every Mystery Unexplained

LISA MASON

There are people who confuse magic and illusion with the work of would-be spiritualists, most of whom have been proven to be charlatans. Harry Houdini certainly wanted to believe in the spirit world, to the extent that he promised his beloved wife that, should he die before her—which he did—he would do everything possible to communicate with her from the other side. They tried and failed to make contact.

Am I a believer?

The best I can say is that I'm a skeptic, but I understand why most of us would like to think that our lives and loves in some way continue beyond the grave.

Because the theme is universal, I was particularly pleased when Lisa Mason chose to use it in her story. Also because I am a longtime Harry Kellar fan, and it is from him that she draws the quote for her title. I know that you will agree that this is a charming story. More than that I can't, or rather won't say, for like Kellar and Mason, I, too, prefer to leave "Every Mystery Unexplained."

—DC

Every Mystery Unexplained

"As long as the human mind delights in mysteries, so long it will love magic and magicians . . . I would say to all beginners, 'Keep three things in mind—

First—Practice constantly new sleights, novel devices, and invent new combinations of old feats. You must always have something new wherewith to dazzle.

Second—Make your work artistic by clothing each illusion with all the glamour and shadows of fairyland and the suggestions of incantations and supernatural powers in order to prepare the observer's mind for a mystery. . . .

Third—Leave every mystery unexplained.'"

—HARRY KELLAR
"The Greatest Magician in the World, 1887"

MY FATHER IS DONE with the doves and colored scarves by the time he gets to the spirit show. "And now, ladies and gentlemen," Uncle Brady says, his voice as sonorous as a Shakespearean ghost. "Professor Flint will endeavor through his astonishing, miraculous, and mysterious psychic powers to establish communication with the Spirits of the Dead!"

"Endeavor to establish communication with the Dead," I whisper to Mr. Pannini, the booking agent for the Tivoli Theater, as we watch from the wings. "A pity he seldom endeavors to establish communication with me."

The audience shifts and titters, restless in the early evening, which is

269

awfully cold and gloomy even for fog-haunted San Francisco. Gaslights flicker, leaking fumes into the chill damp air. The smell of mold clings to the dark scarlet velvet of abundant curtains, a sepulchral smell that leaves me uneasy.

"The old man is a boiled shirt, then, is he?" Pannini says, grinning. Pannini is a dapper, clove-scented dandy in pin-striped gabardine, hair slicked beneath his bowler, a large curled mustache adorning his lip. Some ten years my senior, I suppose, with the air of the rake about him. My father dislikes him intensely, of course. "Nothing a young gentleman like yourself cannot handle, I wager."

"I endure," I say, "the dutiful son." I like Pannini. He slips me a Mecca cigarette. I puff, quick and guilty. My father has forbidden me to smoke. My father has forbidden me to grow a mustache till I reach the age of one and twenty. Extravagant mustaches are the rage for gentlemen in our year of 1895, a requirement of fashion despite other trifling concerns like the bank panic, massive unemployment, and civil unrest throughout our great nation of America. What lady will consider me without a mustache? I chafe at each passing day of these next nine months, shave the scant fuzz from my lip—dutiful son—and speculate pessimistically on what poor bristles may be produced when Pop's injunction has expired.

Onstage, my father arduously prepares himself to establish communication with the Spirits of the Dead. Of Pop's many talents, this is one of his best: the dramatic preparation for impending dire difficulty. Uncle Brady assists him, sloughing off his chartreuse cutaway coat, all the while seeing to the huge plate of glass and preparing the sword. As for my father, he effects much rolling of eyes, rolling up of sleeves, girding of loins. He kneads his forehead, unleashing psychic powers.

A pity he had not prepared so well for my mother's death.

Someone in the audience snores with an exaggerated gargle. A heckler? A pack of hoodlums in scruffy top hats tip rotgut in the back row. There has been an air of uncertainty, perhaps even of desperation, since we first arrived in San Francisco. No one in the far West honors paper money now; you must have gold or silver. Only half the seats are filled in the Tivoli tonight.

"He ain't Houdini, eh?" Pannini says, not unkindly.

"Nope," I say.

No, not that young rascal, the dexterous Harry Houdini. No one can top Houdini, who with his wild antics has spoiled audiences from St. Pete's to Nome. Everyone wants to see "Metamorphosis," in which the monsieur and the mademoiselle, each bound at the wrists and ankles, exchange places in the box in three seconds flat.

"I know exactly how Houdini does 'Metamorphosis,'" I say, bragging. Pannini raises his eyebrows. "The box trick has been around since before I was born."

"The box trick?" Pannini says.

But I cannot reveal how over the years the box trick has been swiftly improved, ingeniously improvised, and presented again and again, fresh as the morning dew. I cannot reveal how Houdini's "Metamorphosis" is done, not even if I wanted to.

"Box trick?" Pannini prompts, intrigued by my hesitation.

"Sorry," I say. "We magicians have a code."

"A code?"

"A code of secrecy."

"Ah, a code," Pannini says and shrugs. "Well, don't look so glum, Danny. In this town, they're nuts for the *opera*. It's a fair crowd for the Tivoli. For a magic act."

Now I shrug, drawing deeply on the Mecca.

"The old man has got to get himself a pretty heifer," Pannini says. "That'll draw 'em."

"We had a beautiful lady in the act," I say, "once."

"Did you?" Pannini says, suddenly animated. "Well, trot her out, sir!"

"She died," I say, "last spring." I fling the Mecca to the floor, stomp it out. My father will raise Cain when he smells tobacco on my breath.

"Sorry," Pannini says. When I look again, he's gone.

My father has got a good act. Not a *great* act, perhaps, but a very good act. He's worked on this act, in its various permutations, for all the twenty years I have walked upon the earth and before then, too, according to Uncle Brady. My father is not a young rascal like Houdini, but a graying man whom some people mistake for my grandfather. Yet Pop has not lost his touch, in my opinion. In my opinion—and as his only son and heir apparent, I'm entitled to my opinion—it's a lousy crowd in San Francisco for the astonishing, the miraculous, the mysterious Professor Flint.

Then again nothing seems right to me since my mother died.

As usual, my father takes up the sword and commences feints and thrusts. In the sulfuric glare of the limelights, I can see sweat pooling over the starched wing collar that strangles his neck, soaking through his fancy brocade vest like a bloodstain. I used to worry about Pop's health. He always was a scrawny bird. Scrofula and consumption ran in his side of the family. Sometimes it seemed to me that the exertions of the stage, not to mention the cognitive and financial uncertainties of magic, would do him in.

Since my mother died, though, I don't worry so much about my father any more. He turned out to be the strong one, after all. Which only goes to show, you never can tell from the looks of things what the truth is or what is an illusion.

Now my father sheaths the sword into its scabbard. This preliminary action sequence is intended to arouse any flagging interest among the gentlemen in the audience. Gentlemen are by nature restless, easily bored, not to mention skeptical. Sure enough, one of the hoodlums in the back row yells, "Bloody well get on with it, man!"

But my father never concedes to a quick, cheap thrill. No, there are ladies and children in the audience—usually there are, anyway, though such tender persons appear to be singularly lacking at the Tivoli Theater tonight. Ladies and children of sensitive sensibilities may be alarmed by Professor Flint's aggressive antics. They may pause, they may press gentle fingertips to pale throats, they may wonder if the next mystery will be too much for them to bear.

It is for this portion of the audience that my father sheaths the sword. A portion lacking in its own economic power, lacking in dignity and opportunity, as my mother used to lecture me only too often. But a portion endowed with the power of trembling lips, of fluttering eyelashes, of little cries of joy or alarm, of those gentle, pale fingertips, just as she, my mother, was so amply endowed. It is for them, then, that my father trots out the dancing handkerchief.

Frankly, I think the dancing handkerchief is rather a silly illusion. I am always surprised how much they love it.

Uncle Brady and I take our positions in the wings. Need I say that all of the Tivoli's stagehands, Pannini the booking agent, and everyone else who is not privy to our techniques, have been summarily banned? Need I say that Uncle Brady and I sprint like souls possessed to our respective positions at each wing abutting the stage? Need I hint that the handkerchief is much like a marionette, only different? Need I add that, like wizards intent on bewitching this sample of poor suffering humanity, we pick up the wonderfully simple and devilishly clever . . . devices? They *are* devices; there is no person on earth *once clearly shown* who would ever make any mistake *how* . . . How, in this case, the dancing handkerchief dances.

Pop spouts his patter. "But first, ladies and gentlemen, I will endeavor to show that the power of Life goes beyond Death, beyond the grave itself. Ladies and gentlemen, I will endeavor to demonstrate this miraculous Life power utilizing the most ordinary of personal accoutrements."

My father has got one of those masterful voices, of course, and the ability to project his humorous and ironic personality clear out into the great opera houses, the cavernous theaters, the carnival tents pitched in dusty Dakota grass. But the air seems thick in the Tivoli tonight. Suddenly, I feel a chill sweep through the theater like the draft from a back door left carelessly ajar.

"Does anyone," my father says, "have a handkerchief? Of purest white silk, if you please?"

In this surly crowd, reeking of cheap whiskey and incipient rowdiness, I fear that no person in attendance is genteel enough to possess the requested accoutrement. The chill deepens. Clear across the stage, I can see Uncle Brady twist his head about, glance behind him, at me, out there. He can feel that peculiar draft, too.

As I squint past the limelights, I suddenly see one of the very few ladies in the audience stand, work her way to the aisle, and approach the stage. I heave with relief. Across the stage, Uncle Brady pantomimes wiping his brow. What a lady she is, too, tall and slim, in rustling burgundy taffeta. Her abundant coiffure spills down around her face and tilts above her forehead at a saucy angle, one curl coiled on her high curved cheek. She brandishes a white silk handkerchief in fingers as elegant as a Dresden doll's. She smiles at my father, who readily acknowledges her charm. She glances around, seeking her neighbors' approval of her boldness. Her large eyes, deep and sparkling, happen to find mine as I peek out from the wings. I am quite sure I can detect her scent, the rich musk of red roses.

"*Da,*" she says to my father. Her voice is one of those husky, purring contraltos. "I have a handkerchief."

And then she winks at me.

I duck out of sight. Pop will have my hide if he suspects one of the audience saw me skulking about in the wings. He proceeds apace with the illusion, however, deftly knotting one corner of the lady's white silk handkerchief. When he's done, the handkerchief looks just like a little ghost with a peaked head and a drooping body. He tosses the handkerchief to the floor of the stage, casually leaning over to rearrange it and attach . . . never mind. Like a marionette, as I've said. That's all you need to know.

"Thus I will prove, ladies and gentlemen," my father says, "within each little thing, such as a mere handkerchief from this lovely lady, that the Dead can truly come *alive,*" and off we go, Uncle Brady and me, making that little knot dance and flip across the stage. First, the handkerchief raises its lifeless head, struggles to become animated, and then—pardon me—gives up the ghost, and falls slack again. My father coaxes it, and the handkerchief rises once more, growing more vigorous, finally standing upright and lively. The ghost hops into Pop's hands, protests his restraint, leaps down and capers across the stage. Pop seizes the handkerchief, hands it back to the lady as it still bobs its head. She cries out. Pop takes it back, unties the knot, and releases a mere lifeless handkerchief to the lady. She beams and displays her erstwhile ghost to her neighbors. Everyone in the front rows leans forward, entranced.

Like I said, they love it.

"Thank you, madame," Pop says. "What is your name, please?"

"I am Zena Troubetzskoy," she says.

"Bloody well get on with it, man!" the hoodlum in the back row yells again. His pals guffaw.

"Madame Troubetzskoy," my father says and takes her handkerchief again and produces from it a sparkling fresh red rose. He hands silk and bloom back to her.

Zena blushes. As I peek from the wing again, I can see a deep flush infuse her cheeks like a sudden fever. "Can you really communicate with the Dead, Professor Flint?" she asks.

"I can," Pop says.

Liar, I think. The enmity between magicians and spiritualist mediums revolves around this very point. No one has established communication with the Dead. No one has proven the soul survives. Mediums deceive people with cruel lies, with illusions any magician can readily replicate. Maskelyne, the Royal Illusionist, exposed the Davenport brothers' spirit cabinet as nothing more than a box trick. Anderson, the Great Wizard of the North, could produce better table-tipping and spirit raps than the Fox sisters. If my father really could establish communication with the Spirits of the Dead, don't you think he would have contacted my mother?

But what else is my father to say? "No, not really"? He cannot say that, not in front of an audience. A magician must never reveal the secrets of his illusions, must never explain the mystery though there is no mystery. That is our code of secrecy.

Still, I am uncomfortable with Pop's charade, his dissemblement. Is he any different than one of those deceitful mediums?

Perhaps I am not cut out to be a magician, after all.

If Zena Troubetzskoy is perturbed by my father's lie, however, she gives no sign. "How marvelous," she simply says and drifts back into the darkness beyond the limelights.

Now the little rented orchestra strikes up a lively tune. Uncle Brady rushes onstage to assist Pop, while I toss the ghost getup over my suit and sprint to my appointed place behind the plate of glass which is situated . . . Situated just so; situated beneath a strategically placed spotlight. Situated so that when light and darkness are arranged precisely right, when the physics of reflection and refraction are manipulated, you will see an apparition appear from nowhere on the stage with Professor Flint. You will see the apparition joust with him in a death-defying duel. You will see him pierce the apparition clear through with his sword, at which point you will see the apparition disappear before your very eyes.

All right, perhaps the ghost duel is not so death-defying. Not like that young rascal Houdini who trusses himself up like an animal bound for slaughter or swallows needles. Nor is the ghost duel original to my father since Pepper pioneered the illusion and others have presented it in various permutations such as "The Blue Room" or "The Room of Mortality," in which a skeleton in a coffin transforms into a beautiful woman and withers to bones again. Still, I think the ghost duel is the high point of Professor Flint's act.

I never tired of watching this illusion back in the days when my mother played the ghost. When I was a kid, I used to love when Pop intoned his Grand Invocation of the Spirits of the Dead, and the ghost appeared—just like that!—floating right over the stage. And you could *feel* how the audience began to believe. Ladies would weep. Some gentlemen would toot their noses, while others would gasp, filled with fear or shock or the wonder of it all. The wonder that Death itself *could* be overcome. One time in Cheyenne someone called out, "Praise the Lord!" and someone else yelled, "Amen!"

What a ghost my mother was! Pop would throw down a leather glove, whip his sword from its scabbard, challenge the apparition to a duel. The apparition would fling down its own white silk glove, would produce its own weapon. And off they would go, leaping and sparring like musketeers. My mother was so charming and lively and graceful that the ladies would stop weeping, the gentlemen would stop tooting in their handkerchiefs. These hardy souls of our young nation of America, these people who daily faced consumption and childbirth and fever, they would gaze at that lively ghost, and they would smile. I could see joy steal like a thief into their hearts, and it was *magic*. For a moment they ceased their grieving because for a moment they could see that the Dead weren't gone after all. Why, the Dead were positively lively on the other side and, if anyone should be mourned for, it was the living who still wept. Who could not find peace.

I am not nearly as charming a ghost as my mother once was, but I can spar, I can feint, and the duel has got this audience going at last. I can hear cheers and exclamations of encouragement from where . . .

From the place where I accomplish my part of the illusion. Pop pierces me through the heart, and I vanish, and it's over. Professor Flint's astonishing, miraculous, and mysterious act is over for tonight. I cast off my ghost getup, dash up onto the stage. The audience stands, applauds. Mr. Pannini gives me the thumbs-up.

I can see the relief on my father's face. He is the sort of man who makes a meticulous accounting of each triumph and failure, however small. The failures disturb him far more than the triumphs ever give him satisfaction. Uncle Brady beams and bows, but he gives a little shake of his head, a sort of cringe to his shoulder, and I know what he is thinking. He's thinking nothing is the same since the accident took my mother's life last spring.

The woman in burgundy taffeta rushes up to the stage, clapping furiously, her red rose tucked behind her ear. Zena Troubetzskoy says, "How marvelous!"

Uncle Brady is already up, bending over our sputtering campfire, brewing gritty coffee in a dented pot, when I wake in the dawn. I am aching, shivering, and my mouth tastes of soot.

"Rise and shine, Danny," Uncle Brady says, grinning. "You look like death warmed over, son."

We have been on the road for a long time. I am accustomed to sleeping on the ground or in the back of our wagon, accustomed to roots and rocks and rough boards pressing into my spine and ribs. Years ago, my father invested in an enormous M.P. Henderson freight wagon with a canvas tent top, a regular house on wheels built for durability, not speed. We need a team of four young sturdy draft horses to pull it. Much of the customized interior is devoted to the transportation of our equipment. I am accustomed to my narrow bunk, the lack of privacy, the sweltering heat or the numbing chill.

But I have yearned for months for this engagement in San Francisco. Something in me secretly hoped for a little relief. There are magnificent hotels in San Francisco, hotels as fine as the best in New York City, London, or Paris. What I would give for just one night at the Palace or Lucky Baldwin's, for a real stuffed mattress, a down pillow, a blazing fireplace, a hot bath. A cup of coffee brewed by one of the hotel chefs whose culinary reputations are repeated among us vagabonds of the far West in the reverent hushed tones reserved for legends and miracles.

But though Pop could probably afford just one night at the Palace for him and me, though Pop struggles grimly with encroaching arthritis and surely yearns for a hot bath and some comfort more than I do, the magnificent hotels of San Francisco are unlikely to permit Uncle Brady to stay in the same suite as us. Uncle Brady is as deft with my father's craft as any of the best; he assists my father with our books of account and the management of our tour. He is my dearest friend; he was my mother's most faithful companion even before she met my father. But Uncle Brady's complexion is the color of the coffee he's brewing. The magnificent hotels are likely to request that Uncle Brady stay in servants' quarters, if they even permit him to stay as a guest at all. And that is unacceptable to my father. My father has never permitted anything but the best treatment for Uncle Brady, treatment equal to any hospitality offered to him or me. Pop may be a boiled shirt, but Uncle Brady tells me my father has insisted upon this policy since Uncle Brady journeyed north with my mother from their ruined home in Georgia in that terrible year before I was born.

And so we camp for the night in the field at Fourth Street and Mission, where the medicine shows and quack peddlers and dime museums have set up campgrounds. The field is a carnival by day and a shindig by night hosted by some of the most disreputable scoundrels in the far West. I have spent the wee hours leaning up against a wheel of our wagon, wrapped in a reeking, moth-eaten, buffalo-skin blanket, a derringer in one hand, a large brass bell in the other. My father did not expect me to kill or even fend off a hostile intruder, of course. If I or our horses were assaulted, I was instructed to shoot into the air and ring the bell like mad. Instead I fell into a poor facsimile of sleep, tormented by a dream about the gypsies we encountered outside of Cheyenne. I kept seeing Leilani, taunting me.

My father extracts himself from our wagon with all the brittle dignity of a nobleman come to survey his hinterlands. Does he say good morning as I am painfully rousing myself? Does he inquire about my well-being?

"You smoked a cigarette last night, Daniel," is the first thing my father says to me, turning a baleful glance in my direction as he seizes the mug Uncle Brady proffers and tosses scalding coffee onto his tongue. He does not wince or grimace at the taste or heat.

"Beg pardon?" I say.

"When you turn twenty-one, you may do as you please, sir," he says in a tone that leads me to suspect I will have little more freedom than I do at twenty. "You may give over your health to wrack and ruin. You may cast away all I have taught you, cast away your livelihood and your well-being, cast your soul to the Devil himself. But till then, sir, till then, as long as you are in my company . . ."

"Professor," Uncle Brady says quietly. "Could we please discuss the state of our affairs?"

At any other time, I would have secretly smiled at Uncle Brady for getting me off the hook. I would have thrown him a wink or a thumbs-up behind my father's back. But I know that the state of our affairs in San Francisco is rather less than salubrious. I collect my own mug of grit from Uncle Brady, crouch by the fire, and brace myself for the bad news.

"We're broke," Uncle Brady says. "Nearly broke."

"Broke?" I say, incredulous. "I thought we cleared ten thousand dollars in Tacoma."

"An agent from Tacoma showed up yesterday afternoon, as we feared," Uncle Brady says.

"I saw no agent," my father says.

"I didn't want to worry you, Professor, before a performance," Uncle Brady says. "The theater wasn't insured. The fire cleaned them out."

"It wasn't our fault!" I say, but I know that's not strictly true. Pop kept kegs of methylated spirits for fireworks effects. A cigarette discarded by some careless stranger sent everything up in flames, including much of our equipment. I suppose we were lucky to get out alive and unscathed. Worst of all, the accursed pane of plate glass, which we tote about in the wagon swaddled more protectively than a newborn baby, got shattered. Uncle Brady had to wire ahead to San Francisco for a new pane.

My father is impassive. "You reimbursed the agent?"

"Of course, Professor," Uncle Brady says. "We must do that if we're ever to play in Tacoma again. Then there's the new plate glass. All the trunks from Europe. The magic portfolio. The vanishing birdcage, the Chinese lanterns, the enchanted demon's head, the flip-over boxes, the feathered bouquets. Well, you know, Professor. Not to mention the costumes."

My father grunts, I groan. Forget a night at the Palace. My stomach rumbles. I have not eaten, I realize, since yesterday noon, and that meal was some leathery beef jerky washed down with hard well water. Traitorous thoughts fill my head. Perhaps I could secure employment as a waiter in San Francisco. At least I could get something decent to eat.

My father only says, "I am grateful our suppliers have been so helpful, prompt, skillful, and courteous. And trustworthy. We could not have gone on with the show without them."

"Nevertheless," Uncle Brady says, "we are broke. Nearly broke. We haven't enough to hire a new assistant."

278

"Pop," I say, "I'm *hungry*."

"Go feed the horses," my father says, unmoved by my distress. To Uncle Brady, "And the take from the show last night?"

"The theater was half-full," Uncle Brady says.

"A pretty poor show for Professor Flint," I say, still insulted.

"And the take?" my father says calmly.

"Won't cover our traveling expenses from Tacoma by even half," Uncle Brady says grimly.

"That's just great," I say, cranky from my awful night. I struggle to my feet, heart simmering with rebellion. "You may both go starve and good luck to you. I'm tired of magic. I'm not cut out to be a magician, anyway. I shall seek my own fortune in San Francisco."

"Maybe the boy should go find some day work, professor," Uncle Brady says. "We'll have to rehearse without him."

"If you're through with your coffee, Daniel," my father says, ignoring my fit of pique as well as Uncle Brady's suggestion, which only makes me madder, "go feed the horses like I told you."

"I've got a bill here for fifty dollars," Uncle Brady says, shuffling through a thick stack of papers. "It's forty days overdue, professor. We'll get no more credit from the Chicago Magic Company if we don't . . ."

"Go feed the bloody horses yourself, Pop," I say, quick anger boiling in my chest. "I won't *stand* for this any . . ."

"I beg your pardon, gentlemen," says a husky, purring contralto voice. "Forgive me for interrupting your breakfast."

We all turn, mouths gaping. Zena Troubetzskoy strolls up to the edge of our campfire and stands, smiling serenely. Have I mentioned how beautiful she is in her burgundy taffeta, the red rose still tucked behind her ear? When I meet her gaze, she gives me a surreptitious wink.

"What breakfast," I mutter. Still, my anger evaporates before that flirtatious wink. She is not a girl of my age but an older woman, yet my pulse quickens all the same.

My father casts a look at me that could choke a horse. He stands and bows graciously. "Madame Troubetzskoy."

"You remember me, sir?"

"Naturally. What can we do for you, madame?" He flips his hand at me; *go get her a stool to sit on.* I hop to it, retrieving one from the back of our wagon.

She sits, warming her hands over the campfire. "Professor Flint," she says at last, "last night you said you can communicate with the Spirits of the Dead. Didn't you?"

Uncle Brady and I trade glances. My father clears his throat. "So I did."

279

"Then, Professor Flint, I would like to ask you if you could attempt to communicate with my dear husband. I have something I need to tell him."

My father takes her hand. "My dear Madame Troubetzskoy . . ."

"Please call me Zena."

"Zena. I am a magician, Zena, not a spiritualist medium."

"And that's marvelous, Professor. Whatever you wish to call yourself is fine with me."

"Zena." My father kneels at her feet and lowers his voice. "We are not before an audience now, so I must tell you something in the strictest confidence."

"Yes?" Her eyes shine with anticipation.

"I am a magician, as I've said. What I do, what we do up there on the stage. It's all . . . an illusion."

Her face darkens. "Oh, please, I implore you, Professor."

"An illusion, madame. It isn't real!"

"But you told me you can communicate with the Dead. You told me you have psychic powers. You *told* me."

My father glances at Uncle Brady and me, his mouth screwed up as though he has bitten on a lemon. My father does not consider anything he does in his act to be a lie. He never misrepresents himself. The audience *knows* it's magic. The audience *knows* it's an illusion. But this lovely woman in burgundy taffeta has taken him at his word. And he does not want to confess that he lied, even if he did. He does not want to admit to false pretenses. He cannot bear being exposed like poor old Anderson, the Great Wizard of the North, who effortlessly knew people's intimate secrets onstage but got so addled with drink one night that he could not find his way home.

"I said I *endeavor* to communicate with the Dead," he scrupulously corrects her.

"Then endeavor for me," she says earnestly. "Oh please, won't you try? You have more power than you know, Professor."

"Bosh," my father says, but he glows with pleasure at her praise nonetheless. Account for each triumph, however small; that's Pop. I roll my eyes in disgust at Uncle Brady, who shrugs and looks away.

"I'll pay you, of course," she says. She fumbles in her burgundy satin purse and extracts a handful of gleaming gold coins.

Need I say our eyes bugged out? "Mercy," Uncle Brady whispers and takes two of the coins from Zena's outstretched palm, gives one to me. It turns out not to be a coin at all but a fat, irregular lozenge of pure gold, soft to the tooth, heavy in the hand, without the smell of inferior metals. The sort of unmarked token gamblers, robbers, or miners carry in the far West and may be better than minted money because you can cash it in at any assay office or bank, trade it for goods or services. The piece I hold in my hand could be worth fifty dollars alone.

My father clears his throat again. "Madame Zena," he says, "would you like to sit at a séance?"

"Oh, please!" she says, and bounces on her stool like a child told she will get a palomino pony for Christmas.

On the one hand, I am now quite disgusted with my father for stepping over the ethical line drawn between magicians and mediums. On the other hand, I am proud of him for the sacrifices he is willing to make for our show. The sacrifices he makes for his family. I don't really want to work as a waiter in some restaurant. I am Daniel Flint, the eminent Professor Flint's only son and heir apparent. I have been immersed in the business of magic my whole life, starting when my father plucked me in my diapers out of a magic portfolio and told me to wave at the audience. One day he will pass the mantle of magic to me.

Uncle Brady and I dash to the wagon as my father serves Zena coffee and chats with her, commenting on the new day. His voice booms over the campgrounds. My father has made his decision. Uncle Brady and I trade grins. We are not displeased.

"This gonna be tricky, son," Uncle Brady says. "We don't know a thing about her."

I hold up the gold piece. "We know *this.*"

The deceitful spiritualist mediums who permit people to believe that they establish communication with the Spirits of the Dead do plenty of research before they work their illusions. They know much about those who come to sit at a séance. They possess the con artist's knack of parlaying what they learn on the spur of the moment into more information, more confidence. Mediums use plenty of tricks and devices and effects to make people believe they are contacting the Dead. Mediums use the Room of Mortality illusion; they use the box trick. Let no one ever be deceived about that.

We feverishly set up the tiny dining area in the back of our wagon with a table, chairs. We position false walls gleaned from backdrops. I'm feeling better and better about this turn of events. In truth, rigging up a parlor to produce a fake séance for an audience of one is quite simple for us. Excitement chases away the last dregs of my discontent. Gold; the lady has got gold.

"What else do we know?" Uncle Brady quizzes me. When my father is hard on me, Uncle Brady is forgiving. When my father is a boiled shirt, Uncle Brady pats me on the back. When my father imposes his rules and injunctions, Uncle Brady gently takes me by the hand and leads me down the paths of new knowledge. I love my father; I adore Uncle Brady. I have always called this handsome, dark-skinned man "Uncle Brady." So did my mother. For that matter, so does Professor Flint.

I grin, intrigued by this new game. "She's married."

"And widowed," Uncle Brady coaches me.

"She's Russian," I say. "Plenty of Russians in California, aren't there?"

"Russians settled in this territory forty years ago," Uncle Brady says. "Lots of gold miners."

"And she's beautiful," I say.

"Um-hm." Uncle Brady wiggles his eyebrows up and down.

I laugh. "Wears perfume, scent of red roses, I think. Nice touch, Pop giving her the red rose. Where did he get it, anyway? We haven't paid the florist."

Uncle Brady shrugs. "The dress is nice," he says, "but not quite in the height of fashion."

"Still, she's got to be rich," I say. "Look at that gold!" I produce my token. "Gamblers carry these, and robbers, and miners. Gold miners, Uncle Brady."

"They're coming." Uncle Brady ducks behind the false walls, leaving me to brush crumbs and dust from the table. I take Zena Troubetzskoy's hand as she climbs into the wagon. My father follows. My father instantly produces a red silk rose, a prop slightly the worse for wear that we've had stashed in our inventory for a long time.

"Oh, no," Zena murmurs, patting the bloom tucked behind her ear. That red rose, a real one, still looks fresh. "You need not try to amuse me, Professor Flint. I merely want to speak with my husband."

My father glances at me for a split second but I can see the frisson of panic in his eyes. "Go get a candle, Daniel."

I unobtrusively relieve Zena of her burgundy satin purse, excuse myself for a moment, and duck behind the false walls as my father continues to chat with her. Uncle Brady seizes the purse. We have no intention of relieving the lady of any more gold than she has freely relinquished. Instead, silently, carefully, we empty the purse, looking for information. A lady's purse typically contains a calling card, a monogrammed handkerchief, perhaps a photograph of the dearly departed. A pressed corsage would be superb, a letter even better, but I would settle for any sort of personal effect that would provide a clue regarding who Zena Troubetzskoy is. Cosmetics, liver pills, a receipt from her dressmaker, a label on the purse itself. All I need are a few clues, which I will convey to my father through the simple device of . . . Suffice it to say, we have ways of conveying information to each other which Zena could not possibly detect.

But there is nothing. Nothing but the purse itself—no label—and the plain white silk handkerchief she lent to my father last night. And the gold; more gold tokens, quite a stash of them.

I slip back into our makeshift parlor, restore the purse to the lady, set candlestick and candle in the center of our table. I signal my father regarding the paucity of our findings. I sit. My father lights the candle and closes the canvas flap over the back of our wagon, plunging the parlor into darkness dimly lit by candlelight. We three join hands.

"I shall now endeavor to establish communication with the Spirits of the Dead," my father says, throws back his head, and closes his eyes, unleashing psychic powers. Uncle Brady sets to work behind the false walls, producing a cool breeze that makes our candle flame flicker.

Zena's hand begins to tremble violently in mine. "Oh, Nickie," she whispers under her breath.

Before my father can utter a word, I murmur, "Nickie?"

"Oh, yes!" Zena cries. "Nikita, is that you?"

"'Tis I, my rose," I say, unable to stop. "'Tis Nikita."

My father blinks at me, but he dare not scowl.

"I'm so sorry, Nickie," Zena says. Tears stream from her eyes. "I never meant to leave you. I never meant to leave you in the mountains, the awful mountains."

"The mountains," I say.

"Here I am in my dress with a rose in my hair," Zena says.

"You look beautiful as always," I say.

"I abandoned you there. I never cared about the gold, not really. I just wanted to be near you. Yet I abandoned you."

"I forgive you, Zena," I say. "I know you didn't mean to abandon me."

"Do you, Nickie? Do you really?"

"Of course, my rose."

"All I've ever wanted since is your forgiveness."

"I forgive you," I say. "I love you, Zena. Always and forever."

She begins to sob in earnest now, withdrawing her hands from mine and my father's and covering her face. My father blows out the candle and stands, throws back the canvas flap. Morning sunlight and fresh chilly air pour into our wagon. Zena finds her white silk handkerchief and dabs at her eyes. My father is impassive. I cannot read his face when he glances at me.

"Thank you," she says to me, pressing my hand. "Thank you so much."

"I am honored to assist you," I say. I confess I am pleased with myself, despite the lady's distress. I read her like a book. Perhaps I am cut out to be a magician, after all.

"May I come back tomorrow?" she says to my father.

"I think not, Madame Zena," my father says. "We are not spiritualist mediums."

"But see how talented your son is? I *knew* he was."

"But this is not what we do, you see," my father says. Do I detect a small sour note of envy in his tone? Only a moment ago, he was the talented one. "We must rehearse, we are expecting a shipment of new equipment, we . . ."

"Oh please, Professor," she says so plaintively that only a man with a heart of stone would refuse her. She dips into her purse, extracts another gold token, tucks it into my hand, closes my fingers over it. Only a fool would refuse her.

My father is no fool. "Very well," he says. "Tomorrow."

And off she goes, her burgundy taffeta rustling over the dusty grass.

"Daniel," my father says sternly as he and Uncle Brady tear down the false walls and stack them carefully around the plate glass. I sit at the table, mulling over my small triumph.

"Ah yes, the horses," I say and scramble to my task. I am ashamed of my earlier outburst. Perhaps my father will let the incident go unremarked, but, knowing Pop, that's not likely.

"Feed the horses," my father says, "then go downtown."

"I didn't mean it, Pop," I say. "I don't know the first thing about being a waiter."

"They say waiting tables is a skilled trade," Uncle Brady says. He throws a look of sympathy in my direction.

"Go downtown," my father repeats and shakes his finger at me. "She'll want more than a few lucky guesses from you tomorrow. You had better go and earn your gold. Better see what you can find out about Zena Troubetzskoy."

And what do I find out about Zena Troubetzskoy? That if a lady wants to vanish in this city of three hundred thousand souls, she can do so without a trace.

I go to the main police station at Fifth and Market, but she isn't a wanted criminal—as far as I know—and she isn't missing. I had seen her only this morning. I go to the post office at Battery Street but when the clerk runs his finger down the directory, he can find no listing for Zena Troubetzskoy. The telephone exchange in San Francisco is still in the planning stages since only a few thousand households own telephones. The telegraph company cannot help me if I don't know her whereabouts in the first place. The messenger services have no record of delivering to a Zena Troubetzskoy. Those messenger boys know more than the cops about people in town. One young man actually does remember the lovely lady in burgundy taffeta; he'd attended Professor Flint's performance last night. I scrutinize his guilty bloodshot eyes, haggard face. Was he one of the hoodlums in the back row? "Perhaps she'll show up again for your father's performance," he suggests, which isn't impossible but doesn't help much with my task at hand.

Could she be a transient then, a tourist, a vagabond? I decide to check the hotels, starting with the Palace. My father appropriated our gold tokens, including the one Zena personally tucked in my hand, and traded me some coins that he miraculously produced from his empty boodle bag. Broke, indeed. What other funds has my father squirreled away? I decide our circumstances are not so dire, after all. I am desperate for lunch. I deserve the Palace after my performance this morning. My first small triumph in a long time.

The Palace Hotel is the crown jewel of Market Street, the first luxury hotel on the West Coast. Miles of Persian carpets, crystal chandeliers. I step into the Garden Court, where the air smells like a florist shop and a string quartet is playing Tschaikovsky. The maître d' in an immaculate tuxedo grants me a withering glance. I brush off my topcoat nervously, tug at my unruly hair, which is nearly as curly and thick as Uncle Brady's. I take a menu. Oyster omelettes, asparagus in aspic, cracked crab with drawn butter, Lady Baltimore cake. I attempt not to appear like some backwater rube but I am agog at this exotic cuisine and salivating with curiosity till I glance at the prices; mercy. Perhaps I should check with the guest register and be on my way. I turn to go and bump right into her.

"Danny Flint," Zena says as though we are long-lost friends. In a gesture so intimate I feel a blush rush to my face, she straightens my tie, smooths her fingers through my hair. She smiles at me like a beautiful aunt would flirt with her favorite nephew. "You look grand," she says, instantly intuiting my distress. "Will you lunch with me, Danny?"

"I . . . I . . . that is, Madame Troubetzskoy, I don't have enough . . ."

"Nonsense," she says, pulling me back into the Garden Court and summoning the maître d'. "And call me Zena."

She orders a huge quantity of dishes and drinks, including lobster and champagne. She tucks into the food with such gusto that I soon forget my shyness. I pour a bit of champagne. "My father would have my hide if he saw me drinking," I tell her.

She throws back her head and laughs. The string quartet strikes up "The Sleeping Beauty Waltz." She extends her hand. "Will you dance with me, Danny?"

"I don't know how," I say.

"I'll teach you," she says.

That little sip of champagne loosens my reserve. "All right," I say bravely, and we stand, go to the dance floor. She positions my hand at her waist, takes my other hand in her own, and off we go. "One two three, one two three," she coaches. I get the hang of it at once. We whirl and swoop across the Garden Court, laughing. Her skin is smooth and cool, her waist slim and firm. She feels as light as a bird in my arms.

"Every man should know how to dance," she declares. "But you especially, Danny Flint."

"Why me especially?" I say, thoroughly enjoying myself.

"Knowing how to dance will give you grace on the stage when you step into your father's shoes one day," she says.

"I don't wish to step into my father's shoes," I say abruptly. "I wish to wear my own shoes, thank you." I break off from her and go back to our seats. Dishes litter the table, but my appetite has vanished.

She sits and helps herself to lobster and asparagus, but she is subdued, troubled. "I said the wrong thing."

"Never mind," I say.

"Dancing will give you grace when you go upon the stage," she repeats doggedly. "And perhaps dancing will make you happy again, too. Perhaps you will lose your sadness."

"Am I sad?" I joke.

"*Da,*" she says. "I can see it in your face."

"But I'm not."

"*Da,* you are." She leans forward. The other diners fade away, the room seems to vanish. "Why are you so sad, Danny?"

"There was an accident last spring," I say curtly. "My mother died."

"I'm sorry," she says quietly.

"I'm so angry with her!" I practically yell. "I'm so angry about what she did to me!"

"What happened?" Zena says.

What happened? What happened was that the astonishing, miraculous, mysterious Professor Flint decided to take his traveling show on a sojourn through the Great Plains. We played the dusty cowtowns, the dead ends, the tenderloins, clearing a thousand dollars here, five hundred dollars there. Was it worth it? The heat and the cold, the dust and the torrential rain, the sullen silent audiences and the drunken rowdy ones. My favorite horse turning his leg in a pothole, and my father having to put him down with the revolver. My mother quietly crying in the wagon. Hardtack and salt pork and millet gruel so dreadful I often preferred to go hungry. We were always afraid to drink the water. My father said dysentery and cholera came from bad water, could kill you in a couple of days, and no medicine could save you. I feared I would go blind studying by candlelight the topics my father assigned to me in our *Encyclopedia Britannica,* which I stored beneath my bunk. Then there were the thieves, the gamblers, the con men, the gunmen. The Indian Wars might have been over, but violence and cruelty and greed still stalked through the endless flatlands, waited in ambush in the mountains. My father taught my mother and me how to use the derringer.

When we got to Cheyenne, we saw our first gypsies, a caravan of tinkers drifting through the West in gaudy, spangled wagons. They possessed their own panoply of illusions and trickery. Curious about us, the gypsies came to our magic shows and to our campgrounds. My father and Uncle Brady discussed horses with several of the men and permitted their best driver to examine our horses' hooves. My mother took a violent dislike to them, though. She took care to fend off their attentions, refused gifts of homebrew from the women.

"You stay away from those tinkers," she warned me.

Nevertheless, I met Leilani. Black hair to her waist, which she wore unbound in a windswept mane. "Brown eyes," she teased me, her own so dark they were black and sparkled like that volcanic stone called obsidian. Sturdy from hard work, Leilani was neither tubercularly thin nor indolently plump. She wore bright loose dresses cinched at the waist by a scarlet satin belt. Bracelets of copper clattered on her wrists. Her smile glittered; one of her front teeth was pure gold.

"But she's my age," I told my mother.

"She's older than you know, Dan," my mother said. "She's playing with you."

"I'm not a simpleton, Mama," I said.

"She's vulgar and cheap." This, when my mother sat clothed in a ragged cotton housedress, darning our socks, as Uncle Brady, in nothing but suspenders and trousers, helped her wash and mend our costumes.

"You're not exactly the belle of the ball yourself," I said. Could have bit my tongue with my meanness. My mother was every bit as beautiful and meticulously coiffed as the belle of Atlanta she once was, despite the ragged cotton housedress. Perhaps even because of it. I often saw Uncle Brady helping her with her hair, with the buttons on the back of her dress.

I remember Uncle Brady's reproachful look. I remember how my mother looked at me then, tears glinting in her eyes, fury and frustration and something else I could not name etched into her fine features. She would not dignify my insult with a reply. Instead she said, "Dan, what do you see in her?"

"I don't know," I said. "I can't explain."

But I knew what it was, or at least I thought I did. Leilani was beautiful, she was young, she was wild, she was free. I had never met any girl like her. She wore thin bright hoops in her ears, a little hoop through one nostril, a long fine chain that plunged from her neck into her neckline and down into her bodice. Her skin was the color of oak leaves shed in the autumn. I could not stay away.

A thunderstorm had blown in from the Rockies that night when Leilani came for me on her Appaloosa mare. The show was over; we were moving on to Denver. My father was sick with worry about the pane of plate glass, traveling up into the mountains. I'd been packing up our gear with Uncle Brady. He and my mother were quarreling behind my father's back about something, I can't remember what. I could not tolerate the tension, the ugly mood. I stepped outside the theater for a breath of fresh air.

And there she was. She did not ride sidesaddle. She rode astride. She wore fancy tooled boots with silver-tipped toes.

"So, brown eyes," Leilani said. "You and your folks are blowing this cowtown tonight?"

I stroked that Appaloosa's sweaty neck. "Yep," I said. Leilani smelled of leather and some smoky perfume.

"You can't leave without your fortune," she said.

"My fortune?" I said.

"You got to let me read your palm, brown eyes. How will you know what tomorrow brings for you, eh?" She threw back her head and laughed.

I mounted the mare behind Leilani. Together we rode to the edge of Cheyenne, where the tinkers had set up camp. Together we slid off the mare and stood tangled with each other as the storm unleashed its fury and the wind whipped her hair. The tinkers had built up huge campfires and covered them with open tents of flapping fabrics. People huddled around the fires, passing wine bottles and enjoying the storm's exhilaration.

Together we found her family's wagon, together we climbed inside. Together we tumbled into a heap of blankets laid on straw. She kissed me in the dark as rain pelted the roof. She tore at my jacket, my shirt.

Suddenly a bright light assaulted my eyes. My mother stood over us, a lantern in her hand raised like a judgment. "Take your hands off my son," my mother said in a booming voice. She did not shriek; she did not scream. Yet the force of her fury, the determination of her will, projected over the entire tinkers' camp. Men murmured, women laughed.

I jumped up at once, fumbling with the buttons on my trousers, searching for my shirt. My mother stood over me with her lantern as I retrieved the rest of my clothes. I remember I checked to see whether my wallet was still in my pocket. The wallet had dislodged and fallen to the floor. I retrieved the fold of leather, checked the pocket for my coins.

All through this reckoning, Leilani lay silently in her tumble of blankets. But as I stepped from her wagon, disheveled and chastened, Leilani began to laugh. She began to guffaw. "Mama's boy," she called out. "Did you forget your shirt, mama's boy?"

"Let's go, Dan," my mother said.

Leilani hurled out of her wagon after us, her bosom gleaming in the firelight, her face streaked with rain and sweat. Her mouth was a rictus of contempt, of ridicule. "Did you lose your wallet, mama's boy? Did you lose your cherry, mama's boy?"

I walked away from the tinkers' camp led by my mother like a docile puppy as the laughter of Leilani and her people seared my ears.

My mother had ridden one of the horses. She had seen me leave with Leilani and galloped after me.

I whirled on her, infuriated. "How could you, Mama?"

"How could I what?" she hurled back. "Protect my son from that hussy?"

"You humiliated me," I said.

"I saved you," she said.

"I don't want your salvation. I never asked for your salvation."

"I know better, Dan," she said, tears starting in her eyes.

"I am not your little boy. You are not my mother," I said. "I disown you. Get out of my sight."

"Dan," she said.

"Get on the horse and go," I said. "Get out of here. I will make my own way in life, Mama, thank you very much. And you can tell Pop the same."

"Dan," she said.

"I said *go!*"

"And so your mother went," Zena Troubetzskoy says. The luncheon crowd in the Garden Court has disappeared. Waiters bustle over tables, cart dishes away. The string quartet is taking a break. The maître d' scowls at us till Zena orders a tray of the desserts du jour.

"She got on the horse," I say. "It was raining like mad. The road was slick. The horse slipped, she fell, and then the horse fell, too. My father had to put that horse down. And she . . . she was all crushed inside. After brooding in the woods for a while and realizing there was nowhere I wanted to go, I walked to town in the rain. She died before I got back."

The maître d' approaches us at last. "I beg your pardon, madame and sir, but we have no more desserts for lunch. We are closing the Garden Court in preparation for the dinner hour. I must ask you to leave."

Zena takes care of the bill in gold. We rise and stroll out of the Palace Hotel. Zena turns to me and says, "Till we meet again, Danny Flint." She straightens my tie, touches my hair. "Goodbye," she says. "Thank you for the dance."

"Goodbye," I say.

I wonder what it feels like to be all crushed inside. I wonder what my mother felt. I wonder what she thought of me. I wonder if she was as angry with me as I was with her. I wonder if she was as sorry about what happened that night as I was. As I am to this day. I wonder if she grieved that she could not apologize to me as I am desolate that I never got to apologize to her. *I disown you,* I said. But I never got to say goodbye.

My father is ecstatic when I make my appearance in the late afternoon for rehearsal at the Tivoli Theater.

Uncle Brady is arguing with the conductor of the rented orchestra. At first I am afraid my father will ask what I have been doing with myself all day, which is nothing much except exercising my legs on the hills of San Francisco. To my surprise, though, he does not quiz me. "Daniel," he says, producing the gold token Zena tucked into my palm that morning. "I want you to look at this."

"All right," I say, nonplussed by my father's excitement. Nothing much perturbs my father. When a horse must be put down, he gets out the revolver. When my mother died, he went into seclusion and drew the curtains around his bunk in our Henderson wagon. He waited out his grief. Yet each night, in each town, Professor Flint went on with the show, though nothing was the same without my mother as his assistant. Uncle Brady, on the other hand, cried for a long time. My father even forgave him when Uncle Brady started taking a drink now and then.

290

"*Look,*" my father insists, displaying the gold token on his palm. I look.

I see a faint legend imprinted on that gold, something I never noticed before. "I didn't see this," I protest, but my father waves away my deficiency.

"Uncle Brady and I didn't either," he confesses. "Yet the legend is on every one of the tokens she gave us this morning. The clerk at the assay office brought it to my attention. It's as if it appeared out of nowhere. I felt like a bloody fool."

Uncle Brady joins us. "What did you find out about the lady, son?" he asks me.

"Nothing much," I say, secretly ashamed that I had talked all about myself without finding out more about Zena. Uncle Brady regards me with his astute brown eyes. Sometimes I feel like I am looking into my own soul when I look at Uncle Brady. I know I am shifting my own eyes around. I am acting like a lying child, but I don't want to tell him or my father about my lunch with Zena at the Palace Hotel. Some things have got to belong just to me.

"That won't help," Uncle Brady says. He takes the token from my father. "See that? Says 'No Return.'"

"What does it mean?" I say.

"It's a registered claim: the 'No Return,'" Uncle Brady says. "The assay office told the professor it was a mine north of Hangtown."

"A gold mine," my father says. "During the Rush."

"Looks like our Madame Troubetzskoy must be the heiress to a gold mine," Uncle Brady says. "Her husband must have been a miner. Just like you said, Danny."

"Lucky guess, huh," I say.

"Of course, she could be a thief," my father points out.

"The mountains," Uncle Brady says. "The awful mountains." Uncle Brady's eyes glimmer and, for a moment, I wonder if he believes I've got the power of communicating with the Spirits of the Dead. "I don't believe she's a thief, Professor."

"*Real* lucky guess," I say.

"An excellent application of your intuition, Daniel," my father says, "just like I taught you." To Uncle Brady, "I suppose it's no concern of ours if she's a thief. She compensated *us*. We're not in the spiritualism business, but if the lady wants to sit at a séance with Daniel and if he can continue to assuage her guilt and grief, he has my blessing."

"And we get more gold," Uncle Brady says.

"Which he will have fairly earned," my father says tartly, ignoring Uncle Brady's sarcasm. "I cashed in the tokens but for this one at the assay office. They hadn't seen the like in forty years. We've cleared the debts from our misfortune in Tacoma. We may clear a profit in San Francisco, after all."

"And we'll assuage her guilt and grief," Uncle Brady says and sprints to the stage where some lunk of a stagehand is roughly handling our precious plate glass.

"You've done well, Daniel," my father says and stiffly shakes my hand. My father never hugs me like Uncle Brady does. For that matter, my father never helped my mother with her hair or the buttons on the back of her dress. But my father is a good man. A kind man behind his cold facade. In truth, after all our petty squabbles, I have never begrudged my father the strictures of his personality. Professor Flint is an astonishing magician. Perhaps not a *great* magician, but a mysterious one.

I turn to go and bump right into *her.*

"Danny, Professor Flint," Zena says. We both start guiltily. She takes my father's hand. Resplendent in her burgundy taffeta, she looks as fresh and crisp as the rose tucked behind her ear. "I want to ask a favor of you, Professor Flint."

"I shall do my best, madame," my father says.

"You must let Danny take his place upon the stage," she says. "He is no longer just your assistant."

My father sputters, but he is helpless before her charming entreaty. "What would you like to do, Daniel?" he says.

Before I can defer to my father's judgment, she answers. She answers not unlike my mother who often knew what I was thinking before I knew it myself, who often spoke for me before I knew what I wanted to say myself. Zena Troubetzskoy says, "Danny would be wonderful dueling with the ghost. Onstage, that is."

My father and I trade looks. How does she know that *I* am usually the ghost? How does she know I am not onstage? And if she knows I am not onstage, what exactly *does* she know? How would a gold mine heiress know about Pepper's ghost illusion? For that matter, how would a gold thief?

Could she be spying on us?

But my father only says calmly, "Very well."

"Do you promise?" she says. "I'll come to the performance tonight if you promise."

My father hesitates. "I promise," he says. Concedes to me, "You shall do the duel." Professor Flint loathes to give up even one moment of center stage. But I'm his only son and heir apparent. One day he'll pass the mantle of magic to me. He could start now.

The cheerless fog that has dogged San Francisco since we came has miraculously burned away in the afternoon sun. The evening sky is clear and spangled with stars. The Tivoli Theater is nearly filled with an enthusiastic audience tonight. Perhaps our reputation is spreading. Perhaps the fliers my father can now afford have nudged our reputation along, too. "Advertising conquered the West better than any gun," my mother always said. In the space of this afternoon, my father commissioned fliers to be drawn and printed by Parker's Advertising Agency, sent bundles to the messenger services. The boys have distributed them along the cocktail route where the gentlemen of the city take their ease. Mr. Pannini is grinning, a red-haired miss clinging to his arm. Professor Flint has got them going with our new mechanical rosebush well before the ghost duel. The applause has us all in a flush. Uncle Brady is beaming. We make that dancing handkerchief *dance.* The ladies laugh, the children exclaim, even the gentlemen chuckle and ooh and aah. But I still cannot see Zena Troubetzskoy in the audience beyond the sulfuric glare of the limelights. I keep looking, but I cannot see her.

Uncle Brady says in his voice as sonorous as a Shakespearean ghost, "And now, ladies and gentlemen, Daniel Flint, the professor's son"— Uncle Brady glances back at me as I wait in the wings in my smart gabardine and fancy brocade vest—"what I mean to say is, the eminent, the talented, the amazing Danny Flint will endeavor through his astonishing, miraculous, and mysterious psychic powers to establish communication with the Spirits of the Dead!"

The orchestra strikes up its lively tune. I know my father is in the place where the illusion takes place, clad in the ghost getup and striking away at me. Zena Troubetzskoy was right about one thing. Learning to dance does help me spar with the ghost. I trust I don't reveal too much if I say that I cannot actually see the apparition from onstage. Pepper's ghost illusion is enacted by the magician with a certain faith in the assistant. A tremendous amount of faith. The magician onstage may bask in the eyes of the audience, but the assistant must make the right moves. The assistant hidden in the place where the illusion transpires is the only one who knows how to move because the assistant is the only one who sees the whole scheme of things.

Need I say I step out to enthusiastic applause? Need I say I commence the duel with all the youthful strength and dexterity within me? Need I say that what the audience sees is a ferocious apparition, appearing out of nowhere and challenging my very mortality with deftness and vigor?

Then everyone gasps, and I see her: a gauzy woman in burgundy steps onto the stage with me. She motions to my father: cease and desist the duel. She motions for my hand to take hold of her waist, takes my hand in her illusory hand. We begin to waltz. She leaps, floating into thin air, vaults over me like an acrobat, and lands on my other side. Whereupon we embrace again and waltz. The rented orchestra grinds to a halt, then strikes up some scratchy Tschaikovsky. Someone yells from the audience, "Oh my God!" and someone else says, "How beautiful!" We spin, we dance, we glide. I don't know how she is doing this illusion. Uncle Brady in the wings is rolling his eyes, I don't know what my father is doing, but I waltz for all I'm worth. At last she breaks away from me and bows and vanishes.

The applause is thunderous.

When Zena Troubetzskoy shows up at our campfire on Fourth Street the next morning, my father invites her for a last cup of coffee. When we finish with the séance, he intends to tell her to beat it.

"Yes, Daniel is very talented," my father says. "He has been talented since the day he was born." My father banters with Zena in the cold, clear morning while Uncle Brady and I set up our little makeshift parlor for the last séance.

"Sure, we'll take three more pieces of her gold," Uncle Brady says. "We'll be able to buy that magic lantern from the Chicago Magic Company."

I am distressed. "She's not a spy," I tell him as we position the fake walls in our Henderson wagon. "I don't believe it. Anyway, Pop possesses nothing original."

"Hold on there, Danny. San Francisco is thick with spiritualist mediums," Uncle Brady says. "They are not as knowledgeable as magicians. Don't think for one moment there are not many who would steal the secrets of Professor Flint's illusions."

"But she's not like that. I know it!"

"Didn't you say she's a transient? Has no fixed address in San Francisco?"

"Not that I could find, but I'm not a detective. And neither do we," I say. "How did she do her illusion?"

"I don't know," Uncle Brady says. "She knows some magic, that's for sure."

I sit before the mirror, sprucing up my threadbare suit for this last performance. Uncle Brady takes the clothes brush from me, whisks my gabardine. He sits on the stool behind me and fusses with my hair.

After an awkward silence, Uncle Brady says, "Don't let the lady fool you, Danny. This Zena Troubetzskoy. We don't really know who she is. What she is."

"You sound just like my mother," I say. "Just like her. That night."

"Danny," Uncle Brady says, refolding my collar. "I know you're mad at your mother. You think she humiliated you. But that tinker girl and her people, they don't even remember you. They're off to the next cowtown or dead end. Your mother was just trying to protect you. What she did was for you."

"All for me," I say. I cannot conceal the bitterness in my tone. "All for the mama's boy."

"I knew your mother," Uncle Brady says, "for a long time."

"I've heard this story," I say, unappeased. "I've heard this story a hundred times. How the two of you came up from Atlanta. In the terrible year before I was born."

"That's right, we came up from Atlanta," Uncle Brady says. "That's right it was a terrible year. The carpetbaggers and the renegades and the scoundrels were pillaging Georgia. Things were so terrible, Danny, you cannot know. There were those who'd gone sour from the war of the rebellion. They went looking to make trouble. Good men like my own brother and my cousin were hanged for nothing. Good people like your mother's family, who sheltered my family, were harried and harassed. Times got ugly. A boy like me no older than you, Danny, and educated alongside your mother by kin you will never know, could not walk down the street without fearing for his life."

Startled, I look up at Uncle Brady in the mirror as he sits behind me, patiently brushing my coat.

"Oh, I was young and wild and impulsive," Uncle Brady says, which makes me laugh since he is nothing like that at all. "Yes, I was," he insists, "and your mother was young, too. We hated Georgia, hated what the war had done to people. Hated what we had left when it was over. The violence, the anger, the cruelty. And so we left, she and I. Left our home behind. We traveled together, she and I. We went up to Ohio. The running and the fear! Your mother was sick. We ran out of everything but hope. And there, in Cincinnati, we met your father. Well, you know. You know how beautiful your mother was."

I study my Uncle Brady behind me in the mirror. He has large brown eyes; so do I. He has wide curving cheekbones, a fullness to his lip, that tough curly hair. So do I. I am also as pale as my mother was, and my curly hair is auburn, not black. My mother had one of those fine Southern noses, and so do I. In spite of my pig-headedness, I possess, undeservedly, her grace.

"You see, son," Uncle Brady says, "your mother didn't want you to make a mistake with that tinker girl. She didn't want you to do what she did. Do something you might regret. Something that could have made your lot hard when you're so young. When your whole life is ahead of you."

"Uncle Brady," I say, gazing at him in the mirror, gazing at my own reflection. "Did my mother regret having me?"

"Of course not," he says. "Your mother loved you more than the sun and the moon. But we were lucky, Danny. We were lucky. Professor Flint turned out to be a kind and practical man. An educated man. An enlightened man. He adored your mother. He had no other family. I guess you could say he was a lonely man. You know Pop. He took us in. All of us."

"Including me," I say.

"Including me," Uncle Brady says. "Danny, the professor loves you very much, even if sometimes you think he is a boiled shirt."

I nod as my father, the boiled shirt, escorts Zena Troubetzskoy into our wagon. He is stern, resolute. We four sit at the table, tense and unsure. A little ripple of shock runs up my spine. I do not know how she danced with me last night on the stage. Apparently she knows some illusion we do not.

"Will you communicate with my dear husband today?" she says innocently.

I start to say, "No Return, my rose," but my father interrupts, "The No Return stake was claimed by one Nikita Troubetzskoy, madame. The assay office says Mr. Troubetzskoy took away three quarters of a million in gold. Yet we have found no record of you in San Francisco."

Zena's eyes glaze with tears. "I want to speak with Nickie," she says, and turns to me. "Danny? Please?"

"Madame," my father says, "we appreciate your assistance in our hour of need. We appreciate your gold, but we'll take no more of it. You're either a thief, a fraud, a lunatic, or a spy. Myself, I think you're a spy."

"A spy?" Zena says, touching fingertips to her pale throat.

"I do not know for whom," my father says. "Obviously someone too lazy or too stupid to design his own illusions."

"Ah, come on, Pop," I say, embarrassed. "Zena is my friend."

"I think not," my father says. To her, "Stay away from my son, madame. No mystery is to be explained to the likes of you."

With a cry, Zena jumps up from the chair, flees from our wagon. My father throws open the canvas flap. We watch her hurry across the dusty lot and turn the corner at Fourth Street and Market.

"Follow that woman," he commands me. "I went down to the main post office this morning and examined the directory myself." He shakes his finger at me. "Never trust clerks, Daniel, you must look for yourself. There is no Zena Troubetzskoy in San Francisco, but there is a Nikita."

"What?" Uncle Brady and I say at the same time.

"Nikita Troubetzskoy lives on Russian Hill to this day," my father says, "at 963 Chestnut Street. Now follow her, sir. Find out who she's spying for."

I dash across the grass, turn that same corner, but Zena is gone by the time I get there. Market Street bustles with elegant broughams and rockaways, cabs and trade wagons adorned with reproductions of famous paintings or other figments of the muralist's fancy. Men in bowlers or top hats stroll the streets, proper ladies promenade in dark colors, sporting ladies sashay in bright ones. Zena would not be easy to miss in her bustling scarlet taffeta. But she is nowhere in sight.

I pause, at a loss, breath choking in my throat. Nikita Troubetzskoy, alive? Living on Russian Hill? Is Zena a lunatic, then, wandering the streets asking for her husband? Nikita Troubetzskoy must be a very old man if he was a miner in the Rush. Perhaps he is a scoundrel. Perhaps he abuses his pretty young wife. Perhaps he has driven her mad. I have heard of such tragedies. Perhaps, too, Zena is a little older than she appears. My mother, the belle from Atlanta, scrupulously avoided sun on her face and rich food. She was as slim and smooth and fresh as girls half her age.

I feel torn in two. A thousand questions tumble through my mind. If the woman claiming to be Zena Troubetzskoy is a spy or a fraud, then Nikita will not know her. And if she *is* his wife, I need to know why she is perpetuating this hoax. I need to know if she's mad, if she stole from him, or if she should be brought back home.

I trudge north up the long, slow slope of Columbus Avenue. I am nearly at North Point by the time I find the corner of Chestnut Street. Russian Hill is an awesome precipice, angling up to the sky. I loosen my collar, unbutton my vest, sling my topcoat over my shoulder. I am winded by the time I gain the summit. To the south and east and west, I can see the whole city of San Francisco spread at my feet. To the north, the whole bay from the Contra Costa to the shoulders of the Golden Gate and out to the endless sea. Despite the spectacular view, however, few dwellings crouch at the very top. Who would want to brave that climb every day? Even the cable cars have not yet conquered this hill. The summit is as lonely as a dune.

I walk half a block down the dirt road and there it is: 963 Chestnut Street. A big, ramshackle Stick-Eastlake mansion with cracked paint and rotting gingerbread. Several side windows are boarded up as though the place has been abandoned. Golden poppies and purple hydrangea bloom chaotically amid weeds, Queen Anne's lace, mint, and sea-bent grass. A rusty iron gate hangs halfway off its hinges and bangs back and forth in the brisk sea breeze. Perhaps Nikita Troubetzskoy is dead, after all, and no one has thought to take his name out of the postal directory.

Yet a trickle of smoke winds out of the chimney and disperses into the sky. An old horse with a gray-speckled muzzle pokes its head from a little stable in back. Heart pounding in my throat, I climb the rickety front stairs to the porch, seize the plain brass door knocker, and announce myself.

Boom, boom, boom. My raps echo into the interior of the house and fall silent as though muffled by the sheer neglect of the place. I wait a long time. Impatient, I climb back down the stairs and circle around the back. Every window not boarded up is securely swathed inside by heavy dark curtains. I peer in, guilty as a Peeping Tom, but cannot see a thing. I rap again at the tradesmen's door. Nothing. I turn to go, disappointment needling my heart.

Suddenly the tradesmen's door whips open, and a scowling old man confronts me. A little withered person, he wears a rumpled suit of heavy black wool, a red rose incongruously stuck in his lapel. What is left of his hair is combed over his bald pate. He regards me with furious gray eyes.

"No solicitors," he says and makes to slam the door shut.

I press my hand on the glass. "I'm not a solicitor, sir. I'm here to see Mr. Nikita Troubetzskoy."

"What about?"

"Are you Mr. Troubetzskoy?"

He draws himself up, enraged. "Certainly not."

"Then I'd like to see Mr. Troubetzskoy."

"What about?" he repeats, narrowing his eyes.

"I . . ." I draw myself up, too. "That is confidential, sir."

"Pah," he says but he lets me into a small, neat kitchen sparsely furnished with a simple wood table and two chairs. We clatter down a hallway past a dozen closed doors, finally gaining the front parlor. A man sits with his back to me in a large burgundy leather chair, swaddled in heavy blankets, staring at a smoldering fire in the soot-caked fireplace.

The room is sweltering. The air smells of ashes and the cloying scent of decaying roses. A vase of drooping blooms sits on a side table. A wide flat circular pan like the ones miners use to sift water coming down from a sluice sits on the floor, spilling over with gold pieces. More nuggets of gold lie scattered on the floor. Thick curtains furred with dust are tightly drawn. The only illumination comes from the fire. Two other doors, one on either side of the parlor, are thrown open, revealing the rooms beyond and their drawn curtains. Eerie white shapes hulk in those rooms like apparitions. I realize with a start that the furniture is draped with sheets.

"This gentleman is here to see you," says the little old man, vastly annoyed at my intrusion.

"Who is he?" says the man in the chair. His voice is deep and soft, almost a whisper.

"Who are you?" the little old man demands.

"I am Daniel Flint," I say to the man in the chair. "Please, Mr. Troubetzskoy. It's about your wife."

The snippy little old man ducks out of the parlor at once.

"My wife?" the man in the chair says and turns. As I suspected, Nikita Troubetzskoy must be in his late sixties. A long, craggy face, a supple mouth turned down at the corners, noble brows, a shock of thick, white hair. But his eyes are not unkind. I am suddenly ashamed of suspecting this man of driving his wife mad.

Suddenly I hear her giggle. "Zena?" I whisper, flabbergasted. And then I *see* her in the room to the left. She waves and ducks behind a draped chair like a child playing hide-and-seek.

Nikita draws the blankets closer around him and stares at me as sternly as my father. "What about my wife?" he says. "What about Zena?"

"Your wife *is* Zena?" I say.

But he only stares at me.

I hear her giggle again. The sound comes from the room on the right. She sits on top of a table, swinging her legs beneath her billowing skirt. As soon as I spot her, she hops off the table and hides behind the door.

Perhaps it is the close heat of the parlor, the thick ashes and the darkness, but I suddenly feel dizzy and a little faint. I pull up a chair and sit. "Mr. Troubetzskoy, what is going on?"

Nikita draws away from me, huddling back in his chair. "Perhaps *you* had better tell *me,* Mr. Flint," he says.

"Look," I say. "I met Zena in town. She asked to sit at a séance with me."

"Are you a medium, Mr. Flint?"

"No! I'm a magician." He stares at me again as though *I* am the lunatic. "Never mind," I say. "The point is, she sat at a séance with me, and she asked to speak with you. She wanted to tell you something."

He nods, and I can see tears pooling in his eyes. "What did she want to tell me?"

I struggle to remember. "She says she's sorry she left you in the mountains. She says she never cared about the gold, not really, she just wanted to be near you. She feels that she abandoned you, and she's sorry."

"I see," Nikita says.

"Mr. Troubetzskoy," I say, my heart leaping with hope and desperation at the same time. "Can't the two of you reconcile? She's sorry for whatever happened between you. Can't you forgive her, sir?"

I hear her sigh. She has run over to the room on the left again. Perhaps a passageway connects them; it's a mansion, after all. She leans against the half-opened door and sighs as though her heart is breaking.

"Mr. Flint," Nikita says, "Zena has done nothing that requires my forgiveness. I never minded her other beaux before we married. She was so beautiful. She would wear a red rose behind her ear. What could I expect? I adored her." He rubs his forehead. "No, if anything, I am the one to blame, Mr. Flint. I was selfish. I wanted her near me. I took her up into the mountains. Do you have any notion how hard it was? How we worked day and night, digging in the rocks? Her hands got all cut up and bruised. When winter came, we nearly starved, nearly froze to death. I still can't get warm after the winters in those mountains." He pulls the blanket up to his chin and shivers. "In the summer, there was fever and not much healthful food to eat, then, either. And after all her suffering, she never could enjoy the fruits of our labors. Mr. Flint," he says, and reaches out and pats my hand. "I wanted her to live in this house with me. I never wanted her to suffer again."

I grin like a maniac at Zena as she lingers at the door, blinking at me sorrowfully. I give her the thumbs-up. "Then Mr. Troubetzskoy," I say with all the self-importance of a matchmaker. "You should know that she wants to be with you again, too."

Nikita throws open his blanket. He is clutching something. A framed tintype, which he hands to me. "How old are you, Mr. Flint?"

"I am nearly twenty-one," I say and stare.

"And are you sure you are not a medium?"

The tintype is of Zena in her ruffled dress, her coiffure tilted at a saucy angle, a curl coiled on her cheek. The red rose tucked behind her ear translates photographically into a soft gray curl. "Yes. No," I whisper. "I don't know."

"Mr. Flint," Nikita says, "I buried Zena with a bouquet of her favorite red roses twenty years before you were born."

We are a rousing success in San Francisco by the last week of our engagement. The astonishing, miraculous, mysterious Professor Flint & Son play to a nearly full house. Mr. Pannini has booked us for a month next spring. We will clear a fine profit. Uncle Brady has sent away for a spirit cabinet from the Chicago Magic Company. We intend to customize the cabinet so that I will appear and disappear, plus play a banjo and a violin with my hands and feet bound. You see, we've worked out this ingenious complex of panels that fit along . . . Never mind. It will be a *great* illusion. Spiritualism is enjoying new popularity this season throughout the far West.

We are headed down to Los Angeles, a small town set among orange groves. Mr. Pannini says you can see flying fish in the ocean. I like that topsy-turvy notion; flying fish. Perhaps I will be inspired to design a new illusion.

"So long," Pannini says, twirling his mustache, as we pack the last of our equipment in the Henderson wagon. "When I see you next, young sir, I expect a proper soup-soaker on that lip of yours and a blue-eyed miss on your elbow."

My father bestows a baleful glance on Pannini and goes to see to our horses. Pop has consumed several cups of coffee after taking his final bow. He wants to drive south in the coolness of this sparkling California night. I'll take his place at the reins at dawn after my own few hours of sleep.

Uncle Brady boards the back of the wagon and carefully checks the pane of plate glass.

"Where on earth are we going to stow that spirit cabinet when we pick it up in Los Angeles?" I say.

"You'll have to sleep in it, Danny, I suppose," Uncle Brady suggests.

"Perhaps you'll have to sleep in it yourself, Uncle Brady," I say. "I'm taller than you now."

We laugh, and then I hear *her* laugh. Uncle Brady and I both turn. And there she is in her rustling burgundy taffeta, standing beneath the gaslight at the corner of California and Dupont streets where the hill swoops up into the sky. She smiles at me and waves.

"Now, son," Uncle Brady says, "that woman is an impostor, after all. The professor says the clerk at the assay office told him the wife of

Nikita Troubetzskoy died of a fever. She went up there with him, and she died in those mountains at the No Return Mine. That was back in '53, over forty years ago."

"I know," I say and start up the hill toward her.

"Danny, she's a con artist," Uncle Brady calls to me. "I don't know what she wants with you. She's a fraud!"

I run up the hill to meet her. I am sweaty and disheveled by the time I reach the corner where she stands.

She gives me a wink, straightens my tie. Her touch is as cool and light as the brush of a bird's wing.

"Are you a fraud, Zena?" I say.

"No," she says.

"Then . . . what are you, really?"

She shrugs and tosses her head. "There's just no explaining some mysteries," she says. She smooths my hair with her fingers. "Perhaps the soul does not survive, Danny. Perhaps there's nothing beyond but darkness and silence. If that's true, if there's nothing, then it does not matter that your mother died with angry words between the two of you. In the end, you've got to know in your heart that she loved you. You've got to know she wanted your forgiveness. And offered her forgiveness, too. That she wanted to say goodbye."

Zena turns, walks across the intersection, and begins to climb the hill on the other side. A slim, pale woman steps out of the shadows. I would know her profile, her meticulous coiffure, anywhere. Zena takes the red rose from behind her ear and hands the bloom to the woman.

"But, Danny," Zena calls to me, "if the soul *does* survive, then she knows. She knows."

The women link arms and climb up the hill, climb into the night sky, stepping on stars as they go.

Just a Little Bug

P. D. CACEK

Because today is yesterday's tomorrow, each moment in time is a confluence of past, present, and future. The first two must be dealt with before the third can contain any hope. I believe that when I dream I am rehearsing my future, but I also know that there can be no future without putting the past to rest. As for dealing with present reality, one of the inevitable parts of life's happenings, and something I fear no less than others do, is experiencing the death of a loved one. The truth is that while most of us don't want to think about it, we do. How, we wonder, is it possible to handle such a loss, and go on.

What I have to believe—and what is confirmed in P. D. Cacek's powerful and painful story—is that emotional survival depends on the mind's capacity to transform what it sees into what it wants to see, to create from our imaginations an illusion more comforting than reality.

—DC

Just a Little Bug

"YOU ALMOST READY?"

Kate stood in the doorway and felt her fingers dig into the thin, summer-weight sweatshirt she was carrying. She never understood why they kept hospitals so cold.

Like walking into a tomb.

The memory of standing next to her father's hospital bed (*watching him die*) shivered its way up her spine.

NO! She wouldn't think about that. Not now. Not ever. Because this wasn't the same thing. This time the doctors were wrong. This time it wasn't her father slipping away. This time it was her *baby* and the doctors were *wrong*.

Kate let go of the air that somehow managed to get trapped in her lungs and smiled. *She looks better today,* Kate reassured herself—just as she'd done every morning for the last six months. *Stronger. Healthier.*

She DOES, dammit.

"Do I gotta go?"

Kate blinked and found herself looking into eyes that were too old and worn-out to belong to a nine-year-old child. *It's just the drugs,* Kate reminded herself as she walked into the sweet/sour/medicine smell of the room.

The sick room.

Her daughter's room.

Carrie Marie McCarthy's room.

Carrie and Kate.

The McCarthy Girls: Stronger than week-old garlic pizza, faster

307

than a speeding skateboard, able to leap insurmountable obstacles with just a blinding smile and the toss of strawberry-blond curls.

Except Carrie's curls had been the first victim of the Chemotherapy War she'd been consigned to. The slightly crooked smile, that once reminded Kate so much of herself, had been the second.

But it was just the drugs.

"Well, of course you have to go, silly," Kate said, trying not to breathe the sick smell in. Trying to keep the smile fastened to her lips.

Trying to pretend everything was going to be fine.

Trying.

"What would Dr. John say if his most favorite girlfriend in the whole world didn't show up for her appointment?"

The pale, almost-colorless eyes rolled beneath the floppy "hippie" hat they'd found the day the last of her hair fell out.

"He'd be happy," Carrie whispered, her voice almost lost in the soft, constant hiss from the oxygen tube strapped to her face. "That way he wouldn't have to see me die."

Kate's nails dug through the material and found the skin on her forearm—left four burning scratches before she forced herself to laugh.

Forced. As if the bright pink-and-white, stuffed animal–cluttered, disinfected, oxygen-rich, sick-smell room was only a set from some prime-time sitcom and she was laughing on cue.

Right before the commercial break.

"Now you really *are* being silly, Carrot-cake," she said as she walked toward the bed. "You're *not* going to die." *You're not you're not you're NOT!* "You just have a little bug. Dr. John told you that, remember?"

"*You have a bug inside you,*" the tall, silver-haired man had told Carrie, scrunching almost in half as he took both her tiny hands in his one and smiled. "*Just a little bug that we're going to SWAT, okay?*"

And Carrie had giggled and tossed her red-gold curls and asked if she was going to have to swallow a flyswatter.

But then the giggles stopped.

And never came back.

Just a bug, they told her . . . like the "flu bugs" and "cold bugs" Kate used to make out of paper bags stuffed with newspaper . . .

Just a bug . . . because telling a child she had cancer was too scary.

It didn't matter if the parents were so scared one of them ran away instead of facing it. And the other one kept forcing herself to laugh.

And pretend. That it really was only a bug.

"I can feel it."

Kate blinked her eyes as if she was waking up (*trying to wake up*) from a bad dream.

"What?"

Carrie looked up and gently touched the center of her narrow chest where the tumor lay, growing like a misplaced embryo. Kate had finally let herself look at the last series of X-rays—had finally seen the malignant shadow that was eating her baby.

Alive.

"I can feel the bug," Carrie whispered, looking serious. Looking old. "I can feel it moving."

Kate swallowed the lump that had formed in her own throat and took too deep a breath. Smelled the odor of disinfectant and medicines and death that hovered in the room.

"Carrie, I want you to listen to me, okay? You . . . you can't feel the bug because it's—" *Too far inside you.* "—it's just a little teeny-weeny, little thing."

Carrie's lower lip inched into a pout.

"No it's not, Mom. Not anymore."

Oh GOD! "All right, that's enough. I don't want to hear any more about the bug, okay?" Kate let her voice drift into a *this is it and I mean it* tone as she held out the sweatshirt. "Now, hurry up and put this on, Dr. John's waiting."

"But it really is moving, Mom." Tears welled almost instantly. "Honest, Momma. Here . . . feel it."

Kate had been able to avoid touching her daughter except for the necessary cleaning and dressing and perfunctory bedtime kiss—until now—because she didn't want to *feel* how little of her daughter the bug had left.

"Carrot-cake," she pleaded, "I promise I'll . . . touch the bug later, but right now we have to—"

"Please? Momma."

Dammit.

Letting the weight of the sweatshirt pull her down, Kate sat on the edge of the *Aladdin* bedspread and laid her palm over the matching cartoon on the front of her daughter's tee shirt. She kept it there just long enough to feel the faint, rhythmic struggling of Carrie's heart.

"Do you *feel* it, Mom?"

Please feel it, her eyes said, please feel the bug.

Kate pulled her hand back quickly—fingers spread, palm up—and gaped at it. As if she really had felt the bug.

"It *tickled*," she lied. Kept lying in whispered, secret tones so the *bug* wouldn't hear. "And you know something, Carrot-cake? I think it's getting smaller."

A look that was almost the old Carrie—wide eyes and crooked smile—blossomed for an instant. And was gone almost as quickly.

"Nah uh . . . the bug's getting bigger and it's moving all the time now, like it can't get comfortable." A single tear finally worked its way out of Carrie's eye and into the hollow of her cheek. "It feels . . . funny. I wish it would just go away."

Oh God, so do I.

Kate pressed her hand back against her daughter's chest and felt the overworked lungs labor despite the constant stream of oxygen. And nodded.

Another lie wouldn't hurt.

Not now.

"It will, baby," she said. "Y'know, I just had another thought . . . maybe the bug knows Dr. John is getting ready to *swat* it. Maybe it's packing up its bug bags right now. Maybe it's *scared*."

Kate was going to embellish the tale a little more when something twisted lazily beneath her hand.

"I don't think so, Momma," Carrie said, as Kate pulled her hand slowly away. "I don't think it's scared of anything."

"A *what?*"

Kate brushed her hair out of her eyes and almost laughed out loud. Would have if they weren't standing in the Waiting Room filled with dying children and their already-grieving parents. Dying children . . . but not hers . . . not Carrie.

"A bug, Dr. John, a *real* bug . . . or *something* alive." Kate pressed her hand against the elderly doctor's white lab coat. "Right here. I felt it *move*, Dr. John, and tumors don't move. So it has to be something else, right? So maybe it's something that you can remove!"

Kate saw her reflection in the doctor's glasses as he stepped closer and placed both his hands over her one . . . the same way he'd held Carrie's hands when he told her the lie about having just a little bug.

But it WASN'T a lie! Kate wanted to scream. *It really IS a "bug" of some kind. I felt it move. I felt it! I felt it!*

"If you felt anything at all," the doctor said softly, "it was probably an air bubble beneath the skin. There's no bug, real or sugar-coated. I've just seen the last series of X-rays, Kate . . . the cancer's metastasized. There's nothing more we can do."

Nothing more we can do
  Nothing more
  nothing

Kate hit the horn hard enough to deepen the heat crack in its plastic housing and cursed.

Silently.

There was more than enough noise already.

The city sounds poured in through the open windows and fought with a stereo that had been cranked up high to compensate. But Kate could still hear her.

Carrie.

Lying across the backseat and puking into the Halloween Happy Meal bucket she'd gotten last year.

B.C . . . *Before Cancer.*

Kate hit the horn again and saw dark eyes glare at her from the rearview mirror in the truck ahead. *Dammit!* If there was *nothing more they could do,* then why did they still give her the Chemo?

And why did they tell her to just take Carrie home when she was *supposed* to stay at the hospital—in a nice, air-conditioned room with crisp sheets and around-the-clock nurses and cool metal bowls she could puke her guts out into so Kate could have a night off.

Away from the cancer.

But it moved.

Kate tightened her grip on the sweat-slick steering wheel and maneuvered the car over another half yard of steaming asphalt.

Carrie was supposed to have stayed in the hospital for observation because they were going to try "something new." That's what Dr. John had told them both.

The *last* time.

This time he had stayed with Carrie throughout the therapy—stroking her thin hands and talking softly . . . so softly that Kate hadn't been able to hear what he was saying. But Carrie had nodded. Solemnly. A little old lady in a floppy hat and cartoon sweatshirt.

This time, after Dr. John told her there was nothing more they could do for her child, he'd hugged Kate and slipped a pill bottle into her hand, saying—

Kate pressed her back against the damp upholstery and crooked her elbow out the window, yelping when the hot metal seared her flesh.

"You okay, Momma?"

Carrie'd heard, even above the noise and nausea. *God, what else had she heard?* Her mother screaming at the doctor that the thing inside her . . . the thing *killing* her really was some kind of bug?

Kate pulled her arm back into the car and tapped the accelerator—moved the car another quarter of a foot.

"Yeah, baby. I'm fine." She glanced into the rearview mirror even though she knew Carrie wouldn't have the strength to sit up. "How're you doing?"

The sound of dry retching answered her.

Kate let her eyes shift down to her purse, thinking that if she stared hard enough she'd be able to see the small amber bottle with its single white tablet.

—saying, "She's put up one hell of a fight, Kate, but her little body's just about worn-out. You know I can't tell you to do this . . . but it might be easier on both of you—her especially—if she just went to sleep."—

To sleep.

Like it would be so easy.

The car jerked and stalled as Kate panic-stopped a few inches off the truck's bumper. God, that's all she needed. Even a minor fender-bender would be more than she could stand.

Taking a deep breath of the exhaust-flavored air, Kate braced her arms and restarted the car. She had to get Carrie home.

To bed.

to sleep

Kate put the car in gear and let the traffic drag them along. A half block away from where she stalled, Kate leaned over and turned the stereo still higher—trying to drown out the lullabies that had begun playing in her head.

"Can I get you something, baby? A popsicle? I've got cherry . . . your favorite."

Kate felt the cool breeze from the swamp cooler licking the sweat off her back as she waited for an answer. They'd moved the air conditioner into Carrie's room right after her first "bug-swatting session" . . . because the "bug juice" had made her skin feel like it was on fire.

But even then, as sick as she was, Carrie had made Kate promise they'd move it back to the front room just as soon as she got better.

Just as soon as the bug got swatted.

once upon a time

"Carrot-cake? Are you asleep?"

The oxygen tube hissed . . . but that was all; and a new, colder chill raced up Kate's spine. Freezing her solid. Making her tiptoe to the bed instead of running.

Making her whisper instead of screaming.

"Baby?"

Carrie was lying on her side, her tiny body almost lost in the *Hard Rock Cafe* tee/night shirt she was wearing, curled around the threadbare teddy that had been her constant companion since birth, one arm bent toward her head—blue-tipped fingers absently making circles on her bare scalp the way they once had made red-gold ringlets.

"The bug's too big, Momma," she said slowly . . . carefully . . . the way she once did when working out a *really hard* math problem. "That's what Dr. John said. He said it's too big and now there's no room left for me."

Kate's own heart felt like it stopped beating then. "No, baby, Dr. John was just fooling around . . ."

"Nah uh."

Carrie dropped her hand to the stuffed toy and hugged it to her chest—pressed it hard against the spot where the "bug" had gotten *too big*.

Kate managed to make it to the edge of the bed before her legs went out from under her. She hoped Carrie couldn't see how her hand was shaking as she reached out and touched the bear. The one and only "class" Kate had attended at the hospital, had recommended that the "Care-giver" (her—*the living*) tell the "Short-Termer" (Carrie—*the dying*) when it became clear that their "departure" (*death*) was imminent.

So they could prepare themselves.

As if they were only going away on a trip.

Bye-bye . . . write when you get there. Have fun.

But no one had been able to tell Kate what the "Care-giver" was supposed to do once the train had pulled out of the station.

"Carrie . . . honey, listen to me." Kate scooted up until she felt her daughter's bony knees jab her thigh. "Dr. John doesn't know everything! There are a lot of *other* doctors we can see. Or maybe we can go get an exterminator."

She'd wanted to make the last part a joke, but her voice had cracked and almost strangled her.

Carrie hadn't noticed.

"What's it like to die, Momma?"

Kate squeezed her eyes shut and shook her head. *No! NO! I'm not ready for this. Not yet . . . Please God . . . not YET!*

"You think the bug'll die?"

Carrie was staring straight ahead when Kate opened her eyes.

"I hope it doesn't," she said, easing her grip on the teddy bear. "It wouldn't be fair if the bug died, too. Would it, Momma?"

Kate reached past the teddy bear and touched the spot just above Carrie's heart. It was just a little bug . . . but if it died there wouldn't be anything left . . .

"No," she said, "it wouldn't."

When Carrie closed her eyes, Kate stood up and balled her hands into fists. *No, it wouldn't be fair . . . but NOTHING was fair any more.* Part of her wanted to scream and pound the walls at the *unfairness* of it, but all she had the strength to do was stand there and watch her daughter's life shut itself off.

Knowing there was not a damned thing she could do about it.

Except make it easier.

"Momma'll be right back, baby."

Kate didn't stop to think . . . didn't stop moving until her fingers found the pill bottle in her purse and closed around it. *Then* she stopped. And looked down. And thought about what she was doing and about all the things *they* would never do—*had* never done—and dropped the bottle back into her purse.

"No."

Failure only happened when you gave up . . . and there were still plenty of things she could do. Hundreds of other doctors who might help. Experimental treatments that could—

Kate spun around, gasping at the sound of shattering glass. *Oh, God.*

Images of Carrie lying on the floor like a broken doll . . . neck twisted, suffocating, knowing only agony in the last moments of her life . . . flooded Kate's mind as she ran back to the room.

"CARRIE!"

The silence seemed louder than the steady hum of the swamp cooler. Louder even than the sound a sliver of glass made when it suddenly came loose and shattered against the top of the cooler, sprinkling down over the other shards from the broken window like frozen rain.

Kate leaned against the doorframe and stared at the discarded *thing* that lay crumpled on Carrie's bed.

It lay on its back. The paper-thin remains of one arm still curled around the old teddy bear, the *Hard Rock* tee mercifully thrown back over the face. As Kate watched, the transparent skin that surrounded the bloodless rent where Carrie's chest had been began to fold in on itself and harden.

Like a cocoon drying out after the butterfly has left.

A cocoon.

It was just a bug after all.

Ignoring the glass beneath her bare feet, Kate rushed to the broken window and leaned out into the dying light. Holding her breath. Listening.

Lifting one hand and waving when she heard it.

There.

Above the perpetual background noise of the city, the soft flutter of wings.

In the Teeth of Glory

DAVE WOLVERTON

I knew Dave Wolverton primarily as a writer of science fiction, more specifically of the best-selling Star Wars novel The Courtship of Princess Leia. *I was, therefore, rather surprised and a little apprehensive when he warned me that what he was writing for this anthology was not a genre story. I shouldn't have been. The story is a character study set in the twilight of an old woman's life. It suggests that there comes a moment, at the end of life, when the delusion of having been a "good person" must be faced head-on.*

—DC

In the Teeth of Glory

"WELL, HENRETTA, HERE YOU ARE, a nice new house to be happy in!" Douglas's teeth flashed in a smile; he smeared his hands across the rear pockets of his pants.

Henretta, who'd been looking out the dusty curtains inspecting the scenery from the window, rolled her eyes toward her great-grandson, narrowing her eyelids to slits. Douglas stood grinning over the boxes he'd brought in, puffing as if winded. Henretta had detected an undertone in his voice—mockery. "Oh, yes, it's a wonderful house!" she crooned. She surveyed his tangled red hair and enormous buttocks. Whoever saw such horrors on a Bloom? In her day *no one* had such a buttocks. A month on her father's ranch would have worked that lard right off! She scowled and tried to think why his words bothered her. "A nice new house to be happy in," he'd said, snotty enough to leave a slime trail. Then she remembered: Douglas had made the same sassy comment when he'd helped her move six months earlier. The kids had been so reluctant to help her move this time. Henretta paused as if to take a breath, "Honestly, that Elaine and Betty at the last place reminded me of a bunch of witches! Oh Doug, you don't know what I went through with those awful women. This place is so nice. I'll be so happy here!"

Henretta's grandson, Bruce, shoved the front door open and made his way into the house with the mop, dustpan, and brooms. He'd caught the tail of the conversation. "Oh, I think you will love it here, Grandma. The park out back is just beautiful. Your neighbors seem really nice, too."

"Oh, you met my neighbors?" Henretta asked, feeling a bit cheated at not having met them first.

319

"Two of them—the old man who lives in the apartment out front, and a lady named Pearly. They invited you to a 'get-acquainted party' tonight at seven in apartment two. Do you want us to help unpack these boxes?" Bruce set the cleaning utensils on the floor.

"No, no. You just scat along. I'll be fine. I can take care of everything," she said, making motions as to shoo an old tomcat off the porch.

"You sure?" Bruce asked.

"Yes, yes, I'll be fine."

Douglas seemed annoyingly relieved at this. Henretta had half a mind to make him stay and work some lard off, but a party at seven gave her less than two hours to prepare. Douglas and Bruce shuffled from the apartment, arms dangling. Henretta herded them to the porch, smiled and waved as they jumped into Bruce's red Ford pickup and drove off. As the dust settled on the gravel drive in front of the apartment, she gazed toward a dark line of oaks across the river. The wind barely stirred the branches. It was quiet. With her front door facing the river, she wouldn't get the street noise from Highway 99. Just a view of the muddy Long Tom River. It could be very lonely here, she thought, or very peaceful. She was lucky Mr. Strunk, the elderly housing man, had told her about this place. Her gaze strayed to the mailbox on the post beside her, to the patch of white poking through the slits. She pulled the mail out—all advertisements and bills addressed to poor Mr. Sullivan.

She took the mail in and hunted through boxes until she found a pen. Then she took the first letter and scrawled *forward to*—to where? she wondered. She just wrote *deceased*. Somebody should know, she thought. After all, Mr. Sullivan was almost a month dead. She wrote *deceased* on the letter from the Lane County Probate Court and on the one from Oregon Utilities. When she reached the ad from Taco Time she began to write *deceased* on it, too, but noticed it was addressed to "Resident" and hesitated. Somehow it seemed important that the people who send these things out know someone had died, so she finished it: *Resident—deceased*.

The day's tasks had been so demanding that at five-thirty Henretta decided to lie down to rest. The apartment was still a mess, but the boys had set the blankets on the bed, which was furnished. Just as she settled on the mattress, Henretta had the queerest thought: What if poor old Mr. Sullivan had died in this bed?

The room chilled. Henretta's heart pounded fiercely in the silence. She imagined the body, sprawled on the bed, turning blue, swelling and stinking for days until someone noticed he was missing. When they found him, his fingers would have been clutching the sheets; they'd have worked them loose with a screwdriver.

She clawed her way out of bed and said a brief prayer, taking some comfort as always from the Lord, then hurried to the living room where the sun shining yellow through the window was bright and pleasant and suffused her with a warm, hazy feeling. The elm tree out by the fence cast its shadow against the white curtains; shadow leaves fluttered reassuringly. After a moment of catching her breath, Henretta decided to nap on the couch. She stretched herself out as luxuriously as a vacationer and closed her eyes. She was just drifting off when a thought latched onto her like a tick: what if Mr. Sullivan had died while napping here on the couch?

"My name is Georgia, Georgia Pearly," the woman announced after Henretta knocked on the door, "and you must be our new neighbor."

"Yes, I'm Henretta Bloom." Henretta stared at Mrs. Pearly unabashedly, as if taking inventory. Georgia Pearly's hair was rather blue in color—the shade of blue you get from a Clairol bottle—and Georgia walked with a cane.

"Bloom. Such a pretty name. It reminds me of spring and flowers blooming," Georgia said. She was more wrinkled than Henretta, shorter and paunchy, with pendulous breasts and cheeks that appeared to have sagged after too much smiling. The last thing Henretta really stared at was the glasses, yellow-tinted bifocals thick as the bottoms of old Mason jars. "And Henretta—why you know, I think we're going to be good friends!"

"Why's that?"

"Because our names both end with *yuh,*" Georgia said.

"My name just ends with *uh,*" Henretta pointed out as Georgia led her through the hall to the kitchen. A man and woman sat at a small kitchen table, slicing eggs for a salad. The rest of their dinner—chicken casserole, peas, and some homemade rolls—was laid out, buffet style.

"This is Dane, your host. He lives here in apartment two," Georgia said, motioning to a tall man, impeccably clean, with a trim moustache and full head of silver hair. His rigid posture lent him an air of dignity.

"Pleased to meet you," Dane said, looking Henretta in the eye.

"Pleased to meet you," she returned, glancing at his arms and chest, thinking, there's still some muscle there.

"And this is Ruth," Georgia announced in a singsong voice, waving flamboyantly toward a thin woman with hair as puffy and white as a cotton ball, who looked as if she'd grown old gracefully but was now on the verge of collapse. "She lives in number one. And everyone, I'd like you to meet our new neighbor, Henretta Bloom."

"It's so nice to meet you!" Ruth said, setting her paring knife on the table as she reached to squeeze hands. "Do you play backgammon? I've been looking for a good partner."

Henretta was momentarily taken aback. She hadn't played backgammon for years and knew it would take practice to return to form. "Well, no; but I'd be happy to learn," she said.

And with that, the evening was off to a wonderful start. They laughed and told their life stories and showed pictures of their children, and grandchildren. Everyone ate just a little too much (except for Georgia, who, as Ruth warned, "has a touch of the diabetes and has to watch her intake"). Ruth extracted a promise of a backgammon game from Henretta, and Georgia was anxious for her to meet Pappy, who lived down the street but couldn't come to dinner because of an ear infection. Dane, it turned out, was quite a fisherman and offered to take Henretta perch fishing down to the park. Although she'd never been fishing, Henretta was eager to go, and she pondered with gratitude on how fortunate she was to still have her figure.

The talk inevitably turned to religion. Dane was a good Baptist and had already been saved fifty years earlier, while Ruth was a Methodist. Georgia, on the other hand was a something of a lapsed Mormon, and while she professed a belief in Christ, Henretta wasn't at all certain that the God's grace would extend to folks like *them*.

Still, Georgia was pleasant enough, and the entire evening was lovely. To top it off, as Georgia and Henretta, whose front doors opened next to each other, walked home, Henretta said, "Tell me, how did poor old Mr. Sullivan die?"

"Oh, he took sick last Christmas while visiting his son in California. The poor man was in a nursing home for three months before he died."

"He died in a nursing home?" Henretta asked distantly.

"Yes, in a nursing home."

"How sad, how terribly sad," Henretta said, relieved to learn that he'd not died in her apartment. She fumbled with her key, unaccountably tired.

At eight the next morning a hippie knocked on the door. Henretta saw his face through the window, stringy gray hair under a dusty brown cowboy hat, wire-rimmed spectacles. At first she hesitated to answer, but he'd seen her and knew she was home, so there was no use pretending she was out. She went to the door and looked out the window. He wore battered blue jeans and a plaid shirt that was so faded it wasn't really any color any more. He wasn't quite what she'd call a dirty hippie. Just some cowboy still lost in the sixties. His beardless face revealed a broad, pleasant smile that wasn't at all deranged or evil-looking, so she answered the door, and found that he was a friendly neighbor boy who liked to garden. His name was Merrill Reuben Silverstein, and Henretta feared he was a Jew.

But he worked hard and didn't charge any money for his gardening. He said it was all his pleasure to do it for free.

That day, Merrill dug and weeded and watered and planted as if the devil held a whip over him. Dane stopped by, and, while Merrill worked planting pansies in the flower beds along the line of juniper trees, Dane broke the dirt clods to catch fishing worms. Henretta fixed brownies and lemonade, then invited them in for a snack. Merrill almost sat on the couch with his muddy pants, but she stopped him and put some newspaper down first. Then Henretta sat in a chair on the other side of the room from the men.

While eating a brownie, Dane suddenly looked up and said, "Say, who's that pretty girl in the picture?" He pointed to a black-and-white photo above the TV in which a dark-haired beauty sat in a wagon filled with pumpkins and dried cornstalks. She wore a banner across her white dress that said "Clover, Utah Harvest Queen, 1934."

"Yeah, I'd pay by the hour to look at a girl like that," Merrill said, winking at Dane.

"Oh, that's just me," Henretta said, ducking her head.

Every evening that week, Dane came over and said, "Hey there, Harvest Queen, want to go fishing?" Then they went to the river. He told jokes and sang old songs. And, as Henretta told Bruce over the phone one day, she began to feel Dane was "the pleasant-est person" she'd met in some time.

Occasionally, Ruth or Georgia tagged along on the fishing trips, but Dane didn't seem to be inviting them. Henretta noticed with pride that it was only *her* door that Dane knocked at before he went fishing. On their third trip, Henretta got up the nerve to put a worm on Dane's hook. She held the worm tightly and poked the hook through it, ignoring the brown worm juice that dripped on her fingers. Dane gently took the hook, and as his hand touched hers, it seemed to linger. From then on it became a regular thing for Henretta to bait Dane's hook.

Ruth taught Henretta to play backgammon and was amazed at how fast she learned. Henretta beat her on the fourth game. Georgia began to stop by in the late mornings, around tennish, and moped around and griped about her swollen feet, the mushy vegetables down at River Market, the latest atrocities committed by Islamic Fundamentalists, and this and that, then went home to watch soap operas.

At the end of exactly one week in her new apartment, Georgia and Ruth invited Henretta to a "laundry party." When they came over, Henretta pointed out that they were just the "partying-est bunch of girls" she'd ever met. She got her laundry bag and they walked to the laundromat together. All the way there, Georgia raved about how well Pappy was recovering from his ear infection and about how it was high time Henretta met Pappy. Between talking and hobbling along with her laundry, poor Georgia could hardly gasp. Ruth and Henretta made her rest several times for fear she'd collapse. Georgia was so insistent that Henretta meet Pappy that Henretta finally agreed to get up at eight in the morning to meet him at his favorite bus stop bench.

The laundromat was hot and humid, with lots of nice new washers and dryers with shiny chrome trim. The ladies quickly dumped their clothes in the wash. Henretta noticed that the floors were free of dust bunnies and the garbage cans were lined with trash bags. Paintings of Indians on horses decorated the walls. This was the kind of place Henretta liked to give her business to, and she informed everyone of this fact several times. Georgia caught everyone up on the latest gossip from the soap operas, then it was time to do the drying. Both Henretta and Ruth put their clothes in the dryer, but Georgia just put hers back in her laundry bag.

"Whatever are you doing with your laundry?" Ruth asked.

"I'm going to take it home and dry it on the clothesline," Georgia said with a hint of a pout.

"You're in no condition to lug that big, heavy sack of clothes home," Ruth said.

"She's right, honey," Henretta put in. With her weight problems, walking on that cane, Georgia would never be able to carry those wet clothes.

"I like my clothes dried on the clothesline," Georgia said. "They catch the scent of the pines."

Henretta rattled her brain trying to remember where the nearest pine tree was, but Ruth ignored the statement and blurted, "You said that two months ago—but remember what happened: that black Lab pup next door pulled *all* your clothes off the line and ripped and muddied them."

"Well, I'll just hang them higher."

"You hold on," Ruth said, putting fifty cents into an empty dryer. "I'll go ahead and dry those for you, dear."

"No!" Georgia shouted. "I'll take care of my own wash. You keep away!"

"Why me? Why do you always get mad at me?" Ruth asked.

"Why me?" Chester had asked, reaching up from the bed, his fingers searching till they caught Henretta's wrist.

"Ouch, hon, you're pinching me," she pleaded. She'd reached over the bed rail and tried to pry his fingers open, to caress and reassure him and pry his fingers loose at the same time. But his fingers squeezed tighter and his whole body jerked in spasm. He began panting. Henretta's eyes widened and she suddenly thought, he's having a heart attack. He's dying. But then she realized he wouldn't die, because he had never died—whenever it had happened before he hadn't died, and so he wouldn't die now. Chester's breath came in shallow gasps. Henretta prayed softly and tried to keep him from hyperventilating by humming softly.

A second spasm brought a sneer to Chester's lips. His eyes bulged and did a little dance, as if he could see again and was watching fireflies dip and leap in the darkness. His back arched off the bed. His mouth opened and he gasped; his face turned dark red. Henretta made a noise that sounded like she said "squeak." She thought of running for help, but didn't. The spasm eased and he leaned back a little more peacefully. She would take care of him, she thought, and pray, hoping she wouldn't lose all of their retirement to the doctors, just in case it was a false alarm.

"Hold on! Hold on to me!" Henretta urged, clasping his hand in hers. Chester clamped her fingers tight enough to leave bruises.

He began to shake, as if he were sobbing. His breaths were too shallow, she thought, not deep enough to sustain a man with his frame. She rose from her chair, struggled free from his grasp, then leaned over his body and hugged him. Sweat clung to his armpits and back; she smelled what seemed a lifetime of sweat that had soaked into his blue pajamas. His face turned from red to purple and Henretta suddenly realized he might really die. He didn't seem to be breathing at all. She closed her eyes, tried to feel him, to hear if he was breathing. She imagined she could feel more than that—she could feel his spirit, that essence that put light in his eyes, draining like water from a broken teacup.

325

She wondered who would come to greet him—his dead brother perhaps, or maybe angels. A lot of people said they saw angels when they died, and she wished desperately that she knew what he saw.

She tried to travel out from herself, to imagine him there before her, and reach a little way into the darkness with him. And it seemed to work. She had wondered if she'd see angels, but instead she envisioned something odd—like silken strands, or like tentacles of light, hooked just above her belly. She was trying to find Chester, to pray for him and hold him, and with these strands she groped for him. She called and he was there, a dim, throbbing egg-shaped mass, and she saw his tentacles of light stretched, being pulled through the darkness toward a distant nebulous cloud of glory. It was as if he were some horse-drawn sled, and those tentacles of light were the lines, pulling him away from her.

Henretta reached out with her own tentacles of light, twined those tentacles around him, caressing, and tried to tug him back to safety. She could feel his spirit in her grasp, warm and fluttering. *It's a miracle, it's a miracle,* she thought, believing she'd got him. But Chester trembled and sighed a sigh so deep it spoke of perfect surrender. With a vicious lunge, he was dragged away through the darkness, toward that great light, and Henretta knew in that second that if she held on, she too would be drawn away, pulled from her body in an untimely death. So she released him.

And he was gone.

He's dead, she thought. *He left just like that. Like he didn't even care. Or like he couldn't stop himself.*

Henretta stepped back and timidly stared at the husk her husband had lived in; his half-open eyes were turning glassy. Sluggish thoughts paraded around her mind like drugged elephants in a circus ring. She mouthed the words to a prayer, "Yea though I walk through the Valley of the Shadow, I shall fear no evil. . . ."

She put a hand over her lips, suddenly terrified by what people would think. Because her strange effort had failed, they would accuse her of having done nothing.

The world would hate her if she did nothing. She jumped from her chair, rushed down the corridor, scanning rooms as she passed. Empty-eyed geriatrics lay on beds, asleep or staring at walls. The more active ones gummed food from trays while watching the five o'clock news; one woman craned her neck and called for help as Henretta passed. Patients strapped in wheelchairs dotted the hall.

When she got halfway down the south corridor, her tears began to flow. The hall blurred. *Damn you, damn you for leaving me like this,* she thought, and then she realized that her thought was a sin. Chester had been a good man, a faithful man whose sure hope was founded upon the rock of the Gospel of Jesus Christ. He was the kind of man who always helped his neighbors, someone who actually liked to teach Boy Scouts. And everyone agreed he was special. He'd had more goodness in him, more faith, than Henretta had ever had. He'd looked forward with calm assurance to salvation, to that day when he would rise in clouds of glory at the rapture.

Surely God had gathered him along with the Saints to his bosom, as a loving Heavenly Father would. God would have been eager for a good man like that. That must have been the reason Chester died.

But it disturbed Henretta, that final look in Chester's face: he'd been ripped from her. Torn violently. He hadn't gone willingly, the way she imagined a good Christian should, peacefully returning to his Father.

And so she feared for the welfare of his soul. She tried to put the thought from her mind, to unthink it, make it as if it had never been. She felt her way along the corridor, holding the shiny metal handrail as if she were some doddering thing. She whispered a litany: "It is better this way; it is better this way." The last stroke had left Chester blind and nearly deaf; it was better that death take him suddenly than that he should have to feel his way slowly to the grave. So this early death was a gift from God, who was manifesting His mercy.

She found herself standing at a counter in front of an aide station attended by a young blonde with a trio of pimples on her chin. "I think my husband is dead," Henretta said, staring beyond the counter at a potato sack of a woman who sat frowning in a chair.

"Because you don't know your own place!" Georgia shouted in answer to the question.

Ruth backed away from the dryer and whimpered. All through the drying cycle, Ruth and Georgia glared at each other and refused to speak. Henretta stared at the floor. When the clothes were dry, the women folded and packed them in silence.

Georgia puffed and sweated on the way home, carrying that big bag of wet clothes. She put her cane in her laundry bag and hobbled along without it. Henretta walked behind, watching the wet clothes sway with Georgia's every step.

Henretta suddenly blurted: "You know, when my husband Chester was dying, he pulled my arm so hard that for a moment I thought he was trying to pull me into the grave with him." Then she added more solemnly, "When he died, he did pull a part of me into that grave." Neither Georgia nor Ruth responded, but Henretta was glad she'd said it. It was one of her favorite things to tell people, it sounded so pitiful, and she was glad she remembered it after all these years so she could say it to them.

The night was hot, and Henretta dreamed of a roast burning in the oven. At 3:00 A.M. she kicked off her heavy winter quilt. When she rose just before sunrise, her eyes were puffy and swollen. She decided to take a walk while it was yet cool.

She stepped out of her apartment and headed down the gravel road to the park. She passed the corner of Georgia's apartment and saw, right there on the clothesline between the blouses and nylons, Georgia's panties waving in the breeze like banners, flapping like flags!

How could Georgia do such a thing? Didn't she have any taste? Didn't she have any decency? People would drive by and see her personals on the clothesline. And what's more, they might think those big panties were Henretta's.

Henretta was disgusted. Something had to be done. She waltzed around in a full circle, looking over the sleeping town, making sure no one was watching. No one walked the street, but one car barreled down Highway 99. Henretta watched the car turn the corner and head north of town, then sneaked toward the clothesline.

When she reached Georgia's window, she hunched and tiptoed beneath it. A twig snapped. She froze in place. Across the street, the Martinellis' tabby cat jumped onto the porch. It glared at Henretta knowingly, like some witch's cat from a story, then arched its back, lay down, and yawned. Henretta hurried over to the clothesline, yanked all five pairs of panties down and wadded them in her fist, hoping no one would see.

But what to do with them? She looked for a hole or a drainage pipe to hide them in, but there was nothing—then she saw the garbage cans by Ruth's apartment. She hurried to the garbage cans and shoved the panties in a milk carton, where they were well hidden.

"You'll just love Pappy," Georgia promised later that morning as they walked to the bus stop. Georgia tapped her cane on the ground and twirled it in the air as they walked. "Everybody loves him—even his family. He lives with his granddaughter, you know. He's got sixty thousand dollars in the bank. He was really smart to save it that way. Kids nowadays will only let you live with them if you have money in the bank."

"Hmmmh," Henretta nodded. Everyone Henretta knew said the same type of thing about kids today, so just as a dig she said, "Maybe it's his personality. Maybe his kids like him because of that."

"Well, there he is!" Georgia said, pointing to a silver-haired, bearded man on a bench.

Henretta paused to look at Georgia, amazed at the tone of her voice. Why that crazy old woman is in love! Henretta thought as she followed Georgia to the bench.

Pappy stood up and began tucking in his shirt when he saw the girls. "Mornin', Georgia," he yelled, scratching his ear. Henretta noticed that though his clothes were wrinkled, they seemed to be clean—an opinion she wouldn't have hazarded about his body.

"Good morning, Pappy," Georgia yelled in reply. "I brought a friend along for you to meet."

"Oh, do I know you?" Pappy yelled at Henretta.

"No, I brought her for you to meet. This is Henretta Bloom," Georgia yelled.

"Henra who?"

"Henretta Bloom," Georgia yelled louder.

"Oh," Pappy said, obviously befuddled by the name. "Pleased to meet you. How old are you?"

Henretta looked back and forth between Pappy and Georgia, not sure whether to answer.

"You'll have to speak up. He can't hear well," Georgia said.

"I'm seventy-six," Henretta yelled.

"Oh, I'm ninety-two!" Pappy said. "You'll have to call me Pappy, 'cause you're not as old as I am. If you was as old as I am, you could call me John!"

"It's nice to meet you, Pappy," Henretta said. Then they all sat down on the bench. Henretta and Pappy each sat on one end of the bench, Georgia in the middle.

Pappy crossed his legs and intently watched cars pass on Highway 99 and didn't say a word, though he often cleared his throat. Henretta waited for something to happen for a few moments, but nothing did. Georgia surreptitiously took Pappy's hand and placed it on her knee, and she sat stroking and squeezing it. Pappy pretended not to notice. Instead, he scratched with his free hand.

First he'd scratch his thigh, then he'd scratch his belly, then his chin, and on around to the back of his neck. It wasn't rapid scratching, but slow, methodical scratching—barely noticeable unless you watched for it. Henretta became convinced he had fleas.

Georgia and Pappy were content to slouch on the bench and watch cars until, suddenly, at eight-fifteen, Pappy perked up like a hound that hears a noise in the night. He craned his neck, gazing down the street. Georgia stiffened. Henretta searched for the object of their attention without luck till Pappy spoke.

"Cara, come marry me!" he yelled. A young girl—with lavender eye shadow, three rings in each ear, greasy red hair combed straight up, and pants as black and shiny as tar—stopped forty feet from the bus stop. She stared at Pappy and chewed bubble gum.

"Come marry me. I love you!" Pappy yelled. Cara glanced back over her shoulder, then turned to Pappy. She leaned her head to the side, blew a purple bubble, and popped it. Bright silver earrings glittered at her ears. *Oh, she's a tough-acting cookie,* Henretta thought, noticing that the girl's face was turning red.

"I love you! We could make wild love!" Pappy insisted.

"Give me a break, you pervert," the girl said.

"I love you! I promise I'll die on the honeymoon and leave you all my money," Pappy yelled. He struggled from the bench, opened his arms wide as if for her to rush to him.

"Drop dead, ya old fart, or my brothers will beat the crap out of you!" Cara said. She curled a heavy chain around her fist, sauntered past Pappy and the ladies on the bench.

"Come back! Come and marry me. I promise to die on the honeymoon!" Pappy yelled, breaking into hoarse laughter as Cara passed. The back of the girl's neck was bright as a burn. Georgia seemed genuinely tickled by the whole affair, giggling and slapping Pappy's back and wringing his hand.

As Cara walked down the street, Pappy watched her behind. "She's no fun," he said, chuckling. "Still, she's a real looker." He settled back down on the bench.

"I'll marry you, you old cradle robber," Georgia giggled. Pappy looked away.

"Nope. I'm gonna marry me one of those young-uns," Pappy said, after a while.

"Why not someone your own age?" Georgia asked.

"Because an old woman ain't a woman: she's neuter, good for nothing. No one keeps an old mare around. But a stallion now, a stallion's worth his oats forever."

"Shame on you for saying that," Georgia said, playfully slapping Pappy. She laughed and began wringing his hand as if it were a washrag. Pappy reached over and squeezed her knee, chuckled, then turned and looked down the street as two more girls approached, neither of them older than thirteen.

Henretta poked Georgia in the ribs with an elbow and whispered, "Does he do this all the time?"

"Every morning, when it's warm enough," Georgia said.

"And you sit here with him?"

"Well of course," Georgia said, "Nobody really minds. They laugh about it. Even the kids laugh about it. Pappy has a great sense of humor!" The two girls slowed as they neared, watching Pappy in dread.

"Here they come," Pappy crooned, straightening his back a little, catching his breath as he prepared to yell. When Georgia and Pappy had their backs turned, Henretta quietly slid off the bench, heading home.

When she reached the house, Merrill, the Jewish cowboy-hippie, was in the yard on his knees, digging among the strawberries with a hand shovel. He sweated profusely and Henretta saw that under his long, curly hair his head was beet-red from sunburn. She walked over and stood where her shadow would cross his path. "Never grow old, Merrill," she intoned solemnly. "Never grow old."

"Why's that?" Merrill asked, looking up, catching sweat with his tongue as it rolled down around his lip.

"Because, old people are so nasty, Merrill. Naaasssty!"

"But you're not nasty, Henretta," Merrill said.

Henretta took a step backward. "Oh yes I am," she affirmed. "I'm just a nasty old lady." Yet she bit her lower lip, hoping that he would contradict her, needing his assurance.

"Hen-retta," Merrill said, with just the right note of reproof. Henretta gazed down at him for a moment, then scurried off to the kitchen to make him some iced tea.

The sun was setting across the river. The night breeze picked up as cool air sped from the hills. A bullfrog croaked in the rushes on the near bank. Dane sat in his easy chair watching his bobber, red in the light of the setting sun, quiver among small waves. Henretta sat on the grass beside him, fanning herself with the *Reader's Digest*. Ruth had come down from the apartment and stood behind them.

"Well, Georgia's talking to me again," Ruth said. "I didn't think she'd talk to me for a week—she was so mad last night when we got back from the laundry. But she started talking to me just a while ago."

"What did she say?" Dane asked since it was obvious she wanted to tell.

"Someone stole her panties off the clothesline!" Ruth whispered.

"Naw!" Dane said.

"Yep, that's just what happened!" Ruth said.

"Maybe that black dog pulled them down," Henretta offered.

"And leave everything else? No!" Ruth said. "If you ask me, some pervert took 'em!"

"Probably so," Dane agreed. A bat swooped low and nabbed a mayfly from the air. Dane slowly reeled in his line, hoping for one last bite before it got dark. "Probably so."

In her dream Henretta reached to put some ointment on her husband Chester. Another ulcer had formed on the back of his neck. *He's becoming one large bedsore,* she thought. She prodded it.

"Why me?" Chester said, groping for Henretta's arm. In his world of silence and blackness, nothing was left but the joy of touch. His hand flapped about feebly until it met flesh, then he clenched her arm.

"Ouch, hon, you're hurting me!" Henretta said, trying to pry open his fingers. But the fingers wouldn't come loose. Chester's whole body jerked in spasm. His back arced off the bed. Henretta looked in his face, saw the sneer of pain, and realized he'd die. She tried to pry free, but his fingers pulled, they pulled. He was trying to pull her into the grave. He wanted her to take his place in the grave! Sirens screamed. The ambulance was on its way!

Henretta woke to a shrill siren. She listened to it come up the road and waited for it to pass, but the siren wound down to silence in front of the apartments. From her bed she saw faint light flash on the living room windows, red and blue, red and blue. Pulling her bathrobe over her nightgown, she hurried to see for whom the ambulance had come.

Dane lay on the stretcher; Ruth hovered over him, smoothing his hair, whispering, "It's all right. You're all right. We'll take good care of you." Henretta ran to the stretcher, too, but a paramedic gently forced her back, then inserted a catheter in Dane's wrist. Dane stared straight ahead, eyes unfocused, body slack.

"What's wrong?" Henretta asked the paramedic as he put some medical supplies into a metal box.

"Stroke."

Henretta watched the paramedics load Dane into the ambulance. Ruth followed them and jumped in back before they drove away. Georgia walked up beside Henretta.

"What happened?" Henretta asked as the flashing lights of the ambulance sped down the street, around the bend, and out of town toward Corvallis.

"Dane had a stroke," Georgia whispered.

Henretta imagined herself lying on the floor, gasping for breath, dying of a stroke, with no one to help her. "But how did anyone find out? How did they know?"

Georgia gave Henretta a glance. "Ruth called them."

"How did Ruth know?" Henretta asked in surprise.

Georgia pursed her lips. She looked at the gravel at the roadside, stirred it with the point of her toe. Next door, the light on Merrill's porch flicked on. Henretta's mouth silently opened in an O as realization struck. Georgia said, "It's a good thing, too. There's no telling how long he would have lain there if Ruth hadn't been with him!" Georgia said.

"Dane and Ruth?" Henretta mumbled, as Georgia took her arm and led her to the house.

Dane had a cerebral hemorrhage and was partly paralyzed in his right arm and left leg. He couldn't eat well and had difficulty speaking, so Ruth took a hotel room and stayed to help him. Every day, Georgia suggested Henretta call her grandson so he could drive them to the hospital for a visit.

"We could go up to the hospital and take Dane a card; then we could stop off at Blessed Bessie's and donate some things. I've got dresses just turning to rags in my closet! We should hurry to Blessed Bessie's before the moths eat everything up!" Georgia would say. But Henretta preferred to sit in her room all day and watch the "Price is Right" and "Wheel of Fortune."

She quit walking the three hundred yards down to the park. Merrill came each morning to work in the garden, and was remarkably good company. Henretta found him rather old-fashioned. He loved to garden like nobody she'd ever seen before. He'd planted azaleas all along the walk to her apartment, along with some flower she'd never heard of. And in the sunny spot just inside the juniper hedge, he'd planted a row of something called cannabis indica, which he said had wonderful buds in the fall. He kept goats in his backyard, and every morning he milked them and made his own butter, and he used their dung for fertilizer. He grew peppermint and spearmint and dried them to make tea, just as Henretta's mother had done. He even canned his own "organically grown" vegetables.

One day, Henretta was sitting in her rocker on the porch, writing a letter to her sister, Daniella. Merrill was spreading goat manure around the cannabis plants, which were still rather short, when his face tilted up and he smiled at her.

"Hear that?" he asked.

Henretta listened for a moment; a truck passed on the road behind the apartment, drowning out any other noise. "What?" Henretta asked.

"Birds. Baby birds," Merrill said. He got up, checked the eaves around the apartment. Sure enough, just above the fence that separated Henretta's yard from Dane's, a mud–nest clung to the wall. A swallow came to the nest to feed the chicks, and each time it came Henretta could see the little heads of the chicks pop over the rim of the nest as they peeped.

"Aren't summers wonderful?" Merrill said. "All the grass is green, the sun shines on the leaves, and the animals come to life!"

Henretta thought a moment. "No, no they're not! I've lived through enough, I should know. Summers are just lies. They make you think everything is warm and wonderful, then turn cold on you. I should know. All my summers I thought would never end have turned to poison in my veins!"

She waited for Merrill to make a soothing reply, but he just opened his mouth, working his jaws as he tried to think. Henretta stomped away, leaving him to gape like a goldfish.

In thirteen days, Dane returned from the hospital. Ruth didn't even pretend she wasn't living with him. As soon as they got home she moved into his apartment and set up house. She said it was because Dane had a hard time swallowing and needed help with the speaking exercises the therapist had given him. "And he needs help dressing," Henretta slyly told Merrill.

Henretta decided to avoid Ruth and Dane for a week, but a week became a month and a month became two. Somehow she felt Ruth and Dane were tricksters. When she talked to Bruce on the phone, that's just what she called them: "those two tricksters."

And so Henretta looked elsewhere for friends. She tried the Congregational Church in town, but there really wasn't anyone there that she felt she could get close to. Some folks brought their grand-mothers, but they were from all over the countryside, miles away, and Henretta couldn't visit them. It was a lonely time for Henretta, and so she read her Bible. Jesus was still her friend and her comforter.

After two months Dane began to walk a bit and often journeyed down to the park to look out over the river. Henretta would see him there, his back bent, right arm drooping, the summer sun bleaching his hair whiter every day. Sometimes he stopped by if Henretta happened to be in the yard. At those times he would silently watch her. His conversations were mostly hellos and goodbyes, slurred to the point of being almost unrecognizable. Yet day by day he slowly recovered.

At the end of July Ruth brought over the backgammon board and insisted Henretta play. Henretta decided to play as viciously as she could, blocking with every move and sending Ruth's pieces home whenever possible. However, Ruth didn't seem interested in the game at all; she chatted all the way through it. Henretta was amazed at how vibrant she looked.

"Have you seen how *cute* Georgia's been acting lately?" Ruth asked, moving seven spaces.

"Hmmm, what do you mean?" Henretta asked, rolling double threes.

"What do I mean? Why, for days she's been saying, 'let's drive up to Corvallis and stop at Blessed Bessie's! I've got a few things to drop off! Let's stop at Blessed Bessie's!'"

"Hmmm. What do you think it means?" Henretta asked. She rolled double ones, and was able to block two rows with her pieces while sending one of Ruth's men home.

"What does it mean? Why, it means she doesn't have any underwear!"

Henretta looked up from the board and frowned. "No underwear?"

"Of course not! Remember when she lost her underwear off the clothesline? Well, she's gone months without a pair of panties!"

"Couldn't she walk down to River Market and buy some?"

"Of course not! River Market doesn't carry panties. Besides, she doesn't have any income but Social Security. She can't afford them! She couldn't even afford to dry them in the washer. That's why she wants to go to Blessed Bessie's to pick up free clothes!"

That night was the hottest of the year. Henretta lay in bed till ten, but found she was sweating so much that she went to the living room, opened the window, and lay on the couch. In a moment, she heard muted voices and a laugh. Her head was near the wall, and she realized she was hearing noises from Dane's bedroom. She lay for a long time, trying to still her breath so she could catch any sound of squeaking springs, but heard only Dane and Ruth's whispers.

* * *

In the morning Henretta woke with a headache. The day promised to be hot as a bee sting, dry as yesterday's biscuits. Soon Georgia came by and asked if the Harvest Queen wanted to go fishing. Dane finally felt well enough, and they were all going to make a picnic of it. Henretta said "yes," and promised to bring drinks, then lay on the couch with an ice-pack on her head.

At six, Henretta lugged lemonade down to the park. She was dizzy with pain, and trudging down that road made her feel as if she were wading in mud. Down by the river, among the shade of the willows, that's where they all were. Dane and Ruth sat in folding chairs; Georgia sat on a bench next to Pappy, fanning him with a newspaper while pretending to fan herself; Merrill, off by himself, watched dragonflies buzz through the rushes; half-naked kids were everywhere, eating watermelon and spitting the seeds at each other.

"Hi, Henretta!" everyone said as she approached. Henretta nodded but held her ears, explaining she had a headache. Everyone understood, and they were all nice as pie; Georgia laid a blanket on the ground for her and Ruth offered an aspirin from her purse. Henretta was normally against taking medications, but she gave in and took the aspirin.

Then they backed off and told her to rest. She lay on the ground, gazing up at the willow leaves that fluttered in the slight breeze, turning green and yellow, green and yellow, depending on how they twisted. Dane said something that must have been funny—everyone broke into a harsh laughter that quickly subsided. Henretta watched the leaves and felt as if she were floating, floating down a river in the bottom of a boat that trembled in the waves and spun in lazy circles. Then she slept.

"All right, you lucky contestants, now is your big opportunity! If you answer your question correctly you could be our lucky *Grand Prize Winner!*" the announcer shouted jovially. A great red curtain stood behind Henretta; a podium stood before her; an audience, off in the shadows, screamed hysterically. Two other podiums sat at her right: Pappy hunched over the far one, blinking stupidly and trying to smooth wrinkles from his clothes. Georgia was in the middle, her hair a blaze of blue in the lights; she looked fatter than usual and leaned heavily on her cane. Henretta couldn't see the announcer's face because of glaring camera lights. A drumroll began, the audience quieted.

"Contestant number one," the announcer said, "here is your question:" Pappy straightened and looked studious. The announcer asked, "Who knows what evil lurks in the hearts of men?"

Oh damn, Henretta thought, *I hope my question is that easy—he'll probably say something stupid, like* God *or something.* Pappy stood without answering. Georgia clutched her cane and Henretta could see that she was tempted to cheat and give Pappy the answer. Henretta's heart nearly stopped for fear he'd miss the question. Pappy pulled a smile at the last second before the buzzer sounded. "The Shadow knows!"

"Hooray!" the crowd screamed and whistled. Henretta jumped and clapped.

"That's right! That's right!" the announcer yelled. "Jay, tell Pappy what he's won!" The crowd hushed in anticipation.

"A neewww set of hearing aids!" Jay squealed. The crowd roared its delight. Henretta nearly wept for joy and Georgia's face glowed at the good news. A shapely redhead in a blue bathing suit paraded by, carrying a poster of the hearing aids. Pappy stared at her every wiggle and bounce. "That's right Pappy, you're the lucky winner of these brand-new Audiotronic 910 hearing aids. These new Audiotronic hearing aids are smaller and lighter weight, with a special earpiece designed for greater wearability. With your new hearing aids, you'll also get a year's supply of batteries! *Free* from Audiotronics! With Audiotronics, you'll soon be hearing *whispers!*" With the word *whisper,* Jay's voice lowered to a false whisper. The lights above Pappy dimmed while the lights above Georgia brightened.

"And now, Georgia Pearly, for your question!" the announcer said. Georgia stiffened, her sagging face frowned in concentration. "Georgia Pearly, who stole your *underwear?*"

The crowd gasped; Georgia looked from side to side in confusion. Henretta's heart pounded and she wanted to scream "Not me! Not me! Don't look at me!" Finally, Georgia looked straight forward and said, "A perverted dog stole them."

Henretta held her breath and waited to see if the announcer knew who really stole Georgia's underwear. She was sure that the crowd knew, that every person out in those shadows could see the guilt written on her face. But the announcer had a smile in his voice and yelled, "That's right Georgia! A perverted dog stole your underwear!" The crowd cheered and whistled, Henretta clapped her hands and smiled in relief. "Jay, tell Georgia what she's won!"

"Georgia, you've won"—Jay paused—"a new pair of wooden legs!"

The audience screamed in delight. From the shadows a pair of shiny plastic legs came flying through the air; Georgia caught them, cradling them in her arms like a bouquet of roses. She cried, "Thank you, thank you."

"That's right Georgia, your dancing days aren't over! With this new pair of legs from Davis Corporation, you'll be waltzing well into your nineties! Molded from the finest lightweight plastic, and crafted with the finest stainless steel frame, joints, and braces, you'll be walking—and yes—even dancing in comfort on your new wooden legs, from Davis Corporation: The finest in prosthetic devices for over fifty years!"

"Oh thank you," Georgia said, then confided to the audience out in the shadows, "These will come in handy: I've got the diabetes, you know."

Henretta gazed at the wooden legs and thought about how appropriate it all was: hearing aids and wooden legs—just what they needed! Not all that fancy crap like sailboats and trips to Acapulco. The clapping subsided; the lights around Georgia faded. Only Henretta was left in the light. The drum roll began.

"Now, Henretta, our final question!" the announcer said. "Henretta, who won the battle of the Little Bighorn!"

Henretta thought for a moment, then screamed, "The Indians!"

"That's right, Henretta! The Indians! And you're our *Grand Prize Winner* today!" The audience screamed and cheered. Horns blasted. Golden glitter fell from the air, shimmering in the TV lights. "Jay, tell Henretta what she's won!"

"Right, Bob! Well, Henretta, here it is! Your Grand Prize! Henretta Bloom, you have won . . . your very own—*mausoleum!*" Cries of astonishment and delight greeted Henretta as she staggered forward. A beautiful building of white stone rolled on stage. Fluted Greek columns with sculpted cherubs near the top supported a creamy white roof. A fountain burst from a stone at one corner of the building. A stream flowed away from it. Henretta marveled at it.

"Yes, Henretta," Jay said, "your own private mausoleum! You won't be eating dirt and breathing worms with your friends! You'll be resting in your own, pleasant, climate-controled mausoleum from Christian Brother's Mortuary! This handsome building comes complete with recordings of your favorite music, to be piped into your room for eternity." Henretta walked up the steps of the building and peered in the open door. Light shone from beautiful plum-colored walls; an orchestra played "The Blue Danube." She entered and stared at the coffin in the middle of the room. "And, your package also includes this beautiful coffin!" Jay continued. "This handsome, stainless-steel coffin with genuine silk sheets and pillowcases will let you rest in comfort forever! And the beautiful leaded crystal cover will let your loved ones view you with ease!"

Henretta approached the coffin and gazed at the bright floral pattern of the silk. She imagined how nice it would be to lie there, how the cares of the world would slide off her if she lay down. The thought brought tears to her eyes.

"Well, Henretta, how do you like your new mausoleum?" the announcer asked; his voice was not magnified through a microphone. Instead, it sounded as if Jay had walked into the room with her for a private chat. His voice came from the direction of the door.

"Oh, it's wonderful!" Henretta said with a sniff.

"We're glad you like it!" Henretta glimpsed the announcer's shadow as he approached, heard his feet softly scuff the carpet. The applause died; anticipation fluttered in the air. Henretta heard a rasping noise— the glass lid of the coffin sliding open. "And now, Henretta, it's time to get in," the announcer said.

Henretta turned to face him. The rest of the room was distinctly visible but the announcer stood in shadows. "I won't get in there. It's not time yet!"

"Go ahead. Get in," the shadowy announcer said, stepping closer. Henretta could hear tension in his voice. She looked around the room. All the doors had disappeared.

"Go ahead. Get in," the announcer said. A noise like a drum roll began, only tinnier—more of a rattle. Henretta looked at the announcer and realized his microphone was really a rattle—an Indian rattle. She stepped back. The announcer lurched closer; a shaft of light fell across his hand. She saw that he was indeed holding a rattle, but it wasn't the rattle that made the noise, it was bones! The flesh was rotted off the announcer's hand and his bones were rattling! With a flash of insight she realized that the announcer was Malcolm Blackfeather, an Indian worker who'd taken sick and died in the bunkhouse at her father's ranch. He'd come to get her!

"Indians! Indians!" Henretta screamed, flailing her arms.

"Indians?" Ruth asked.

Henretta opened her eyes and looked up at the willow leaves fluttering overhead. Everyone was chuckling. She clenched her fist to her heart until it stopped pounding.

"Oh, I've had a horrible dream!" she said.

"About Indians," Georgia clucked.

Henretta glared at Georgia for the teasing, then got up and smoothed her dress. Evening was coming on. She'd slept at least an hour. Everyone was quiet. Dane had his fishing pole, and he stood on the riverbank, casting out into the water. Merrill and most of the picnickers from town had left. Henretta began to walk over to the water's edge, but Georgia put her finger to her lips, gesturing Henretta to greater silence, so she tiptoed.

When she reached the water, she looked out over the river. It had grown dark and shadowed in places. It was peaceful. She stared across the river for some time, then happened to glance down in the water.

"Look! There's a fish!" she said, pointing to a little purple-backed crappie that swam just below the surface. "And there's another! And another!"

"Shhh . . ." Ruth hissed, waving toward Dane, who was slowly reeling his bait through a school of fish. Henretta looked out over the water, and suddenly realized with awe that in every shadow, everywhere she looked, the purple fish were rising to the surface. There were crappie and bass and bluegills—more fish than she could ever remember having seen. *More fish,* she thought to herself, *than the days of my life.*

A breeze kicked up; willow leaves rattled. Fish boiled to the surface, then disappeared underwater. Henretta wondered what made them behave that way, then looked at the willow tree: from the limbs of the tree, little silk webs dangled, glittering silver in the sunlight. From each strand of silver hung a tiny green inchworm. She watched as the wind gusted again, and strands of silver swayed in the wind, swayed out over the wide water, then back to land, then back out over the water. Some of the strands of silver snapped.

"Aaaa . . . aggh," Pappy said quietly, making sound effects for the falling caterpillars. The fish rose to the surface. The water boiled as they grabbed the inchworms, dove again. Dane reeled his worm past the nose of a largemouth bass; the fish lunged, took the worm in its mouth. Dane set the hook with a jerk of his rod; the gears in his reel ground like an alarm clock as he pulled the fish in.

Henretta was appalled at the way Pappy made fun of the dying worms. *He's just a dirty old man with dirty fingernails and fleas,* she thought, *so I'll just say something about it.* She said: "Wouldn't it be horrible to die that way; to be swinging out over the water, hoping never to fall in, then to fall in, just to have the fish eat you?"

Pappy didn't hear her, but Georgia and Ruth both nodded. Dane jerked the fish from the water. Its gills swelled wide as it gasped for breath. Henretta could see the gills, strand on strand of red, through the gill slits. Suddenly Dane got the strangest grin on his face. Henretta wondered what he could be thinking, then realized he smiled sideways because of the paralysis.

"I just 'membered somthin'," Dane slurred. "You yellin' 'bout Indians, then talking 'bout these worms put it to mind. Seems there's these Yaqui Indians that believe somethin' funny. They believe there's this magical cord that hooks you up to everthin' alive. And when you die, that cord snaps, and your spirit falls through a dark place to this place of great light. When you reach that light you feel all warm and wonderful for a minute.

"Then God comes. And he eats you. They think the whole reason for living is so God can eat your spirit. And he only lets us grow old so that our spirits will grow sour and ripe with bitterness, cause that's what he likes to eat. Ain't that kind of a strange thing to believe?"

Georgia laughed, but Henretta grew pale. It was bad enough when people questioned faith, or when Henretta wondered if God would be kind enough to forgive her sins. But to have people talk about pagan beliefs so, to have them talk about such frightening pagan beliefs—her heart hammered and she drew ragged breaths. And she remembered how Chester had died, with that silver cord being yanked from her into the keen, cold light.

She looked up and down the river, trying to decide which way to run.

She looked back toward Ruth and Georgia; both of them laughed at her and pointed. Dane stood, fishing rod in hand, and stared in bewilderment, as if wondering what was going through her mind.

Henretta crossed her arms over her breasts, covering herself protectively, ran toward the house.

"Indians!" Georgia yelled. Henretta spun, mad enough to rip out Georgia's blue hair. Georgia held her belly and cackled; Ruth snickered. Even Dane betrayed an amused smile.

"You—" Henretta started to scream, but couldn't think of a curse word, "I know what kind of person you are! What have you been wearing since you lost your panties?" Georgia would try to lie—then Henretta would confront her with the ugly truth.

"Why, I've just been making do without," Georgia answered.

"Hah! Did you hear that?" Henretta asked the others.

"So?" Dane said calmly, "I haven't worn underwear in years. Have I Ruth?"

"No, he hasn't," Ruth solemnly testified.

Henretta gagged. She fled for home. *How horrible!* she thought. *How horrible! How could I have thought I was falling in love with him? with that horrible man without underwear—the man with the ghastly smile?* Then she realized it was because of the stroke, because of the ghastly smile, that she couldn't love him. *When Chester died, he pulled a part of me into the grave with him,* Henretta told herself with grim satisfaction. *He pulled in that part of me that would let me love a man when he's down.*

341

As she reached the gravel lane that led to the house, she wondered about the story Dane had told about God. And she began muttering fervent prayers, all disconnected from her thoughts, "Oh, my Lord Jesus, God, come for me. Take me in rapture . . . forgive me my sins— I give them all to you. All of them. All of them to you. My love, my love, my love, I don't want them any more. Oh, shit, god damn it— please, please, please save me!"

But as she prayed, she considered what Dane had said. Is that the way God is? she wondered. It felt so right. So perfect. And it rattled her to the core of her soul.

"Bruce, Bruce, you've got to help me!" Henretta pleaded over the phone between ragged sobs. "You've got to move me! Please, Bruce, I can't put up with those horrible neighbors any more! These Mormons and Jews and witches. I can't! You have to come move me!"

Henretta waited in the house after the phone call, secretly watching the people down at the river. A crowd of them had gathered like crows. And all of her neighbors were sitting together and sitting with strange picnickers with smoky barbecues. All of them were laughing. She knew what they were laughing at. Oh yes, she'd put on quite a show! She knew what they were laughing at. She sang softly, fervently, "Shall We Gather at the River?" as she watched from the corner of the window, behind the curtain, so no one would see.

The sun was setting. Henretta watched out the window in the gathering darkness. The whole crowd was still down by the river. Soon the sun would be down and this horrible day would be over, she thought. People were lighting campfires; people were singing. A small Mexican boy walked up from the park, up the dusty road. He wore red shorts and a man's white shirt, which was open. His bare feet kicked up little clouds of dust as he ambled along the roadside, away from the sharp gravel at the road's center. Henretta watched as he passed her living room window. Then she went to get a drink. Afterward, she peeked out the window toward Merrill's house, but the Mexican boy wasn't there—nor did any dust clouds indicate that he'd passed the house.

She ran to the front door, jerked it open. The fuzzy-headed Mexican boy stood in her flower beds, an innocent smile on his face, penis in hand, urinating. Henretta wanted to say something, to curse him or tell him to go away, but Henretta and the Mexican boy just watched each other as the boy finished urinating, shook his penis off, put it in his pants, and ran.

Henretta slammed her door and locked it. Through the window she watched the Mexican boy run down to the park, and waited to see who talked to him. But no one she knew approached him—not Ruth, not Georgia, not Pappy, Merrill, or Dane. None of them went to the Mexican boy and patted him on the head and gave him a quarter as she expected they would. None of them even looked at him. Yet it was obvious, it was obvious, that one of them had put him up to it. One of them had told the Mexican boy to pee on her flowers. But which one? Or was it one? Could they have done it all together? Could they have gotten together and sent him as an emissary?

Henretta sat on the couch and wondered, turning it, like a coin, over and over in her mind. Outside, darkness deepened; shadow leaves fluttered on the white curtain. Could someone else have sent the Mexican boy? Someone greater than the picnickers, greater even than the whole town?

Henretta rose from the couch and walked out the front door, opened it. She stood on the porch and looked west, beyond the highway, above the mountains.

It was there! It was there—just as she had known it would be! A vast menacing shape loomed on the edge of night. On the horizon a solitary thunderhead glowed dark purple in the waning light; the red sun suffused the lower billows with a crimson, gilled effect.

"So, is this the way of it?" she asked, trying to keep calm, but the bile rose to her throat, and the wonder of what she saw was like an icy spike that struck from the top of her head down through her back to the soles of her feet. The sheer terror made it feel as if all her bones were disconnected, as if her arms and legs and fingers could fall away. She could not move, could hardly draw a breath. For so many years she'd been trying to convince herself that she was the right brand of Christian, that she'd never considered the possibility that beyond the Valley of the Shadow something ghastly prowled, something that all her panicked supplications could not shelter her from.

But on the horizon, she saw the proof of it. It had come for her. "Oh, damn it," she whined. Christ would not come for her trailing clouds of the righteous in their white robes. Hers would be a dark rapture. She gasped, "Oh, Chester, oh shit in hell!" And then she felt the bitter gall of all her wasted summers congealing in her veins, and she screamed. "You—you think you're God? You think you'll get me?"

"I've felt you nibbling on me!" she accused, wanting to pretend that somehow, on some deeper level, she'd had a premonition of what was coming. "I don't see what you get from it!" She waited, as if for an answer, but Dane had already warned her that God loved to eat them when they were old and bitter, as bitter as she was now. Henretta vowed at the top of her lungs, "This worm won't wiggle for you! This worm won't dance or fall! You just try to get me. *Just come on over here!*"

Townspeople down by the river turned to wonder at Henretta's gabbling sounds as she stood on her porch and shook her fist, threatening the sky.

Suddenly a shadow fell over her house—over her—as a thunderhead blocked the falling sun. And something majestic happened: Henretta grabbed her shoulder as if in pain, then danced crazily forward two steps and vaulted off the porch toward the horizon—a leap of an amazing height for an old woman. Just at that moment, a finger of lightning flashed in the near hills, so that Henretta's white hair and pale body were kissed by glorious, unnatural light just as she reached the top of her arc.

Then Henretta crumpled like a duck shot in flight and dropped into a tiny pile among the bed of pink pansies at the foot of her porch.

Out past the shimmering lights of the city, out beyond the gloaming pine forests on the hills, the thunderhead drifted over the mountains, out to meet the darkness, like a great purple skyfish swimming off into the night.

The Last Vanish

MATTHEW COSTELLO

One of the stock pieces in an illusionist's trade is making things disappear. I've done a few little tricks along those lines myself. In illusionists' parlance, that's known as a Vanish.

While I suppose I've pulled off some pretty big Vanishes, Matthew Costello has a very big appearance to his credit; he is the writer of The 7th Guest, *what is to date the largest selling CD-ROM title in the history of that burgeoning industry.*

I knew before he told me that Matt also dabbles in magic, else how could he have known that, in the silence between the Vanish and the Applause, the echo of a single question hangs in the air: "Where did it go?"

That question lies at the heart of Matthew Costello's story.

—DC

The Last Vanish

IT WAS A WARNING. I KNOW THAT NOW.

And the warning came well before I hit it big, before the world of magic finally started paying off.

I was doing a birthday show for a bunch of rug rats. Kids, four, five . . . who could tell how old they were? All I knew was that they were real little brats who didn't need *any* sleight of hand to be fooled.

I made a quarter vanish.

And one littler boy, sitting so close to me that I was sure he caught me palming the coin, looked up, his lips tight, his eyes wide, and said—

"Where did it go?"

I smiled.

"What do you mean?"

"The nickel—" he said. I guess all coins were the same to him. "Where is it?"

I smiled, getting ready to change a red kerchief into a rainbow of colors.

"It's gone," I said. "I made it *vanish.*"

The boy's face was implacable, worried.

"But where is it . . . where is it now?"

The kid was having an anxiety attack over the missing quarter.

"Nowhere, kiddo . . . why it's—"

And I reached out and snatched the quarter from behind his ear.

"—here. Now, for my next trick—"

And I remembered that I proceeded to the scarf trick. But there was no change on the little boy's face. He still wasn't happy, he still was concerned.

Where did it go?

Funny . . . it was the first time anyone ever asked me that question.

Where did it go?

I didn't know then—but there was an answer to that question.

Take a big jump ahead in time.

After I hit it big, after I got a "career."

I was in New York and I decided to visit the Athena Restaurant, a magician's hangout in the Big Apple, a home away from home for illusionists.

It wasn't something I did much any more. I was way too big a star to waste time sitting in the greasy spoon.

But I had some time to kill. So I thought I'd touch base with the old magicians who clogged the Athena's back tables, slurping chicken soup and swapping war stories from the resorts.

The Athena used to be across from Tannen's, the magician's mecca. Tannen's Magic Shop had since moved—but it didn't matter. The old pros still came to the Athena.

Maybe it was nostalgia that made me go, or maybe it was show-boating. Maybe I wanted to say to these old borscht belt illusionists, Hey, old-timers, look how far I've come. Catch me on Letterman? I'm doing the MGM Grand next week. And, wouldn't you just kill to know how I do the Chair Illusion?

I walked past the counter area, and the smell of a hundred breakfasts rushed by, hitting me with a warm storm-force wind of greasy food, fried potatoes, bacon and eggs. No Heart Healthy cuisine here.

I looked in the back.

There were magicians there, of course, never the same faces. Couldn't be sure who might be up in the Catskills making the trek from one Grade B resort to another.

I walked straight to the back tables.

For a moment no one looked up. No. That would be too obvious, too much recognition for my newfound fame.

Then Harry Feld, nearly bald, wearing a too-black rug, glanced up at me, his lips testing his scalding tea.

"Ho, ho. Ho—look who rejoins us. The great Tommy Fina. Mr. Vegas, *Mr.* Atlantic City!"

Then the others looked up, most of them probably "between gigs." I saw a young kid, sitting at Feld's table, hoping for a magical crumb from the "master." Feld, dubbed "Mr. Wonder" back when Atlantic City's Steel Pier was open for business, nodded to me.

"Been reading about you, kid." Another nod. "You've been doing the really big houses, eh?"

I smiled. I took a breath. "Things . . . have been going well."

Then I felt Gary Hayes studying me. He was a respectable mentalist with a few neat illusions. But he was strictly small-time. "That's a helluva trick, Tom," Gary pronounced. "That goddamn Chair Vanish of yours is terrific."

I pulled up a chair, and searched for one of the hairy-armed waitresses who prowled the sea of tables that constituted the dining room of the Athena.

"Helluva trick . . ." he repeated.

My scan for a waitress was bringing no fruit. Like a cop, there's never one around when you need one.

"Yeah," Mr. Wonder bellowed in his rich baritone. "So, tell us, kid—how you do it?"

They were referring to my Chair Illusion. It was my speciality, my ticket to the big rooms. Someone sits down in a chair, and I cover them with a black satin sheet, and then—poof! The person disappears before the audience's eyes.

Not that making people vanish was new. But this trick, *my* trick, was done in the open. No black curtains nearby, no mirrored walls. Just a chair, a sheet, some jokey patter—

And then the person was gone.

"Damn good illusion," Gary said.

I felt his bitterness. It was "damn good," as in—why the hell can't *I* do a trick that good, and where do *I* get the money together for what has to be some very tricky and pricey hardware.

"Catch me on Letterman?" I said.

Mr. Wonder shook his head. "Too late for me, kid. I don't even stay up for my own shows anymore." He collapsed, coughing with hysterical laughter at his own joke.

Gary kept looking at me. He measured his words—then spoke.

"You know something, Tommy . . . I don't see it. I don't see how you do that Chair Illusion."

A waitress finally appeared at my elbow. From central casting, on cue she popped her gum in my ear, a Chelsea version of "what will it be, sir?"

I ignored the question and turned to the woman.

"Cup of coffee and a Danish."

Another pop, and she laboriously scribbled down my order as if it was a seven-course dinner.

When I looked back, the other magicians were listening to another of Feld's tales of magic's past. But Gary was still looking at me. He wasn't happy about my success. That much was obvious. Professional jealousy, I assumed.

I smiled at him. "So, get any good gigs lately?"

He shook his head.

"No, Tommy. Nothing until December."

Holiday in the Catskills for old Gary. A bad Crosby and Hope movie. The Road to Nowhere. While I'd be doing a week at the MGM Grand in Vegas.

"Things will pick up," I pronounced. "They always do."

But they didn't always pick up. Things didn't always get better.

I looked over at Mr. Wonder. He fanned some cards. Another old-timer shook his head at the old trick, but the kid beside Mr. Wonder, the dutiful acolyte at the feet of a master, watched the close-up magic with attentive eyes.

In that moment, Gary slid his chair closer to mine.

"Tommy, I wanna know . . . how do you do it?"

I shook my head. "Hey, man—what are you doing, I can't tell—"

He grabbed my arm. "Where did you learn it? Who taught it to you? You can tell me. God, I showed you a dozen tricks—"

It was a mistake coming here. This was my past. I should have known that.

"Look, I can't. All right?" I shrugged off his claw-like hand.

"I could do that trick—" he said, a spray of spittle punctuating his point. "I could do it . . . even better."

I smiled. "Maybe you could . . . maybe you could."

My coffee and Danish arrived, and the moment passed. At the time I thought it was nothing, just a nasty episode effectively signalling that one phase of my life was over. That's all.

But I was quite wrong there.

Then, I was away from New York for a couple of months straight, touring in Vegas, Atlantic City, Reno, followed by a three-week gig in Los Angeles. Could life have been better?

I didn't think so.

Then one night in Vegas I was talking to the pudgy close-up magician who worked the small room of the new tropical-themed hotel, The Caribe. And he told me some incredible news.

Gary Hayes was *hot*. The Amazing Gary Hayes was wowing audiences again.

The stubby magician showed me a clipping from *The Black Hat,* a small newsletter for professional magicians. I read the article. Gary was performing a new Vanish that was killing audiences. Knocking them absolutely dead.

Even the description of the bit seemed powerful.

In full view of an audience, Gary covered a volunteer from the audience with a satin sheet. The person then *floated* over the heads of the audience before exploding into a brief fireball—and vanishing.

The illusion sounded fantastic.

Certainly more exciting than simply making someone disappear from a chair.

There was a photo, too—Gary standing next to a sheet suspended in the air. His eyes looked bright and alert. He looked debonair. God, even a bit . . . *amazing.*

I would have liked to see the trick some time. Check out the unlikely competition.

I thanked the close-up magician, who went back to card tricks and snatching coins from the ears of jaded slot players.

It was months later when I was back in New York and responded to the siren call of the Athena.

Walking over there, I acted causal.

But I really hoped to see the newly successful Gary Hayes.

Suddenly, I was the one desperately curious about his amazing illusion and his sudden success. Perhaps—this time—we might exchange secrets. Or so I would let him think.

I walked into the Greek greasy spoon, and the whole tired crowd was there, with some new young acolytes.

But no Gary. I asked Mr. Wonder about him.

"Ah—we don't see much of *him* any more. That's for sure. Not since he became 'Mr. Big Shot.'"

"He's in New York?"

"Sure. He did that TV show last night, and he starts a week-long gig in the city tonight. Sure, Mr. Big Shot's in town, but no way he's coming to see us."

I tried hard to hide my disappointment.

Then the door opened, a rolling ball of frigid January air barreled into the restaurant.

I turned to look and, damn, there he was, wearing a sleek camel hair overcoat, pulling leather gloves off his hands. The gray was gone from Gary's temples, and his face was ruddy and tan. He looked positively reborn.

He smiled—a bit nervously I thought. And, seeing me, he walked over to the table.

Before I could say anything, he touched my shoulder.

"I hoped you'd be here, Tommy. I knew you were back in New York." He took a breath. "I wanted to talk."

"Me, too," I said. "I've been following your success. Way to go, guy."

He threw his expensive gloves onto the greasy tabletop. "Sure."

Mr. Wonder stood up and shook Gary's hand. I watched everyone treat the reborn magician with newfound respect. There was a special awe they reserved for a magical phoenix rising from its ashes.

As for me—I was just curious what he wanted to talk about.

Maybe I even suspected what he wanted to talk about.

Still, his words soon chilled me far more than the near zero temperature that clung to Manhattan.

I walked Gary back to his hotel.

No longer did he hang his hat in the seedy Hamilton House, a flophouse that was a midway point between somewhere and oblivion. No, now he was ensconced in the Warwick, a nice, old-world hotel.

We walked together . . . and he spoke as if he was pleading for his life.

"I thought it was all over, Tommy. No career, no life. Nothing." He turned to me. "I couldn't compete, not with the big acts, not with the kind of stuff you do. How could I play the big rooms with my little act?"

He stopped on a corner. The light changed from red to green—but Gary didn't walk.

"Then I met someone—"

"Come on, man," I said to him. "Let's keep walking. It's too damn cold to—"

He grabbed my arm, and looked right at me. "I met someone, after one of my little gigs . . ." he licked his lips. Now I could see that the old magician's eyes were bloodshot, haunted. "He—he said he could get me a trick like—" he waved a hand through the air—"no other trick. A fantastic illusion. One of a kind."

He looked at me as if I might think he was crazy, that I wouldn't believe his story.

I tried to let him know that it was okay. *I understand . . . go on.*

The light was about to change again, so I pulled Gary across the street. He didn't need any prompting from me to make him continue his story.

He nodded to himself. "And it was, you know—the best Vanish, Tommy. God, it was incredible, breathtaking. The audience couldn't believe it . . . *I* couldn't believe it. The effect was wondrous."

We were on Forty-seventh, only blocks from the hotel. I hadn't said more than ten words to the man, and still he rambled on, constantly checking that I was with him, following his tale.

Which, of course, I did.

"I mean, to see someone float above the audience's head and then—" he snapped his fingers—"vanish! It was incredible . . . absolutely incredible."

Then he stopped talking on the crowded street. Seems like New York streets are never empty no matter how frigid they get.

"So . . ." I said slowly. "What's the problem?"

He looked at me, and now I could see his eyes for what they were. I saw the terror. I recognized that look.

"It's not an illusion, Tommy."

A woman walked by us and stared at us, eavesdropping. I was keenly aware of the person listening to us.

I grinned. "What the hell are you talking about?"

His face was rigid, set, looking right at me. "It's not a damn illusion. The people, the"—he forced a weird grin—"*volunteers*—really vanish."

I looked away. Going to the Athena had been a mistake. Some things have to be put behind you, and, yessiree, Gary was obviously one of them.

"Come on, man, give it a break."

He came close, and through his cologne I smelled something else. Like flop sweat . . . only a hundred times worse. I felt cornered by Gary. But I was used to that feeling.

"No—*you* don't get it. I didn't understand how the illusion worked, Tommy. And that's because it isn't a damn illusion."

"So you really make people vanish?"

He shook his head. "No. Not vanish. They go someplace else, this other place and—"

"Where? Brooklyn?"

Where do things go . . . when they vanish?

Same question a kid asks at a magic show.

Gary grabbed me by the shoulders. "Listen to me, will you? Will you listen to me, damn it? I need your help, Tommy. I thought you of all people would understand. Something *happens* to those people . . . they float in the air, and then they're *gone*."

People on the street passed us, looking at us . . .

"And what about their relatives, their next of kin?"

"But that's part of it. I only pick people who are alone, a traveling salesman, someone who stopped into the show alone for a few drinks. Somehow I can tell." He took a breath. "And I make them go away."

"And you don't know where they go?"

He squinted, looking at me. "No. I've—I've seen the place where they go. I've had dreams . . . nightmares. There's this world, a place . . . a dimension. And they go there, the people I make vanish."

The icy wind whipped around us on that street. Was it possible to get any colder?

I didn't think so.

"They wait there. God, the people I make disappear stand there with these strange plants, the sick colors in the sky, while something comes for them. Arms reach out from the sick-looking foliage, and, God, Tommy, they begin screaming. They know it isn't a trick any more, that it's all real. In my nightmares I hear them scream."

How long had we been standing there? A few minutes? An hour? It was impossible for me to tell.

I raised my hands to him, a frightened old man. No, he was beyond frightened. Terrified. I patted his shoulder.

I said to him:

"So why are you telling me this? How come you're telling me this?"

He licked his lips again.

"I—I was told . . . I have to do the trick each show." He made a sick grin. "Gotta keep that place stocked, you know. And I can't—don't want to do it any more. I can't stand it."

I nodded. Anyone picking up a piece of our conversation would think that we were both crazy. I was aware of that. We could be *heard*. No telling who was listening.

"So then I got this idea, a plan to get away."

"An escape plan?"

He grabbed my arm and squeezed it hard.

"Don't make fun of me! But listen . . . here's the idea. Tonight—when it's time for me to perform my Vanish—I want to call *you* up on stage. You can be a guest, you do your Chair Illusion . . . using me. Use your machinery, and make me *disappear*. Trick them so I can get away."

It was a crazy idea. But no more crazy than anything else Gary had told me. I thought that he might fall to his knees begging if I said no.

Couldn't be that cruel, I thought.

Not standing here on Fifth Avenue.

"Okay," I said. "I'll do it. *Now* can we go to the Warwick and get a drink?"

He took my hand and shook it. "Sure, Tommy. And thanks . . ."

The Last Vanish

*　*　*

The club was called London 1888, a year which didn't ring any bells of significance for me.

I asked a cute waitress dressed in a bodice-displaying dress suitable for a Victorian-era tart about the name.

She grinned. "Oh, 1888 was the year that Jack the Ripper made his last kill. Never caught him, y'know."

"Cheers," I said taking my martini from her. "Here's to old Jack." I took a healthy sip.

The house was full. Gary was enjoying a career revival that would bring most older magicians to tears . . . and yet he was backstage, terrified to perform his act. It was sad, pathetic.

The props for my guest gig were already backstage. So I settled into a chair to enjoy the first forty-five minutes or so of Gary's act.

Which had me yawning in matter of minutes. It was old stuff, nothing that we all hadn't seen and done for decades. There were kerchiefs that changed color, cards that "magically" rose out of the deck, and a newspaper that, when cut in half, remained in one piece.

Pretty mundane stuff.

I sensed that the audience was waiting for the big trick, the illusion that brought them to the club in the first place. They didn't yet know that they were about to be disappointed.

As the moment got closer, Gary grew shakier and shakier. At one point, working with some vanishing balls and silver tumblers, his hands shook so bad that one metal tumbler went flying to the floor. Some people giggled.

Then he looked out at the audience, searching for me.

"I—I have a special surprise. Tonight, as a special treat, my good friend and great young magician Tommy Fina will perform one of the great illusions of our time, the Chair Vanish. Ladies and Gentleman, I give you—"

A spotlight swung around to catch me standing up, waving to the audience, acknowledging their applause.

"—Tommy Fina!"

The applause followed me up to the stage.

I was not exactly unknown. And after Gary's lackluster performance, they could only look upon me with great relief.

I took a bow on the stage.

"And not only will the Chair Illusion be performed," Gary said, smiling nervously, "—right before your eyes—but guess who will be disappearing?"

The audience guessed, and there was a smattering of snide applause.

I took a step forward, taking charge.

First, I did the polite thing.

"Ladies and Gentlemen, the Amazing Gary Hayes!"

Drawing the old-timer some unenthusiastic applause.

Gary's young assistant wheeled out my chair.

"Now Gary, I know you've seen me do this trick before. But you've never experienced it. Is that correct?"

He nodded. As soon as the chair was in place, he wasted no time scuttling his butt into it. I saw him checking for the hidden apparatus which would mask his departure, his getaway. It was going to be like that scene in *The Sound of Music* where the Von Trapp children vanish one-by-one from the Nazi authorities.

I looked out into the glaring lights, at the hidden audience. Was Gary's mysterious benefactor out there, the one who gave him the illusion, the person who watched him all the time?

"I'm ready," Gary said.

I turned back to him. Gary held onto the edge of the chair as though it was an ejection seat.

"Very good," I began, continuing my normal patter, unwilling to rush and cheat the audience of the complete effect. "You understand, Gary, that I will cover you . . ." the assistant was at my side with the black covering, "with this dark satin cloth. I will turn the chair around once, twice—and on the third turn you will—" I looked out to the audience, grinning—"be gone."

He nodded.

"Very well!" I took the cloth from the assistant, and snapped it out to the audience, sending a million tiny dust motes flying in the bright lights.

I then let it fall dramatically onto Gary, until he was a black outline on a black stage, the dark material sucking in the light. As every magician knew, black isn't really a pigment. Black absorbs all colors of light. What we see is that nothingness, so very helpful for illusions.

"Are you okay?" I asked.

The black shape nodded, an eerie-looking thing.

"Great." I walked behind the chair. Was someone's eyes on me, I wondered, watching me so carefully? Who knew.

I gave the chair one spin. Gary returned to his normal position, facing the audience.

"One," I said. Then I gave him another spin. The black material fluttered as the chair spun.

"Two." I paused a second, and leaned close to the chair . . . all part of the routine. "Are you still okay, Gary?"

358

Again, he nodded.

I looked out to the audience, grinning. "Good, because now it's time to say—*goodbye* . . ."

I gave the chair one final spin, twisting my body away from it like a toreador.

The chair came to rest.

And the black shape was still there.

I looked out to the audience, What was wrong? my face said. Did I screw it up? I slowly reached out to grab the material. My fingers closed on it.

"Gary—" I said, with concern dripping from my voice. The black shape didn't move. "Are you—"

I whipped the cloth off, revealing a completely empty chair.

Thunderous applause. I bowed. I bowed again, and true to the magician's dictum, after one final bow, I left the stage with the audience clamoring for more.

I hurried to my hotel. I grabbed a pair of tiny scotches from the minibar.

I postponed going to bed as long as possible. I ran through Letterman, then the new Tom Snyder late-night show, before reading the new Koontz novel well past 3:00 A.M.

I could still feel the audience, their eyes glued to the stage, eager to catch any misstep, wanting to uncover the magician's "trick." Then there was always that mystification that overtook the disappointment in not seeing the secret.

Not much different than my first shows and the little kid who asked about the disappearing quarter "where'd it go?"

Where do the disappearing things go?

Maybe not the best question to ask.

I postponed sleep . . . until I couldn't postpone it any more.

The book tumbled from my hands and the unread pages flopped to the right. I was too tired to get up and shut off the light. It felt soothing to simply fall asleep.

Until the dream started.

Until I *saw* the world, the greenish-purple undergrowth, the twisted plants all curled in on themselves as if they were all one giant living thing.

A world I had seen on other nights.

And I saw Gary—

Still wearing his performance tux. A good old illusionist of the old school still wearing the formal magician's uniform. And in my dream I thought, any rabbits in that suit, Gary? Anything to eat in case you get—

He was shaking.

From fear, from the temperature? Hard to tell.

But as I watched him . . . imagined him . . . I saw that he *knew* where he was. Just as he knew what that sound was when the vines and leafy purple things parted, when he finally heard the sounds of things moving towards him.

He turned around.

Not a good idea, I thought. Having witnessed many scenes like this before. Not too damn good an idea, Gary old man.

Because now he saw them coming for him, the slithery things with long, tubelike arms. The little mouths at the end, the teeth-like hooks, snapping at the alien air.

I had to watch.

In case I ever got any ideas.

In case I got too concerned like Gary, upset with all the people . . . *vanishing* during my trick.

They took their time with him, the arms flying onto different parts of his body. He yelled, beating at the arms. To no avail, of course.

Any rabbits in that suit, Gary?

More arms appeared, more screams from Gary that slowly turned into whimpering. The sound of cutting, feeding . . .

I had to watch.

In case I got any ideas.

And when the nightmare was over, when the vision had ended . . . it faded, as if it were only a bad dream.

I slept peacefully, until well past noon.

I didn't have a show that night. A night off.

And that—was a good thing.

Indigo Moon

JANET BERLINER

*With special thanks to Stancil
"Winnie-the-Pooh" Johnson, M.D.*

*On stage, transformation illusions trade a man for a woman;
swap faces and bodies; even change humans into beasts. In my
own version, I am suspended ten feet in the air, while below me
a beautiful woman stands on a platform at mid-stage. She raises
a cloth above her head, and instantly we trade places.*

*In Janet's story, a tribute to this, her favorite type of illusion,
we meet two souls who have experience in this process. They
shared a sin long ago; now they chase each other through the ages,
swapping whole bodies once in a blue moon, seeking vengeance,
until finally they perform the ultimate transformation.*

*In the end, this story says that anything the obsessed mind
can conceive, it can achieve. It also tells us again that when two
elements meet, the result is often greater than the two parts
taken separately.*

—DC

Indigo Moon

I SMILED. The tall, bearded man they called the Jackal returned the smile and adjusted the screws on his elaborate oak carving board. The metal pierced the meat and the blood flowed warm and red.

"I'm curious, Mr. Ramirez—"

"Carlos, please."

The Jackal lifted a ten-inch Solingen knife from its case and drew it carefully, knowingly, over its companion sharpening stone. I watched his hands. Long and tapered, they moved with a sureness born of much practice. I imagined them playing with my flesh and shivered. It had been a long time since I'd found myself so attracted to any man. I looked at the red velvet chaise in the corner of the Victoria Club's private dining room, visualized the seduction scene in *Funny Girl,* and reminded myself that Carlos Ramirez was my opponent.

No matter how great the temptation, I could not allow myself to succumb to my old weakness and go to bed with him . . . not unless I was willing to relinquish control. He had corrupted me once; I could not give him the chance to take on my strength again, not when I was so close to the last stage of my journey. I had come too far to let him blunt my resolve. For the moment, I held the advantage over the world's top assassin. I would keep it that way, no matter what argument my primal hormones gave me. If I indulged myself, I could only lose.

Still, I did need to seduce him into playing my game. What better way . . .

With enormous effort of will, I shook myself free of the bondage of old memories: a small, bare room and a narrow cot; his monk's habit crumpled on the floor, mine pulled to my thighs, our bodies coupling

365

to the music of a Gregorian chant floating in through the barred window from the monastery's quadrangle.

"Do you visit London often?" I asked. "They seem to know you well here, at the Victoria." My glance strayed to the knife in his hand. "Well enough to—"

"To allow me to carve the meat myself," he said, smiling as he finished my sentence. "I dine—and play—here several times a year. And, yes, I have entertained other lovely women in this room. You *are* very lovely, Miss Harris, not to speak of being an outrageous poker player . . . an irresistible combination."

"You call *me* an outrageous player! Just a few hours ago, you made the most flamboyant play I've ever seen. You took a small fortune off me with that crazy play of yours."

"I did no less than you would have done," he said.

"I don't know." I shook my head slightly. "I'm not sure I would have had the audacity to pay four hundred pounds—one hundred pounds a card—to draw four to a joker."

"The way you bet, I knew you had at worst a six-four," he said. "That meant I needed a wheel to beat you. There was a lot of money in that pot—"

"Forty thousand pounds. Before the draw."

"I wanted to win," he said.

"Isn't that what we all want?" I asked, letting him assume the obvious, that I needed the money, and the enhancement to my player's reputation brought by that kind of a win at London's Victoria Club, home of the highest stakes non-tournament lo-ball poker game in the world. *In good time, Carlos Ramirez,* I thought, you will learn the true reason I made sure I was in that game. Losing to you was small payment. I was gambling for much higher stakes.

"Do you need the money that much, or is it winning itself that . . . turns you on?"

Clearly aware of how attractive I found him, Carlos Ramirez— womanizer, gambler, assassin extraordinaire—smiled at me again. I was pleased. If he thought me vulnerable to his charm, he would desire me, and I could absorb him all the sooner. If only he didn't look so good in a tuxedo—

Like me, Carlos had a preference for black and white; unlike me, he did not remember why. We were two studies in chiaroscuro—he and I—linked by the infant's body we had buried together in the monastery walls. Our child.

Would revenge, I wondered, be as sweet as its anticipation?

Would it be sweetest if I told him—

I resisted the temptation. Better this way, I thought. Let him think me simply a professional card player with a penchant for men with his elusive combination of skill and *panache*. There was no need for him to be aware of how carefully I had planned to play at the tables with him, or to learn, yet, that I knew everything about him—what he wanted, who he was, who he had been. If there was more, I would know that, too, once this night was over. Already, just being in his physical presence had taught me something. I could hear his voices—the selves he had accumulated—arguing with him, saying they were tired of Carlos' life and ready to enter a new vessel. He would not hear of it. Jackal he was, and Jackal he would remain.

That was why he had accepted the U.N.'s offer of amnesty and protection in exchange for information and his promise to retire from the world of international terrorism, I thought, pleased with my discovery. This was his compromise, his way to avoid being forced to abandon Carlos, whose perfect performance of business and pleasure so suited his needs.

"You handle that knife with great expertise," I dared, as he continued with the carving. I would have liked to add, *as well as the Ripper might have done,* but I held my tongue.

"Are you interested in knives, Miss Harris?"

"I'm interested in people who wield them . . . well," I said.

"Like Jack the Ripper?"

I must have looked as startled as I felt because he laughed out loud at the expression on my face.

"I regard Jack as a perfectionist responding to imperfection by ridding the world of it," I said quickly.

"You didn't think he saw himself as evil." His eyes said *Brava* and I knew my analysis had not been far off the mark.

"I believe he saw himself as a God-fearing man, doing God's work," I said, toying with Carlos. "You told me earlier that you are a mercenary. Do you think of yourself as evil?"

"Mercenaries are beyond good and evil."

He glanced at himself in the beveled mirror behind me, then lowered the knife and stared into my eyes. I looked down and fiddled with my ring, allowing him time to examine me. I knew I was exciting to look at. My soft brown hair lay loosely about my shoulders, and the intimate lighting softened the years.

"You bear a striking resemblance to Garbo," he said. "How old are you, Marta?"

"Ageless." I gestured at my cassette recorder with a manicured hand. "Mind if I turn this on?"

He nodded his agreement. I saw that he had noticed my Lucrezia Borgia ring. Poor Lucy . . . so pretty, and so badly maligned.

"You appear to be interested in killers, Miss Harris," he said.

Holding the carving knife like a violinist's bow, he drew it gently across the rump. The blade, properly sharp, slipped effortlessly through the meat. Red beads clung to the surface of the knife. The viscosity of the blood seemed to fascinate him. I, too, focussed on the blade and found it a simple matter to enter his mind's eye. . . .

Lamplight flickered on a darkened London street. A man in formal evening attire wiped blood off his cheek with a whore's petticoat, holding his breath to avoid the smell of her cheap perfume. Tossing the garment aside, he walked in the direction of London Bridge.

Like a peculiar mutation of Peeping Tom or Thomasina, I routed my consciousness through the Jackal . . . into the Ripper. I knew I had succeeded when I felt him pulling his cape closer to protect himself against the fog that guarded the night-banks of the Thames; his pleasure at having rid the world of yet another evil woman almost, but not quite, overcame my own revulsion.

Having completed his night's work, Jack resolved to take a short constitutional to work up an appetite before hailing a carriage to Bloomsbury and Colonel Moran's dinner party. I knew I had succeeded in fully submerging my own predispositions when, chancing upon a toy shop, I found myself admiring my bow tie in its window. A row of tin soldiers on the window shelf saluted me and I saluted them back before compulsively adjusting the tie.

When I lowered my hand, the lamplight revealed a blood spot on the heel of my left glove. I was removing the offensive thing when a bobby's whistle disturbed the silence, followed closely by the sound of heavy footfalls on the pavement.

They had found the mutilated woman.

Heart beating a modicum fast, I stepped into the shop's shallow entryway and pressed my body against the door. Thanks to an insufficient lock, I was flung unceremoniously inside. I kicked the door shut and listened. I could hear bobbies everywhere, combing the streets, circling, calling out to one another and closing in on me. I smelled fear rising from my pores, and began to shiver, to shake violently, to convulse.

Hastily, I parted myself from Jack and returned to my post as observer. I watched him search the dark shop until he came upon an expensive French bisque-head character doll on a shelf near the window. Drawn by the boy-doll's black-and-white costume motif, he inhaled, expanded his chest, and forced his soul's atoms to coalesce.

Moments later, the bobbies burst into the shop and found a lifeless body in formal clothing. They had no reason to examine the grinning doll with its slightly open mouth and row of white porcelain teeth. . . .

"Another slice?" Carlos asked.

I had become so engrossed in his past that I had no recollection of having eaten a first helping. "Thank you. Yes," I said. I leaned toward him, advertising breasts barely contained by a low-cut Chanel blouse. Though I dared not consummate my lust, making him want me was my tool of empowerment. Judging by the flush on his cheeks, I was succeeding.

My pleasure at this minor success was short-lived. As I reentered his thoughts, I saw that he was looking at me, but seeing the brown paperweight eyes of the Jumeau doll on the shelf next to him. She was flaunting her Parisian arrogance and inviting him to impale her French belly on a tin soldier's spear.

By now, Jack had come to understand that his choice of the doll as a resting place had been no idle coincidence. The fates, though approving of his fight for the triumph of good over evil, had placed two constraints upon him, as they had upon me: he could only transmigrate on the night of a blue moon, and only into a black-and-white vehicle.

"'G'morning Nanny Brockwell." The shopkeeper emerged from the back to greet an elderly woman. "Aren't *you* looking spruce today! I still say it's a shame to see a handsome woman like you wasting her life on someone else's child. Looking for something unusual in a toy for yer young charge, I suppose. You need a son of yer own, I say."

"Flattery will get you absolutely nowhere, Mr. Johnson," the woman said. But she flushed anyway, and toyed with the lace collar of her black-and-white nanny's uniform. "What's that, there?" she asked, pointing at the doll that housed Jack. It stood on a high shelf, away from the children's peppermint breath and their fingers, ready to poke and pull at anything within reach.

"Made in France," the shopkeeper said. "Those teeth give me the willies. 'Ere, take it. No one else seems to want it. If your Master writes a book about it, tell 'im where you got it. "Wish't the Pooh Bear had come from me. I'd be a bloody rich man by now."

There followed a trip on the train and a brief smell of the country, then the doll was cooped up in a nursery with the jam-sticky fingers of one little boy. He was closeted with a buffoon bear, the whinings of a piglet, a self-deprecating donkey, and a loathsome kangaroo and its ugly offspring—forced to listen to Nanny's nightly retelling of the boy's father's wholesome tales.

On the day of the next blue moon, Jack did the only thing he could.

He wasted no time catapulting himself into the stout physical presence of Nanny Brockwell. As luck would have it, she chose that day to take Christopher Robin to Ashdown Forest, along with Kanga, one of the boy's favorite animals. When she pulled out a picnic basket and began, at once, to tell one of her stories, this taste of what he would have to endure was enough—too much—for Jack; with no choice but to trust in the fates to provide his soul with appropriately chiaroscuro shelter, he again forced his soul's atoms to coalesce. His spirit rose trembling into the air. Soaring with him, I could see the Nanny and her charge below. . . .

"You keep slipping away from me," Carlos said. He laid the knife upon the carving board.

I fiddled with my ring and stared at the meat on my plate. "I'm sorry," I said. "Perhaps I need more champagne."

He reached for the bottle, but I got to it first. Quickly, I refilled my glass, then his.

"I was thinking about power," I said, watching him drink. He was a potentate of sorts, at least in the underworld of assassins. He would miss that, isolated on Robben Island.

"What makes you think I'm going to Robben Island?"

I felt my heart pounding in my chest. Either I was slipping, or he could read my thoughts as well as I could read his.

"I distinctly heard you say Robben Island, Marta."

"An educated guess," I said flippantly. "They say the South African climate is superior." I would have to be more careful.

"You know that I am the Jackal, don't you, Marta? I'd bet you've known all along." He looked amused, but his eyes said *bitch*. "You really are attracted to killers, aren't you." His words were a statement rather than a question. "Very well, then, let me ask you something. Is it impossible to believe that the Jackal's lust for power could be sated?" he asked.

"People don't change," I said flatly, annoyed at myself for complicating matters with the mention of South Africa. Of course that was where he'd intended to go . . . where I would go, once I was wearing his shoes. "If Jack the Ripper were alive now, he'd still be searching for a woman of virtue."

Suddenly I did not wish to think about the element of Carlos that was Jack, for it had occurred to me that the latter's search for that virtuous woman could continue after he was mine. Better to focus on Carlos, I thought.

"You're right," I said, collecting my thoughts as quickly as possible. This is a poker game, I told myself. Just because the stakes are life and death doesn't mean you can't bluff. "I do know who you are."

"When did you find out?"

"I suspected when you called yourself a mercenary. You just confirmed it."

"Does that scare you? Excite you?"

"It fascinates me," I answered, sensing the opening I needed. "Many strange things do. This, for example."

Sliding my fingers into the briefcase I'd placed next to my chair, I pulled out a clipping, a copy of a Naval Operations Directive:

15 MAY. USS NAUTILUS TO NAVOPS, WASH., D.C. PER NAVOP
DIRECTIVE 19652-H4. COLLECTED, PER DIRECTIONS,
NINETEEN 9190 EMPEROR PENGUINS FOR SPECIAL
PROJECT AT BETHESDA NAVAL HOSPITAL. SUBJECTS
THROWING RANDOM OBJECTS AT CREW. APPEARS
TO BE PRELUDE TO ATTACK. ADVISE.

I handed him the clipping. He took it from me, making sure our fingers touched slightly longer than was necessary.

I withdrew quickly and concentrated on the piece of incredibly good fortune that had drawn my terrified host from Ashdown Forest into a plane carrying a man uniformed in black and white. In human form again, he had flown to the Continent. There, every three years or so, he used the time of the blue moon to find new forms and new missions, culminating in the transmigration to which I was obliquely referring through my mention of *Nautilus*.

A transformation into a Patagonian diplomat—debonair and well-liked, but not wise—had taken Carlos on a lengthy expedition to the Antarctic. It was Carlos' misfortune that the diplomat strayed away from his party to examine the phenomenon of a blue moon and died of the cold. Once again forced to leave his host body, Carlos entered the only suitable mobile creature around—a large emperor penguin.

He had hated being confined in the doll; he had refused to be confined in Nanny Brockwell. *This,* he loathed. The creature and the rest of its stinking companions apparently devoted themselves single-mindedly and untiringly to nudging, jostling, and shoving one another. Only the occasional frozen icicle, carefully placed into the guts of a stray female who proved herself unworthy of her mate, relieved his boredom. He saw himself having to move from one penguin host body to another for all eternity and had all but given up when, rising out of the icy waters, came the *Nautilus*.

"You may be interested in the mating habits of emperor penguins,"

Carlos said. "But I'm not." He tossed aside the clipping. "Now, let me tell you what does intrigue me. Your resemblance to Garbo in . . . in . . . ?"

He was edging precariously close to the truth. I was tempted to help him, to blurt out *Mata Hari,* and tell him that I clung to her essence the way he wished to cling to the Jackal's. We were, after all, playing the same transmigratory game—a game of dark and dangerous ritual we had begun together in a Gregorian monastery buried deep in the Black Forest.

Carlos lifted his hand to knead the back of his neck. My instincts pulled me toward him, but I resisted. I held the winning hand, but only if I did not divert from my game plan. I counted the pot: win, and I would command him and all of the others he was and had been; lose, and—

"Headache?" Having made my choice, I found I had to force myself to sound sympathetic.

"Fatigue," he answered. "In response to your question, I don't know anything about that directive. I have read that throwing objects is part of the male emperor penguin mating rite which can only be short-circuited by picking up the objects and striking the penguins with them."

You know all about the *Nautilus,* I thought. Merging with his memory, I paced with him up and down, up and down, great webbed feet flapping along the metal submarine deck . . . envious of the Turkish naval observer, beautiful in his black-and-white attache's uniform . . . plotting to fuse with him and commandeer the submarine—

I detached myself from his memory and rose from my chair. We could continue this on the way to Southhampton tomorrow. His ship—our ship—left at dawn.

"You could stay the night," he said, helping me on with my coat and allowing his fingers to touch my bare shoulders.

"Your fingers." I shivered. "Surprisingly delicate for—"

"For what, Mata? A killer's hands."

His doctored champagne was taking effect and he was slurring his words. That must have been why he'd mispronounced Marta. Or did he somehow know what I was planning? I stilled my momentary panic and turned to look at him. "I'd like to stay, but—" His eyes were hard and I was glad I had not succumbed to my initial desire for him as a bedmate. The window of lust closed.

Through thin, cold lips, he said, "Perhaps we will meet again."

You can bet on it, I thought, as he ushered me to the door. I was tall. My black silk skirt was fashionably slit; I could feel him looking at what I knew to be shapely legs and well-turned ankles. Then he closed the door behind me.

I avoided the lift and walked past the elegant upstairs restaurant and down the steps. Knowing that I was unlikely to see the Victoria Club again, I glanced into the rooms at each level—the Chinese restaurant where I had eaten whenever I wanted a break from an all-night game; the high rollers' room, with its recently added craps tables to pull in American business; the big gaming room for smaller punters. I stopped briefly at the cardroom for one more look at the world's largest stakes Omaha and Lo-Ball games. As always, an amount in excess of thirty thousand pounds lay casually sprawled across the felt on each table.

Pulling my coat closer in a gesture that reminded me of Jack, I walked down one more flight of steps, through the lobby, and into the street. *By now Carlos is picking up the knife,* I thought. *Secreting it under his cummerbund.*

I found it harder to enter his being when I could not see him, but I forced myself in. A wave of nausea hit him, filling my mouth, too, with bile. I swallowed uncomfortably, trying to ignore the dizziness I felt as I took his headache upon myself. He was descending the metal stairs of the fire escape, stepping onto the pavement, seeing double—two cars, two me's.

He moved into the shadow of my auto and leaned against the metal for support. I could see the images he saw in his mind as he imagined himself holding me on the knife's tip and pulling me gently, ever so gently toward him—while the blade invited itself into the soft center of my belly; I could feel his anticipation of pressing his palm across my mouth and whispering lovingly in my ear, bidding me hush.

The visualization was seductive in a way I could never have imagined, and I wondered if, perhaps, I was being a fool. Was this how it would be, later, I wondered? When I fused with Carlos, in all his incarnations, would I still be able to identify my own sensibilities? I sought androgyny, but what would I find? I knew that Carlos and I must merge. Part of me longed to remain separate, an observer; the other part needed to feel what he felt—to *be* him, just this once. I was curious, and not a little anxious, as I forced myself to stay in his consciousness. If nothing disturbed the moment, I could experience his transformation.

But now that I had witnessed Carlos' complex flight through the universe—heard the selves he had accumulated arguing with him, distracting him from the perfect performance of both business and pleasure—I had begun to have doubts. Could I really preserve my essence housed in a male body, with its proclivity for easy violence?

"Carlos?" I balanced myself against him, opened his jacket, and drew out the knife. "You don't really want to use this on me, do you?"

He lacked the strength to pierce through flesh and bones or he would surely have answered my question with the blade, slicing it up into my heart and into my soul. Silently, I thanked Lucrezia for inventing the ring with its poison recess, though despite the rumors she had never used it.

"The champagne," Carlos whispered, staring at the ring.

"If you're worried about dying, rest easy." I tapped the knife absently against chrome and placed my other hand on his cheek. He shivered. "Poor man, you're cold," I said. "We'll soon all be inside where it's warm and cosy."

I glanced up at the moon. *This is it,* I thought. I could feel his dizziness fading. If I did not hurry, he would regain his strength.

Opening the car door, I tossed the knife inside. I snapped open my briefcase and took out a small, pearl-handled revolver. "Pretty little thing, isn't it?" I handed it to him. "Use it on me. We will ply the knife later. Together."

He stared at me blankly. Then understanding dawned. Mata Hari. A firing squad. *My* constraints. He looked up at the sky. There was no blue moon.

"You will not be woman," I said softly.

"You win," he said. Then he leveled the pistol and took aim—

Just before dawn, on the way to Southhampton, the taxi rounded the corner of Petticoat Lane. It was too early even for hawkers and the street was deserted.

"'Ere you are," the driver said. "That there's the alley. No toy shop there. Bombs took it in forty-four."

"Wait here," I said. "I'm coming back."

The driver glanced at me in his rearview mirror. He examined my tuxedo and elegant cape and raised a bushy eyebrow. "The waiting'll cost you, sir," he said.

I was tempted to laugh out loud. I had paid tonight's price with my female form; nothing would ever cost me more dearly. Given a choice, I would certainly have kept the woman's body which had provided me with so much satisfaction.

Picking up the plastic-wrapped package I had placed on the seat next to me, I left the taxi and turned down the alley. Where the toy shop had been stood a designer clothing shop whose well-lit window included a woman's tuxedo.

Pleased by the coincidence, I knelt on the Welcome brushmat, removed the string that held the package together, opened up the package, and surveyed its contents. Marta's liver and spleen, major and minor sentinels, stood guard over a sea of twisted intestines which, in turn, held the stomach in place. Her lungs embraced the heart like a beloved toy. I caressed the heart, licked my fingers, then added the pistol—there would be no further need for it.

Not quite ready to leave, I took out the envelope that held a brief note of farewell I had typed to a friend who worked for the *London Times*. At the top of the page, written in a bold, extravagant, masculine hand, were the words: NEWS RELEASE.

"You all right out there?" the taxi driver called out.

I was afraid he might come to find me or, worse yet, drive off and leave me stranded, so I glanced down at the mat one more time and hurried back to the taxi. When we were en route, I took out the hand-written note and held it up to the light:

THE JACKAL BIDS YOU FAREWELL
Signed *Avatar*

I sat back against the leather seat, lit the cheroot I had found in my pocket, and thought about this metamorphosis—mine and the Jackal's. I knew my fingers must have held the pen, yet I had no memory of having written the words; at best, they provoked in me a mild feeling of *déjà vu*.

Inside our head, Carlos chuckled. When the taxi driver turned around and winked, I realized that I had laughed out loud. We, Carlos and I, had laughed together. There was a knowing in me that came of neither man nor woman, a blending of equals. In a sense, we had both died. Now we were reborn and it no longer mattered who had won the game—Carlos or I. We were androgyne, and more than the sum of our parts.

Author Biographies

Kevin J. Anderson's Jedi Academy trilogy—*Jedi Search, Dark Apprentice*, and *Champions of the Force*—has sold nearly three million copies and are the three top-selling science fiction novels of 1994 (according to Waldenbooks). He is at work on numerous other projects for Lucasfilm, including editing the anthologies, *Tales from the Star Wars Cantina* and *Tales from Jabba's Palace*; a young adult series of six books, Young Jedi Knights, cowritten with his wife Rebecca Moesta, a new hardcover novel, *Darksaber*; a lavish coffee-table art book, *The Illustrated Star Wars Universe*; as well as a twelve-issue comic series for Dark Horse Comics, Dark Lords of the Sith.

In 1994, Anderson's novel *Assemblers of Infinity*—written with Doug Beason—was nominated for the Nebula Award for best science fiction novel. Also that year his solo novel, *Climbing Olympus*, launched a new paperback line from Warner Books and has been published in a fine leatherbound edition from the Easton Press and will be produced unabridged by Books on Tape. Other major novels include *Ill Wind* (also with Beason) and *Blindfold*, both published in 1995.

Janet Berliner (Gluckman) is the coeditor, with Peter, of *Peter S. Beagle's Immortal Unicorn* (HarperPrism, due Fall '95). She also had a hand in Peter S. Beagle's *Unicorn Sonata*, (Turner Publishing, due Fall '96). She recently completed work on *The Michael Crichton Companion*. Among her current projects are *And So Say All Of Us*, an episodic psychological thriller, *Prism*, a dark novel about androgyny; and *Dance of the Python*, a novel in the tradition of H. Rider Haggard; about treachery and witchcraft in modern tribal South Africa.

In 1961, Janet left her native South Africa in protest against apartheid. After living and teaching in New York, she moved to San Francisco's Bay area, where she started her own business as an editorial consultant, lecturer, and writer. She now lives and works in Las Vegas. Her last novel was *Child of the Light*, coauthored with George Guthridge (St. Martin's Press, April 1992). She is under contract to White Wolf Books for *The Madagascar Manifesto*, which completes the Child trilogy.

Janet's short fiction and non-fiction has appeared in many anthologies, magazines, and newspapers, including the *San Francisco Chronicle*. She is the author of the political thriller *Rite of the Dragon*, and coauthor of *The Execution Exchange*, and *Timestalker* (TV Movie-of-the-Week). She served as personal and developmental editor of *Don Sherwood: The Life and Times of "The World's Greatest Disc Jockey"*—a #1 bestseller on the West Coast—and as coordinating writer on The Whole Child series from Enrich.

In her copious free time, she travels (most often to the Caribbean), dances (preferably the lambada), and plays the occasional game of poker.

Larry Bond is 43 and lives with his wife Jeanne and daughters Katie and Julia in Virginia outside Washington, D.C. He is the designer of the *Harpoon* and *Command at Sea* gaming systems and several supplements for the games.

In 1985 he co-authored *Red Storm Rising* with Tom Clancy, and since then has written the novels *Red Phoenix*, *Vortex*, and *Cauldron*. His next novel, *The Enemy Within*, will be published by Warner Books in early 1996.

Harpoon won the H.G. Wells Award, a trade association honor, in both 1981 and 1987 as the best miniature game of the year. It is the only game to win the award twice. The computer version of the game appeared in 1990 and won the Wargame of the Year Award from *Computer Gaming World*.

Ray Bradbury has published some twenty-seven books—novels, stories, plays, essays, and poems—since his first story appeared when he was twenty years old. He began writing for the movies in 1952—with the script for his own *Beast from 20,000 Fathoms*. The next year he wrote the screenplays for *It Came from Outer Space* and *Moby Dick*. And in 1961 he wrote Orson Welles's narration for *King of Kings*. Films have been made of his "The Picasso Summer," *The Illustrated Man, Fahrenheit 451, The Martian Chronicles*, and *Something Wicked This Way Cometh*. The short animated film *Icarus Montgolfier Wright*, based on his story of the history of flight, was nominated for an Academy Award. Since 1985 he has adapted his stories for *The Ray Bradbury Theater* on USA Cable television.

P. D. Cacek was born and raised in the sunny climes of California (many, many years ago), but she recently had her belly-button surgically removed and replaced with an "I ♥ Colorado" bumper sticker. Writing "ghostly" tales since the age of five (a fact that had both family and teachers worried), P. D. has, if the Internal Revenue Service is correct, actually been making a living as a freelance writer for the past ten years.

Still a "ghost" writer by nature, her work has appeared in a number of small-press magazines as well as *Pulphouse, Deathrealm, The Urbanite, Bizarre Bazaar, Bizarre Sex and Other Crimes of Passion, 100 Wicked Little Witches, Newer York, Deathport, Grails: Visitations of the Night,* and *Return to the Twilight Zone*. She is currently editing an anthology of short fiction.

David Copperfield was born in 1956 in Metuchen, New Jersey. His first television special, *The Magic of ABC*, aired in 1977. From then until now, between his yearly CBS specials, and his 500 live performances per year, he has been seen world-wide by more people than any other illusionist in history, including Houdini.

His celebrated feats and sense of theater have won him numerous Emmys and have led him to be twice named "Entertainer of the Year." Six times he has performed for the President of the United States.

Performing professionally at the ripe age of twelve, David became the youngest person ever admitted into the Society of American Magicians. By the age of sixteen, he was teaching magic at New York University. While still in college, David was cast as the lead in *The Magic Man*, in which he sang, danced, acted, and created all the magic in what became the longest running musical in Chicago's history.

David writes all of his own material for his stage shows and his TV specials. Now, having already rewritten the book on magic, he is turning his hand to the writing of fiction.

Author Biographies

Matthew Costello has written for many publications, including *Sports Illustrated*, *Mystery Scene*, and the *Los Angeles Times*. Costello is a contributing editor at *Games* magazine. He has written books on games for Prentice Hall and John Wiley & Sons. His science fiction and fantasy novels include *The Wizard of Tizare* (1990), a best-seller, and *Time of the Fox*, a time-travel thriller for Penguin/ROC. His mainstream thriller, *Homecoming* (called "A killer of a book!" by Dean Koontz) was a nominee for the Best Novel of 1992 Award by The Horror Writers of America, and his short stories regulary appear in bestselling anthologies.

Costello wrote the gothic-horror script for *The 7th Guest*, the number-one bestselling interactive CD-ROM from Virgin and Trilobyte. In June 1995, the novel of *The 7th Guest* will appear. 1996 will bring *Mirage* (Warner Books), a novel and interactive CD-ROM co-authored with F. Paul Wilson. Costello and Wilson also wrote *Bombmeister*, an interactive film for Interfilm Technologies, scheduled for a 1995 release. The two of them create the "bible" for the USA Network's Sci-Fi Channel, *FTL NewsFeed*, a daily news program from the 22nd Century.

Costello lives in Katonah, New York with his wife and three children.

Raymond E. Feist is the international bestselling author of the Riftwar Saga, *Faerie Tale*, and the Empire trilogy. His books have been translated into more than a dozen other languages and he presently has over fifteen million books in print. His newest book, *Rise of a Merchant Prince*, is the second volume of the Serpentwar Saga, and will be published in the fall of 1995. He lives in Rancho Santa Fe, California, with his wife, novelist Kathlyn S. Starbuck, their daughter Jessica, several horses, cats, and assorted wildlife. Feist's hobbies include collecting wine, movies, and art.

Jack Kirby, "The King of Comics," created such well-known characters as The Fantastic Four, Silver Surfer, Captain America, and the X-Men. His artwork inspired generations of comic-book artists. Kirby was one of the greatest influences in creating the modern superhero.

Lesser known to his fans who knew him only as an artist, Kirby was at work on a novel of racial hatred and mysticism set primarily in Mongolia. The novel—titled *The Horde!*—was never completed in final draft, but in the last years of his life, with the advice and assistance of his friend, one-time literary agent and editor Janet Berliner, several sto-

380

ries were culled from his work. Among them, "The Conversion of Tegujai Batir" is Janet's favorite and the one which shows most deeply what was in the heart of Kirby when he was writing.

Dean Koontz's novels have sold over 150 million copies in thirty-seven languages, and eleven have been number-one bestsellers. Though he has never been abducted by aliens, he was a foundling raised in the jungle by a tribe of gorillas among whom he is still affectionately known as "mooma." He now lives with his wife, Gerda, in southern California.

Eric Lustbader was born and raised in New York City. He graduated from Columbia University in 1969. Before becoming the author of such bestselling novels as *The Ninja*, *Angel Eyes*, *Black Blade*, and others, he had a successful career in the music industry. In his fifteen years of work in that field, he wrote about and worked with such artists as Elton John, who later asked Lustbader to write the liner notes for his 1991 box set *To Be Continued . . .* He was also the first person in the United States to predict the success of such stars as Jimi Hendrix, David Bowie, and Santana.

He has also taught in the All-Day Neighborhood School Division of the N.Y.C. Public School system, developing curriculum enrichment for third- and fourth-grade children. He currently lives in Southampton, New York, with his wife Victoria, who works for the Nature Conservancy.

Lustbader is currently hard at work on his next novel.

Lisa Mason graduated Phi Beta Kappa from the University of Michigan School of Literature, Sciences, and Arts. After graduating from the University of Michigan Law School, she practiced law in Washington D.C. and San Francisco. Now she lives in the San Francisco Bay area with graphic designer and fine artist, Tom Robinson, and three cats, and writes fiction full-time.

Mason is the author of four novels: *Arachne*, *Cyberweb*, *Summer of Love*, and *The Golden Nineties*. *Summer of Love* (Bantam Spectra, 1994) is about a far-future time traveler who must return to San Francisco during the summer of 1967 to save the universe. In *The Golden Nineties* (Bantam Spectra, 1995), a time traveler returns to San Francisco during the wild and extravagant 1890s. *Arachne*, *Cyberweb*, and the forthcoming *Spyder*, (William Morrow-AvoNova) are cyberpunk tales set in a future San Francisco.

Her acclaimed short fiction has appeared in numerous publications, including *Omni*, *Full Spectrum*, and *Year's Best Fantasy and Horror*. Most have received Nebula nominations, many have been translated into other languages, and "Tomorrow's Child," (*Omni*, 1989), was optioned for film to Helpern-Meltzer Productions.

Joyce Carol Oates is one of the most distinguished and prolific of American writers. She is the author of 24 novels and collections of stories, poetry, and plays. She won the National Book Award for *Them*; her 1990 novel *Because It Is Bitter, and Because It Is My Heart* earned an NBA nomination; her novel, *Black Water*, was nominated for a National Book Critics Circle Award and the Pulitzer Prize. In 1990, Oates received the REA Award for Achievement in the Short Story. She lives in Princeton, New Jersey, where she is the Roger S. Berlind Distinguished Professor in the Humanities at Princeton University. Her most recent novel, *What I Lived For*, was published by Dutton in the U.S. and was nominated for a PEN/Faulkner Award.

Dave Smeds lives in Santa Rosa, California, with his wife Connie and children, Lerina and Elliott. He is the author of two books, the fantasy novel *The Sorcery Within* and its sequel *The Schemes of Dragons*. His science fiction and fantasy works have appeared in such anthologies as *In the Field of Fire*, *Full Spectrum* (4), *David Copperfield's Tales of the Impossible*, *Return to Avalon*, *Magicks: Sorceries Old and New*, *Dragons of Light*, *Sword and Sorceress* (4, 5, 8, 9, & 11), *Warriors of Blood and Dream*, *Deals with the Devil*, and *Future Earths: Under African Skies*; and in such magazines as *Asimov's Science Fiction*, *The Magazine of Fantasy & Science Fiction*, *Realms of Fantasy*, *Ghosttide*, *Inside Karate*, and *Pulphouse*.

He has also contributed two titles to Faeron Education's series of booklets for remedial reading classes. His erotic works for such magazines as *Penthouse Forum*, *Hot Talk*, and *Club International* led to a Henry Miller Award in 1992. He was the English-language rewriter of *Justy*, a Japanese "manga" science fiction mini-series released in the U.S. by VIZ Comics.

His work, called "stylistically innovative, symbolically daring examples of craftsmanship at the highest level" by the *New York Times Book Review*, has seen print in Great Britain, Germany, France, the Netherlands, Italy, Finland, and Poland.

Before turning to writing, Dave made his living as a graphic artist and typesetter. He holds a third degree black belt in Goju-ryu karate and teaches classes in that art.

Somtow Papinian Sucharitkul (S. P. Somtow) was born in Bangkok and grew up in Europe. He was educated at Eton College and at Cambridge, where he obtained his B.A. and M.A., receiving honors in English and Music. He has published more than twenty-five adult and children's novels, and much short fiction. He made his conducting debut with the Holland Symphony Orchestra at age nineteen, has since conducted, among others, the Cambridge Symphony Orchestra, and has been a director of the Bangkok Opera Society. He writes and directs movies, among them a gothic-punk adaptation of *A Midsummer Night's Dream* starring Timothy Bottoms.

Recently, Somtow handed to his publishers *Vanitas*, the long-awaited sequel to *Vampire Junction*. His semi-autobiographical *Jasmine Nights*, published in 1994 by the British literary publishing house Hamish Hamilton, will be made into a $14 million motion picture, filmed entirely in Thailand, by AFFS. It has just appeared in the U.S. from Wyatt Books/St. Martin's Press, and has received astonishing praise on both sides of the Atlantic.

Somtow's forthcoming writing projects include a new literary novel; a short-story collection from Gollancz, *The Pavilion of Frozen Women*; and a fourth young adult novel, *The Vampire's Beautiful Daughter*.

Lucy Taylor is a full-time writer whose horror fiction has appeared in *Little Deaths, Hotter Blood 4, Northern Frights, Bizarre Dreams, The Mammoth Book of Erotic Horror*, and other anthologies. Her work has also appeared in such publications as *Pulphouse, Palace Corbie, Cemetery Dance, Bizarre Bazaar 92*, and *Passion*. Her collections include *Close to the Bone, The Flesh Artist*, and *Unnatural Acts and Other Stories*. Her novel, *The Safety of Unknown Cites*, has recently been published by Darkside Press.

A former resident of Florida, she lives in the hills outside Boulder, Colorado, with her five cats.

Robert Weinberg sold his first short story when he was a junior in college in 1967 and hasn't stopped writing since. He is the author of sixteeen books and numerous short stories. His recent novel, *Vampire Diary: The Embrace*, written with Mark Rein-Hagen was a hardcover bestseller. As an editor, he has compiled over a hundred anthologies and short-story collections. Along with his writing and editing, Bob serves as vice-president of the Horror Writers Association. He is co-chairman of the Chicago Comic Convention and a member of the board of directors of the World Fantasy Convention. Much of his time recently has been spent working as story consultant for the new HBO cable TV series, *Weird Tales*. Bob lives in Chicago's south suburbs with his wife, Phyllis, son Matt, and over twenty thousand books and magazines.

F. Paul Wilson was born and raised in New Jersey where he misspent his youth playing with matches, poring over *Uncle Scrooge* and E.C. comics, reading Lovecraft, Matheson, Bradbury, and Heinlein, listening to Chuck Berry and Alan Freed on the radio, and watching Soupy Sales and horror movies. (He managed to see *King Kong* 11 times on Million Dollar Movie.)

In 1968 he graduated from Georgetown University. He began selling short fiction while a first-year medical student and has been writing fiction and practicing medicine ever since. He sold a number of comic scripts during the 1970s. His short stories and novelettes have appeared in all the major markets and numerous best-of-the-year collections; his novels have made the national bestseller lists.

He is the author of sixteen novels and the editor of the Horror Writers of America's anthology, *Freak Show*. His first three science fiction novels have been collected in an omnibus edition, *The LaNague Chronicles* by Baen Books. Two of his novels, *The Keep* and *The Tomb*, appeared on the *New York Times* bestseller list. *The Keep* was made into a visually striking but perfectly incomprehensible movie by Paramount in 1983. It opened to deservedly horrendous reviews and died a mercifully quick death. The author takes no responsibility for the film. *Wheels Within Wheels* won the first Prometheus Award in 1979; *The Tomb* received the Porgie Award from *The West Coast Review of Books* as best paperback original of 1984.

Over five million copies of Wilson's books are in print in the U.S.; his work has been translated into eighteen foreign languages.

In 1989 his original teleplay "Glim-Glim" aired on *Monsters*.

In 1992, in collaboration with Matthew Costello, he created the Sci-Fi Channel's *FTL NewsFeed*, a daily one-minute newscast from 150 years in the future that has achieved cult status; they script all the spots (the equivalent of a 4½ hour movie per year). Their interactive script *Bombmeister* (Interfilm) wrapped production in Hollywood in February 1995. Wilson and Costello have also contracted with Time Warner to write *Mirage*, a mystery in both novel and interactive CD-ROM format, to be published simultaneously by Warner Books and Time Warner Interactive in 1996.

And he's still married to his high school sweetheart. They live on the Jersey shore with their two daughters and three cats.

Dave Wolverton began working as a "prize-writer" in college during the 1980s, and quickly won several literary awards. He first hit the bestseller lists in science fiction with his first novel *On My Way To Paradise*, which won the Philip K. Dick Memorial Special Award as one of the best science fiction novels of 1989.

His novels *Serpent Catch* and *Path of the Hero* also received high acclaim. *Star Wars: The Courtship of Princess Leia* placed high on the *New York Times* and London *Times* bestseller lists and was soon followed by the highly successful, *The Golden Queen* (Tor Books, 1994). Dave's next novel, *Beyond the Gate*, was released by Tor in hardcover in the summer of 1995.

Dave has also published short fiction in magazines such as *Asimov's Science Fiction* and *Tomorrow*, and in numerous anthologies.

In 1992, Dave became the coordinating judge for the Writers of the Future contest. Among other things, he edits their anthology and teaches at their workshops. He has been a prison guard, missionary, business manager, farmer, a technical writer and editor, and a pie maker. He currently lives in Oregon with his wife and four children.

Copyrights